INTERFERENCE

BOOK ONE

A.F PRESSON

Copyright © 2021 by A.F. Presson Fiction

First Edition June 2021

ISBN 978-1-7372433-2-8 (Hardback)
ISBN 978-1-7372433-1-1 (Paperback)
ISBN 978-1-7372433-0-4 (Digital)

www.afpresson.com

"There is no magic greater than the power of true love."

-Fitz

❖

"You disgust me, Mercy."

With every chop of the knife, she spat bitterness and hate. I stared at the pitiful, massacred potatoes out of boredom. This was nothing new. Nothing I hadn't heard before.

Mom stood, angrily chopping potatoes and carrots across the counter from where I sat. The ratty yellow apron tied around her narrow waist, her faded brown hair pulled up in a clip she used in the nineties—she always looked the same. My eyes drifted over to the old wooden cabinets where the doors hung crooked by rusty hinges in our small apartment. I'd never known anything else.

"You realize you need to graduate to get a place of your own, right?"

I sighed. "Yes, Mom. I'm aware."

Trust me, I wanted nothing more than to get away from her. It's not that I didn't care about school. My grades were average, and I excelled as an athlete, but the school had suspended me for fighting—for the second time this year. A few months ago, I lost my temper. I still wasn't sure how

Randall Weatherby ended up with a basketball to his head and another to the crotch a few minutes later, but I wouldn't deny it brought a smile to my face.

He liked to taunt me in front of everyone. I never touched him, although I considered hitting him seconds before it happened. He wouldn't run his mouth again anytime soon.

I couldn't explain the incident that morning. One minute Cynthia Matthews made a snarky remark about her boyfriend flirting with the school slut, the next, she held her broken nose screaming like a banshee. I didn't touch her. She knew I wasn't close enough to hit her, but she blamed me anyway. Cynthia had despised me ever since I won the sixth grade spelling bee. There was also the track competition . . . and the tennis tournament. Which is why I'd learn to keep my head down.

Was it my fault? I still didn't know. My frustration and anger brought out something dark and powerful inside of me—different from other girls my age.

"I don't even know what to say to you right now," she mumbled.

That couldn't be right. She always had an insult on the tip of her tongue.

"You're a selfish, horrible girl, and you deserve what's coming to you, that's all I can say."

Ah ha. I knew she'd come up with something.

"You're no better than your repulsive father."

My blood boiled at the mention of my dad. I'd never met him, but I didn't blame him for leaving her. Living with her was just as tortuous as walking into school everyday.

She glanced up. "He was hateful like you."

Chop. Chop. "Selfish." *Chop.*

The hair on my arms bristled, and my nails pressed into my palms as I clenched my fists.

"Arrogant." *Chop.* "Trash." *Chop.*

"I hope he gets what he deserves, just like you will one day."

Chop.

My skin flamed as her words raged inside me. How could she be so cruel? I had to get away from her before I lost my mind. A person could only take so much.

"Probably dead in some alley after he messed with the wrong person."

Chop!

A gruesome scream of pain filled the kitchen. I watched, hypnotized, as the red stream of blood ran off the white countertop and dripped to the floor. It would have been a beautiful contrast if it weren't so grim. She grabbed for her towel, attempting to stop the flow of blood.

"You! I know you did this!"

Her accusation pulled me from my trance, the bloody hand wrapped tightly in a red-soaked cloth. Two small fingertips laid on the cutting board, unmoving with the diced potatoes. Did I do that? No, I couldn't have . . . Could I?

"Me? I'm sitting on the other side of the counter. You can't blame me."

I ran over to help, pulling rags and anything else I could find from the kitchen drawer. She jerked the extra towels from my hand, snarling at my attempt to assist. Tears streamed down her pale face as she scrambled to control the bleeding. I reached for her cell as she pulled it from my grip.

"Get away from me!" she screamed.

I turned and stomped to my room, leaving her to fend for herself. If she wanted a selfish teenager, she'd get one.

"Mark my words, Mercy! I am done with you! You're going to pay for this!"

I stopped in my tracks, tilting my head to the side, and slowly turning back to face her. "Are you threatening me?"

The fear she'd hidden under years of hate showed in the

way she stepped back, cradling her wounded hand to her chest. I almost felt sorry for her. Almost.

I turned away from the miserable excuse of a mother, angry at the part of me that loved her—the part that wanted her to love me.

. . .

ONE WEEK LATER

BRIGHT SUNLIGHT BEAMED through the white, sheer curtains —brightening the pale yellow of my bedroom walls and the popcorn ceiling overhead. After a long night of tossing and turning, I might have slept two hours. My dreams were always vivid, almost lifelike. Lately, it felt as if they morphed into something ominous. The memory of staring into a mirror, watching a knife slide along the front of my neck while my reflection grinned sadistically, brought a feeling of instability that couldn't be healthy.

I stretched my arms over my head in the small twin bed as unfamiliar voices in the living room carried down the hall and piqued my curiosity.

Mom always said eavesdropping was childish and nosy, but I never claimed to be mature, so I cracked the door to listen. We didn't receive visitors often.

"I can't do it anymore. As a single mother, people don't realize how hard it is for me to manage a daughter with mental health issues."

She had to be joking. Mental health issues? Well, maybe. But she wasn't sane herself.

"You're doing the right thing, Ma'am. I can't imagine how difficult this is, but please know that we will do all we can for

Mercy. Insurance and grants cover our program, so we won't expect anything from you."

"I appreciate you reaching out. How did you hear about my daughter?"

A man's voice faltered. "Oh, well sometimes the school counselors call us if they see a student struggling. We're just here to help."

Help? How were they going to help me? My psychotic mother needed therapy, not me. Had I even met the school counselor? I didn't think so. The reality of the conversation hit me. Mental health issues.

She was sending me away.

What I considered intimidation tactics and empty threats had finally become a reality. I closed the door as footsteps clomped down the hall, and I quickly climbed into bed.

"Mercy, wake up. You have visitors. In the living room, right now."

I had no other option. If I didn't go in there, they would come after me. Taking my time, I dressed in my usual jeans and cotton tee, brushing my teeth, and pulling my long dark hair on top of my head in a messy bun.

My gaze took in the small, puke-green bathroom surrounding me. Rust chips crumbled in the sink from the old faucet while the crack in the mirror seemed to grow every day. Who would've thought I'd ever want to stay? I knew deep down I didn't, but it had to be better than an institution, right?

I racked my brain, needing a way out of this. How could I make them see the truth? My feet dragged toward the living room, weighed down by the fear of what she'd done.

Mom huffed. "Well, thank you for gracing us with your presence." Mother stomped past me, leaving me alone with our visitors. She didn't bother introducing them.

Two men in suits and one lady with a kind smile stared

intently, as if they waited for a show to start. I stared back, refusing to give them one. Did they really think I was that bad?

"Mercy? My name is Elise. I work at the Fremont Mental Health Guild in downtown New York, along with Dr. Brian Fitzpatrick and Dr. Gavin Lee. We're here to help, okay?"

Elise was a full-figured woman with dark skin and trustworthy eyes. A calm surrounded her, and I could feel my muscles relax as the tension eased from my spine. My eyes darted from her to the men who remained quiet and I raised my brows in question. Were they going to speak?

"Hi, Mercy. I'm Dr. Brian Fitzpatrick, but you can call me Fitz."

I nodded, so he knew I'd heard him. The man called Fitz studied me, as if he were searching for something. His gaze traveled over my hair, eyes and fidgeting hands, assessing my every move.

"Dr. Gavin Lee. It's a pleasure to meet you."

How different these two men were. Dr. Fitz's short, salt and pepper hair fit his stern and observant expression, where the smiling Dr. Lee had wavy strawberry blonde hair and looked around ten years younger than his associate. He smiled brightly, without intensity or scrutiny.

"I'm Mercy Monroe, and apparently crazy." I shrugged my shoulders, unconcerned. This was my life. A constant battle of defending myself with snarky remarks.

A giggle came from my right, and I turned to see Elise— lips tight—attempting to restrain her laughter. I liked her.

"Mercy, your mother feels as though raising you is too much for her," Fitz said. He leaned forward, clasping his hands between his knees, studying me. His eyes bore into mine as if he waited for a reaction.

I wasn't surprised by his words—she had made this well

known. It still angered me, which typically brought forth an attitude I failed to keep under wraps.

"Yes, Sir. I've noticed her angelic wings aren't as fluffy as they used to be. Probably from living with such a demonic teenager like myself."

Dr. Lee lowered his head, trying to hide his smile. At least he had a sense of humor.

"How would you feel about staying with us? Just for a little while so we can make things easier for both of you." Fitz should have been a politician.

"I've heard of Fremont. You treat crazy people. All I want to do is graduate high school and move out of here. I only have three months left until I turn eighteen, then I can check myself out of your facility. I appreciate your time, but this isn't necessary."

"I'm sorry, but this isn't your decision. You're underage and your Mom has signed the admittance paperwork. You have my word you'll graduate. You'll finish your senior year in our classroom at Fremont." Dr. Lee frowned, as if he hated being the bearer of bad news.

"What? You're saying I don't have a choice?" I jumped at the thud of my duffle bag hitting the hardwood floor behind me.

My mother smiled as if she'd won the lottery. "I've packed. You're all ready to go."

I didn't have to glance in her eyes to know she was still afraid, but she covered it with the knowledge I wouldn't misbehave in the presence of guests. It killed me to know she was right. I wouldn't do anything to make my situation worse. Sadness washed over me at the state of our relationship. My heart was exhausted and for the first time, I wanted to give up.

That's when I made the decision to go peacefully. I needed to get away from this woman so badly, I would live with mental health patients to do it. It honestly couldn't be much different from living with her.

I cleared my throat, struggling to say the words. "Three months. When I turn eighteen, I'm gone."

They regarded each other as if disturbed. Were they waiting for an opportunity to pull out a sedative? A reason to restrain me? I wouldn't give them one.

"You are a surprising young lady," Dr. Lee stated. "All of this talk about how dangerous you are, and you're not even putting up a fight?"

I met Dr. Lee's eyes. "You sound disappointed."

"Maybe a little." He grinned.

❖

2

MERCY- SIX YEARS OLD

"What is she doing here? She's weird." Susie's pretty blonde pig-tails and white lace dress was a stark contrast to the ugly snarl on her face.

"Mommy made me. She said I had to invite everyone." Bethany rolled her eyes dramatically and spun away from the sight of me in her kitchen.

I watched as the frilly ruffles on her pink dress twirled around her—the white silk ribbon tied snug around her waist. Bethany's beautiful red hair hung down in ringlets and I wondered if my hair would curl like that.

I knew they didn't want me there, but Mother wouldn't listen. She told me to make an effort. Blend in. I kept my head bowed, like usual, and refused to make eye contact— just like Mother told me. The thin threads of my cotton shoes were not as pretty as Susie's glitter sandals. What would it be like to wear something like that? I couldn't imagine. Did Susie feel special? Like a princess? I bet she did.

A sharp pain hit the underside of my arm, and I flinched as Mom's fingers twisted my skin. I hated when she pinched, but I never reacted. It would be worse if I did.

"Move, Mercy. You're standing in everyone's way." Her eyes narrowed as a thin brown curl escaped from the banana clip in the back—the one she always wore. She blew the hair out of her face and spun, as if the sight of me nauseated her.

I shuffled toward the corner, admiring the ivory tile floor and pale pink balloons scattered about. I had never seen anything like it, but I'd never been invited to a party before either. It was my first. White and pink streamers twisted above the brown cabinets, while a large poster, painted with Bethany's name, stretched across the wall.

Everyone looked nice. Fancy. My brown wool skirt hung from my hips and covered all but the toes of my worn sneakers. Mother found it at a thrift store downtown and said I would grow into it. I'd tucked my white cotton shirt into the waistband, hoping to keep it from sagging, but continued to pull at the material as it slid down my thin waist.

Self-consciously, I patted my long hair, hoping it wasn't sticking up. I hated it. Susie told me only evil people had hair that dark, so that meant we couldn't be friends. I knew the truth though. I wasn't pretty like those girls. I wasn't good enough.

"Happy Birthday, Princess!" Bethany's mother called out.

Bethany, Susie and several other girls squealed at the sight of the tiered pink cake lined with Strawberries. It was the most beautiful thing I had ever seen. As the girls rushed forward, I stared at the cake in a daze as excitement welled within me. I took a step forward, but Mother jerked me back by the neck of my shirt.

"Where do you think you're going? You're lucky to even be here—don't push it."

I nodded, knowing she was right. I watched the crowd belt out happy birthday and cheer when Bethany blew out her candles. She grinned, proudly. She deserved it—all of it. Everyone loved Bethany. I wished we were friends.

Bethany's mom cut slivers of cake and lined the plates along the counter. I wanted one so badly—I wanted to know what cake tasted like. Would it be savory like meatloaf or did it taste like cornbread? Had I ever wanted anything more? I didn't think so.

I stood in the corner of the kitchen, focusing on the beautiful strawberry cake. My gaze traveled from face to face as they closed their eyes, enjoying every bite of the soft, delicious dessert. The kitchen began to darken, as a gray cloud blocked the rays of sunshine. Bethany's mother glanced out the window, concerned at the sudden change of weather.

Bethany and Suzie ran and bounced around the kitchen, oblivious to anyone else. The loud conversation from parents combined with screaming from excited children collided into sensory overload. I breathed in and out, as the sky darkened and the cake sat on the counter—tempting me.

The thought of a delicious bite pulled the platter closer, as if it longed to reach out to me. Inch by inch, the pink delicacy slid its way across the counter. I glanced over at Mother, but she was preoccupied, faking interest in another's conversation.

Susie sneaked toward the counter, laughing. She grinned at Bethany, then grazed her finger through the sweet icing before sucking it off her finger. It wasn't fair! She'd already had a piece!

Thunder broke across the sky and guests jumped in shock from the sudden lack of electricity. The strawberry layers toppled off the counter, covering Susie and Bethany in pink icing as they screamed in horror.

Kids ran. Parents shouted. The dark kitchen erupted in chaos as hard rain pelted the windows. I took a step toward the dining table, where a half-eaten piece of strawberry cake sat—alone. After glancing around, I slid the plate from the table and crawled underneath, out of sight.

The first taste was magical. A creamy sweetness I'd never experienced. I ate bite after bite, hiding under the large oak table as hysteria continued outside my private bubble of strawberry cake bliss.

. . .

MERCY- THIRTEEN YEARS OLD

THE HOT SPRAY of the shower streamed down my face, washing away the remnants of sleep and fatigue. I hadn't slept well. The nightmares were vivid—too real. Images flashed between dozens of mirrors, drowning, and being chased through a dark forest as I fought for my life. My heart pounded at the thought.

"Happy Birthday to me," I grumbled.

Loud pounding beat against the old wooden door of the bathroom. "Maybe you can save some hot water for the rest of us! Ungrateful child." Mother stomped down the hall, leaving me ashamed for the longer than usual shower. I knew better.

The old faucet groaned as I turned the rusty shower handle and stepped out onto the thin, worn bath rug. Cold air enveloped my wet skin, as chills traveled across my arms and legs. The towel did little against the chilly morning air. It barely covered half my body.

A mild burn—not exactly painful—radiated across my left shoulder. I reached across my chest with my right hand, massaging the ache that began only minutes before. I rolled my shoulders forward, attempting to loosen the muscles in my neck and back. Nothing helped. Lowering the towel, I stepped in front of the mirror to investigate.

I blinked, as if my mind didn't comprehend the reflection. Drop by drop, black specks appeared on my shoulder, as if someone had dripped ink, staining my skin, one speck at a time.

Bam. Bam. Bam.

"Get out, Mercy! Now!"

I jumped, the knock jolting me from my daze. I glanced once more at the small speckled image on my shoulder and swallowed. My mother would think I had gotten a tattoo. She wouldn't believe me.

"Now, Mercy!"

"Be right out, Mom."

I stared at myself in the mirror. I would hide it—as I did everything else. No one saw things move out of frustration or anger. My teachers didn't know I purposely missed questions to blend in. My tennis coach wasn't aware I could have easily won every tournament that year. No one would know about this either.

I walked out of the bathroom wrapped in the small towel and ducked into my bedroom before she returned. I slid into the only pair of jeans that fit—handed down by my mother. I grabbed a sweater and left my hair down to dry. If I didn't hurry, I would miss the bus. I swiped the books and brown paper bag off the counter on my way out the door.

I'd barely caught the bus in time and took my usual seat, relaxing my head against the cracked leather seat in front. Thirteen-years-old. I knew there wouldn't be a card or cake. There would be no gifts. I didn't expect it. In the past, I had hoped there would be an acknowledgement, but it never came. Now, the pure joy of knowing I was one year closer to moving out was enough.

I didn't need anything else.

When I stepped off the bus, a familiar heaviness surrounded me. Not dark or eerie, just an awareness of being watched. Sometimes, I could feel longing in the air, as if someone's sadness penetrated my heart—taking over my emotions. I glanced across the street as busy pedestrians crowded the sidewalks and children made their way toward the school.

I shook off the feeling and headed into class. Something felt different about that day—a change was near. I didn't know whether to be afraid or excited.

Maybe a little of both.

. . .

LIKE ALWAYS, I kept my head down and mouth closed. I knew the other girls would make fun of my clothes and ask if I'd done something to my hair.

Whatever thrills them.

I shuffled from class to class, pushing myself through the day when all I wanted was to run—away from school and home. I started volunteering at the kids club downtown, teaching youth basketball and assisting with homework after school. It gave me purpose. Pride. I'd grown quite fond of the children and made the decision to work with youth after college. Maybe a social worker—to be there for the ones who didn't have anyone else.

When the bell rang for gym class, I hurried down the hall. Nothing satisfied my pent up energy like physical activity. I quickly turned the corner, barreling into a group of students. A firm grip reached out for my elbow, steadying me. I glanced up, startled, to find Michael Bryant grinning mischievously.

The cute, cocky football player just happened to be Bethany Spencer's boyfriend.

I struggled to find words. "I'm . . . I'm so sorry."

"Are you alright?" He grinned—obviously aware of how flustered I'd become.

"She's fine, Michael. No need to worry yourself over her." Bethany flipped her long red hair, cocking one hip to the side. "Don't waste your time."

Michael smiled, apologetically. "See you around, Mercy."

My stomach cramped, tied in knots over the encounter. He'd never spoken to me before. How did he know my name? I nodded and turned away, but loud cackling followed me down the hall. I refused to turn around and give them the satisfaction of my hurtful gaze. No—I would ignore them like always. At least I would try.

By the time I reached the locker room, I could barely contain the tears—the five minute walk from algebra to the gym filled with antagonizing shouts and whispers. I heard my name on their lips, as if ignoring me wasn't enough to please their cruel desire. They needed to torment me.

I pulled the gym clothes from my bag, and hurried into the restroom. Flipping the small metal lock on the door, I kicked my shoes off at the same time a small item slid underneath the door. I froze, as if a bomb threatened to blow the tiny stall to bits.

"Hello?" I called out.

Silence.

As I took in the plastic wrapping in front of me, my heart dropped and sweat broke out across my neck. The threatening tears from before rolled down my cheeks as I quickly slid the jeans down my legs to see for myself. Nausea built as the dark red circle soaked through the back of my pants.

I'd started my period. And everyone knew it.

Panic set in. I unwrapped the small square of what looked to be a bandage or gauze of some sort. I'd hoped for instructions, but I guess most girls had a mother to teach them this part. I didn't. There were no intimate, private discussions about becoming a woman. No demonstrations about the proper application of products.

There was only me. It had never been any other way.

I buried my face in my hands, attempting to keep the sobs at bay. Those were my only jeans. What would I wear to school? The laughter and pointing fingers . . . they all knew. Anger built within me like never before. I cleaned myself up, situating the protective pad into my gym shorts. Shoving the clothes into my backpack, I walked out of the locker room with my head high.

I shuffled, somewhat awkwardly, over toward my gym coach. "Coach?"

"Yes, Monroe?" She asked.

"I'm not feeling well. May I be excused?"

Whispers and snickers echoed throughout the gym, but I didn't acknowledge them. I knew they wanted to embarrass me.

Coach turned, meeting their eyes with a stern look. "Is there something you need to tell me?"

It was no use. "No, Ma'am. I would like to go home."

She sighed. "Alright. I'll see you tomorrow."

If only I had walked a little faster. If I'd made it out the door a few seconds earlier, so much disaster could have been prevented. I hurried toward the double doors of the gym when the shrill voice of Bethany rang out across the gym filled with students.

"Wow, Mercy. It looks like you're wearing a diaper under those gym shorts."

A cascade of laughter surrounded her as I froze. Bethany's words penetrated the small sliver of self-confidence I'd worked so hard to hold on to. It began as a tremble inside the building and quickly escalated to a shudder as the bleachers shook against the wood floor.

I shoved through the double doors, my anger almost pulling them from the hinges. As the metal doors slammed closed, every window in the gymnasium shattered on impact. Screams from terrified students filled the air as small slivers of glass clinked against the wood floor. I heard every piece fall.

. . .

I SAT on my bed that evening, thoughts drifting from the tortuous morning to the anxiety-ridden afternoon. It was more than what happened at school. A pivotal moment had arrived—a crossroad shadowed in uncertainty came out of nowhere. I climbed under the covers—as if I could hide from the darkness calling out to me.

My door swung open with a bang, the brass knob slamming against the faded paneling. Mother, dressed in her usual khaki pants and button-up shirt stood with one hand on her hip, frowning.

"I heard there was an incident at school. Want to tell me about it?"

I swallowed, but knew to play dumb. I always did. "I left early. I wasn't feeling well."

"The news reported an explosion at the gym, possibly a gas leak. Are you sure you don't have something you wanna say?" Her mouth sneered in disgust, as if she knew I was to blame.

"Like I said, I left early."

She exhaled. I imagined her somewhat disappointed in the fact she couldn't punish me. "Hmph. You better keep your head down. I don't need anything else from you, Little Miss."

Mom jerked the old door closed, as a small piece of wood splintered against the shag carpet. I exhaled, relieved she was gone.

Something had changed in me that day. A power I didn't understand and couldn't reach grew with each passing hour. I shoved the covers back, and pushed away from the comfort of my bed. My hand grazed the black and white quilt as I slowly stepped toward the window.

It felt as if I expected someone to be waiting for me—watching me. An ominous shadow closed in until my chest tightened. There was pain—someone, somewhere suffered a tortuous pain I would never be able to comprehend. But who? I closed my eyes as their life slowly faded, taking a piece of me with them. After several minutes, the connection broke and they were gone. My heart broke on my thirteenth birthday, for someone I didn't even know.

I'd never felt more alone or confused. The knowledge of what I was capable of terrified me. It erupted into an avalanche of self-doubt and fear. I didn't want to be different.

I vowed to ignore the powerful pull threatening to take control over my life.

Hide it—for as long as I lived.

❀

3

FREMONT- PRESENT DAY

J waited, just like the past few nights. Sitting on the floor, beside my bedroom door at Fremont, I listened for movement, voices, or anything to let me know they were still awake. From the small rectangle windows that met the ceiling, the lights flickered above me—then blackness enveloped the hallway.

The bedside table had been stocked with literary fiction before I arrived. Jane Austen, John Steinbeck and Charles Dickens—the greats. I didn't care that I had read them before. They transported me to a different time and place.

I craved it.

Easing the door open, I clutched a small flashlight I had found in the closet alongside a copy of Pride and Prejudice. I would take the only path I knew, the one I memorized on arrival. I snuck out into the hallway, easing the heavy wooden door closed without a sound. Then, I tip-toed across the hardwood floor toward the old metal elevator to the ground floor.

Fremont was located in an old brick building a few blocks from Greenwich Avenue. Adorned with industrial-style light fixtures, exposed brick walls, and dark hardwood floors, it wasn't quite what I expected. There were no padded rooms, white-uniformed orderlies, or electric shock therapy. I found myself disappointed about the last one . . . Who wouldn't want to see that?

The guild held a sense of grandeur—a posh but classic style few buildings maintained after years of renovations. The character and rich history intrigued me, but apparently not enough to come out of my room. I'd secluded myself from the rest of the institution, studying and taking my meals in the comfort of isolation.

Over the years, I'd grown tired of trying to fit in. The last thing I wanted to do was socialize. Snarky comments stood guard in front of my wall of emotional solitude. It was easier that way. I'd become someone I didn't know, just to survive. I didn't need a new crowd of people to clash with when I'd only be there a few months. It was easier to be alone.

Leaving the elevator, I took notice of the large set of front doors on my right and quickly turned left toward the court-yard. I slid the bolt lock free on the back door and stepped out into the chilly night air.

The narrow brick path disappeared into a garden, surrounded by tall evergreen trees. I had discovered the secluded area the night before when the need for fresh air became too strong to ignore. In the far back corner, beside a thick cypress tree, a worn down spot in the landscaping led to a large smooth rock—perfect for reading—hidden behind a wall of shrubs and bushes.

I stayed out over two hours the night before engrossed in a novel—forgetting about what lay ahead. My own perfect, private. . .

"Can I help you?"

I glanced up, startled, by the deep voice in front of me . . . sitting on *my* rock. "You're on my rock."

"Your rock?" he asked.

"Well, yes. I sat out here for two hours last night. We bonded. Talked. Cried. We're committed now." I tried to sound sincere.

The dark of night obscured his facial features, but a sliver of moonlight lit up the black of his eyes—tinged in red. His lips tightened, holding back a grin. "I feel like a third wheel. I've been cheated on. You see, I've been coming out to this very spot to look at the stars for over two years."

I nodded with sympathy I didn't feel. He couldn't expect me to give up my spot so easily. I didn't have anything else. "You seem like the kind of guy that might have several spots. You know—not fully committed to any of them. Surely you can find another to suit your tastes."

His eyes narrowed at my words. Was he as handsome in the light as he was shadowed by the night sky? I needed to step away before he found a way to humiliate me—they always did.

"I'm more of a one-spot kinda guy. I get attached. This particular location is not only hidden from the other residents, but provides a clear view of the big dipper. Do you know how special that is?"

I exhaled. The jerk would not move. "Well, as much as I would love to waste my time arguing with you, I need to be searching for a new hideaway. Goodnight." I turned to leave, disheartened.

"What are you reading?"

I froze, but refused to turn around. "Jane Austen."

"Fan of Mr. Darcy, huh?" There was humor in his tone.

"Maybe. Not many gentlemen around anymore, so maybe I like to fantasize."

He chuckled. I heard a rustling of bushes, then a tall shadow stood beside my shorter one. "I wouldn't deprive you of a quiet place to read. They're hard to come by."

He walked toward the house, and I heard him utter, "Goodnight, Elizabeth Bennett."

I didn't reply. I couldn't. There were no hateful sneers, no ugly comebacks. He'd given up his peace and quiet . . . for mine. But why? I shook off the strange encounter and sat on the cool smooth stone I'd looked forward to all day.

I wanted nothing more than to get lost in the life of Mr. Bingley, Jane, or even Mr. Collins—but I couldn't stop thinking about the tall, dark-eyed stranger that had shown kindness instead of ridicule.

. . .

"THANK you for meeting me today, Mercy," Fitz mumbled while shuffling through paperwork. "I wanted to give you a couple of days to settle in and get comfortable. Unfortunately, Stella tells me you're refusing to leave your room. Except for your nightly courtyard visit. Is that true?"

My shocked gaze met his. The nurse, Stella, reminded me of my mother—snarky, skinny, and apparently a tattle-tale. I nodded. No use denying it. "Yeah. Pretty much."

He tilted his head forward, his brows furrowed. "Would you like to talk about it?"

"What?" I asked.

"The reason you're shutting yourself off from everyone." He tapped his pen against the desk, waiting for an explanation.

"Oh, that. No, I'm good, thanks."

"Come on, Mercy. Give me something here." Fitz leaned back in his chair, crossing his arms over his chest.

What did he want me to say?

"Why does there have to be some deep, dark reason for staying in my room? Maybe, I'm not good with people. What's wrong with that?"

He exhaled and rubbed his eyes as if I exhausted him. "Are you sleeping at night?"

I cleared my throat. "Sometimes."

"Why not every night?"

"I don't know. You tell me . . . doctor." I grinned.

The staring contest began—Fitz versus Mercy. The confidence in the way he locked eyes with me, scrutinizing my weaknesses, impressed me, but he'd never challenged someone as stubborn as myself. I was sure of it. After a few minutes, Fitz submitted and looked down at his paperwork. The inner Mercy pumped her fist.

"I'm sure your mother is missing you right now," he called out.

"Really? Has she called to check on me?" Hope swelled within me at the thought of her realizing her mistake, but I knew it wouldn't happen.

Biting the side of his lip, he lowered his head and mumbled, "Good point."

He knew she didn't care. At least he didn't pretend otherwise. Fitz scored bonus points for being honest.

He tossed his pen on the desk. "I'll let you know as soon as I hear from her, alright?"

"Don't bother. I just want to graduate and get on with my life."

"I heard you flew through a week's worth of classwork yesterday. At this rate, you'll finish your senior year in half the time."

"I've recently had some free time on my hands."

I didn't intend on being abrasive. None of this was his fault. If I could control what came out of my mouth, my life might have gone a little smoother. Anger simmered inside of me like a volcano ready to erupt. Innocent people like Fitz needed to stay clear.

"Looks like your grades are stellar. Tell me, what kept you in the average grade range at school? You're apparently far brighter than you let on, Ms. Monroe."

I didn't speak, mainly because the answer embarrassed me. Sometimes blending in with the average kids smoothed the rough path of public school. If I could avoid standing out in the crowd, I didn't care what my grades were. Fitz stared at me across his desk, chewing on the side of his lip. He eventually gave up on receiving an answer.

"Here's what I want you to do. Focus on finishing your assignments. Let's get that done and out of the way. Then, I'll help you apply to the colleges you're interested in. I may even have some contacts to help things go smoothly."

I sat up in my seat, surprised. "Really? You're going to help me get into college?"

"No, you have to do that. I'm going to help speed things along, but . . ."

Oh, no. Fitz wanted something. I should have known.

"But what?" I asked.

"For the next few months, you will interact with other residents. When I say interact, I mean I would like for them to keep their fingers." He glared, making sure I understood, then continued. "You will eat with everyone else, take part in group activities, and pretend to like people. Do we have a deal?"

There wasn't much to consider. Getting out of the house and into college was all I'd ever wanted. "Alright, Fitz. I'll play."

He clasped his hands in front of him, pleased. "Great. We found you a roommate."

"I'm sorry, what?"

"A roommate. She will be arriving tomorrow. Might be

good for both of you ladies to get to know each other. You know, have someone to talk to."

"About what? Fitz, I'm not the kind of girl who needs to confide in others about my current brand of tampons or the cute boy down the hall. That isn't me. I actually enjoy being alone. I'm splendid company."

He smiled at my snide comment. This man didn't rile at all. "I'm sure you are, but this isn't only for your benefit. It's for Nora's as well. You wouldn't want to do anything to impair another, would you?"

He played dirty.

My lips tightened at his words. I looked up at the ceiling, refraining from saying what I really wanted. I took a deep breath then looked at Fitz. "No, Sir. If that is what's best for her, then count me in."

"Wonderful. See you at dinner."

I made my way down the hall, somewhat pouty, passing an open door to the activities center. There were maybe eight to ten teenagers reading, playing video games, and listening to music. Everyone walked around without escorts —talking on their phones. What kind of facility were they running? It seemed more like a college dorm, but unfortunately, the professors lived there too. There would be no wild parties, but there were rumors of crazy card games on Friday nights.

I could hardly wait.

My gaze ran across each one, wondering who they were —where they came from—until a tall, muscular guy with black hair and olive skin caught my attention.

At first I thought he was older, more mature, by his size and strong facial features, but his age was evident in his youthful gaze. A stare that betrayed him as he took me in from head to toe. We made eye contact for a few seconds before I remembered the dark depths of that gaze. The courtyard. He gave up his private spot for me.

To keep from looking dewy-eyed, I pasted an unnecessarily stern look on my face and stomped away, uncomfortable. Something about him was too . . . intense. I'd been attracted to guys before, but he unnerved me.

I hurried down the hall, eager to return to my solitude. Turning the black iron doorknob to my room, I gave the wooden door a push and stepped into my room. I shut it quickly and leaned back against the frame, taking in the solitary chamber I'd call home for the next three months.

In May, I would turn eighteen. Two months, three weeks and five days to go. Tension eased from my shoulders, and I breathed deeper at the thought of being on my own. I turned to the right side of the room—bare except a twin bed and dresser. The one Nora would soon occupy.

I had agreed to everything else. He could've at least given me privacy. I didn't need a roommate, and I couldn't see how I could be any help to her.

Hasn't he met me?

I crashed down on the bed, then rolled my eyes at my foolishness. "Get over it," I whispered.

I closed my eyes as the mattress softly molded around my body. I nestled into my favorite quilt from home. The black and white geometric design, hand sewn by my grandmother who I'd never met, had been my father's. Something about the blanket comforted me. I'd never slept without it in seventeen years.

The wooden bedside table housed a black lamp and the only picture I possessed of my dad. The quilt and the picture were all I'd asked for after seventeen years in that house. What clothes I owned, I had bought myself after babysitting for our neighbor last summer.

We never went shopping for new clothes—Mom handed

down her old ones to me. Eventually, I tired of the snickers and comments. She and I were not the same size.

Even at my age, I stood taller and curvier. She didn't care if they made fun of me, but I did. I cared more than I should have. So, I worked hard to save up for my first shopping trip. I went alone after she refused to go and I even had enough money to have my long hair cut and styled. The stylist took additional time to show me how to tame the wavy tresses. That had to be one of the happiest memories of my life. I felt pretty that day, normal even.

Walking into school the following Monday with my new jeans and peplum top, there were no embarrassing comments. No finger-pointing or dirty looks. I realized what everyone else must have felt like, and the comfort of blending in overwhelmed me. I have never forgotten running into the bathroom stall, in tears from the relief of not being the center of negative attention.

I opened my eyes from the memory and bare white walls reminded me I had nothing. I imagined the other residents had covered their walls with family pictures or concert posters. I felt so empty, like I had missed out on life. The need to get out on my own and build a future for myself outweighed everything else. I also knew nothing in life went as planned, and a tiny voice in the back of my mind warned me not to get my hopes up. Why? I didn't know.

A high-pitched bell chimed in the hallway, signaling dinner. Since I arrived, they'd been kind enough to bring a tray to my room. After my conversation with Fitz, I didn't see that happening again. He'd be in the dining hall and would expect me to show. I promised I would try. I didn't belong at Fremont, and the only way for me to get out of there was to prove it.

If I planned on going all-in, I'd at least look decent. The 'homeless and hadn't washed my hair this week' look wasn't my best. I jumped in the shower, hoping to look less depressed. Considering the time, I braided my hair over one shoulder. After throwing on my favorite jeans and Beatles tee, I chewed the side of my lip, contemplating the pale face staring back at me in the mirror.

I've never liked makeup. Mascara made my hazel eyes pop, and my already full lips looked even better with gloss. That's all I ever used. I enjoyed being a minimalist. I tried the total makeover once and counted down the hours before I could wash the thick layers from my face.

I applied my usual basics, hoping the added color would liven up my appearance. I walked out of my en-suite bathroom, giving myself a mental pep-talk.

You're an attractive girl, Mercy. Be beautiful on the inside too. Blend in.

Keep your mouth shut.

❦

4

*S*weat coated my palms and regret haunted me for not spraying one more round of deodorant. Ridiculous—it felt like the first day of school all over again. I entered the main dining hall, where eight round tables were scattered throughout the center. Exposed brick along the outside wall bordered large windows overlooking the city.

The same hardwood floors from the hallway continued into the dining room, adding warmth. I assumed the swinging doors on the right led to the kitchen and dirty dishes would go to the stations in the corner. Of course, I was last to arrive. The ruckus of conversation simmered as residents took notice of me standing awkwardly in the doorway.

"Mercy, I'm so happy to see you." Elise stood, weaving around the crowded tables.

My smile tightened. "Well, Fitz didn't give me much of a choice."

She grinned, but didn't comment. I wouldn't put it past her to have a part in all of this. "Have a seat, and I'll let them know you're having dinner with us, alright?"

"Yeah, okay. Thanks."

I searched the room for an empty chair, as curious eyes met mine. It was the exact situation I wanted to avoid. One table in particular, sat empty except for a single teenage boy —wild red curly hair, his barely-there chin peeking out from under his plump cheeks, and a button-up shirt fastened under his neck—tight enough to cut off his flow of oxygen.

He looked safe. Plus, sitting with him seemed like the polite thing to do. I stepped in his direction, and a voice stopped me in my tracks.

"You don't want to do that—trust me."

My head spun toward the table on my right, and a young guy with a dark complexion and buzzed head smirked. Even from a sitting position, his lean body appeared somewhat muscular under the fitted shirt. His dark almond eyes gleamed with mischief as his sexy smirk —a beacon of warning—could woo any teenage girl in the vicinity.

"Excuse me?" I looked around to see if he'd been speaking to someone else.

"That's Cyrus, and if he doesn't know you, then he could be allergic to you. Just the thought of you sitting beside him will give him hives and breathing issues. It can get ugly until he's desensitized himself and knows you're safe."

He studied me intently, taking a bite from his crisp red apple.

I stared at the strange man like he had lost his mind. Then, I remembered we were in an institution and decided to go with it. At least he was civil.

"Well, no need for that, I guess. Especially since I don't carry an epi-pen for our dear Cyrus. Is there a chance you're allergic to strangers?" I asked.

"If I'm ever allergic to beautiful women, just put me out of my misery." The sexy smile on this one shouted trouble.

"Would you like to sit down?" He pulled the chair out beside him.

I breathed a sigh of relief. So far so good. "Thank you. I'm Mercy."

"I'm Ren. Is this your first day?"

"I arrived a few days ago."

Saying it out loud embarrassed me. Ren frowned, opened his mouth to speak, then closed it again. I could understand his confusion. It would be hard to miss someone new in a place this size. A flush of heat ran up my neck. "I'm an introvert."

"Ah, okay. Well, I hope you won't keep yourself hidden from me."

He was definitely flirting with me. I wiped my sweaty palms down the front of my jeans. When was the last time someone came onto me? I had only dated one boy in school, and it didn't last long. He grew tired of the hateful looks and comments I'd grown accustomed to over the years.

Needless to say, I was out of my element.

"Ren, leave the girl alone. You don't have to pounce in the first few seconds. Look around, not a lot of competition," a voice across the table rang out.

A gorgeous girl with dark ebony skin and remarkable fashion sense smirked at Ren. She wore a green floral dress under a fitted brown leather jacket. Short curly ringlets and long lashes highlighted her high cheekbones and straight nose.

"Hi, Mercy. I'm Neela."

"It's nice to meet you, Neela." Classy and chic, I couldn't help but envy her confidence. "I love your style," I told her.

Her eyes widened. "And you're my new best friend. What room do they have you in?"

"Seven."

Neela's eyes lit up. "A single. Sweet."

My shoulders slumped. "It is until tomorrow. I'm apparently getting a roommate."

"I'm not surprised. There are more girls than guys here. Most of them have singles. We aren't so lucky." She slumped. "Your roommate can't be any worse than mine. Trust me."

A thin, older woman walked up with a plate of food and sat it down in front of me without a word. I turned to thank her, but she had vanished. The swinging door to the kitchen settling into place. How did she get away that quickly?

Staring down at my plate, I couldn't help but be impressed. Roasted chicken with green beans and rice with a slice of lemon meringue pie for dessert. My mom couldn't boil an egg—or chop potatoes.

Thoughts of delicious food dissipated as shouting pulled our attention toward the corner of the dining hall. A thin, blonde-headed boy threw down a stack of cards, red-faced and angry, toward a shorter guy with curly black hair. Overhead lights flickered as two boys stood from their table, shoving each other.

Other residents jumped up to stop the fight as a loud crack of thunder shook the building. I could have sworn the sun shone against a backdrop of blue clouds moments before.

"What's going on here?" Dr. Lee shouted.

Everyone froze. The storm drifted away in mere seconds and the overhead lights stabilized. I watched as Dr. Lee escorted the boys from the room and everyone sat down as if it was just another day. It ended as quickly as it began.

Memories surfaced . . . sitting under a large oak table eating cake while a large crack of thunder shook everything around me. I pushed the image to the back of my mind. This wasn't like that. They were normal—not like me.

I turned my attention back to Neela, and in the corner of my eye, Ren grazed his finger through the top of my meringue. She gave him a dirty look and stared at my dessert. Preparing to scold Ren, I looked back at my plate, but the meringue looked to be untouched. My gaze darted across the table, but Neela avoided eye contact. What just happened? Did I do that?

Ignoring the baffling incident would be more comfortable than confronting him. Neela and Ren made small talk, but the table had gotten awkward since the boys argument, not to mention the meringue incident. I stood to take my dishes to the station, and as I spun, I bumped into someone with their head down, focusing on their phone. The phone fumbled, flying out of their hand, and slid across the wood floor.

"What is wrong with you? Watch where you're going!" a high-pitched voice shouted.

Ah, yes. I knew this type. Long blonde hair, big blue doe eyes, an inch of makeup with a designer purse on her arm. Who carried a handbag in an institution? Yes, I had lots of experience here. Be tactful, Mercy, I told myself. She wouldn't run over me—I stopped tucking my tail and running after the gym incident years ago.

I smiled sweetly. "Nice to meet you as well. I'm Mercy, by the way. You did have your eyes glued to your phone."

Her mouth fell open in shock, and someone behind me gasped. "How dare you waltz in here and talk to me that way. Do you have any idea who you are dealing with, Missy?"

"Mercy. My name is Mercy. I apologize if this offends you, but I don't care who you are."

I had to control my temper. Fitz wanted everyone to keep their fingers.

Cassie opened her mouth, then closed it again as if unsure how to respond. When she realized we'd drawn an audience, she narrowed her eyes. "You little b. . ." she yelled, but was soon cut off by a deep voice from the doorway. A voice I recognized.

"Cassie, what's going on?"

I looked up to see the guy from the activities lounge—the same one from the courtyard. Of course, he would be even more attractive up close. An overwhelming desire pulled at me, and I had to plant my feet so I didn't gravitate toward him. I'd never felt anything like it.

"Oh, Drake," Cassie cried.

The toddler, Cassie, collapsed in Drake's arms dramatically. He soothed her—rubbing her back and holding her close, but appeared bored and indifferent.

"This horrible girl, Missy, ran all over me, and you won't believe the things she said!" She threw her hand on her chest in shock at . . . well, I wasn't sure.

"Mercy. My name is Mercy." I don't know why I bothered to correct her.

"Calm down. I'm sure it was an accident," Drake assured her.

I rolled my eyes and sighed.

"It wasn't! I know it wasn't!" Cassie cried.

I clenched my fists, struggling to hide my anger. Fear coursed through me at the thought of losing control in front of everyone.

"Cassie, here's your phone. Are you okay? I saw the whole thing, and I was so worried about you," a squeaky voice called out.

I looked over at the boy they referred to as Cyrus, and his eyes twinkled as they settled on the beautiful Cassie. He had it bad.

"Thank you, Cyrus. I'm glad someone is here for me!" Cassie stomped off toward the hall and left us all staring at each other awkwardly.

"That would be my roommate," Neela whispered. "I wish I could say it gets better, but it doesn't."

Silence filled the dining hall as everyone's gaze focused on the floor or empty plates in front of them—anywhere but the new girl that caused a scene.

Drake sighed. "Look—I'm sorry. What's your name again?"

My blood boiled at his tone. The air felt thick and electric, as though my anger charged the room. Dishes clanged loudly against each other in the corner, but no one stood at the station.

Calm down.

"Mercy. My name is Mercy. You're David, right?"

He smirked at my attitude. "Drake."

"Oh, I'm sorry, Derek. I'm terrible with names."

He ignored my jab. "I apologize about Cassie. She isn't always emotionally stable, and she tends to rile easily."

An arm wrapped around my shoulders, somewhat too familiar for my liking. I didn't know these people well enough for physical contact.

"Tell your girlfriend to back off, Drake. If she wants to antagonize Mercy, you and I are going to have issues."

Was Ren marking his territory? It sure felt that way. I mean, I barely knew the guy. My body froze at his words—my mind unable to think of a response. Having someone at my back, to defend me, was something I'd never had before. But I knew it most likely stemmed from the fact he was interested in me.

Drake's eyes narrowed at Ren, and something that felt like rage brewed under the surface.

How did I know what he was feeling?

He looked down at Ren's arm around my shoulders, then his eyes met mine. "Noted."

Drake spun and left the dining hall in a mood similar to Cassie's.

Ren dropped his arm from around my shoulders. "Ignore them, Mercy. Everyone else does," Ren whispered. "Well, except for Cyrus. Poor guy is in love with Cassie."

I couldn't respond. My hands shook and breathing became difficult, but I managed to get back to my room before running into anyone else. Cassie was only one person —everyone else had been kind. I appreciated the connections I'd made with Neela and Ren, although Ren was somewhat too friendly. He really was handsome, but I'd never reacted to anyone like I did Drake. My body gravitated to him like a magnet. I might have been interested if I hadn't been so embarrassed.

Fremont honestly didn't seem so bad. For the first time, I had a conversation over dinner without being yelled at or chastised. I had a chance at friendship. How could three days at a mental facility offer more comfort than seventeen years at home?

When I finally fell asleep, the nightmares began. That night, the glow of angry fire blinded me. Bright red and orange flames licked the ground at my feet. Instead of burning, the blaze created a golden protective circle. All of a sudden, someone blew it out like a candle. A dense fog, filled with aggression and spite seeped toward me, then split as beasts ascended over a hill ahead. Hundreds of strange creatures that looked like evil boars surged toward me.

I heard the psychotic cackle of a woman and the sweet, familiar whisper of a girl, "Mercy, run."

My heart pounded, and my clothes clung to my skin as I leapt from bed. Gasping for air, I replayed the nightmare in my mind, determined to remember every detail. The warning from the sweet voice of a girl stood out among everything else. Who was that? It felt so real, and something inside me knew that voice. My nightmares usually consisted of the same—dark forests, drowning, unfamiliar reflections. It was strange that I'd never dreamt of fire before. Not until that night.

The clock on the wall ticked, mocking me—only five o'clock in the morning. There wasn't a chance I could go back to sleep—adrenaline still coursed through my veins from the dream. Stretching to relieve the coiled tension in my back, I did what I always do after a nightmare. I pushed my body physically. If I didn't stay active, frustration would take over, threatening to spill out on those around me.

Not to mention, I would be overweight. Even at my age, my curves rivaled most women, and if I didn't exercise, I would gain quickly. I would never be the petite girl that graced the covers of magazines, but I fought to stay healthy and in shape.

Near the end of my push-ups, a scraping sound pulled my attention toward the door. White paper slid underneath with large bold print at the top that read, "Schedule."

Schedule? Okay, Fitz. Now you've gone too far. I scrolled down the page, looking for anything that didn't make me want to curl into a ball. After breakfast, we were supposed to convene for studies in the activity lounge. Then, straight to physical education on the indoor tennis court. A tennis court? That I would enjoy. Lunch, therapy, activities, free time, etc. It was all mapped out. *You can do this, Mercy. Breathe.*

Hopefully a hot shower would calm me down. On the way to the bathroom, I tried to determine which was worse, the dream or the schedule. The nightmare continued to replay in my mind as I undressed—my fingers reaching over my back, brushing against the tattoo on my left shoulder. I could almost feel the heat rising from my skin. The ink I'd never wanted—the tattoo I'd never shown to anyone.

I recalled the fear on my thirteenth birthday, when I woke up with the tattoo seeping through slowly—like a towel soaking up spilled liquid. I panicked, afraid something was wrong with me, but not enough to confide in my mother. Every day, the black ink grew darker until the perfect image of a flame formed on my skin. I'd never been able to figure out what it meant, and last night was the first time I'd ever dreamt of fire.

I kept the flame hidden, always choosing tops that covered my shoulders so people wouldn't notice. At times, I wished I knew what it meant, but mostly I tried to ignore it. Pretend it didn't exist. I knew I couldn't do that forever.

Since I awoke early that morning, I had time to blow-dry my long dark hair and choose an appropriate outfit. I'd be lying if I said I didn't care what anyone thought. I may have felt that way the day before, but something quickly changed. I opened the small closet and pulled out my black short sleeve romper. Cute, but casual.

It said, "I'm not trying to impress you, but I work hard to be able to wear something like this."

Perfect.

As I left the bathroom, a quiet knock came from the door. Elise stood with a worried expression on her face. "We didn't want to startle you, Mercy, but your roommate has arrived. We need to lay her down."

Lay her down? She didn't walk?

"Oh, sure. Come on in."

I stepped back and held the door open while Dr. Lee carried a tiny blonde girl in his arms. I couldn't see her face, but I didn't have to. She wasn't in the best condition.

"Can I do something to help?"

"I think we can handle this, Mercy. You go ahead and meet the others for breakfast," Elise whispered.

I nodded and turned toward the door to give them

privacy. The delicate, frail girl might be more at ease without me gawking anyway. Before walking out, I glanced over my shoulder at the small huddled form on the twin bed. Something dark surrounded her, and I could not only sense it but feel it on my skin. Chills ran over me like a wave as I shook them off and shut the door.

The quietness of the dining hall surprised me. Cyrus sat at his isolated location in the corner, probably hoping to catch a glimpse of Cassie. Fitz read the paper while sipping on what looked to be hot coffee. A couple of kids I hadn't met sat at a table close to the window where Neela waved me over.

"Hey, Mercy. How'd you sleep?"

"Like always."

She wrinkled her nose. "That bad, huh?"

My eyes widened in surprise. Her intuition surprised me. I didn't have to divulge details for her to understand, and the change was pleasant.

"You look amazing. Imagine if you had a good night's rest." She smirked, and I couldn't keep the smile off my face at her attempt to lighten the mood. Neela's warm presence comforted my anxiety.

"So, we have a tennis court?" I asked.

"Yes. We also have a weight room and a running track on the roof. I love it when tennis is on the schedule."

I nodded, pleased to hear she enjoyed it. "I'm pretty excited myself."

"Oh, I hate tennis." She wrinkled her nose.

Was she trying to confuse me? Didn't she just say she loved it? She paused mid-chew at my change of expression.

"What?" she asked.

"I thought you said you loved it."

"Oh, no. I love it when it's on the schedule. I don't actually love tennis. I like to watch Kellan's fine butt running all over that court, kicking everyone's tale. Girl, that man is sweet to watch."

I couldn't help but smile. "I don't believe I've met Kellan."

"You'd remember. Kellan will be mine one day, he just doesn't know it yet."

"I can't imagine anyone turning you down, Neela."

She grinned, then shook her head. "We flirt, but I haven't made a move. It can be a touchy thing in Fremont, relationships I mean."

"Drake and Cassie seem to make it work." I peeked up at her, hoping she didn't pick up on my curiosity.

"Yes and no. Cassie says they are, but Drake has never acknowledged it. I think sometimes he goes along with it to keep her calm. Drake doesn't do well with intense emotions. He would rather appease her, so he doesn't have to deal with her outbursts."

"Interesting." He didn't come across like the type to go along with something he didn't want.

"You should room with her. She talks about him nonstop, but I rarely see him stop by. The girl gets on my last nerve."

"Hmm." I didn't know what else to say.

She stared over her juice as if her thoughts were drifting somewhere else. An older lady set a plate down in front of me, filled with oatmeal, fruit, and bacon as I studied Neela.

I waved my spoon in the air toward her. "What? You look like you have something on your mind."

She shrugged, and sipped her juice. "Drake seemed pretty focused on you last night. It isn't like him."

"I didn't notice," I lied, shoving bacon into my mouth.

"You didn't notice? I highly doubt that." She narrowed her eyes across the table.

I looked around to make sure no one else was listening. "I've known you less than twenty-four hours, and you are by far the most perceptive person I've ever met."

She smiled, enjoying the compliment. "Ren has it bad for you. There is some serious competition brewing, for sure."

"I'm not interested in a complicated relationship right now. I want to get through these next three months and get on with my life."

"What happens in three months?"

"I turn eighteen, and I'm free to check myself out."

Neela didn't respond, just tilted her head to the side and pursed her lips as though she doubted my words. She opened her mouth and closed it again, then picked up her juice to finish it. Neela protected her mind like a vault.

The loud click of heels on wood had us both turning in our seats. Of course, who else would wear stilettos at seven in the morning—Cassie.

I sighed. "I think I've lost my appetite. See you later." I did not need another run-in with her.

"Bye, Mercy." Neela called out.

The dishes clanged together as I piled them at the station, then walked toward the door as quickly as possible to avoid any early morning drama.

"Leaving so soon?" Her voice crawled under my skin.

I brushed by her without a word, crashing into Drake.

He wrapped his arm around my lower back to steady me. Every nerve in my body electrified at his touch. His eyes searched mine with curiosity as if puzzled. We were unable to back away—unable to speak. No one else existed at that moment. Drake's jaw clenched as if keeping himself from moving closer. I could see the struggle in his eyes.

How long had we been standing there? Did anyone notice?

"Drake!" A shrill voice rang out.

His head jerked up at the high-pitched squeal.

"I've been calling you over and over. Missy is leaving, aren't you, Missy?" Cassie yelled.

I swallowed, confused by the desire for a guy I didn't even know. "Um, yes. I'm just . . . I'm just leaving," I whispered.

I took a step back, and his hand fell away, leaving my back cold. Drake's gaze heated as he looked me over from head to toe. I forced myself to step around him and make my escape before I said something awkward. I pulled the schedule from my pocket, cursing myself along the way.

Smooth, Mercy. Real smooth.

. . .

BOOKSHELVES LINED an entire wall of the activity lounge with tables pushed up against the windows. Laptops were available, along with a tutor to help with our studies. The room had been separated by several couches and recliners, and the opposite side of the space was covered a large shag rug with two gaming chairs. A popcorn machine, air hockey table, and big-screen television demanded most of the attention. Not as horrible as I first imagined.

I sat down to work on the history and literature homework my teacher prepared. A few more students came in to study, but it never felt crowded or loud. Everyone's schedule must have been staggered to help the noise level at any given time. I tried to focus on the western civilization passage in front of me, but thoughts of Drake flooded my mind like a tsunami.

What happened back there? He seemed equally perplexed over our connection. Should I confront him? I feared that he'd deny it, making me look as though I had lost my mind. Let's face it, I didn't need any help in that department. I'd spent most of my life avoiding situations just like that.

Studying felt pointless—I slammed my book closed and went in search of the tennis court. I needed something to take my mind off him.

Wandering around the hall, I found someone that pointed me in the right direction. The floor below Fremont housed the athletic equipment. I jogged down the stairs and walked into a state-of-the-art indoor tennis court, locker room, pool, and weight room. Impressive. They might have given me a tour if I had come out of my room when I arrived.

Private showers, locker rooms, and towels were readily available. I pushed through the doors of the women's locker room and met two more residents coming out. One held the door open for me and smiled. My expression was probably a mixture of disbelief and mistrust as they grinned brightly. The idea that someone could be so polite wasn't one I'd grown accustomed to. I forced myself to stop acting like a suspicious maniac and nodded.

I found my name at the end of the back row of lockers. A set of shorts, a t-shirt and shoes sat inside. They made sure I had everything I needed. The shorts were a little small, so they fit snug on my backside, but the top fit perfectly. They were comfortable, so I'd be able to move without feeling too restricted.

I walked out to the court where a tall, athletic-looking guy warmed up alone. Dark brown skin, strong shoulders, and a sexy smile—Neela told me about him.

"Ah, ha. My first victim of the day. Please step forward," he said.

"Me?" I looked around, somewhat confused.

An older gentleman stepped toward me with his hand out in invitation. "I'm Coach Rogers. You must be Mercy. Your coach at Davis High School had very nice things to say about you."

I shook his hand, appreciating the firm grip and eye contact. Coach Rogers immediately came across as genuine.

"Thank you. I've been looking forward to this."

"Well, Kellan needs some competition. Most kids favor the weight room or the track. I'm too old to play anymore."

"Yeah he is," Kellan shouted.

Coach Rogers rolled his eyes. "Please do your worst."

"Let's do it," I said.

"Come on, Sassy. I got this. Best out of three sets?" Kellan smiled and bounced with anticipation.

I smirked. "If you're ready to be taken down a few notches, I'm game."

Our match started like any other—feeling each other out —watching for habits that would give us the upper hand. He had a precise swing, packed full of power. Kellan won the first set . . . barely. I continued to learn his game, find the patterns, then easily won the next.

More and more people shuffled in during the match. Ren sat on the floor with his arms resting on his knees, obvious enjoyment on his face. Neela's eyes appeared downcast— almost tormented, struggling between cheering me on and rooting for her crush.

"Is this going to be over soon? Some of us have important things to do." Cassie studied her perfect manicure, as if the boredom of the match was too much for her to bear.

Drake stood against the far wall with his arms crossed over his chest, watching me. I didn't want to consider how awful I looked right then. The red flush of my face, the wet shirt stuck to my sweaty back, hair falling from my ponytail.

Beautiful, I thought.

All at once, Kellan hit the ball too far to my right, and it should have whizzed past me. I dove for it, but it was too far away. The ball never touched my racket. No *thwack* echoed in the air from the contact, but the ball sailed back toward Kellan, almost on demand.

My mind froze, attempting to make sense of what happened. How did I do that? Whispering in the corner of the room broke through my confused state as Fitz and Drake spoke quietly away from the others. I could have sworn I heard my name from Drake's lips, but how is that possible from across the court? The ball flew past me, as Kellan laughed from the other side of the court.

Distractions were costing me points. Frustration built, and my heart rate picked up. Clouds covered the bright sunlight through the windows, and thunder rolled in the distance. Neela jerked her head toward Ren, and he shrugged his shoulders, mouthing what looked like 'not me' toward Neela. Brushing off everything around me, I attempted to focus.

On my next swing, I hit the ball as hard as possible, and it grazed Kellan's cheek. He avoided getting hit head on, but couldn't stop the ball.

"That girl's strong." I heard from the sideline.

"I guess so. Her arms are bigger than Cyrus's," another mumbled.

Chuckling followed. I immediately cringed at their words as petite Cassie walked up beside Drake—she looked to be a size two.

"Girl, don't hurt his pretty face. You know how I feel about it," Neela called out.

I grinned at her comment. "I'll do my best."

It amazed me how evenly matched we were. Kellan's speed surpassed anyone I had ever played. Match point—Kellan whacked the ball from his corner of the court, and I saw my move. I swung back, giving it all I had, and it sailed to the opposite corner from him. The match was over. He stood shocked, panting hard and sweating. Our audience paused, and some took a step back as though a threat approached. I walked over to Kellan's side of the court and stuck my hand out to show respect.

"Great game, Kellan. You're the best I've played against."

He stared down at my hand, then looked up at Coach Rogers. Coach nodded, and Kellan stepped forward. His hand came up and hit mine, then he turned and threw his racket against the wall as hard as he could. The speed and force behind the throw bent the frame of the racket on impact. I had never seen anything like it. He jogged out of the room without looking back.

My eyes widened in shock. Coach Rogers and Neela made their way over to me with sympathetic smiles.

"Don't take it personally, Mercy. Kellan has severe anxiety when he loses to anyone. Giving you five at the end of the match was a huge step for him."

"Why didn't you tell me? I would have gone easy on him and let him win."

"Now that wouldn't help him, would it?" Coach patted me on the shoulder and followed after Kellan.

"You were amazing out there!"

"Neela, I've never seen anyone that strong. Kellan destroyed his racket. He must have been holding back on the court."

Neela bit the side of her lip, then covered her unease with a smile. "I think his temper got out of hand after losing. Coach is right, Mercy. This is good for him."

"I hope you're right."

"I am, trust me. Try not to worry. We haven't had anyone around in a long time to give him a run for his money. I'll, um. I'll meet you for lunch?" She turned to leave, not waiting on my response.

As everyone filed out of the room, I turned—my gaze traveling over the courts, recalling the match.

Fear prickled the back of my mind as the realization hit me. I wasn't shielding myself like I normally did when emotional or frustrated. It was dangerous. They would see right through me, know I was different, then I'd never get out of there.

❖

5

*A*fter the match, I walked next door to the large indoor pool. Sitting on the side, I slid my shoes off, then socks, before slipping my feet into the cool water. Something about it calmed me. I closed my eyes and took a deep breath, filling my lungs to capacity.

"Everything alright?"

I jumped, then exhaled at the sight of Drake standing beside me. "I'm good."

He nodded thoughtfully, then walked over to where I sat. "Heck of a game. Have you always played tennis?"

Why did he make me so nervous? "Tennis, basketball, swimming . . . Anything that will keep my mind occupied."

He nodded, as if he understood. His dark gaze penetrated a piece of my soul that no one had reached in . . . forever. My senses were all of a sudden consumed with Drake. Did he know the effect he had on me?

"Occupied, huh?" he asked. "Are you the type that needs to stay busy?" He smirked as if joking, but somehow I knew it was a serious question.

"Aren't we all?" I asked.

"Nope. There's nothing I love more than to retreat to a quiet place and think of nothing at all." Drake stared out across the water without looking at it. "Thoughts. Feelings. Pain. Just close your eyes and breathe until there's . . . nothing."

I exhaled. "That sounds—peaceful. I wish I could, but I'm not that person. I like to keep my mind and body moving. I struggle to stay still."

Drake narrowed his eyes above me. "What are you running from?"

I jerked my head back, surprised by the question. "I'm not running from anything."

He chuckled as he turned away, but I could hear his faint whisper as if his mouth grazed my ear. "You're running."

. . .

MY TOES GLIDED through the water as I contemplated Drake's words. Was I running from the inevitable? Whatever set me apart from the others simmered, threatening to boil over at any moment. Did he know that? Did Fitz? Fremont obviously didn't operate like an institution, but what were they exactly?

I glanced up at the clock and knew I'd have to meet Neela soon, but I couldn't eat lunch smelling like sweat. The doorknob to my room squeaked as I turned it slowly. Light from the hall spilled into the dark bedroom, and I closed the door swiftly to make my way to the shower. I tip-toed past my new roommate, still asleep. The last thing I wanted to do was wake her. I had the romper I'd worn that morning, so thankfully I didn't have to dig around for clothes.

I stepped out of the shower, putting my hair into a bun, and stepped back into my clothes. I stared at the reflection in the mirror, and it almost felt a little odd to see an unfamiliar smile on such a familiar face. The guild wasn't unbearable. Of course, the only thing I had to compare it to was living with my mother.

Sneaking out of the bathroom, I jumped at the sight of Nora, sitting on her bed with her head down. A sheet of pale blonde hair hung loose like a curtain. Her thin, hunched frame shook all over—whether from cold or fear, I didn't know.

"Oh, you scared me. I'm sorry if I woke you," I whispered.

Silence.

"My name is Mercy. Is there something I can get you?"

Silence.

I squatted down on one knee in front of her. "I'm new here also, so I understand if you want to be alone—but, if you need anything . . ."

The pale blonde head slowly raised. My breath caught in my throat at the sight of her sunken cheekbones, fair skin and light blue eyes that were rimmed with the darkest circles I'd ever seen.

"Pain," she whispered.

"Pain? You're in pain?"

"No. You. You carry so much pain. I can feel it."

I stood up, the move making me stumble backward.

Nora watched me, her eyes absorbing every move, every expression as if I fascinated her. She tilted her head, curiously. "You have an honest heart. It's sad that no one has cared enough to notice."

I took another step back, hitting the wall behind me.

"Don't be afraid of me," Nora whispered.

"How do you know anything about me?"

"You don't have a clue, do you?" She studied my face intently. "How difficult it must have been growing up in the dark. You don't know."

I stepped forward. "Know what?"

Nora's silence cut through the air between us like a knife. Tension coiled in my shoulders as the seconds passed, waiting on her answer.

She whispered, "I think I need to lie back down."

Nora curled up in the center of the bed and closed her eyes. Within seconds, her breathing evened out and I knew she'd fallen asleep.

I backed away from her bed as if she'd wake and attack me. She honestly didn't appear dangerous, but the tone in her voice caused an icy chill to run up my spine. How did she know anything about me? My mind focused on the ultimate question—who were these people and what were they capable of?

. . .

"YOU'RE SAYING she could read your mind?" Neela asked while walking around the courtyard after lunch. Her forehead wrinkled in confusion, but her eyes weren't surprised. Not even a little.

"Not exactly. It was more than that." I shook my head. "It's hard to explain."

"She sounds exhausted and confused, Mercy. I wouldn't worry about it. I'm sure things will all make sense soon."

"What do you mean?" I asked.

Neela looked down at the ground, uncomfortable. "I

mean, I'm sure you'll figure her out. You know, living with her and all." She cleared her throat and changed the subject.

Neela had shut down on me. Again.

"How's your classwork?" She asked.

"Almost finished. Fitz is helping me apply to college. I never thought it would be possible. Then again, I never imagined any of this. One day, Mom forced me to leave for Fremont—the next, I have college plans and friends to talk to." I nudged her elbow and she grinned.

"I'm glad you're here, Mercy. Not as glad as others, but I'm still pretty high up there." Neela chuckled and wagged her brows.

"Ren." I sighed.

"Not just him, Sister." She nodded toward the second story window where Drake stood—watching me.

I narrowed my eyes. "Don't start."

Neela snickered. "Alright, I won't say anything. But neither of you are fooling anyone."

. . .

AFTER NEELA LEFT FOR THERAPY, I sat outside for hours. Although a crisp wind blew through the air, the warmth of the sun renewed me—relaxed me. I closed my eyes, thinking of how far I'd come. In one week, my future felt brighter and the loneliness subsided. The people surrounding me felt like friends, like I belonged with them.

A small stem of self-assurance gradually blossomed into confidence. No matter the obstacles, I would overcome the fear and allow myself to be happy. I didn't have all the answers, but I knew it was a good start.

Dinner would be served soon, so I headed back toward my room to check in on my roommate. Maybe she was confused. Maybe she could read my mind. Either way, being different was something I could relate to and I would make the effort to get to know her.

When I entered the room, the petite blond sat hunched on the side of her bed. Her dark rimmed eyes, slightly brighter than when I left, peeked up in my direction.

"I wanted to check on you—see if you need anything."

"I don't think so, but thank you, Mercy. I'm Elinora James. You can call me Nora."

Her words from before echoed in my mind. I shook off the questions and reminded myself to give her a chance. "I'm headed to the main hall for dinner. Are you hungry? Thirsty?"

Nora shook her head. "I don't think I can eat. I don't feel well."

"Can I bring you something?" I offered.

"That would be nice, thank you."

I nodded, backing up slowly toward the door. "I'll be right back."

I walked toward the main hall, hoping to find Fitz or Elise. I didn't want them to think I'd gone back on my word —especially if they saw me carrying food to my room. Luckily, they were sitting together at a table when I walked in.

"Mercy, how are you? Don't forget you have therapy with Dr. Lee after dinner," Elise reminded me.

"I'm good, thanks. I wanted to make sure it would be alright if I ate in my room today. Nora is awake and doesn't feel up to walking around yet."

"So, you're having dinner with her?" They looked at each other skeptically.

"Yes, if that's alright."

"I think that's very kind. Stella is sorting the trays, so let her know."

I walked over to nurse hag and informed her I needed two trays to go. She eyed me up and down then cut her eyes toward Elise. She grumbled as she turned to pack our food.

"Make that three," a voice called out.

I turned to see Neela waiting.

She winked. "I'm coming too."

I hoped Nora would appreciate getting to know us without everyone around. She seemed so . . . emotional. As we entered, Nora looked up, brows pulled together, inching back in her bed as if she were afraid. She and Neela stared intently at each other for a few seconds, as though they were having a silent conversation. Nora's face relaxed, and the tension left her small frame.

Neela piled up on my bed and we ate silently for a few minutes, until the lack of conversation became awkward.

"Do you have a big family, Nora?" I asked.

"Yes. I hate my family."

I felt the sting of those words deep within my chest.

I sighed at the thought. "I know what that's like."

"Yes." Nora glanced up, deep in thought. "I believe you do."

Again, her ability to see right through me left me feeling somewhat emotionally violated. I attempted to focus on Neela.

"What about you, Neela?" I asked.

She grinned. "I'm lucky. I have very supportive parents and siblings. Two older brothers, so I'm their princess." Although there was happiness in her tone, she looked away as though it was difficult to talk about.

"I have a sister," Nora said quietly. "She's the princess in my family. The normal one. The pretty one. The child that makes my parents proud. I'm here at Fremont now, so I'm not tarnishing their country club reputation." She took small bites of her sandwich, but didn't seem present. Her eyes were heavy—her mind consumed with thoughts she didn't share.

"What types of things do you like to do?" I asked.

Nora glanced up, and an expression of surprise crossed her pale face. "I've never been asked that before. I guess . . . I like to read. A good story can quiet the emotions. It can get overwhelming at times."

Her answer confused me, but I didn't push for details. Neela offered her information about the book collection in the library downstairs, as well as the activities lounge, and the quiet spots to read in the building. I made a note of these for myself in case I needed to get away. After checking the clock, I excused myself so I didn't miss my therapy session.

Before closing the door, I glanced back at the two girls piled up on the beds—whispering. Something strange bonded them, but I'd never had friends before and the possibility of it drowned out the peculiar way they seemed to connect. I smiled—just thankful to have someone to talk to for the first time in my life. I didn't care how strange they seemed.

. . .

How long had I been sitting in Dr. Lee's office? He asked the same questions Fitz did, but Dr. Lee asked about my nightmares. Fitz only asked if I slept well.

"How did you know I'm having nightmares?" I asked.

He glanced down at my file. "Well, it must be here in your chart from where we discussed it earlier."

"We've never discussed it. I'm sure of it." I hadn't told anyone about my nightmares.

"Does that mean you still have them?"

I didn't answer.

He sighed, as if I exhausted him. "Talk to me. Please."

"Yes, I'm having nightmares."

"Do you want to talk about them? Are they the same every time? Are you hurting anyone in your dreams?"

My mouth fell open. "Why would you ask me that?"

"Because of what happened with your mother."

I sat up straight, defensive, even though I knew he was right. "I would never hurt my mother. You don't know what you're talking about."

"Then tell me what happened. All I have is her report."

"Fine. I got upset, that's all. She said some truly horrible things to me, and I felt like my insides were about to explode, but I never touched her. She chopped her fingers off by accident. You have my word."

He leaned back in his chair, his hand rubbing back and forth along his chin. "And the problems at school?"

I swallowed as sweat beaded across the back of my neck. "What problems are you referring to?"

"The gym explosion. Fights. Unexplained broken noses." Dr. Lee picked up the file in front of him. "A volleyball came out of nowhere and knocked a girl to the ground. After she stumbled to her feet, she tripped and broke her tooth on the gym floor."

"Alaina was always tripping over her own two feet. I had nothing to do with that," I said, defensively.

He raised his brows in question. "And the volleyball?"

My eyes traveled to the window, away from his penetrating gaze. Was I responsible for it? Alaina was only happy if I left the gym in tears. I recalled the emotion bubbling up inside at her every word that day. That's all I remembered—I shook my head as I continued to study the gray skyline. "I don't kn, I mean . . . I didn't mean to," I whispered.

"I believe you, Mercy. I believe you." Dr. Lee sat up straight and lowered his voice. "Look, I know this is hard. I only want to help you. Sometimes Fitz can be hard to talk to, so just know you can come to me. No matter what, alright?"

I nodded. "Thank you."

"We're going to be good friends, Mercy. I just know it."

⟨⊙⟩

6

*C*ommunity service. Why did I have to do community service? I didn't do anything wrong. Fitz said it wasn't punishment. Fremont offered several hours a month to the surrounding neighborhoods. It felt like punishment. Every week, he sent three or four to an area that needed attention. We were assigned to clean up trash and create a more appealing environment.

Whatever. This wasn't in the brochure.

I couldn't believe I'd been at the guild for almost a month. Most of my time was spent with Nora and Neela, although I'd grown quite fond of my time on the court with Kellan. It thrilled me to have friends for the first time in my life. We'd walk along the back lawn, chatting about recently read books or the latest gossip between residents. I couldn't remember a time I felt so normal—so included. I continued to fend off Ren's advances, mainly because my connection to Drake only strengthened. I didn't understand it, but I also couldn't ignore it.

We'd run into each other in the library on occasion, espe-cially on those crystal clear nights when the stars begged to be noticed. That's when I would find Drake, laying on his back underneath the sky. Peace surrounded him during those moments and made him even more attractive. We didn't speak more than a few minutes at a time, but I fought to break away—to leave the connection behind.

It didn't matter how far apart we were or how much we tried to avoid it, our eyes always found the other across the room. When he did get close, I felt a stirring inside. As if the control I kept over the darkness within wavered in his presence. Like fuel on a fire.

Seeing him with Cassie felt wrong and I fought to hide my jealousy around her. On top of that, the storm clouds did nothing for my mood. My stress heightened when it rained, and then I couldn't seem to climb out of the pit I'd dug. Although surrounded by company I enjoyed, I still felt disconnected from an essential part of myself.

I had completed most of my school work to graduate, so that accomplishment helped my mood somewhat. After finals the following week, I would be ready to apply for college. True to his word, Fitz dropped a dozen college applications off at my door that morning. How many people could say they finished their senior year in a mental institution?

Exactly.

"Mercy. Earth to Mercy."

I looked up at Fitz, standing in front of the guild with a clipboard.

"Did you hear your assignment?" He asked.

"No, sorry. I was planning my escape."

He lowered his glasses, unamused. "I want you and Drake to take these streets in Chinatown. Neela, you and Ren take these toward Little Italy." He handed us print-outs, informing us where to go. "See how much you can get done in three hours, then come straight back. Got it?"

"Yes, Sir." I mumbled.

Wonderful. Three hours with the guy I wanted to kiss and slap at the same time. Was I being punished? That had to be it.

"You ready?" Drake asked.

"Yep."

"We can take the subway if you like. It'll be quicker," he offered.

"Sounds good."

I looked around for an escort—a Fremont employee—anyone not admitted to the institution for a mental disorder. We were going alone, and I found that to be odd.

Everything about this place is odd.

Gratefulness overpowered my curiosity, so I kept my mouth shut. The freedom would be nice. I felt as though Fitz and Dr. Lee were constantly watching me—waiting for something to happen. I'd kept my anger under control though . . . for the most part.

Crisp spring air blew across my skin as the savory smell of food carts assaulted my nose. I missed walking the city streets every day, watching the men and women rush through the busy crowd in their own world—ignoring thousands around them. The streets were packed. Car horns honked, people jaywalked, a naked guy stood in a filthy alley. Typical day in New York.

Walking down the steps to the closest subway, along with Neela and Ren, we dodged the crowd departing from the previous train. Ren pouted over my assignment with Drake—discontent obvious by his narrowed eyes and tight-lipped smile. Drake hadn't mentioned it once.

Ren spoke up. "I don't see why we can't switch if we want. I mean, Mercy might not want to spend the morning with you. It's not like you've been very inviting toward her."

Neela rolled her eyes at Ren's sad attempt to swap partners. Drake whipped around, his eyes landing on me.

"Do you have a problem spending the morning with me?"

"Oh, um. Well, no. Yes, I mean—No, I don't."

I'd apparently forgotten English.

Drake looked toward Ren, "She's fine. Now, shut it."

Ren never replied, but sulked as we hurried to scan our Metro cards. We rushed onto the train, doors nipping at our back as they shut tight.

"That was close," Neela said while squeezing between passengers.

It was standing room only, and Drake struggled to maneuver his way to the map to determine our next stop. "We jumped on the blue line, so let's get off at Canal Street and walk over to Chinatown."

No one disagreed, so we all remained quiet. Especially since Drake appeared more on edge than usual.

As Canal Street lit up the display, we hurried off the train and walked over to the street we were assigned. Neela and Ren still had a couple of extra blocks to go, so Neela waved as she followed Ren to the crosswalk. When Drake wasn't looking, she wagged her eyebrows up and down.

She's such a child.

I wagged mine back for good measure.

"See you guys at Fremont," I called out.

Ren stomped off without a word.

"You know, he's going to pout about this for days." I grinned at the thought.

"This isn't about your boyfriend. It's community service," Drake snapped.

I whipped my head around. "Whoa, excuse me?"

Drake didn't answer. He kept walking as though I hadn't spoken at all.

I grabbed his arm to stop him, and the familiar pull shot through me. "Ren is not my boyfriend."

His eyes darkened the longer I held onto him. He nodded, so I knew he heard me, then spun back around.

"What about Cassie?" I asked.

"What about her?"

"How does she feel about her boyfriend spending the morning with Missy?"

Drake chuckled. "I don't know. I don't tell Cassie anything about myself or the plans I have for the day."

"What do you talk about?" I asked.

"Her. We always talk about her."

Ok, that sounded like a miserable conversation.

Drake stopped to pull garbage bags and gloves from his backpack. The streets Fitz assigned to us were overcrowded and covered in trash from the previous weekend. We worked well together, gathering garbage and taking bags to a public dumpster. I avoided personal questions since that seemed to bring out the worst in him.

"Favorite baseball team?" I asked.

"Well, duh. The Yankees."

"Basketball?"

Drake gave me a look that said I should try harder. "The Nets, of course."

"Ok, I have a good one for you. Your favorite college football team." I smiled, waiting for his response.

He stopped to think about that one, but I knew he had an answer when the grin appeared.

"Come on. Tell me." I begged.

"I don't have one."

I rolled my eyes. "Yes, you do. You have to tell me."

"Alright. Being from New York, this is top secret stuff. You can't tell anyone this. Do you promise?" he asked.

"I promise."

"Alabama." He mumbled it so softly, I almost didn't hear him.

"Alright, I get it." They had an incredible football program. I'd give him that.

"You get it?"

"Well, yes. Saban totally turned that program around. They have the best running backs in the country, and the upcoming quarterback is going to be tight."

Drake grinned, but didn't respond.

I threw my hands up, guilty, "I know, I'm more like a dude sometimes."

"I like it. Not dudes. You, I mean. I like spending time with you." He looked down, as if he couldn't meet my eyes. "What about you?" he asked. "Who are your favorite teams?"

Yeah, this was easy for me.

"Braves, Warriors, Patriots, Predators, Raphael Nadal, and Serena Williams."

"Wow, I'm impressed. You even threw hockey in there. You're my kind of girl."

The comment thrilled me, and I grinned up at Drake.

He realized what slipped out and looked down abruptly. "We better get moving if we hope to finish this block."

We spent another hour cleaning, then walked past an empty alley littered with paper bags and bottles.

"I'll make a quick sweep here and be back in two minutes," I said.

Drake's gaze searched the alley and his brow furrowed when he glanced back at me. "You're sure?"

"Yeah, I'm good. Be back in a flash."

As soon as I stepped into the shadows, an eeriness floated through the alley that took my breath. Only a small strip of sunlight peeking through the buildings interrupted the darkness within. The rustle of bags and clanging of bottles were the only sounds, as I scooped up the discarded garbage.

How much effort did it really take to throw something in a trash can? I found the dumpster sitting in the back corner. Glancing toward the entrance, I didn't spot Drake anywhere, so I assumed he had moved along. When I lifted the lid of the dumpster to throw the trash inside, a strange voice drifted through the silence.

"You shouldn't be here."

Startled, I jumped, releasing my hold on the lid. The loud bang amplified my fear, and I spun as though I'd have to defend myself. A dark shadow in the corner captured my attention, and I fumbled back toward the main street.

Once again I heard, "You shouldn't be here."

"Who's there? I know karate, so you really don't want to mess with me." Of course I didn't, but they didn't know that.

"You're lying."

Damn.

"Even if you did, it's not the karate that I'd fear from you."

A black hood fell back, and an older man sat on the nasty street, his back against the brick wall. His long thick robe tied in the front and his head was shaved smooth.

"Ah. You don't have a clue. Do you?" he asked.

The man had lost his mind. I had officially arrived in crazy-town. "Clue about what, Sir?"

He chuckled. "The flame on your back. The mysterious mark on his."

I stepped away as if the old man had burned me, and hit my back against the hard, rough brick wall. "How do you know that?"

"I know more than you can imagine. I can teach you, but you have to find yourself before you can learn from me. Find yourself, Mercy. Look deep within."

Drake called out from the entryway, "Mercy, you all done here? We really need to move."

I glanced back at the old man, and a pile of loose bricks

and trash were all that remained. I spun as if he'd somehow snuck behind me. He was gone. My heart pounded against my chest as I searched up and down the alley. "Did you see that man?"

"What man? Are you alright? Did someone bother you?"

"Yes, but he wasn't a threat. I'm just . . . not sure where he went." I stepped toward Drake, looking back into the alley once more before continuing. It was empty.

"Our time is up, wanna catch the train back?" he asked.

"Sure," I answered, scanning the area one last time.

I smelled disgusting. Heat and garbage did not mix well, and a long shower would be the only thing that would help. We made our way back down Canal Street toward the subway. The streets were packed, and I had to stay close to Drake, so I didn't lose him. The creepy man in the alley weighed heavily on my mind. How did he know about the flame? I couldn't shake the need to find him—question him.

The train came into view, and we jumped on it the minute the doors opened. Loads of people shuffled out, and it looked as though Drake and I would be the only ones riding. I peered over at him, one brow raised. I'd never seen it this empty in the middle of the day.

"There isn't a bomb threat we aren't aware of, right?"

Drake didn't speak, but looked around on high alert. He grabbed my hand and bolted for the sliding door, but we were too late. When the train jolted forward, Drake gripped me by the arm, leading me down the aisle to a closed-in area in the corner.

His gaze met mine. "Stay behind me, alright? I need you to promise to listen to me."

My eyes widened at his words. "What's going on?"

"I don't have time to explain. Do you trust me, Mercy?"

I looked into his intense black gaze and knew the answer without thinking. "Of course."

Drake stood in front of me in a defensive position, looking from door to door. Confusion and paranoia caused me to question everything, but I trusted him.

Chill bumps ran across my arms, but it had nothing to do with the cold. A charge, almost electric, vibrated throughout the air—anger combined with hurt and revenge. It was hard to describe. It felt as if the emotions radiated from Drake, and even then I struggled to comprehend the reason behind them.

As the door at the opposite end slid open, two guys stepped forward, dressed in all black. They looked like everyday men—early twenties, clean-shaved and average build—but something told me they weren't. They were anything but normal. Their black outfits were loose and unrestrictive and a lazy confidence existed in their smirks. The one on the right stepped forward with his arms crossed, his sadistic gaze landing on me.

"Don't look at her. You look at me." Drake demanded.

What started as an ache, pulled at the back of my neck and radiated toward my skull. A terrible squeezing pressure throbbed inside my head, and I hit the floor, holding both sides of my temples. My vision blurred until there was only blackness. Trapped in an isolating darkness, feeling nothing but pain, I couldn't think—I could barely breathe.

"Hang on, Mercy," Drake called out.

I could have laid there for minutes or hours—I had no clue. The throbbing slowly dissipated, and I sat up, disoriented. The men remained focused on getting past Drake. The sliding door on the other side revealed several more men, anxious to attack. I slid back against the wall, curled in a corner protecting myself. The pain in my head was somewhat relieved, but still lingered enough to weaken me.

Two guys came toward us, but it only took one uppercut from Drake on the first guy. He swept the second, the man's feet flew out from under him, and Drake landed on top. He knocked him out with a punch, so forceful, I feared he'd broken the guy's neck. I'd never seen anything so violent— but I couldn't look away. Drake backed up protectively toward me, waiting for the next threat. Several more came forward, but were swiftly dealt with.

I stood up, gripping the back of his shirt with trembling hands. The pain moved to the front of my head and I leaned against him, fighting against the pressure. I knew he could feel my fear as I clung to his back. Drake was solid, unmoving, and unafraid.

"Who else is here?" Drake asked. "I think we all know you aren't capable of any real power."

The man sneered at Drake's remark. "You can't keep her protected, Moreno. You know how this ends."

"I'm not so sure about that, but I'm willing to go with this a little longer if you are." Drake's body hummed as the air around us thickened, making it hard to breathe. A look of fear and confusion came over the men, and their hands flew out, feeling around for what they couldn't see.

"Damn it, everything is black!" One of the men shouted while keeping his fists out, protecting himself. "He's a sensory interferer," he warned.

"My legs. I can't feel my legs!" the others screamed as they crumbled to the floor in front of us. The doors opened once again, and a group of men ran through, caging us in. One in particular stepped forward, a cocky grin on a somewhat familiar face. Had I met him before? He wore the same type of uniform, except in gray, with a long robe over his shoulders. His dark eyes met mine, even though his words were for Drake.

"Drake, it's been too long. Good to see you."

"Not long enough. And, good? That's amusing," Drake chuckled, not at all winded from the fight.

67

"Want to know what I find amusing? You. You're convinced you can protect that woman. Aadya's never going to stop until she's dead, you know that. After I tear you limb from limb, I'm going to take my time doing the same to her— of course I'll have a little fun first."

Drake stepped forward. "I'd like to see you try. I'm warning you—" Drake froze mid-sentence. "Mercy?"

My hands gripped Drake's shirt as anger built within him. I could sense it all around me and the intensity took my breath away. The thought of someone harming Drake, and threatening my life was too much for my—already on edge— nerves to handle. Drake glanced behind him, feeling the change within me. Everything I'd kept buried my entire life, all of the darkness and power, clawed its way forward.

"Mercy? What are you doing?"

The air vibrated, and my hands shook uncontrollably. The men took a step back, eyes darting around the train as the car trembled from the unknown force. All at once, the man in gray stepped forward and my arms tensed at my side, palms and fingers splayed wide. A ripple in the air originated from where I stood and exploded outward through the men in front of us.

As if in slow motion, Drake spun, covering my body with his own as windows exploded on all sides of the train and men flew backward, hitting the wall of the car. After several quiet seconds, he pulled me to a standing position as we took in the destruction around us.

The subway glided to a stop, and the doors opened for the new passengers to board. There weren't any, and I found myself even more confused about what just happened. Drake grabbed my arm and pulled me out of the train before the door closed. Looking behind me, I could feel the angry glare of the man who threatened us. He was pissed. Drake didn't slow at all as we ran up the stairs onto the sidewalk. He weaved through the crowd, knocking people to the side, focused on getting us out of there.

There were so many questions I wanted to ask. I knew it wasn't the best time, but anxiety overpowered any sense of reason I had. I jerked on his hand, and he spun to face me, searching for the threat. Drake looked down, his eyes full of worry. "Mercy, we need to. . ."

"What's happening to me?" I couldn't keep my lip from quivering or stop the tears that fell from my eyes. I'd never been an emotional person, but the fear of being the dangerous woman my mother accused me of terrified me.

His hand cupped the side of my cheek, as his thumb wiped a tear from my face. Drake's dark eyes softened at the sight of my distress. "Trust me, we need to get off the street."

I nodded, and he turned to continue his pace through the crowded streets.

The old red brick of Fremont came into view, as Fitz paced on the top step—waiting for us. Drake gripped my hand as if he feared I'd disappear. Someone to the side of the door caught my attention, and I realized Fitz wasn't alone. Cassie waited for her boyfriend to return, and she looked furious. Causing Drake more problems today wasn't on my to-do list, so I tried to slide my hand away, but he held tight, refusing to let me go.

"What happened? You were supposed to be back hours ago." Fitz shouted.

Hours?

Walking straight past Cassie without a glance, Drake whispered, "Custos."

Fitz paused, staring after Drake, then snapped out of it and quickly followed us into the building, ignoring the stares and whispers in the hall.

We shuffled into Fitz's office as he entered behind us and slammed the clipboard on the desk. I sat down, for fear of

69

collapsing. The flush of his face and tight line of his mouth made him look older—more intimidating. "I don't understand," Fitz called out. "We don't even know if she's the one they're looking for. There's nothing concrete to prove it."

"I know." Drake exhaled, as if annoyed.

Fitz crossed his arms over his chest. "How many?"

Drake shook his head. "I don't know, maybe eight to ten?"

"Eight to ten? Are you joking? Aadya must be desperate. And you handled all of them?"

"Well, not all of them." Drake looked over at me.

Fitz glanced back and forth between us. "Mercy, are you all right?"

"Yes, I'm fine." I shook my head. "No. No, I'm not fine!" I stood and began pacing the room.

Fitz bobbed his head in understanding. "I want you to go lay down a little while, alright? You've been through quite an ordeal today."

I spun toward him, surprised. "You don't want to hear what happened?"

Fitz waved toward the door. "Drake can take care of the details. You get some rest."

He's getting rid of me, I thought.

A familiar tremble traveled through my body as the lights flickered overhead. "Look, I'm not that gullible. I know you want to speak in private, and that's fine—but don't think I believe we went through a normal, everyday mugging on the subway. That was not normal! What Drake did to those guys wasn't normal! What I did . . ."

"Mercy, calm down," Fitz said.

"Don't tell me to calm down!"

Drake pulled my body against his, wrapping his arms around me—holding me. The current that always pulled us together felt five times stronger right then, and I relaxed instantly. I breathed in and out slowly, the strong earthy scent of him filling my lungs. My body needed that . . . needed him.

The office door swung open with a loud bang, and I jerked away from Drake at the sight of a rage-filled Cassie. Frizzy hair framed her fuming red face and she looked as though she could fall to the floor in a tantrum at any moment. "How dare you? How dare you try to steal my boyfriend!"

"Cassie . . ." Drake tried to calm her down, but there was no use.

"I don't want to hear from you either. Do you have any idea how worried I've been today? When I heard during lunch that you'd left with Missy, I fell apart!"

"At lunch? We've been gone since seven this morning," I offered.

Cassie's eyes widened and a vein protruded in the center of her forehead as she breathed in, attempting to control her anger.

"Mercy, go ahead and get some rest. We'll talk some more during our next therapy session," Fitz ordered.

"I'm sick of being in the dark. If you don't give me answers, I'll find someone who will." I stomped out the door without another word.

. . .

I OPENED the door to my room, and Nora sat huddled on the bed, as if stressed and worried.

"Mercy! I've been tied up in knots. When Neela said you hadn't returned, I pictured the most horrible things."

I stared at Nora, visibly shaken over my absence. I'd

never had real friends before, and I struggled to trust the relationships as easily as they did. I seemed to always look for an ulterior motive to their kindness, or anticipate the day they would realize I wasn't worthy of their close-knit group. I could fight it all I wanted, but something tied me to them. I prayed every night for it to hold strong, the bond fueling my determination to be a better person—to love harder.

Nora wrapped her arms around me as my body trembled from all that happened. She held onto me for several minutes, and the fear and tension eased, replaced by a calm and warm sensation. Peace washed over me and my eyes closed, relaxed by her presence.

She leaned back, studying me. "Better?"

I swore the dark circles under her eyes were much worse than when I first walked in. "Yes. Thank you."

"What happened?" Sitting on my bed, she continued to hold my hand while I spoke.

"I don't know. We were cornered by these men on the subway. They threatened us. This is going to sound crazy, but I think Drake did something to them. Something like— well, something like a superhero would do."

"A superhero?" Nora's face scrunched up with confusion.

"I know it sounds crazy, but the boy has mad skills. I wish I could understand what happened. I spent most of the time on the floor with a severe migraine. Before it was over, something happened to me. It was like built-up energy released and stunned everyone." I shook my head. "I promise I'm not making it up."

She grinned. "Of course you're not. But I'm getting the feeling your fear and anxiety started before this. Am I right? There's something else you aren't sharing."

"How do you do that? How do you always know how I'm feeling or what's on my mind. You and Neela both."

"We just know you, I guess. So tell me, what else has you shaken?"

I had a tendency to hide things from people—important or significant things. I couldn't do that forever. I needed to rely on my friends, people that I'd never had before. I trusted Nora and Neela, and something inside pushed me to open up to them.

"I walked into an empty alleyway to pick up trash and ran across an older man huddled by a dumpster."

"That's awful." Nora's face fell.

"He knew things about me." I already felt like a crazy person talking about this. Now I had confided in a crazy person about my crazy visitor.

Nora tilted her head. "He knew things? What things, Mercy? You can talk to me."

"He said I had to find myself. He also knew a private detail I've never told another soul."

"Can you tell me?" Her eyes widened, waiting for me to divulge my secrets.

"Nora, if I tell you—you'll think I've lost my mind."

She shook her head. "You have my word, that will never happen."

I knew she meant every word she said, but I still felt out of sorts discussing it. "I have a tattoo."

She stared, waiting patiently for the dark secret. "Ok, well. I have several friends with tattoos. I can see how it could be stressful, especially if you regret it."

"No, I don't have a real tattoo."

"Mercy, I swear if you are playing with me right now. . ."

"Look, when I turned thirteen, something changed. I felt different. These black spots under my skin grew darker. It didn't hurt, just a burning sensation. Eventually, it turned into a tattoo on my shoulder."

"You've shown no one this tattoo before?" she asked.

"No, never."

"Can I see it now?"

I reluctantly stood up, pulling my shirt over my head. Taking a deep breath, I turned so Nora could inspect the ink.

A gasp, then I heard the words, "Allegato" from her lips. Her small finger traced the outline of the flame, as I nervously waited. "Rage Fire," she whispered.

"Rage Fire? What are you talking about?"

She snapped out of her daze and covered the surprised expression on her face. "It reminds me of something I've seen in a book. Very cool looking, Mercy. Are you sure you didn't pay to have it done?"

"No, I swear. What do you think it means?" I asked.

"Who knows? Something tells me it will all make sense one day, though. So, let's not stress about it, alright?"

"How can I not? Nora, something is wrong with me. A darkness is building up inside and I'm terrified someone will get hurt." I threw my hands over my face, and tears rolled down my cheeks.

Nora stepped forward. "Mercy, listen to me. I know you're confused, but I'm here. Okay? I'm not afraid of you."

I exhaled then met her eyes. "Maybe you should be."

❖

"*D*o you want to talk about it?" Neela asked.

"No, but thank you. I love wallowing in my own pity." This wasn't a lie. "I'll be fine, I promise." Thunder rolled in the distance. "It looks like it might be a rough one," I said, gazing out the window.

Neela's eyes focused on me, as if I were a puzzle for her to solve. "That's what I'm afraid of."

Drake and Fitz were keeping essential details from me. If it had something to do with me, then I deserved to know. Hard rain pelted the windows outside the dining hall. The weather had been in sync with my mood lately.

I'd taken one bite of my lunch and pushed the plate aside. I had to get out of there. "I think I may go downstairs to get a jump on tennis practice. The exercise may help my mood."

Neela nodded. "Yeah, okay. I'll see you there."

Tension pulled at my muscles, my body humming with the need to hit something. Pushing through the stairwell door, Kellan hobbled toward me on a crutch.

"Oh, no! What happened?" Please, Lord. Please don't take my tennis partner, I prayed.

"Don't go worrying your pretty little head about me, Mercy. I'll be back to kickin' your fine butt soon enough. It's just a sprain."

"Well, I'm glad to hear it, but I'm sorry we can't play. I need to hit something in a bad way," I grumbled.

"I have someone lined up, Mercy. Try not to be too hard on em'," Coach yelled across the court.

"I'll do my best."

Yeah, right. I changed clothes in the locker room and pulled my hair on top of my head so it didn't get in the way. Stretching my neck from side to side, I swung my shoulders back and forth to warm up. I walked out to the court, finding Ren on the other side, smiling from ear to ear.

"Hey there, hot stuff. Are you ready for some of this action?"

"Ren, I don't want to hear any whining when I finish with you today."

He grinned. "Bring it, Mercy. I'm ready."

Ren was so not ready. I won three sets straight. He never had a chance. The match was so easy, it did nothing to calm the rage within. The rain fell harder, and Neela stared out the window, her eyes narrowed on the storm clouds above.

Coach Rogers yelled, "Next up! Dunivant, get out here."

He had to be joking. I looked over at Coach with an expression he knew all too well.

"Shut it, Monroe. I'm running out of options for you today."

Cassie strutted toward the other end of the court with a smirk the size of Texas. She could swing—Daddy, no doubt, paid for lessons at the country club. But it wasn't enough to score on me. Plus, the girl couldn't run without falling.

"Cassie, are you alright? You're favoring your right shoulder," Coach called out.

"I'm fine, thank you for asking Coach. I'll get Drake to rub it for me tonight. He gives the best massages."

Don't hit her. Don't hit her. Don't hit her. I whispered the words to myself over and over, attempting to control my temper.

"All the stress Missy put me under a couple of days ago caused horrible knots in my shoulders. Drake spent all night rubbing them out. He is such a doll."

A heavy pressure built inside my head, and I shook off the tension. Thunder rolled overhead, and my grip on the tennis racket became uncomfortable. I welcomed the bite of pain in my palm.

Neela paced back and forth, uncomfortable. "Cassie, that's enough. You've made your point."

"Who asked you, Neela? Everyone knows your family abandoned you because they couldn't stand you. When's the last time you had a visitor? Hmm?"

Neela's fists balled up at Cassie's words, but she controlled her anger. She did better than me.

Unfortunately for Cassie, she continued talking. "I care as much for you as I do for Missy. Trash. Both of you."

The ball sailed past her once again, and she spun toward me growling, the hate and bitterness obvious. Cassie once again regained her composure as she positioned herself to serve the ball.

"No wonder Drake said you were a circus freak. A crazy, unstable, fat, unattractive freak." Her racket smacked against the ball, her words fueling the force behind her serve.

Several things happened at once. I threw my racket to the ground, full of disbelief and hurt, as lightning struck overhead. The loud boom shook the building, and the lights shut off, along with my sanity. Dim sunlight shone through the gray clouds, illuminating Cassie's sneer. My palm flung out in front of me and stopped the tennis ball mid-air. I heard gasps and my name being called, but my focus never wavered from Cassie.

Her words cut me. It didn't matter if they weren't true. My heart wanted Drake, and she threatened any chance I had with him. The possessive part of me wouldn't back down, no matter what anyone said. I had lost control.

My head throbbed and a flush worked its way up my neck, as she grinned at my obvious hurt. All of the resentment and hate built up over the years came surging forward, and with one flick of my wrist, the ball propelled itself toward Cassie's face. The loud crunch of a broken nose echoed throughout the tennis court, and blood splattered her pristine white skirt. Her mouth opened as if a scream filled the air, but I heard nothing except the pounding of my heart.

My gaze traveled to the tennis racket lying on the ground, and I forced it up, launching it toward her face, not yet satisfied that she had learned her lesson. A satisfaction stirred within as I watched the racket spin in slow motion to her side of the court. I ignored everyone and everything around me. The head of the racket nailed her in the mouth, causing broken teeth to fly out in front of her. It wasn't enough. She hadn't learned. How far would I have to go until I felt relief?

A steady hand came around from behind me and pulled me against a hard body. Drake softly whispered in my ear, "That's enough, Mercy. Let go of the anger and breathe."

Drake broke through the storm, and I looked around at what I'd done. My body collapsed against his as he held me up. I was a monster.

The room became hazy, as though it was out of focus. Broken teeth slowly floated from the floor and put themselves back together, secure in Cassie's mouth. My racket spun backward toward my side of the court and laid where I first tossed it. Droplets of blood gathered together from the bright white skirt and flowed like a stream back into the broken nose.

Cassie's mouth closed, the sobs no longer screeching through the air, and her nasal bone snapped back into place as though it never happened. The ball sailed back toward me from the previous serve. I glanced around the room, convinced it was all a dream. Elise stood there with her palm out, turning her hand counter-clockwise.

Then, it hit me—she had somehow turned back time. Cassie stood frozen in place—as if unaware of the events at hand. Everyone else watched as Elise reversed the damage I'd done. The room began to spin, and I felt myself losing consciousness. My vision began to fade and everything went dark.

. . .

WATER DRIPPED down the side of my head, the cold sensation causing chills across my skin. I blinked against the bright light, as sharp pains shot through my temples.

"Mercy? Can you hear me?" Nora asked.

"What happened?" I tried to sit up, but I'd never felt so weak.

She placed her hand behind my back and helped me raise forward.

"Would you like my take or Cassie's? Because mine is much more interesting than hers," Neela called from across the room.

"Um, what . . . what did Cassie say?"

"She smoked you on the court, and you couldn't handle it.

79

You apparently faked passing out to get Drake's attention." She smiled.

"And your take?" I asked.

Her expression turned soft as her eyes and mouth relaxed. "We have a lot to talk about, Mercy," Neela responded.

She knew I was different. Just like I knew there were others here that were different. Neela, Drake, Ren, Elise, and I suspected Nora as well. How many others?

"We want to help you, but Fitz asked to speak with you first. He feels as though you deserve an explanation from him," Nora whispered.

I nodded. "Fitz is right."

Neela stood from the bed. "I'm going to the kitchen, see if I can find you a snack. I'm sure you need it."

"Thanks, Neela."

I wasn't sure if the kitchen run was an excuse to get away from me, but I hoped not. These were my closest friends, and I needed them.

"Stop worrying," Nora called out.

"How do you know I'm worrying?" I squinted my eyes suspiciously.

"I think you know by now."

I threw my hands up in the air. "You're a superhero, too."

Nora grinned. "Not so much a superhero, but I have gifts —like you."

"You knew before today, though, didn't you? About me?"

"I knew the moment we met. We can talk more after you speak with Fitz, alright? He was adamant about speaking with you alone."

Loud screaming throughout the hall interrupted our conversation. What sounded like hitting, kicking, and fighting echoed down to our room. Nora and I both stood to investigate. We peered out the door to find Dr. Lee, along with Stella, wrestling a teenage boy down to the ground.

"You don't know what you're doing! They're coming, and you have to protect everyone! They're going to kill you all! Listen . . . Listen to . . . me." His voice faded as his body relaxed.

Stella pulled a syringe from his arm. They had to sedate him—he was bound to hurt someone. Dr. Lee glanced up, frowning at the sight of us gawking.

"Go back to your room, ladies. We don't need an audience. This fellow has been through enough."

Nora and I shut the door, both letting the scene in the hallway sink in.

"What was that about?" she asked.

I shrugged. "I think we have a new patient at Fremont."

. . .

THE NEXT DAY, I stopped by Fitz's office three times, but he seemed to always be occupied. He promised he would find me after his meeting that day so we could talk. I sat frustrated in the lounge, unable to focus on anything else. Energy coursed through me like never before, and I struggled to sit still in the activity lounge.

"Are you going to the track with me today? The fresh air will be nice." I asked.

Neela looked up over her book, then glanced toward Nora. "Are you talking to her or me?"

"You."

"Why not her?" she asked.

I felt as though the answer was obvious. "Because she won't go. I have a chance with you since Kellan will be there."

Neela nodded. "True. Okay, I'm in, but I'm walking. Stop trying to make me run."

"Deal." I grinned.

I dragged Neela toward the locker room to change, only to find Cassie admiring herself from different angles in the mirror.

"Missy, how are you? I'm sorry if I was too hard on you yesterday. I'll take it easy on the track today." She sashayed out of the room, and I glared blank-faced at Neela.

She busted out laughing, holding her stomach as if the chuckle caused her pain. I gave her a few minutes, but she still hadn't regained control. Tears rolled down her cheeks.

"Can I ask what has you so tickled?"

She took a deep breath, a sad attempt at regaining control. "I wish I'd had my phone yesterday. To get a picture of her with a broken nose and no teeth!" She cracked up again, and I fought the bubble of laughter that made its way up my throat.

I leaned forward and whispered, "So, I'm not going crazy? Elise erased what I had done, right?"

Neela nodded. "She's gifted, Mercy."

"So Cassie doesn't remember? Everyone else watched Elise reverse my temper tantrum."

Neela chewed her lip, as if trying not to say too much. She sighed. "Not everyone is in tune with their power. That is what gives us the ability to see the truth in the time change. Time is affected, but our gift shields our minds from it."

"So, Cassie has a disconnect from her power? She's gifted as well?"

"That's right. Fitz will explain it, I promise. We grew up studying our gifts, Mercy. You have a lot to learn in a short

82

amount of time and he's worried about it overwhelming you."

Neela turned toward her locker as she pulled the cotton shirt over her head.

I froze at the sight. "What is that?" I asked.

"What?"

"You know what. The mark on your shoulder. What is that?" My voice echoed across the locker room.

She exhaled loudly and reluctantly turned to face me. I could tell she didn't want to say too much.

"Can I at least see it?" I asked.

"Sure." She turned so I could see the tattoo up close. Neela's mark looked like an eye—almost whimsical. Not creepy like I would've imagined.

"It's beautiful, Neela."

"Thanks. Can I see yours?"

My eyes narrowed. "How did you . . ."

"Your reaction to mine told me what I needed to know. Can I?"

I lifted my shirt, and like Nora, Neela gasped. "I've never seen that before. I'm not sure what to call it," she whispered.

I turned back to face her. "Nora called it Rage Fire."

Her eyes met mine, curiosity evident by the tilt of her head. "Does she know what it means? Is it elemental?"

"If she knows, she didn't tell me."

"I'm sure Fitz can shed some light on all of this for you. I would love to hear his opinion, so keep me in the loop."

I groaned, annoyed. "If he doesn't explain things, you and Nora will have to. I'm not waiting any longer. I have a right to know."

"Deal," she agreed.

. . .

NEELA LEFT to go upstairs while I finished changing. The mild weather felt lovely that day, so the roof was a perfect place to jog due to the breeze. Tables and chairs were arranged in the four corners of the roof with herbs and flower gardens along the outside edge. A rubber-like material ran from one end of the building to the other—offering a decent jogging track. Most of the students were taking advantage of the pleasant weather, especially since we'd had so much rain the past few days.

When I walked toward the track, Neela and Drake stood in the corner, talking privately. Drake stared at his feet with a grim expression on his face—hands on his hips. He looked upset. She leaned in to whisper something, but he took off along the track, leaving Neela mid-sentence. She tried to call out, but he didn't acknowledge her.

I stretched my legs, warming up for my run, and tried to time it where I could speak to Drake. As he came around the bend, I jogged into the space right behind him. He pushed himself harder, and I could feel his frustration. Picking up speed, I jogged beside him, but he never looked my way. He knew I was there. We always knew.

"I wanted to speak with you about yesterday," I called out.

"Nothing to talk about."

I tried again. "I . . . um, thank you. Thank you for calming me down."

"Well, I didn't want my girlfriend's face busted up anymore, so it seemed like the right thing to do," he snapped.

That was the first time Drake had publicly declared Cassie as his girlfriend, and the words caused an angry stir inside my chest. I licked my lips and looked away, unsure how to respond.

"Is that really the reason?" I asked.

"It looks like Ren is warming up. It may be more appropriate for you to jog with your boyfriend."

The hits kept coming. I stopped running and grabbed onto his arm, forcing him to face me as other runners darted around us. "Tell me those words aren't like a knife to your chest."

Drake closed his eyes and took a deep breath. He held back, but I wasn't sure why.

I pushed again. "Tell me and I'll drop it. I won't mention it again."

Silence.

"Tell me!"

"I can't." He turned away and continued running alone.

I stood there, unsure of what to do next. Why did I care? I'd known this guy for less than two months, but it didn't feel that way. We were connected and I needed to know why.

"Hey, hotness. Wanna race?" Ren ran up beside me, gently squeezing the back of my neck.

"Sure, Ren. Let's go."

We ran for a half-hour before people started sitting down, catching their breath. Ren made it forty-five minutes before he quit. Drake and I were the only ones left, refusing to stop. We kept our pace on opposite sides of the track, so we didn't come in contact with each other. An hour passed and Coach yelled for everyone to get ready for lunch. Everyone started shuffling down the stairs, but we never stopped.

"Last call! Moreno! Monroe! Let's go!"

Coach Rogers eventually gave up and went inside. Fitz walked to the roof and sat in a chair beside the track, taking in the scene before him. Two hours. He let us go for two hours before he called us over. We both jogged toward Fitz—his gaze darting between us as if he sensed the tension.

"Drake, come see me this evening."

"I'm not scheduled with you this evening."

Fitz lowered his glasses and a stern expression crossed his face. "Come. See. Me. This. Evening. Got it?"

"Yes, sir." Drake spun toward the stairs without another word.

He turned toward me and exhaled. "I thought meeting with you out here might be nice. I tire of that stuffy office, you know."

I stayed quiet. He knew what I expected from him—the truth.

"Elise told me what happened yesterday. I wanted to apologize for not preparing you before now. I've only tried to protect you, Mercy. You must know that. You're a little different, so I wasn't even sure what I was preparing you for."

"And now?" I asked.

"I have a better idea than I did. Sometimes I think I know exactly who you are and other times I don't have a clue." Fitz rubbed his eyes as if exhausted. "It's becoming easier now that your power is progressing."

"I'm tired of being in the dark. I have a right to know."

"Alright, I'll tell you what I can." He sat up straight as if the conversation made unnerved him. "This world that you know is a small piece of the puzzle. It hasn't always been this way for us."

"Us?"

He sighed. "Regalians."

I tilted my head to the side and narrowed my eyes. I didn't know what to say.

"Hundreds of years ago, our people lived as one. All are human, but some are born with extraordinary gifts, one of the six gifts. The ungifted begrudged us, Mercy. In their resentful view, we were an interference of nature. Because of that, they banished us from living alongside them."

"Couldn't you have resisted? You have power and they don't."

"It would have been a world war, Mercy, and our people only wanted security for our families. So, the two highest Elders, from Ireland and Italy, created a hidden underground world so we could live peacefully. They called it Seregalo. Meaning, *Six Gifts*."

"I feel like you could be high right now. Are you?" I raised one brow in question.

He stared, blank-faced. "Were you high yesterday when you broke Cassie's nose?"

Point taken. "Please continue."

He nodded. "One individual has never ruled alone. We've always worked together as a council. The most powerful has always held the highest rank over the Elders until someone even more gifted came along. Our people felt like it was nature demanding a time for change."

I shook my head. "How do they know that?"

"Our current leader, Aadya, was born forty years ago. Out of the six gifts, she holds the power to wield three. That's unheard of. Most are only born with one. The day of her birth, a ripple of energy ran through the land, and our people acknowledged when she came of age, she would be the next in line to lead." Fitz paused, allowing me time to process his words.

"What happened then?" I asked.

"At sixteen, she was the highest-ranking official among the Elders. Power-hungry, she demanded more say than the others until she created a rift among our people. Those that refused to live under her authority were told to leave."

I couldn't comprehend that level of maliciousness. "That's awful. Where did they go?"

"New York, Ireland, India . . . Wherever they could seek refuge," he explained. "When Aadya was twenty-three, a powerful surge ran through the land once again, declaring another had been born. Aadya was so afraid of being removed from the throne she created, she sent a group of Custos to find the child and kill it."

"Custos? I've heard the word before—from Drake."

"Yes, that's right." Fitz sat back in his chair, waiting on me to process his words.

"What are they exactly . . . the Custos? Are they gifted?"

"No, they weren't born with powers. Or powers that they could use, anyway. Imagine being born into a gifted family, only to find out you're the only one unable to contribute—unable to protect. It would destroy your esteem," Fitz said.

"So Regalians can join the Custos if they aren't powerful?"

"The men could, yes. The women would be cast out of Seregalo at a young age. Which is why I felt so strongly about helping where I could. It isn't right."

"I'm so confused," I admitted.

"Aadya created the Custos when she decided she needed an army to do her bidding. Pulling from the weakest, most defeated Regalians in our city probably seemed like the perfect scenario to her. They craved purpose. And most of the time, their combat training is enough for two of them to overpower a gifted individual. Unless it's someone as powerful as you or Drake, which isn't typical."

"So if they aren't born gifted, do they not have a purpose?" I asked.

"Tell me, what did you think your life's purpose was before you found out who you were?" Fitz tilted his head to the side, curious.

It felt like a lifetime ago. "I wanted to work in child protective services. You know, help kids find a home where they could feel safe."

He smiled. "They're purpose is like any other person on this planet, Mercy. Nurse, teacher, electrician . . . they are human. Regalian blood doesn't change that. God created us all, but some of us were born with rare gifts. Aadya might not treat them as such, but it's true."

"This is a lot to take in at one time, Fitz."

"I can't imagine."

"So, you're telling me I'm a Regalian, born with a special gift, and I should have lived happily ever after in Seregalo, except I'm not, and her guards came after me on a train because they believe I'm a threat?"

His brow wrinkled in confusion. "Well, yes, Sort of."

I threw my hands up in the air. "Maybe I am high."

He smiled. "I know this is all a bit much. Learning this at one time, and later in life than most, must be overwhelming."

It did overwhelm me, but not in a negative way. It felt as though I'd been given the final pieces of a lifelong puzzle. "Why is there a familiarity in all of this? I've never heard any of it before, but I don't doubt the truth of it."

Fitz nodded. "Because it's in your blood. It's who you are."

"And who is that? I've never been closer to discovering who I truly am, yet I feel more lost than ever. I don't understand my gift or how to control it."

"You're a tough case to crack, Mercy. You have what they refer to as interference of energy, or psychokinesis. You use the energy around you to move objects against nature. Which is also what makes you stronger and faster—the manipulation of energy. The issue is that you only seem to be able to use it when you are in a highly emotional state, which can become very dangerous. I believe that's what caused your mother's accident, the energy eruption on the subway, and again on the tennis court with Cassie. I've asked Neela to work with you, and she's agreed to help."

"Neela? She has the same gift?" I asked.

"She does," he answered.

"Does everyone at Fremont have gifts?"

"Everyone at Fremont is Regalian, but not all have a

connection with their power," he explained. "Dr. Lee and I started Fremont with the vision of helping everyone—powerful or not. That's what we've done. Some Regalians are born with latent power or a gift their mind refuses to tap into. It's a stressful process if it doesn't come easy. For some, it takes years, and others can never access it—like Custos. Most of the Regalians in New York moved here after the rift in Seregalo, so they're alone. We're here to help if we can."

"So Cassie, Kellan, Cyrus . . . they're all gifted as well?"

"Yes, but struggling. That's why they're here. That's also why Cassie wasn't aware of the shift in time yesterday. Some have a broken connection we are trying to mend."

I didn't like Cassie, but I felt bad about her lack of power. Feeling less than those around you was something I could relate to.

"Neela also brought something else to my attention. Elemental interference has the power to manipulate air, fire, water, and earth. So it would be quite easy for someone with this gift to control the weather. She is noticing a correlation between your moods and our sudden increase of storms. She's convinced you hold more than one gift."

Fitz focused on my face, waiting for a reaction from me before he continued. "I've suspected this, but I wanted to give you as much time as possible to learn and grow in your power. We're running out of time, Mercy. Aadya must sense how strong you are if she is sending Custos for you. As your power strengthens, it will be easier for other Regalians to find you. If there's a chance one of my students is the next chosen leader, then I have to protect them. Our future depends on it."

"What are you saying? That it could be me?" My stomach dropped.

"Yes. That's exactly what I'm saying."

❖

8

*F*itz went back inside, but I couldn't. Not yet. I wasn't sure how long I'd sat on the rooftop, looking out across the top of the endless brick and concrete surrounding me. New York was all I'd ever known, and the possibility of not belonging caused an ache deep inside. I wasn't entirely sure if I mourned for the city I loved, or the city I should've grown up in.

Nevertheless, the pain was present, and I hadn't been able to process it. The thought occurred to me that someone in my family had been gifted. If my mom had power, she would have used it against me. My dad? A grandparent?

"Are you going to stay out here all night?" Dr. Lee walked toward me, smiling. "How ya doin' kid?"

My troubled eyes said it all.

"That bad, huh?" he asked.

"I've never felt so confused, excited, and exhausted in all my life. How can that be?"

"I'm not sure because I've met your mom. Can't get much worse than that."

I cracked a smile. "Haha."

Dr. Lee took a seat beside me, staring out over the city. "That was not a joke." His elbow nudged mine. "You know you can talk to me, right?"

"I wouldn't know where to start. There's so much I need to learn."

"We'll help you with that. As we learn more about your power, we can help you find your source, and keep you safe while you learn to use it," he assured me.

"My source? How do I find it?"

"You want to try right now? You've been through a lot, so I understand if you want to wait."

"Yes. Definitely." I sat up straight, eager to get started.

He smiled and bobbed his head in agreement.

"Close your eyes. Now, take in a few deep breaths and try to relax."

After I reluctantly closed my eyes, I breathed in my nose and out my mouth, attempting to rid my body of the coiled tension I'd built up. My shoulders settled, and my spine loosened.

"Now, the most important thing to remember is your source of power is a connection between your heart and mind. A fuse, so to speak, that everyday people are not born with. An absence or overabundance of your heart's involvement can be dangerous. In your case, too much of your heart is connected to your gift, and your emotions threaten your control. Try to calm yourself, so your fuse doesn't blow. Understand?"

"Yes, that makes sense."

"Good. Now, focus. Find the connection that houses your gift and discover the mental and emotional balance it needs to thrive. Search within yourself for the strength you never knew existed. Don't forget to breathe."

I concentrated on the pit of my stomach, working up toward my chest—waiting for an inkling of what he'd described. I felt nothing. Just an emptiness. A black hole inside of me for all the hate and resentment to pile up. I opened my eyes in defeat.

"Keep trying, Mercy. If it were easy, then you would've already found it when you were younger. Some spend their entire life trying to master the very thing that makes them who they are. It takes years of understanding and patience that someone has ripped away from you." He stood to leave. "I'll give you some privacy. We have therapy scheduled tomorrow—we can try again."

"Dr. Lee?" I called out.

He tilted his head in question. "Yes?"

"What is your gift?"

Grinning mischievously, he said, "Subconscious interference."

It hit me. So, that's how he knew about my nightmares. My eyes narrowed, and he grinned mischievously.

"Goodnight, Mercy."

. . .

SLEEP HAD NEVER BEEN A FRIEND. Even as a child, I would lie awake at night dreading the possibility of another nightmare. That night was no different. When I wasn't counting sheep, I searched tirelessly for my fuse. I needed a little spark—a hint to lead me in the right direction. There was nothing. My body relented to exhaustion a couple of hours before sunrise, and I slept through breakfast. A dip in the bed caused me to stir.

"Wake up. We have training to do."

My eyes squinted and I struggled to focus on Neela. Her

excitement was obvious and I grinned at the contagious energy.

"You're going to help me figure this out?" I asked.

She nodded. "I am."

"You have quite a task ahead of you."

"I'm up for it," she assured me. "We all are."

"We?" I already knew the answer to that question, but I needed her to say it.

"Myself, Nora, Ren, and Drake."

How did they talk Drake into helping? He'd made his wishes known the evening before.

Neela knew me all too well. "He wants to help you, Mercy."

"I'll take all the help I can get. Let me clean up, and we can get started," I said.

"Dress comfortably and meet me on the roof," she called out.

Dr. Lee explained I needed to calm my inner emotions and relax to use my gift. So, before I walked out of the room, I took a few minutes to breathe and stretch my wound-up body. I wanted to soak up the knowledge, experience, or anything else my friends could offer to help me understand the ability I was born with.

An uncomfortable silence surrounded me as I walked out onto the rooftop. Bare, except the four serious-looking faces that sat beside the track. Choosing this area for that reason was smart—everyone had a class or session elsewhere, so they wouldn't be a distraction.

"Alright, let's do this," I called out with more excitement than I felt.

"Have a seat, Mercy." Neela pulled out another chair and motioned for me to join them. "Let's find out how much you know before we start."

"Yeah, sure. That makes sense." The seriousness of the group heightened my anxiety.

"Fitz said he explained some things last night, but I'm not sure how in-depth he went. We have a few questions for you, that way we'll have a starting point," she explained.

"Okay. . ." My mind instantly wanted to know how much he didn't tell me.

"Don't be nervous, Mercy. We're here for you, remember?" Ren smiled at me with that smug grin of his. "How many gifts do Regalians possess?"

"Six, but typically one gift per person. Except for Aadya—she has three," I answered like a proud student.

"Good. Name them." Ren's head tilted back, eyes squinting while he focused on my response.

I thought back to everything I'd seen and heard over the past week. "Dr. Lee has the gift of subconscious interference, and I witnessed Elise turning back time. I remember hearing the term sensory interferer on the subway with Drake that day. Fitz thinks I'm capable of energy and elemental interference. I'm not familiar with the other one."

"Wait. Fitz thinks you have two gifts?" Nora looked skeptical, but Neela nodded in agreement.

"Or more," I replied.

Neela explained, "I witnessed the rain and wind change based on Mercy's mood more than once. We saw what she did to Cassie on the tennis court."

I cut my eyes to where Drake sat quietly, but he didn't react.

Nora couldn't contain her enthusiasm, she grinned brightly and sat on the edge of her seat. "That's amazing. I've never met someone with more than one gift before."

Ren raised his hand to halt the discussion, trying to get the lesson back on track. "Mercy, the six gifts of interference are time, subconscious, emotion, sensory, psychokinesis, and elemental. I'm elemental, Nora is emotional, Drake is sensory, and Neela is psychokinetic. You have a wide variety of power and experience here to guide you."

I took in every person surrounding me, seeing them with fresh eyes—a new perspective. Remembering the warmth flooding my body when I received a hug from Nora. Or the group of Custos going blind when they went up against Drake. The realization of the truth brought so much clarity to my time at Fremont.

"We want you to sit in the center so we can surround you with our magic to force yours to the surface. A gift like Nora's could help calm your emotions so you can focus on the spark," Neela assured me. She watched as if she expected this to be too much for me to handle.

"What happens . . . I . . . I just don't want to hurt anyone," I admitted.

Ren chuckled as if that was absurd. "What makes you think you could hurt us?"

"Did you see Cassie's face? And before that, I cut my mother's fingers off."

The silence around the group made me wish I'd kept that last one to myself.

"One step at a time, alright? I promise we'll go slow," Ren told me.

Neela directed me to a chair in the center where I sat with sweaty, clenched fists. I had to remind myself that they were my closest friends—my support system.

"Close your eyes and try to unwind," Nora whispered.

Breathing in and out slowly, I tried to block out any outside noise. If you've ever been to New York, you know how difficult that can be. To my surprise, the cooing of the pigeons dissipated, and the sirens were no longer wailing down the street. What was happening? Then it hit me—

Drake had blocked out the surrounding distractions with sensory interference.

The rushing of blood and pounding of my heart was louder than anything else around me. I searched for my center, my purpose. Again, I came up empty. This time, an awful throbbing pain started in the back of my skull and made its way forward. I opened my eyes, throwing my palms up on the side of my head.

"It's no use," I admitted. "I can't do this for five minutes before I get a migraine."

Neela leaned forward, her forehead wrinkled with concern, "Mercy, it's been over two hours."

"Hilarious. I literally closed my eyes a few minutes ago. I felt Drake filter out the noise level, and a calm came over me —there was nothing after that."

Neela nodded. "Yes, Drake and Nora did attempt to help, but look at them. Do they look the same to you?"

I glanced over at Nora, and the black rings that now rimmed her eyes were not there a few minutes ago. Then Drake beside her, covered in sweat.

"Is that what happens when you use your gift? I'm so sorry. I didn't know."

"Nature always takes in return, but we bounce back quickly. It's worth it if we can help you," Nora said with a kind smile. She leaned forward, "Close your eyes again, I'd like to try something. There could be a component of your power that you are missing or haven't discovered yet. We're going to try to direct you."

I closed my eyes, and like before, the noise drifted away, and the fear of failure eased from my mind.

All at once, their hands came in contact with my shoulders, arms, and knees, and I felt a surge deep inside of me. They were using their power to feed mine, and it made me hyper-aware of my surroundings. I could feel a warmth traveling in from every limb, especially on my right knee. A burning hot sensation that wasn't unpleasant, just louder, caused my pulse to skyrocket. My body reacted differently to the touch, and I fought to dampen the effects.

A flame flickered. A small orange flash that happened so fast, I almost missed it. Dr. Lee was wrong, this wasn't a connection *between* my heart and mind—the source was rooted deep in my heart. And it wasn't a fuse—it was a fire.

I stood abruptly at the realization, and Nora watched with a pleased expression, "Nice work, Mercy. Now that you found it, let's learn to control it."

I looked to my right, determined to know who my body responded to so fiercely. I should have known. Drake's dark eyes met mine, and we took a deep breath in sync. The connection broke as Ren spun me to face him.

"This is freakin' awesome, Mercy. Tell us, how did you finally do it? Did you feel one of us lead you, or did it just happen?"

Glancing back at Drake, I remembered what he said to me on the rooftop last night. He wanted me to move on. He already had a girlfriend.

"It just happened, I guess," I lied.

Neela beamed. "Whatever sparked it, the hardest part is over. Now we can move forward with your training."

"It's strange, Dr. Lee kept referring to my source as a fuse or spark. It was buried deep inside my heart, and it was nothing like a fuse."

"What did it feel like to you?" Nora asked.

"A flame. A tiny flame that roared when linked with everyone's power."

"Wait, a flame? Like the one on your back?" Nora asked.

"You have a flame on your back?" Ren asked, intrigued.

"An Allegato mark. Show them," Nora said.

Excitement ran through the group. All except Drake, who

appeared agitated and determined to stare a hole into the building under his feet. I turned and pulled the back of my shirt up so they could see the mark.

"We never got around to discussing this last night, so I still don't know what it means," I explained.

Silence and nervousness surrounded me, overpowering the anger radiating from Drake. I pulled the back of my shirt down and turned to face them. Considering how quiet everyone was, I thought they may have left.

"So? What does it mean?" I asked.

Drake's eyes narrowed angrily, but Ren seemed rather proud.

Neela spoke softly, "Allegato marks represent one of the six gifts, Mercy. For example, sensory is represented by an eye. An hourglass for time. Elemental has always been represented by water. I'm not saying your mark doesn't symbolize the elements, I just haven't seen it before."

"Nora, you said something about Rage Fire. What does that mean?"

"I've not been able to find the exact history of it, but I've seen a picture in an old Regalian text my grandmother kept. Apparently, it hasn't been seen in over a hundred years."

"So, what? It portrays our gifts? You said yourself that I may have an elemental gift. Maybe that's what it symbolizes."

"It doesn't represent your gift," Neela explained. "Allegato is another word for attached. An Allegato mark represents the gift of your soul mate." Everyone stood very quiet. "We wear the mark of our other half, Mercy."

Her explanation sunk in. It meant I belonged with someone, the soul mate for my power. The flame represented someone else's gift. Drake was a sensory interferer, and my mark symbolized fire. My stomach dropped, and I fought tears.

Neela's arm wrapped around my shoulders, and she whispered softly in my ear, "Not here, Mercy."

I tucked my emotions away, and my eyes dried immediately.

"I think it's another way to represent the elements," Ren said with satisfaction in his voice.

Having the gift of elemental interference, he would think that.

The scraping of metal on concrete interrupted Ren's opinion. Drake's chair slid back as he stood and stomped off toward the stairwell without another word.

"I'm going to check on him," Nora said.

"I need to go also, I have a meeting with Fitz." Ren leaned in and kissed me on the cheek before he left.

Lovely. Now he thinks we're betrothed.

I turned toward Neela, something from yesterday weighing heavily on my mind. "Your mark is an eye. It's sensory, isn't it? You're mated to a sensory interferer."

She didn't want to answer. She knew I'd be upset.

"That doesn't mean I am supposed to be with Drake, Mercy. There are hundreds of Regalians out there with sensory interference. Just like it doesn't mean you are meant for Ren."

I nodded my understanding, but my heart mourned. I wanted it to be Drake.

"Drake knew about your mark. When I realized yesterday that your Allegato wasn't sensory, I gave him a heads up. That's why he was so angry last night. I didn't want him finding out in front of everyone else—that would've been cruel," she admitted.

"Are you happy that I don't wear his mark? You carry it, maybe that eliminates me as competition."

Her eyes narrowed. "You're upset. You don't mean that.

Plus, it doesn't work that way. If we were meant to be together, there would be no competition."

My anger deflated. I knew she wasn't that type of person, but my frustration wanted to lash out—punish someone. "I'm sorry. I'm confused and disappointed."

"I know you are. I've seen the way you look at each other and I was hopeful for you both. Now that Regalians are so spread out, some never find their other half."

"Does Drake have a mark?"

"If he does, he's never shared." She honestly looked disappointed for me. "Give Ren a chance, Mercy. If he's your other half, you may not have sensed it yet, because you've been so caught up in Drake."

I knew her words made sense, but something told me it wasn't Ren.

"Alright, Neela. I'll try."

. . .

IRONICALLY, I slept very well that night. The training exhausted me mentally and physically. My eyes opened the next morning—my vision crisp and clear. If I focused, I swear I could hear the sound of the steady beat of Nora's heart. A sense of change washed over me, as if I'd been reborn. I took a quick shower and stepped into my favorite jeans and a tank. I left my hair down and had just walked into the bedroom when Nora peered at me with tired, narrowed eyes.

"You have a visitor at the door."

"Who is it?" I asked.

"Ren."

There it was again, the confusion and disappointment that my heart wouldn't relinquish. *You promised Neela you would try.*

Pasting a smile on my face I didn't quite feel, I opened the door to a smirking Ren. His eyes sparkled with mischief.

His presence confused me. "You're here early. What's up?"

"There is somewhere I'd like to take you."

My eyes narrowed suspiciously. "Are we allowed?"

"I got permission to take you to breakfast, but we have to come straight back," he explained.

"Getting out of Fremont for a bit sounds wonderful. Let me grab my jacket."

I stepped back into the room, pulling the hoodie from my closet. Nora didn't comment, but I didn't expect her to. She knew I struggled with Ren. He offered me his arm, and I took it graciously. As I closed the door, we turned and immediately ran into Drake, his posture tense as if ready to pounce.

"Sorry, man. We're heading out for breakfast. Can I bring you back something?"

"No, thanks. I've lost my appetite." Drake circled around us, seemingly annoyed with life at the moment. I understood.

The bite of the morning air hit my face as we exited the guild. Conversation didn't flow as easily with Ren. Every time I considered asking a question, I changed my mind, trying to come up with something more interesting. Pigeons broke through the uncomfortable silence as I focused on the uneven cracks in the sidewalk beneath our feet. Most businesses were still closed, although the bagel carts were full steam ahead. It was a peaceful morning.

We walked a couple of blocks north and stopped in front of a store decorated in pink and teal. "You will never find a better blueberry scone in all of New York. The owner is originally from Nebraska and grew up in a family of bakers."

I looked up at the feminine pink striped awning, and the swirled teal letters on the window. "Arin's Bake Shop."

"It'll change your life," he told me.

My eyes widened and I grinned at his enthusiasm. "I'm hard to impress, you know."

"I'm up for the challenge." Ren smirked as he held the door open for me.

We chose a seat by the window, and a young woman with her dark brown hair in a loose bun greeted us from the counter. Her bright green eyes stood out against the coral pink of her dress. After discussing the latest menu options, she persuaded me to try her famous scones with a seasonal spicy mocha. The woman knew her way around a scone. She continued bringing out samples of her latest creations, coercing us into trying the sweet delicacies. The atmosphere was an escape from the hustle of the city streets, and I hadn't been that relaxed since I arrived at Fremont. Ren's eyes studied me, deep in thought.

"What?" I asked with a mouthful of scone. "Do I have something on my face?"

"No." He grinned. "You're at ease. No tension, no confusion, or anxiety. I didn't think you could be more beautiful, but I was wrong."

My coffee mug froze against my lips. Had anyone ever said anything like that to me before? I didn't remember it if they had.

"Wow, Ren. That is very sweet. I'm not even sure what to say."

"You don't have to say anything. I'm just glad you're here." He smirked as if he were proud of himself.

I glanced away from the intense scrutiny of Ren's gaze.

Say something. Change the subject.

"Tell me about yourself. Your family and where you grew up," I told him.

"Alright. Dad and Ma live in Brooklyn. I have a large family nearby on my father's side, but Ma is from Japan, so that side of the family is still overseas. I'm an only child, but it never felt like it growing up. I had cousins everywhere. I loved it. My gift comes from my father's side, he is Regalian, and Ma is not."

"So, I guess he never found his other half?"

"She died very young. Honestly, I couldn't imagine anyone better for my father than Ma. You can't tell me they aren't meant to be." He smiled at the thought.

"That's interesting," I whispered. "Did she struggle to understand your gift?"

"She's trying. Dad knew Fremont would be the best place for me, with guidance from Fitz. Ma doesn't understand why I can't train at home, and she's been heartbroken since I left."

"That's sad and sweet at the same time. I knew you had a unique blend of features, but I wasn't sure about your heritage."

"What about you? You've said little about your folks—besides the fact you cut your mom's fingers off. . ." One eyebrow raised in question.

"Well, funny story really . . . I didn't actually cut them off myself. Anger overpowered everything else in the moment, and she cut them off while chopping potatoes. I didn't realize I had an out-of-control gift at the time. She's a horrible person, Ren. We've never gotten along. Not saying I didn't feel bad about it, of course, I did."

Well, sort of.

"I hate to hear that about your mom. What about your dad?" he questioned.

"He left when I was an infant. Probably to get away from her." I turned up the mug, finishing the rest of my mocha.

"I'm sorry, Mercy. I'm not sure how I'd cope if I didn't have anyone to help with my gift. You turned out remarkable considering."

"Thanks, Ren. You're pretty incredible yourself."

"I hate for breakfast to end, but I promised Fitz I'd have you back quickly."

I absorbed the softness of his smile, the affection in his eyes. "This has been wonderful, Ren. It's the first time I've felt normal in a while. Thank you."

Ren smiled but didn't respond. He didn't need to. We stood to leave, and he took my hand as we exited the bakeshop. I let him, even though my instinct was to pull away. We weren't there for long, but already the city streets were waking up. Several more cars were on the road, and the occasional jogger would dodge us on the sidewalk.

The massive doors to Fremont opened, and Dr. Lee leaned against the doorframe with his hands in his pockets. "Mercy, I need you to come with me. You have a visitor."

"Who would visit me?" Oh no. Please say it isn't so.

"Your mom," he answered.

My mother sat, wearing her usual tan slacks and cream cardigan, in a dark brown leather chair in front of Dr. Lee's desk—her hand still bandaged, and a disgusted sneer across her face at the sight of me. Dr. Lee raised the blinds to brighten the room, and warmth from the sun radiated into the small space. In the distance, a dark cloud hovered.

"Mom, what brings you by?"

"Apparently, they require a parental visit. Ridiculous policy," she spat.

"Oh, I see. After meeting you, I assumed they'd realize that isn't necessary in my case."

"Don't get smart with me. I fully intend to sign the paperwork to keep you here an additional six months after turning eighteen, with weekly electroshock therapy sessions. You aren't capable of making your own decisions, and I won't have you back in my house until they get you straight." She tilted her chin high, as if she had the upper hand.

"You don't have to worry about that, Mom. I don't plan on coming home. Ever." I shrugged.

"Mrs. Monroe, Mercy is excelling at Fremont. She's finished her high school finals, an amazing athlete, she has close friends. You should be very proud," Dr. Lee added.

"Proud? You've got to be joking. Look at her. She reminds me of her father. Selfish, arrogant, and lazy."

Thunder rolled outside of the window, and I reminded myself to stay calm and breathe. Dr. Lee slowly reached for his letter opener and slid it into the top drawer of his desk. Good call.

"Why are you here? Why did you bother coming at all? You care nothing about me, you never have. I would've been better off going with my dad instead of enduring your presence for the last seventeen years!" This was quickly going downhill.

"I wish he would've taken you! Then you could have perished right along with both of them! That's what you deserve!" she screamed.

The room turned silent as rain pelted against the window. Sadness crept its way inside of me at her words.

I whispered. "Perished? What are you talking about?"

She stood, and the venom behind her next words surprised me. "Noah and Annabel Monroe."

Dr. Lee stood abruptly. His eyes widened as if the information he'd been waiting for had just been revealed.

"You didn't really think I was your mother, did you? That I could ever birth something as vile as you?" She stepped around me, never taking her eyes off my face. "I hope they come for you. I hope you get what you deserve, just as they did," she whispered.

The door slammed, and I fell back into the chair in shock. What just happened?

"Mercy, listen to me. The things she said, well—I need to speak to Fitz immediately. Are you alright? Let me help you back to your room," Dr. Lee fumbled over his words.

My room. Nora and Neela were, no doubt, waiting for me to return to offer their support. They knew how I felt about my mom—or who I thought was my Mom. I couldn't see them right now. I needed to be alone.

"Can I wait here? I need to think."

"Of course. I'll be right back."

Noah and Annabel Monroe. Someone killed my parents. I needed to know what happened—how I ended up with that heinous woman. Strangely enough, there was peace peeking through the confusion and pain. It hit me—the relief of knowing I didn't come from her. Knowing I wasn't her spawn and I could be better. Warm salty tears left paths down my cheeks as I tried to balance the gratefulness of not belonging to her with the mourning of the only mother I knew.

Fitz ran into the office with Dr. Lee. Hair disheveled, sweat on his brow, and what looked to be tears in his eyes. He stared as if seeing me for the first time.

"I knew it was you all along."

꘎

9

"*W*hat are you talking about?"

Shaking his head in disbelief, he looked as though he could hardly believe it. "I've been looking for you, Mercy. For years."

"But you're the one who brought me to Fremont."

"Well, yes, but I didn't know it was you. I'd hoped, but I couldn't be sure," he explained.

"Fitz, I know I ask this often, but are you high?"

"I promise I'll explain everything when I return." Fitz spun to leave the office.

I've heard that before. "You're leaving? Where are you going?"

"I need to speak to your mo . . . to, um, Mrs. Monroe first. I promise I'll be back as soon as I can."

Fitz and Dr. Lee quickly departed, and left me alone to sort through the haze of confusion my heart and mind were wading through. What was going on? It was as if the entire world had forgotten to take their medication.

Was I supposed to wait there? I couldn't do that. I needed to find something to occupy my mind and release the energy coursing through my veins. Maybe the gym or pool would be empty, considering it was still early. I left the office in a hurry, and as I turned the corner, I collided with Drake—knocking a book from his hand.

"I'm so sorry, I . . . I . . ." I stuttered. I couldn't think straight.

"Are you alright?" he asked.

I didn't answer, I couldn't for fear of crying.

He didn't hesitate to wrap his arms around me, even when he knew he shouldn't. He led me back into Dr. Lee's office out of view, concern flooding the dark brown of his eyes.

His palm cupped the side of my face. "What's wrong? Tell me what happened."

I shook my head, unable to explain. I opened my mouth and closed it. Drake gave up on words and leaned forward, pulling me into his chest. My heart slowed, as the smell and warmth of him relaxed me. At once, the confusion drifted and contentment settled within me.

He held me for several minutes, his arms tightening—his nose and lips buried in my hair. Neither of us wanted to let go.

"If you need to talk, you know where I am. Okay?" he asked.

I nodded. Once again, I leaned further into him, our proximity fueling the attraction. His chest expanded, breathing me in. My anxiety eased, and I pulled back slightly. We were too close, and we both knew it.

"Thank you. I really appreciate it," I said.

"I haven't been there for you like I should. I'm sorry." He brushed a hair from my face. "I'll do better."

We stood frozen, inches apart. It would be so easy to lean forward—feel the warmth of his lips on mine. But he wasn't mine.

Backing away, I nodded and quickly left the office to change into my Fremont swimsuit.

I flipped the switch, and the sound of the overhead lights echoed throughout the empty room. I walked around the pool, staring at the blue glass-like water as though it called out to me. I threw my towel to the side and dove in headfirst. I needed the release—craved it. My mind struggled to process everything, and I couldn't do that around my friends.

I stretched my body as my arms stroked the water and my legs kicked in a steady rhythm, which I knew I could keep up for a long while. Turning my head from side to side, I took deep breaths of air and closed my eyes. Focus on the movements—forget everything else. I tried to clear my mind, but Drake interrupted my line of thought, as he always seemed to do.

Why did I feel so strongly for him if he wasn't mine? I'd never been in love, and I wouldn't pretend to be an expert, but I'd never had an instant connection with anyone in my life.

The muscles in my thighs cramped. I welcomed the stinging pain. I couldn't be sure how long I'd been out there, but I knew I had swam at least twenty laps. Swapping to a backstroke, I worked a different muscle group and pushed my body as hard as possible. The conversation with the woman I thought was my mom replayed inside my head. Even if she wasn't my mother, she raised me. It hurt that she felt so little for me. I'd spent my entire life with her—I knew nothing else. Couldn't my parents have found someone that had a heart?

Swim harder.

You're selfish.

Don't quit.

You're lazy.

Push forward.

You're arrogant.

The water thrashed against me and pulled at my body as if it knew I was all of those things. It became more challenging to move, as if I were in a pool of syrup instead of water. A wave crashed down on top of my head, and I barely got a breath before it knocked me under once again.

You deserve to die, just like your parents.

Maybe I should've let the water take me. The waves created a cyclone that spun around my body from one side of the pool to the other, refusing to set me free. My foot pushed against the bottom of the pool, and I surged up, needing to breathe.

You're not worthy.

I kicked my legs harder to swim to the surface until I heard the most heartbreaking truth of all.

He'll never be yours.

I stopped kicking and my arms floated out to my side. My mind gave in to all the pain and bitterness. A heavy weight pushed down on my chest as though an anchor forced me to the bottom of the pool. My life should have been different. A loving mother and father should have raised me. They would have taught me everything I'd ever needed to know about my gift. I would have never questioned if I was worthy of anything or doubted my abilities.

Most of all, I wanted to be with the one my heart called out to. Even at seventeen years old, I knew who that was.

Dark eyes stared down into the blue depths around me. Drake. My heart swelled at the sight of him standing on the edge. The water calmed, and I swam to the surface. He angrily grabbed my arm and pulled me from the pool.

"What was that?" Drake screamed.

Nora's eyes darkened, and her hands shook as she placed a towel around my shoulders. Drenched and gasping for air, Ren lay on his back by the pool.

"What happened? What's going on?" I asked, confused.

Drake gripped the sides of my face and forced me to look at him. "Mercy, we've been trying to get you out of the water for over an hour. We thought we'd lost you."

"What?" My head tilted to the side, trying to make sense of his words.

"Ren tried to use his gift to control the water, and he couldn't budge it. What were you doing?" Nora asked.

I thought back at everything going through my head in the pool. It all felt like a dream. I recalled giving in. I remembered letting the water take control.

"I've never seen that before, never felt anything like it." Nora, shaking and weak, looked as though she was close to tears.

"Never felt what?" I asked.

"Despair. Hopelessness. You were literally drowning in your own emotions, and you weren't doing anything to stop it." A single tear fell down her cheek as she watched me, as if she remembered the torture I'd put myself through.

"I . . . I'm so sorry. I would never put any of you in danger. Please, tell me you know that," I pleaded.

Drake scoffed. "You think we're upset because you put us in danger?" He leaned in close, whispering, "I'd give my life for you, Mercy, but I need to know that you'll do everything in your power to survive. No matter what happens. If you don't do it for yourself, do it for me." Drake stormed off, leaving me speechless.

Ren helped Nora to her feet.

I stepped toward them. "Nora, I'm so sorry. I didn't even know what was happening."

She swallowed and took a deep breath. "I know you didn't. That's what scares me. I'm worried about what will happen if you don't learn to control your powers, Mercy."

Ren wrapped his arms around my shoulder and kissed

my forehead. "I'm going to help Nora back to her room, and then I'll be back."

I shook my head, focused on the settling ripples of the pool. "I think . . . I need to be alone."

Ren's brows shot up. "I'm not going to leave—"

"I'm okay, now. I promise." I smiled to assure him.

He nodded, but didn't look pleased. "Don't get back in the water. Promise?"

"I promise."

I watched as Ren assisted Nora back to our room, leaving me baffled at what happened.

I sat on the lounge chair by the pool after they left, wrapped up in a large towel. Lights glistened over the surface of the water that had been angry with me minutes before. I should never have jumped in with my emotions that high. I could've killed my friends, people that would have given their life for me.

"I heard I might find you here," Fitz called out. "I received a rundown of what happened in the water."

"I didn't mean for it to happen," I whispered, my eyes never leaving the pool.

"I know." He sat in the lounge chair beside me and paused, as if trying to find the words he came there to say. "I feel it's my responsibility to protect you. I only wish I could have done it sooner."

Finally, I turned to face him. "What are you talking about?"

"The only way I can make up for lost time is to teach you everything your father would've wanted me to." Fitz's words surprised me.

"You knew my father?" My voice echoed against the concrete walls around me.

"He was my best friend, Mercy. Noah Monroe grew up in Seregalo with me. Long story short, he and his wife moved to

New York before you were born. It devastated me, and I felt as though I'd lost my family. The day you were born, Regalians across the world sensed the wave of power, but one of our elders detected Monroe blood. He made the mistake of telling the council, including Aadya. Your parents tried to shield you from Aadya, but there was a terrible attack by the Custos, and you supposedly died along with Noah and Annabel. When you turned thirteen, we all felt the ripple again and knew you were alive."

"So, she really isn't my mother? It's true?"

"Yes, it's true," said Fitz.

"How did I end up with her?"

"That's the part I didn't understand. I had a long talk with her today, so I could piece the puzzle together. Apparently, she's the non-gifted half-sister to Noah. Banished from Seregalo because she was born without power. They must have kept her birth a secret—I don't remember Noah having a sister. They sent her away at an early age and she remembers very little of our world. She has major resentment toward Noah, and that has carried over onto you," he explained.

"So that explains why she despises me."

"I'm sorry," he muttered.

"It's not your fault."

"Noah panicked when he realized the extent of your power, and he knew Aadya would come for you. She said Noah showed up on her doorstep offering an obscene amount of money to hide you and raise you as hers. She was unmarried and struggling, so she accepted. Plus, Aadya would've never suspected her."

"My parents were trying to protect me? They loved me?"

"Oh, heavens, yes. Your father was over the moon when Annabel was expecting. When I heard the rumor of his death in New York, I felt like a part of me died right along with him. I came here searching for you, and found over fifty babies with the last name Monroe. And, there was no guarantee that your name hadn't changed. All I could do was wait and hope that if you survived, your power would surface."

I shook my head, confused. "How did you find me?"

"Dr. Lee was the one who heard about the trouble a Monroe girl was dealing with at school. One of his contacts reached out to him, so we investigated. I had my suspicions, but I couldn't be certain you were the one, not until today."

I had so many questions. But one stood out among everything else. "What were they like? My parents, I mean."

Fitz grinned. "Your father was cocky." He chuckled at the memory. "Never backed down from a fight, and trust me, there were plenty." His eyes grazed over each of my features. "Your mother was from Ireland, beautiful red hair and green eyes. Your dad had dark hair, like you."

"And their gifts?" I asked. I wanted to know everything.

"She carried emotional interference, and your father was sensory. If the elder was correct, you could be the one that has all six. The only one ever born to have all six, Mercy."

"I've only shown power in two, right?"

"So far, but that means nothing. They wouldn't all surface at the same time," he explained.

"There is so much I don't understand. If I don't learn how to control my power, someone is going to get hurt. I'll do whatever it takes, just tell me how to master it."

"Practice, Mercy. Over and over every day. Come see me tomorrow, I want to go over some things with you, alright?"

"Okay, Fitz. I'll be there."

I sat by the pool much longer than I intended after Fitz left. I needed some time alone. It was late when I crept down the hallway as quietly as possible, but the planks of the hardwood creaked under my feet. A door to my left eased open, and Ren stepped out, looking side to side.

"Mercy, I was hoping to catch you. Are you okay?"

"I'm fine, Ren. Sorry about earlier, though. I would never put you or the others in danger."

He nodded. "We all know that. You'll figure this out, I promise."

He wrapped his arms around me before I anticipated the gesture. Ren pressed my body into his—holding me—showing me kindness and support. Warm lips grazed across my cheek, then he softly whispered, "Good night."

I had to get away from there. The last thing I wanted was for him to get the wrong idea.

My door whined as I pushed against the wooden frame. My vision struggled to adjust to the darkness before I could move around the room. Nora lay on her back in the tiny bed across from me. I couldn't tell if she was asleep, so I moved as quietly as possible.

Shedding my clothes on the floor, I climbed into bed and stared at the ceiling for the answers my mind demanded.

Hurt. Deception. Abandoned. Dangerous.

Those four words did the tango around my head, keeping me from going to sleep. I don't even know the damn tango.

"Most people don't understand that pain is relative." Nora's small voice drifted across the room, pulling me from my daze.

"Sorry, what?"

"Pain. It's different for everyone. Not everyone responds to pain the same way, you know. Take Neela, for example, you'd never know she struggles to paste that pretty smile on her face every day. But the worry over her family keeps her in knots. Ren loves you even though he barely knows you, but deep down, he knows you don't feel the same way. Drake is angry. Angry at the world, and he has every right to be. And I'm . . . well, I'm broken. There are days I feel as though I'll never be whole again."

"Nora, you're not broken. You're the strongest person I

know."

"Have I ever told you about my parents?" she asked.

"Not a lot, no."

"My father is a lawyer and country club member in upstate New York. Reputation is everything to my parents, and we never left home unless we were photo-ready. As I got older, my gift grew stronger. Mom drove herself crazy, trying to hide the dark circles under my eyes, so I became a pro at applying concealer at thirteen. I embarrassed my family. My father said I looked like a drug addict in our family portrait, and he tore it to shreds. He said I was a freak."

My heart ached for Nora. "Are you the only one in your family with power?" I asked.

"My maternal grandmother was an emotion interferer. Everyone said she was crazy, and that I inherited the lunacy," she mumbled.

"I'm so sorry."

Not knowing about my gift was difficult. Being treated like that, by the people who should have loved her, must have been horrible. Tendrils of guilt wrapped around my heart for moping about my situation.

"Sometimes, it felt as though we were being prepared for politics. Maybe we were. He hosted a high-society benefit in the country club ballroom recently, and the place buzzed with business partners and golfing buddies. Out of everything that happened that night, the thing that stood out was the multiple trays of golden champagne, sparkling against the lights. I remember thinking how magical it all seemed. My little sister played in the corner with another girl, so I ran to the restroom before dinner. I had to hurry. I knew what would happen if I wasn't there when my dad began his speech."

Nora spoke as though I wasn't in the room. Staring at the

ceiling as if memories were playing out on the white sheetrock above her. Her voice got smaller and cracked halfway through her story.

"When I opened the door to leave the restroom, I ran into a man entering. He introduced himself and shook my hand politely, but his smile shined too bright—his eyes dark and eerie. Something felt wrong. The combination of wealth and alcohol created an illusion of invincibility for those men. He forced me back into the bathroom, telling me to be very quiet. His wide, fake smile couldn't hide his intention. His hands reached for my hair, rubbing it between his fingers. Then, his hand traveled down my arm, and I felt it. I felt all the emotions raging through him in that moment and I grew nauseous."

Nora took a shaky breath, crying as she relived her horror.

"The aggression and lack of concern—the guilt-free, sick mind standing in front of me tore at my soul. I sensed it all—everything he hungered for. I screamed at the top of my lungs and kicked him as hard as I could. It shook him enough for me to get out the door. I ran out into the silent ballroom with my father in the middle of his speech. Hearing my scream, everyone turned in my direction. My father was furious."

I shook my head, angry and baffled at the same time. "Surely after you told him what happened. . ."

"You would think so, but the man denied everything and said I attacked him for no reason. I even tried explaining everything to my mother before bed that night, and she told me if it were true, then it would have been better for me to keep my mouth shut, for my father's reputation. Mom said, 'It's not all about you, Elinora.'"

"Oh, Nora. How can she say that? You did the right thing. I can't imagine what could have happened to you."

"They brought me here the next day and told Fitz to do his worst. I'm happy here, Mercy. Happier than I've been in a long time. My sister is everything they could ever want in a daughter. They don't need me, anyway," she admitted.

I didn't know what to say. The pain and suffering that she endured the last few months were more than I'd dealt with my entire life. Nora felt everything—every single emotion we were all dealing with, on top of her own struggles. I only dealt with mine, and my world felt as though it would collapse all around me. *Pain is relative.*

At that moment, something came alive in me. Grief for the family that didn't care enough, sadness for the people hurting around me, and gratefulness that someone found their gift through the pain I carried. . .

Then I realized, those weren't my feelings at all. Those were Nora's emotions that I'd absorbed. I'd used emotional interference. I looked across the dark room. I couldn't see her, but I could feel her pride.

I struggled to find the right words. "You and Neela are my family, and we're yours. I can't thank you enough for sharing this with me. I'm sorry for the pain you had to go through, but I'm grateful for the lesson. As soon as I truly grasped I wasn't the only one hurting, I opened myself up to your pain. I could feel it, Nora. I could feel you."

Nora was silent for several minutes.

"Get some sleep, Mercy. Tomorrow's a new day for you."

. . .

FIVE O'CLOCK IN THE MORNING. I must have been insane. I woke up in the middle of the night with a crazy idea in my

119

head, and couldn't let it go. I dressed in dark leggings with a black hoodie pulled up over my head. I assumed this would be the appropriate attire for someone trying to sneak out of a building. If nothing else, I looked chill.

Fremont was quiet that morning—only the banging of pots and pans from the kitchen staff heard from the hallway. I flipped the lock on the heavy front door and eased it open just enough to squeeze through. I paused on the top step, absorbing the cool morning air. Without the usual traffic, the streets were bare.

Bagel carts rolled awkwardly onto the sidewalks, and garbage trucks banged against heavy dumpsters. This was my favorite time of the day. Everything came back to life and rose with the sun. A crispness in the air and a musty scent in the streets surrounded me. Maybe that's the garbage, I thought, as I hurried down the front steps before someone saw me sneaking out.

Mornings on the subway were just as nerve-wracking as late nights, for me anyway. Something about the abandoned stations and trash blowing across the cold concrete—as if it's all that remained of life. It wouldn't be this way for long though, maybe another hour or two before the city came to life.

I jumped on the blue line along with a few other early risers. An older lady with bluish-gray hair held a shaky dog that peaked out from her purse. She handed everyone pumpkin candy from last year's Halloween stash. A tall black man in a suit sat engaged on his cell phone and a teenager, around my age, huddled in the corner with headphones.

Remembering the route I took with Drake, I jumped off on Canal Street and walked over toward China Town. Coming up on the street we had worked so hard to clean, littered with trash, caused my heart to ache. Up ahead, I recognized the alleyway and quickly scanned the area before

I walked down the dark, enclosed space. The last thing I wanted was getting caught in a dangerous situation.

Again, empty bottles and brown paper bags littered the alley. I checked both sides of the dumpster but came up empty. *This is a stupid idea.*

I kicked a loose brick to the side and stomped toward the entrance.

"You shouldn't be here," a voice called out.

I paused mid-step, waiting to see if I had imagined it.

"Leave," he demanded.

I turned to see the black-clothed bundle sitting by a trash bin.

"Leave, Mercy Monroe."

"How do you know who I am?" I asked.

"That's a simple question. Can you do no better?"

"Screw you." That was a perfectly reasonable question.

A psychotic cackle erupted throughout the alley. The fact he found me funny surprised me. Most people didn't.

"I need help . . . controlling my power. I don't know what I'm doing," I admitted.

The hood fell from around his face, and he tilted his head toward me. "A wise Regalian knows when to ask for help. A fool is proud."

"I'm afraid I'll hurt someone if I can't control it." I took a shaky breath, praying he would help me.

"That's not all you're afraid of, is it?" he asked.

"No. I'm . . . I'm afraid of failing." Relief coursed through me after admitting it out loud. "I feel like everyone expects so much from me."

He grinned, motioning for me to sit across from him. Both hands opened in front of his lap, asking for mine. I slipped my slender hands inside his older, shaky ones. The intensity in his eyes and amused grin caused an uncomfortable chill to run up my spine.

"You've grown since I saw you last. Your source burns brightly, Regalian, but you haven't learned to control it. If you can't find balance, it will consume you and everyone around you."

"How? How do I do that?" I asked.

"Each Regalian discovers their power differently, in their own time. Not to mention you have more than one to command."

His words fueled my anxiety. "Can you help me, yes or no?"

"I can try if you like. It won't be easy."

I nodded once for him to continue.

His eyes closed, so I shut mine, but opened one now and again to peer at him. Might as well be weird together. My palms were hot, and a tingling sensation traveled up my arms. The exertion of power thickened the air around us as I gasped for air. It started as a hum, as he hovered on the surface of my subconscious, his intentions unknown.

A stabbing pain shot through my spine and caused my back to arch forward. I froze from the agony and wasn't able to move if I wanted to. I could sense his presence searching me, invading my mind and heart with disturbing interest. We weren't alone. Someone else violated my subconscious with him, impatiently waiting for me to reveal my strengths and weaknesses. My skull ached as though it would crack under the pressure of his assault.

I pushed against the pain, and a burning sensation built in my chest as terror consumed me. The flame was out of my control, and no matter how hard I tried, I couldn't dampen it. A searing heat worked its way up my neck, as my cheeks flamed hot. Dizziness and exhaustion devoured my mind, but I wouldn't give in.

Pressure surrounded me, pushing me away from the threat of the mysterious man and the unknown presence invading my thoughts. A tug of war was in play as he reeled me back in, holding onto my freedom by a string. At once, a powerful internal force flung me backward, and I shook off the last of the hold. An empty space against the brick wall was all that remained in front of me. Blood dripped from my nose as I looked around the alley, the air thick with the aftermath of magic.

I placed one foot flat on the ground, attempting to stand, but fell back against the rough brick wall. Blood continued dripping from my nose, and double vision kept me from standing up straight. Fremont—I could make it to Fremont. The brick wall guided me out of the alley, and I stumbled my way toward Canal Street.

I knew what everyone thought of me, and sadly not uncommon to see on the street—a troubled, drunk girl. Eyes shifted back to personal business, wanting nothing to do with the girl who was obviously bad news.

Compassion as usual.

Closing one eye helped. I finally located the subway, and a kind homeless man balanced me by my elbow to board the rail. Sympathy filled his eyes, and I felt ashamed I had put myself in that situation. Something about the man looked familiar, but the blurred vision made me doubt myself. At my stop, he offered to assist me further. I declined and thanked him for the rare act of kindness. I staggered the rest of the way to the guild, the top of the red brick building coming into view.

The throbbing behind my eyes worsened with each step, as my hands felt their way up the concrete steps. Angry shouts and accusations could be heard from the other side of the door, and I could make out Drake's rage-filled voice. I turned the doorknob, praying I'd step inside before I passed out.

"You told me you would protect her! You said I didn't have to worry! Where is she?" Drake yelled.

Nora's head jerked up at the creak of the door, "Mercy! Are you. . .?"

Ungracefully, I collapsed, and everything went black.

. . .

IT WAS dark when I opened my eyes, but I recognized my soft mattress and old quilt tucked around me. Nora's small form lay visible under her blankets. Even though she slept, I could sense her emotions. She worried about her friends, and guilt overwhelmed me for being reckless. Thankfully, the brutal throbbing in my head subsided.

I wasn't sure what I expected when I approached the man for help, but definitely not the suffering I experienced. My chest expanded on a deep breath, and I exhaled loudly, releasing the pent-up tension.

Do you ever learn? Evidently not.

I closed my eyes to everything around me so I could focus on my source. Amazing how the flicker was so visible now, the tiny orange flame so eager to burn bright. The old man's motives were not kind, but I've never been so attuned to my gift. The anticipation of starting the day buzzed through me, and I couldn't lay still any longer. I tip-toed across the room, letting Nora sleep as long as possible.

Someone must have taken me out of the blood-stained hoodie—only the cotton shirt I usually slept in remained. They had cleaned me up, and I honestly looked much better than I expected. As soon as I decided to brush my teeth, the toothbrush flew out of the cup and shot straight into my mouth, gagging me. I yanked it out, breathing heavily and staring at the possessed object. What just happened?

My eyes inspected the brush, and I hesitantly reached for the toothpaste. I'd never battled a tube before, but it was evident the toothpaste didn't plan to go gently. By the time Nora opened the bathroom door, toothpaste covered the countertop and floor, fighting for its liberty. My palm flung forward from frustration, and the tube and brush both flew against the mirror.

"Mercy? Are you all right?" Nora asked.

"No. No, I'm not. All I want to do is brush my teeth, and I can't even do that!" I yelled.

"Maybe I should grab Neela. This looks like her territory." She quickly left me for back-up.

A couple of minutes went by when the door slowly opened. Two familiar faces peeked in, no doubt surveying for flying objects.

"Doin' okay in here? I heard you got attacked by a toothbrush," Neela said, grinning.

I sat with my knees to my chest, paranoid I'd kill someone if I moved. "I don't know what's happening to me, Neela. That old man, he did something to me in the alley."

Neela squatted down in front of me. "Mercy, what are you talking about?"

"I'm so sorry, I know I shouldn't have gone without you, but I had to know if he could help me. I'm not sure what happened out there, but something awakened inside of me."

Neela and Nora looked at each other with wide eyes. "What old man? When?" Nora asked.

"Earlier. When I came through the door and passed out. You were there, Nora."

Nora stared at me, her brows pulled in as she shook her head. "Mercy, I have no idea what you're talking about."

"*Mercy*, explain what happened again."

I sat in Fitz's office—cornered by him and Dr. Lee. "I've already told you twice." My patience had worn thin. It irritated me that everyone acted like I had lost my mind. I glared at Fitz. "You were standing in the hall when I came back. It's kinda hard to miss a blood-covered girl passing out at your feet. I mean, does that happen often?"

Fitz rubbed his chin, deep in thought. "Work with me, Mercy. Think about it. You got out of bed, went on this brief excursion, then woke up in bed. You're a smart girl, what do you think happened?"

The truth of his words broke through my frustration as chills ran across my skin, and my stomach dropped. "Someone used subconscious interference."

"That's right," Dr. Lee spoke up.

"It was all in my head?" I asked.

"Thu Dang." Dr. Lee replied. "I know him from Seregalo."

"Who is Thu Dang?" I asked.

"An Elder that works with Aadya. He's the only one powerful enough to pull this off, and he matches your description. You said it felt as though he wasn't alone. I'm assuming she was with him, spying on you. If they were looking through your eyes, then they know where you are." Dr. Lee's eyes were heavy with concern.

I glanced toward Fitz. "There's something else. A homeless man assisted me on the subway. I couldn't focus well enough to figure it out at the time, but now I think it could have been my father."

"Mercy, she invaded your mind, using anything she could against you. Understand it wasn't real, okay?" Fitz responded.

I nodded once, biting my lip.

"We need to ramp up security until we figure out our next move." Dr. Lee said. "I already have alarms on the doors and windows, but I'll construct wards around the property to deter their power. It won't be easy. I'll also assign nightly guards."

"I'm leaving that in your hands, Gavin. Whatever Thu Dang did to Mercy, he brought forward her gift. She has to get a handle on it before it's too late," Fitz added.

. . .

ELISE DROPPED OFF A NEW SCHEDULE. First, elemental training in the pool, then psychokinesis on the tennis court, and emotional interference on the roof. Fitz decided I needed to strengthen those three before more powers surfaced. I had the sneaking suspicion he thought I was running out of time.

Ren met us in the pool, smiling with that cocky grin I loved. "So, you think you're ready for me now?"

"I don't know, the last time we were out here, I seem to remember you not being ready for me," I replied.

The grin dissipated, and he mumbled under his breath.

"Alright, enough. Get in the pool and quit trash-talking," Fitz demanded. "Mercy, concentrate on the water, the way it moves, looks, flows, everything. I want you to force it toward Ren."

"Force it how? Like splash him?" I asked.

"Ren, demonstrate," Fitz called out.

The water rippled, and soon a small wave formed, rolled toward me, and gently slapped against my chest. My eyes shifted to Ren's face, unimpressed.

"Don't give me that look, Mercy, I'm trying to take it easy on you."

"Mercy, give it a go," Fitz called out.

I focused on the water for several minutes, but nothing happened. My eyes burned from the strain of trying to force it. I ran my palm out in front of me and a ripple formed.

"Nope, that's cheating!" Ren called out.

"How is that cheating?" I asked, outraged.

"You were using psychokinesis, Mercy, a different source. Elemental is forged with your mind and water alone—not the energy around you," Fitz explained. "Keep your hands down."

The water hated me. I didn't know why, but it definitely had something against me.

"Emotions, Mercy. Use your emotions to fuel it." Fitz paced back and forth, watching.

I thought of my family, sacrificing themselves for me. The parents I never knew. I thought of my aunt, who raised me, and it surprised me how the pity for what she'd become replaced the bitterness inside me. The ripples grew and eventually formed a wave I pushed toward Ren.

"Excellent! Now, bigger." Fitz called. "Your powers seem fueled by your connections—people you care deeply for."

"How do you know that?" I raised one brow, suspiciously.

"I could feel your emotions," Fitz admitted.

That answered my question about his gift. I tried over and over, but the water never moved more than a few inches. I almost quit for the day out of frustration when the door opened and a loud screeching voice entered the room. Great. Just what I needed.

"Awe, is Missy taking swim lessons?"

Drake followed Cassie in with a towel, and I realized they were planning a little pool time together. I almost threw up in my mouth.

"Start with the doggy-paddle, Missy. I'm sure you'll be great at that one. Come on, Drake, we can go back to my room." The door closed behind them with a loud bang.

All at once, the water spun, and the force of it almost took me under. A wave rose high into the air and crashed down on top of Ren with a strength fueled by resentment. Poor Ren. He stood, water dripping from his face, as he stared at me with hurtful eyes. He knew exactly what that was about. He turned to jump out of the pool.

"Ren, I. . ."

"We're done for the day." He grabbed his towel and left me standing in the water.

Fitz's eyes were full of sorrow. I couldn't tell if he felt bad for Ren or for me.

"I don't know what's wrong with me. Ren is such a good guy," I told him.

Fitz smiled, sadly. "Doesn't mean he's the one, Mercy."

"My mark is fire. It makes sense." I exhaled and closed my eyes, irritated.

Fitz didn't acknowledge my comment about the fire mark, and I felt as though he was avoiding the topic.

"Mercy, did you know my mark is a heart? The first girl I ever fell in love with had the gift of emotional interference. There is no magic greater than the power of true love. There wasn't a doubt in my mind who I would spend the rest of my life with—until an eye formed on her shoulder. Shortly after, it was apparent who her mate really was. They were so in love. It devastated me and I never found mine—some never do. It's a big world, Mercy. Your mate may not be in Fremont, especially with the rare mark you carry. Give yourself time, okay?"

I nodded, thoughtfully.

Fitz stood to leave, but there was one more thing I needed to know.

"Fitz?"

"Yes?" he asked.

"It was my mom. Wasn't it?"

He looked down toward the floor, then back up at me. "Run on over to the tennis court. Neela will be waiting."

. . .

NEELA STOOD ON ONE SIDE, a tennis ball in one hand. She smiled, a little too giddy, as she sent it zooming toward my head. I stopped it mid-air and sent it flying back her way.

"You ready for more?" she asked.

"Yep, let's do it."

The ball traveled at twice the speed, and it took more effort to return it. She started asking me questions about my nightmares, friends, food, or anything to distract me. It didn't work. I kept focus on the ball, finding creative ways to move it across the court, kinda like kinetic-tennis.

It was when she threw a second object at me that I faltered. I didn't expect it, so when the racket spun toward my head, my focus abandoned the ball and switched to the racket. I felt the crack of the ball against my cheek as my vision blurred. Thankfully, it immediately went numb. Neela ran across the court, apologizing repeatedly.

"Mercy, I'm so sorry! I wouldn't have done that if I thought it would be too much. You were doing so well."

I lowered my hand from my face as I blinked to clear my vision. Neela gasped and covered her mouth with her palm—tears forming in her big brown eyes.

"Heck of a lesson, Neela. Remind me never to cross you."

We stared blank-faced, then burst out laughing at the hilarity of it. Doubled over on the floor, we couldn't regain control, even if we wanted to.

"Mercy, Fitz wants you to take a break before meeting him and Nora on the roof. What's going on?" Ren asked as he walked toward the court.

I held one finger up toward Ren, "Give me just a second."

"Mercy! What the hell happened to your face?" Ren looked angry.

Again, the hysterics overwhelmed us. Ren eventually gave up on getting answers and left, shaking his head in exasperation.

. . .

NEELA BROUGHT a bag of ice for my face before I ran to the roof to meet Nora and Fitz. The swelling had gone down, but a nasty blue haze spread across the left side of my cheek. Surprisingly, I still hadn't felt anything.

"I wasn't sure if you'd make it. Using your powers this much has to drain your energy," Nora called out as she walked toward me.

"I don't feel too bad, honestly."

Nora froze. "Mercy, what happened to your face? That looks horrible!"

Fitz stepped in front of me, turning my face from side to side. He stepped back with his arms crossed in front of his chest, glaring. "Well? Did you learn your lesson?"

I chuckled."Yes, sir. I believe I did."

"Good. It was worth it." He turned away and sat down on the lounger in the corner.

Nora and I followed silently. My battered face agonized her sympathetic nature, and I gave her a half-smile to soothe her distress.

"Alright, round three for the day. Emotions. I expect this one to come naturally for you, Mercy. Your heart seems to be at the root of everything. There are varying degrees of this gift. Nora is more compassionate, and I am more of a realist. Can you tell me what I'm feeling right now?"

I searched his eyes but came up empty.

"You're like a black hole. A black hole without feelings, you heartless beast."

He grinned at my assessment. "Nice, but no. There's feeling in there somewhere," he said, patting his chest. "Try with Nora."

This would be easy, I've been able to read her ever since she told me about her parents. I searched deep, but this time was different. I knew the compassion and love were there, but I didn't have the strength to reach them.

"Something's off," Nora replied. "She's been reading me for days, she should be able to get through easily."

"Mercy, tell me what you're feeling right now. From your head to toe, what's going on?"

"Nothing, Fitz. I promise. I don't feel anything."

His forehead wrinkled in confusion. "Nothing? Even after Neela almost broke your cheekbone?"

"That went numb as soon as it happened. I can't even feel it." I admitted.

"Sensory interference. Your body is protecting itself from pain."

My eyes widened. "What?"

"Your body is using sensory interference to keep you out of pain. Maybe you can't use one source while the other has control."

"So, I can only use one at a time?"

"Looks that way, but I honestly don't know for sure. You may be able to do more as you strengthen. Get some rest, and Nora can work with you tomorrow. We'll see how it goes then."

I sat on the roof for a while after Nora followed Fitz inside to discuss my training plan. Lunchtime came and went, and I remained on the rooftop, contemplating all I'd learned the last few weeks. How does someone's life change so quickly? It felt as though ten minutes had passed when the sun started to set. A bright orange brilliance hidden behind the top of a skyscraper had cast a beautiful glow over the city. Someone entered my peripheral vision, and I spun to find Drake—walking toward me with a brown paper bag.

"Thought you might be hungry." He handed me the sack, and I opened it to find a sandwich and water tucked inside. He sat down beside me, staring out over the skyline.

"Thanks. I haven't had much of an appetite," I admitted. He'd surprised me by coming out there and I wasn't sure what to say.

Drake turned my chin toward his direction, inspecting my face. His eyes darkened, and his thumb ran over the shadow across my cheekbone.

"It doesn't hurt," I whispered.

"Because you're using your power to numb it."

"Learned my lesson, though, didn't I?" I asked, grinning.

He frowned. "I wanted to say I'm sorry about Cassie earlier. She isn't very tactful."

I nodded, not wanting to talk about her—but a question had been bouncing in my head like a ping-pong ball since I met him, and I couldn't contain it any longer. "Why are you with her?" My heart squeezed painfully at the words.

He exhaled before answering. Sirens wailing in the distance and blaring car horns were all I could hear as I waited for his answer.

"I wouldn't say that I'm with her—more like a friend, Mercy. She can be a horrible person, but she is also lonely and lashing out. She has no one, so I let her cling to me."

"You called her your girlfriend on the rooftop that day. I remember."

"Yeah, but I also just found out you wore someone else's mark." His head tilted toward me, and his gaze locked on mine.

I couldn't move. I closed my eyes, trying to ease the knot in the center of my stomach. "I wish things were different," I admitted.

"Me too," he whispered.

"It's strange, you know. My source feeds off you, as though you're a part of me." I didn't tell him anything he didn't already know, but I needed to say it anyway.

"I know. I wish I understood." His hand reached over to hold mine as though he knew I needed the comfort. I felt guilty for how much I craved him—my mate was out there somewhere. Drake released me when I pulled my hand back.

"How long have you been here?" I asked.

Drake shook his head and faked a smile. "This is probably not a story you want to hear."

"Please?" I asked. "Tell me everything."

He exhaled. "Alright. My father, Dorian Moreno, was born in Spain and moved to Seregalo where he met my mother, Victoria. When Aadya went off the rails, they decided to leave before things went downhill. So, they moved to Queens and had my brother, Asher, and then myself."

"So, you were born here?"

"Yep, eighteen-years ago. My father was a sensory interferer and my mother was an emotional interferer. Luckily, my father could work with me, teaching me how to control it from a young age."

"What about your brother?"

"That is more complicated. Asher had . . . difficulty with control. His source would surge forward halfway, then cower back as if it was afraid of itself. Having an emotional gift like my mother, his frustration and anger was over the top because he never fully learned to use it."

"That must have been horrible for him. Where are they now?" The deafening silence that followed made me wish I hadn't asked.

"Around five years ago, there was an attack in New York, close to where we lived. I'm still not sure about the details, but they were both killed, and Asher and I went into foster care."

"Drake, I'm so sorry. I shouldn't have asked."

"It's fine. You have a right to know. Plus, we only stayed in foster care for about a year. We couldn't take it anymore. My brother and I ran away, living on the streets for a couple of years. It wasn't easy. Sleeping under whatever shelter we could find, especially in the winter. Sometimes my gift was the only thing that saved us—stealing food, finding shelter, and even surviving street fights. Asher resented me for it, unable to use his own. He wanted to contribute to our survival, and he felt useless."

"What happened?"

"They ambushed us in an alley one night. Men came at us from all sides, men that I now know to be Custos. They gave us two options, surrender or die. The darkness of the alley, rattling of garbage cans nearby. . . I remember it like it was yesterday. I'm still amazed at how quickly my brother abandoned me for them. When he left my side, all I could focus on was the crunch of gravel under his shoes as he walked away. When he stood in front of me, side by side with them, an evil grin spread across his face. My source exploded at the pain, knocking them flat on their back in the alley, and I escaped."

"Fitz sensed my emotional outburst three streets away and found me that night. As soon as he saw my face, he said, 'Dorian was a close friend of mine. You can trust me."

Nora was right, Drake had several reasons to be angry with the world. "Have you seen Asher since?"

He exhaled. "Just once, with you on the subway."

I thought back to that day, and I remembered the leader— the guy that threatened us. The one that looked familiar. He wasn't nearly as attractive as Drake, but the features were similar. I'd never forget the contempt and bitterness in his voice.

"Drake, that is awful. Thank you for telling me."

For the first time, Drake didn't shield his emotions. He typically protected himself from everyone, letting very little through. He wasn't fighting me right then. I felt a slight throb in my cheek as my sensory gift backed off my injury, then my emotional gift reached forward. Anger at his brother, mourning for his parents, grieving for love lost and longing for me.

I looked up into his eyes and saw him in a new light. Still Drake, but more layers that defined the hard edges and explained the surrounding wall. There was a deeper significance to the way he gazed at me. Unfortunately, this only caused my feelings for him to intensify.

"I don't know what this is between us, Mercy. I've lied awake at night trying to figure it out. If it goes on much longer, I'll take the chance of fighting your other half for you one day. I'm very close to that."

His words confused me. "What about your mate? Do you have a mark?"

"That doesn't matter to me."

I rolled my eyes. "It might one day."

"Whoever she is, I'd put money on you. I wouldn't want to piss you off."

I chuckled at his faith in me. "While that's smart, I still don't want to come between you and your happily ever after, Drake. I want you, but I want what's best for you too."

He offered a weak smile, and defeat showed in the drop of his shoulders.

"Alright, Mercy, but I can't promise I won't break Ren's neck the next time he touches you."

. . .

THE NEXT MORNING Fitz walked into the dining hall with Cassie hot on his heels, grinning with pride. "Hello, everyone, I have exciting news for all of you," Fitz announced.

"We . . . We have exciting news," interrupted Cassie.

"Uh, yes. We have exciting news. Sorry, Cassie."

"No problem, Fitzy. You can continue." Fitz took a deep, calming breath and started again.

"Mr. Dunivant has sent over passes for his box for tomorrow nights Yankees game. It looks as though it holds twelve, so we will take sign-ups first—if over twelve express interest, we will draw names. Obviously, Dr. Lee or I will have to chaperone."

Although I disliked Cassie, a surge of excitement ran through me at the thought of going to a game. I looked over toward Drake, and he smiled at my obvious enthusiasm.

"Time to pull out my Yankees' shirt," Neela said with a naughty grin.

"I didn't think you liked sports," I said, confused.

"Oh, I don't. Kellan does."

I should've known. "I didn't bring my Yankees' shirt—I have a jersey and everything." My aunt probably burned everything I left behind.

All at once, I could feel someone watching me from across the room. The last time I had seen the new kid, he'd been screaming like a banshee in the hallway, but here he sat in the dining hall as if that never happened. He looked up, winked, then back to reading the book in his hand. He was kind of cute, with dark brown wavy hair that curled around his ears, and he carried a sense of confidence that I didn't expect for his age. I could've been wrong, but I felt like he had a particular interest in me.

That's all I needed.

. . .

THE REST of the afternoon was like the day before. Practice. Practice. Practice. My power felt more natural than before, for which I was grateful. The swelling in my cheek had gone down significantly overnight, but the bruising remained. I thought Neela might take it easy on me that day, but nope.

The racket and ball both came flying toward my face again. This time, I pulled the racket up quickly and knocked the ball toward her mischievous smile.

Finding and controlling my gifts consumed me. The pressure of being born powerful didn't mix with teenage hormones and I couldn't decide which was stronger—or more catastrophic. Every free moment, I hid away in a remote corner of the building, determined to find a few quiet minutes to myself. I remembered Drake's words—"Just close your eyes and breathe until there's . . . nothing."

I found myself craving *nothing*.

I stopped by my room after dinner to grab my copy of *Sense and Sensibility*, then hurried out the door. Avoiding Ren had become a nightly mission—he couldn't take a hint and I would have to have a serious conversation with him soon. The connection was one-sided and there was nothing I could do.

After taking the stairwell to the ground floor, I stopped at the back door, absorbing the sight of the courtyard under moonlight. I breathed in, relaxing under the backdrop of stars overhead. Padding barefoot across the grass, I pushed aside the overgrown shrubs and made my way toward the smooth surface of my favorite rock. I laid on my back, staring up at the night sky before diving into the tale of the Dashwoods.

I reached for the novel, only to lay it back down. I froze at the presence of someone nearby and held my breath while attempting to focus. I could feel frustration and longing, but also amusement.

"Don't mind me." A deep voice called out. "I'm just relaxing in my new favorite hideaway."

I twisted from my position on the ground to find Drake, maybe ten feet away. "New favorite, huh? I thought we decided it was never really yours to begin with."

Mischief sparkled in his eyes. "It was always mine." Drake grinned. "Just because you deny it, doesn't change the fact."

I laid down on my back and shook my head. Somehow, I knew he wasn't referring to the rock. "How's it going for you? Your new spot?"

"Lovely actually. There's a worn spot under this tree, so I'm always covered in dirt when I leave. And—if I sit twelve inches to the left, I'm directly under a bird's nest so I get shat on. Can't beat looking up at the stars through these limbs. Nothing like it."

I shook my head and chuckled. "Now I feel horrible. You can share my rock, how is that?"

"Like joint custody?" he asked.

"Sure. I'll even let you have it tonight. See? I can compromise." I pushed up from the ground, but when I stood—he was already there. His lips pulled up into a half-smile.

We didn't speak. We barely breathed. Drake reached up, swiping the wind-blown hair from my face, then grazed his fingers across my cheek. "You need it more than I do. Take your time."

He slowly leaned forward, watching me. I closed my eyes anticipating the feel of his lips on mine. After several seconds, I opened my eyes to a conflicted gaze as he leaned back on his heels. He exhaled and his face fell, as if frustrated with himself. "Goodnight, Mercy." Drake silently slipped from the courtyard without another word.

I threw my head back and sighed. I couldn't continue to push him away—we both knew it. I looked over my shoulder to stop him, tell him I craved him more every day. Explain how our connection terrified me. The back door slammed shut, along with my confidence. Easing down to the ground, I focused on my breathing to calm the pounding of my heart.

"Get it together, Mercy," I told myself.

. . .

AFTER LUNCH THE NEXT DAY, I showered and changed for the ballgame. Only eight signed up to go, so there were plenty of seats. Dr. Lee and Elise would chaperone Drake, Cassie, Ren, Neela, Kellan, and myself. I styled my hair and threw on a pair of jeans with a navy v-neck. That would have to work. As I walked out of the bathroom, Nora glanced up from her book. I could tell by the flannel pajama pants and her freshly washed face that she had decided to stay in.

"Are you sure you don't want to come?"

"Trust me, I'm sure. Baseball is not my thing. Yankee fans are the most emotional people on the planet, and you better have your guard up, or you'll have a migraine."

"Noted." I turned and stopped dead in my tracks.

"Nora, where did that come from?"

"What?"

I picked up the blue Yankees hat from the bed, inspecting it. "This. It wasn't here when I jumped in the shower."

"Not sure. I didn't notice it."

I assumed Neela had brought it after telling her about my lost jersey. I left my hair down and tried the hat on. Perfect fit. "Alright, see you soon."

"Have fun." Nora smiled.

. . .

WE PILED into Fremont's van, and I squeezed in the back with Neela. The girl looked amazing in skinny jeans, a cutoff

Yankees top, and large hoop earrings. For the life of me, I couldn't figure out how Kellan had so much self-control.

Cassie looked to be in a low-cut tank and stilettos, while Drake followed behind her wearing a Yankees shirt.

"Drake, you forgot your hat," Cassie said, panicked.

"It's fine, Cassie," he mumbled.

The hat. I looked over at Neela with a puzzled expression. "What?" she asked.

"Nothing. I—I thought you left this for me. That's all." I pointed toward the hat.

She giggled, "Why would I ever cover this magnificent hair?" She rolled her eyes at my absurdity.

We arrived at the stadium, and Cassie eagerly led us to our box seats. Her father had a buffet set up for dinner and left a note for us to enjoy ourselves. Which I would have done if Cassie would've quit talking. Drake, Ren, Kellan and I were the only ones keeping up with the game while everyone else socialized and snacked. Even Dr. Lee was utterly uninvolved, standing on high alert as he kept a watchful eye around the room.

Ren leaned back and put his arm around my shoulders during the game. I felt Drake's eyes, but didn't acknowledge him. I looked straight ahead, focused on the game. Bases were loaded, and Aaron Judge was next to bat. Anticipation ran through me, and my knee bounced out of nervousness. The crack of the bat echoed throughout the stadium, and the ball flew centerfield over the fence. We all jumped up— cheering as the players made their way to home plate.

Ren picked me up, smiling, and kissed my cheek out of excitement. The rage brewing two seats down felt like tendrils of fire creeping into the room. I pulled away from Ren, smiling politely.

A knock sounded at the door, and Dr. Lee answered. "Mercy, can you come here for a moment?"

I went over to where an older lady stood with a ticket in hand.

"Hello. Are you Mercy Monroe?" she asked sweetly.

I nodded. "Yes, Ma'am. Can I help you?"

"We had a box seat drawing, and you won a batting cage session downstairs after the game."

I shook my head. "You must have the wrong box."

"Do you know many girls named Mercy Monroe?" she asked.

"Well, no. No, I don't."

She handed me the ticket and offered to escort me downstairs.

I looked back toward the field. "The game isn't over."

"You'll need to get down there quick, or lines start forming for autographs."

I looked over to Dr. Lee and he studied the woman, as if considering her offer.

"I'll bring her right back," she promised.

I grinned. "I'll be careful."

Dr. Lee looked at me and nodded once. "Make it quick, okay?"

. . .

I FOLLOWED her down the stairs and through the tunnels to an entrance away from the public. Our steps echoed throughout the empty corridors, and the solitude of the space was eerie. "These halls will get crowded in twenty minutes or so," she said.

She flipped the overhead lights as we walked through the door. I wasn't sure what I expected, but the state-of-the-art equipment and batting cages reflected the professionalism of the program. Two turfed lanes ran down the length of the room with black netting on both sides. A shiver ran through me at the thought of holding a bat, a Yankees bat.

"Wait here, dear. They will be right with you."

"You're leaving?" I asked.

"Just for a moment. I need to grab another winner, but I'll be back," she assured me.

I jumped as the heavy door banged loudly upon closing. I shuffled around the room for several minutes until giving in, picking up a bat propped against the wall. Running my hand down the smooth wood, the excitement of being there over-powered the nervousness of being alone—until the cages went dark without so much as a flicker.

"Hello? Who's there?" I didn't expect anyone to answer, but I had to try.

Footsteps crunched along the turf, and I attempted to use my power to determine their distance. I could feel a man's presence standing to my left, maybe ten feet away. He froze, unmoving, taunting me in the blackness. I sensed resentment —so much hatred and hurt. He wanted revenge, but from what—I couldn't determine.

One step forward.

I took two steps back and clung to the bat in my hand. I detected satisfaction as he located his own bat and dragged it against the wall. The wood of the bat scraping the concrete wreaked havoc on my nerves, already on edge.

"Come on out, Mercy. Just want to talk." Loathing dripped from the familiar voice.

I had to focus. If I got distracted, I'd never be able to recover.

"I heard you liked Morenos. I bet you'd like me, older, more mature, and better looking. Yeah, we'd be good together. I saw how my brother protected you on the train, sweetheart, you must be special. Nothing but the best for Drake." He threw the bat as hard as he could against the wall beside me. I jumped, but kept quiet. I didn't want him to know he frightened me.

I silently crept toward the door, gripping the bat in my shaky hands. I sensed his intention before it happened, and I spun as his hands reached out. Catching the back of my hair, he yanked me against the wall and the bat flew out of my hand. His fingers slowly circled my neck as his thumb grazed back and forth over my pulse. There wasn't one thing about Asher's demeanor that reminded me of Drake. His hot breath, full of excitement, blew across my face and he leaned in, inhaling deeply.

"You smell fantastic, Mercy. I'm sure my brother wouldn't mind if I had a little taste." His hand around my neck squeezed tighter. "He has his hands full with that little blonde, anyway." Asher's nose ran across my jaw line.

My palm flinched at my side as I used the surrounding energy to pick the bat up from the floor. Swirling my index finger, the wood spun faster and faster. As soon as I felt the wetness from Asher's mouth on my neck, the bat struck him in the side of the head, knocking him to the floor.

Asher shook his head, as if dizzy, and grabbed the bat, leaping toward me. My palms splayed out, and his body froze in midair. I flung him back against the wall, then made a break for the door. Running out into the tunnel, the lights blinked and went black, disorienting me. My heart raced as footsteps followed close, but I never faltered. I could barely see the light peeking under the doors ahead, and I busted through them into Drake's arms.

He cupped my face with his hands, eyes full of concern. "What happened?"

Breathing heavily, I could only get out one word, "Ash. . . Asher."

His spine stiffened, then Drake absorbed the sight of the red hand print across my throat. His eyes narrowed. "Stay here."

Sliding down the wall, I attempted to catch my breath as people started filing out of the stadium corridors. A few minutes later, Drake came back frustrated, and I knew Asher had disappeared.

"He's gone," Drake said.

I stood. "How did you know to come find me?"

He shook his head as if he didn't have an answer. "A feeling, I guess. Dr. Lee said you were fine, but I couldn't relax." His thumb rubbed over the marks around my neck. "I'll deal with Asher."

I didn't want him anywhere near Asher. "Let's just go. I don't want to be here anymore."

Drake nodded and led me back toward the box.

. . .

ON THE WAY back to Fremont, Drake kept a close eye on me, and Cassie noticed. She wasn't happy when we walked back to the box together, and she'd been pouting ever since. Drake made up a quick story about me not feeling well, but the look in Dr. Lee's eyes said he knew something went down. I needed rest. Asher depleted my strength, but I was proud that I could defend myself. Fitz would be too.

We filed out of the van, and I made a beeline toward my room. Drake caught me by the elbow, his brows pulled in with concern.

"You're sure you're okay?" he asked.

I tried to smile, but I knew it wasn't convincing. "I need

sleep. I'll feel better tomorrow." Not only exhausted, my emotions were simmering—almost unstable.

He gently released me, giving my arm a squeeze. "Goodnight, Mercy."

"Night, Drake."

As I reached for the doorknob, someone grabbed my arm. I turned, thinking Neela had stopped by to check on me.

Smack!

My head swung to the right as Cassie took a cheap shot across my face, right over the healing bruise on my cheek.

"That will teach you to mess with someone's boyfriend, you little slut!" She yelled.

Heat flooded my chest, and I knew this was going to be out of my hands. My emotions were all over the place, and I had no control as energy surged around me.

I straightened after the slap and backhanded her into the wall. Pictures fell along with her, and she snarled, stumbling to her feet. She didn't learn. People started filling the hall as she grabbed a handful of my hair, trying to hit me again.

She screamed, "He's mine! He doesn't want you!"

I couldn't take it anymore, and something possessive came over me as I conjured all of the energy around me and picked her up by the throat—holding her against the wall.

I vaguely remembered voices yelling my name, then powerful arms pulled me away as I fought to get back toward her. Rage controlled me. They pulled me into a room and the door slammed, shutting me out of the hallway. My back hit the door, and hands cupped the sides of my face.

"Mercy, look at me. Calm down, Babe. Focus on me."

I looked up into black eyes and deflated on the spot. My shoulders sagged, and I gripped the sides of his shirt in my fists. "Drake."

We were breathing hard, our eyes locked. There it was again. The pull that demanded his proximity and refused to relent. The adrenaline from the night remained, fueling my need. He fixated on my mouth, waiting for my permission. I could feel him shift toward me, then back again—dangerously close. His intention and desire was obvious, he only needed to hear the words from me.

I couldn't fight it any longer. "Drake, please," I whispered.

His mouth came down on mine with a hunger I'd never experienced. Something in my heart screamed yes, while my conflicted mind felt sympathy for my future mate. How could I feel guilty about this? Didn't I get a choice?

I chose Drake. Something in the back of my mind knew I always would. His hand traveled up my neck, gently rubbing over Asher's fading fingerprints—then moved to the back of my head, holding my mouth to his. I'd only been kissed once in my life, and it wasn't anything like this. Drake demanded everything from me.

The exhaustion we both felt from trying to deny it had taken its toll, and we refused to fight it any longer. I pulled him closer, running my hands under his shirt—clinging to the heat of his skin. I wanted everything he would give me.

A deep moan vibrated throughout his chest as he pulled back, pressing his forehead to mine. "Do you have any idea how much I want you?" he asked. "It's like nothing I've ever felt before."

I tilted my head back and gently kissed the corner of his mouth. He closed his eyes, and clenched his jaw as if restraining himself.

I whispered, "I can't fight this anymore."

Drake exhaled, as if relieved. "Me either."

"*How* is she? Cassie?" I asked.

"She's fine, Mercy. Lucky that Drake pulled you off her, but fine." Fitz answered. "You want to talk about it?"

"Nothing to say, I guess. I suck at control, apparently."

"You were wound up before she approached you. I felt it as soon as you entered the building. Wanna tell me about that?"

"I had . . . a visitor at the ballgame." I picked fuzz off my shirt sleeve that wasn't there—anything to look casual because I knew Fitz would not take this well.

"A visitor? Someone you know? Mercy?"

"Asher Moreno."

Fitz sat back, struggling to suppress the worry etched on his tense face. "I see." He lowered his head, rubbing the back of his neck. "Does Drake know?"

"Yes."

"Did he hurt you? Where was Gavin?"

"No, I fought him off. Well, kicked his tail, really." A grin spread across my face, and he shook his head, watching me.

"Dr. Lee stayed with everyone else when I went to the batting cages."

"He sent you alone?" Fitz's brows shot up. "I'll have a word with him about that."

"It was my fault," I admitted. "I honestly thought it would be fine."

"While I'm proud you could use your gifts, I'm concerned that you had to. That could have ended badly, you know that, right?"

"I do. I have to keep training, Fitz. There's still so much I need to learn."

"Mercy, I. . ." Fitz's gaze darted to the door, and he abruptly stood as loud pounding and shouting carried into his office.

"What's going on?" I asked from behind him.

We walked out into the hall and had to step back from the force of emotions crashing into us. Ren stood on one side of the hallway, and Drake on the other.

"Ren, I know you're upset, but you had to see this coming a mile away, right?" Drake asked.

A wind tunnel formed around Drake, spinning and keeping him confined.

"She wears my mark!" Ren shouted.

"I don't care who's mark she wears, she belongs with me, and everyone knows it!" Drake's body slammed into the wall repeatedly.

Ren gave everything he had toward punishing him. Anger stirred within Drake, but more than that, I sensed sympathy for Ren. It was never Drake's intention to hurt him.

"Ren, stop this before someone gets hurt," Fitz called out.

"Someone? The only person getting hurt is Drake." Ren smirked.

Drake still wasn't defending himself. The wind tunnel turned full force and smashed his body into the ceiling.

Sheetrock crumbled to the ground, and a crack formed above our heads. The light fixture overhead swung back and forth, threatening to topple, and blood ran down Drake's face from the back of his head. I'd had enough.

"Ren, please!" I shouted.

"What, Mercy? Please, tell me what I can do for our princess. You like this? Does it turn you on to have two guys fighting over you? Who's next? Kellan? Gonna make your way around the guild?"

All at once, Drake swept Ren's feet out from under him, and his head slammed against the floor. Ren's palms flew to his eyes out of panic. Drake stepped in front of me, looking down at Ren.

"I'll take anything you got, all day long. I know it upsets you, but don't ever speak to her that way again. She doesn't deserve it." The anger in Drake's deep voice shook me to the core.

Ren looked up at us from the floor after getting his sight back.

"Drake, give the boy his legs so he can get out of the hallway. I don't have time for more therapy today, so sort your issues." Fitz turned, stomping toward his office.

. . .

I WAITED in the pool for twenty minutes, but Ren never showed. I pushed water around, swirled it, spun it, and even created a massive waterfall with two tiers. The thought of him not forgiving me caused a sharp pain across my chest. I liked Ren and wanted him in my life. Maybe not the way he wanted, but I think we both knew that from the beginning.

He tried to force something that never had a chance. As I dried off, giving up for the day, a voice drifted over from the doorway.

"Quitting so soon?" Ren leaned against the wall, arms crossed over his chest.

I dropped the towel, a relieved smile spreading across my face. "You came. I didn't think you would."

"Would you blame me?"

I shook my head, "No, but I'm glad you did."

Ren walked over to where I stood and dropped his towel on the chair, "I got stuff to do, so let's get to it."

As he stepped around me toward the pool, I wrapped my arms around him, and he relaxed under my embrace. "I made my choice on the first day, Ren. It had nothing to do with you."

He propped his chin on top of my head and hugged me back. "You know I didn't mean anything I said, right?"

"I know," I said. "For the record, this doesn't mean I'm going to take it easy on you today."

Laughter rumbled throughout his chest. "I never expected you would, Mercy Monroe."

. . .

I FELT AWFUL. From my head to my toes—my muscles hurt, and my head pounded. I'd practiced all day and needed time to recharge. Nora said she'd bring dinner back so I could rest. I couldn't imagine how I'd feel when we added the other gifts.

After a small knock, Drake cracked the door open, "Are you dressed? I hoped to catch you changing." He stepped into the room and took in the pathetic, weak excuse of a Regalian spread out across the bed. "You've looked better. I mean, you're still hot, but I've seen you hotter."

"Go away." I pulled the pillow on top of my head. I vaguely heard the water running, but ignored it.

Drake pulled the pillow away and lifted my head into his lap.

"How's your head?" I asked. The memory of him bleeding in the hall still haunted me.

"I'm fine. I'm more concerned about you at the moment."

A cold washcloth laid across my forehead. Right then, I knew choosing him would be the best decision I ever made. He left dinner to check on me. He wanted to take care of me, and I'd never had that before. I felt—complete.

All at once, the aches drifted away, and warmth settled in my joints. I moaned in appreciation, "Best boyfriend ever."

"Is that what I am? We've never really talked about it," he said, softly.

I opened my eyes, studying his face, "You're more to me than that, but there isn't a word for it. So, boyfriend will have to do."

He smiled, "I don't know, I mean, I think I could do better than the average boyfriend."

"Oh yeah? Give it a go." I grinned.

The warmth radiating throughout my body intensified, my muscles turning to mush. As if he knew exactly what I needed and where I needed it.

"Yeah, I mean, that's nice."

My atmosphere changed, and white sand and blue water surrounded me. A soft lapping of waves slapped against my legs as familiar hands massaged sunscreen into my shoulders.

"You've got to be kidding me." I mumbled, relaxed.

Then . . . the smell of freshly baked cinnamon rolls hovered in the air.

"Now you've gone too far."

Drake smirked. "Just trying to be a good boyfriend."

. . .

A HIGH-PITCHED GIGGLE pulled me from sleep. I sat up, glancing over at Nora's side of the room, her small frame huddled under the blankets. It had to be a dream.

"Hehehehe . . ."

I pulled the blankets back, standing, convinced I wasn't going crazy. I wore a large cotton shirt that hung down to my thighs, but it didn't concern me at the moment. The laughter did. Easing the door open, I peeked into the hall, as if a horrid monster would be waiting. Instead, a beautiful red-haired little girl in pink danced across the hardwood floors, her perfect white sandals not making a sound. Her head tilted down, she peered up with bright green eyes and a mischievous grin across her face at the sight of me.

"Where did you come from?" I whispered.

The child's head flew back in laughter as though I'd said something funny and then died as quickly as it began. She bolted down the hall away from me, tempting me to follow. I couldn't hear a sound throughout the dark and empty building, all except the high-pitched giggles up ahead. I tip-toed toward the child and found her in the activities lounge, but to my surprise, two sat before me. Although identically beautiful, the one at my door had an evil presence, while the other a gentle, sweet smile that comforted me.

They sat on the floor, crayons in hand, focused on the

task before them. One looked up with a gentle expression, proud of the work she had accomplished. She held up a picture of a family of four, standing outside on a sunny day. The sun shone down brightly, and flowers bloomed all around them as they stood holding hands.

"That is so pretty!" I praised her. "What do you have over there, little one?"

Again, her eyes shifted upward as she fought a smile. The picture she held up took my breath away. A dark-haired woman with hazel eyes took up the extent of the picture. Red crayon colored over her head and ran down in a chaotic mess across her face. Along the bottom in messy scribbles, she had written, 'Die'.

Laughter erupted out of the child that sounded like a crazed grown woman. I backed up slowly—chills running down my spine.

At once, the cackling died, and her head snapped forward. She screamed, "You can't run from me!"

I turned to escape the evil shriek that resonated from the room and hit a tall hard body. Arms wrapped around me as I fought to get away.

"Hey. Are you alright?" I looked up to the familiar face of the new guy staring down, concerned.

His forehead wrinkled in confusion—he probably thought I'd lost my mind. "You're shaking all over. Should I get someone for you?"

I spun back around, and the dark lounge was empty. All except a single red crayon rolling across the floor.

"I . . . I . . ." I knew what they would think. Poor, crazy Mercy. "I think I need to lay back down, but thank you. What's your name again?"

"Sebastian. You're Mercy, right?"

"That's right. Thank you, Sebastian. I'll see you tomorrow."

155

"Goodnight, Mercy."

. . .

"MERCY, HOW CAN I HELP YOU?"

I stood outside of Fitz's office that day, contemplating whether I should talk to him. I'd begin to knock, then I'd leave, then come back again. I finally gave in after a somewhat vicious pep-talk that ended with me calling myself a coward.

"I need to speak with you."

"Sure, come in and sit. What's up?"

Chewing the side of my lip, unease prickled the back of my neck at the questions bouncing around in my head. Did I really want to know the answer?

"Mercy, I don't have all day. Spit it out." Fitz turned his wrist to check the time, then narrowed his eyes at me.

"Who are the twins?" I asked. I swallowed the lump in my throat, anticipating his answer. I had already worked it out, but I needed him to say it. I'd taken Fitz off guard—he blinked rapidly and cleared his throat. I could tell he didn't intend to have this conversation with me.

"What brought this on?" he asked.

"They visited me in a dream last night. Two little red-haired girls with bright green eyes."

He glanced down at the floor, then back at me. "You're a smart one, aren't you?" His gaze carried a sadness I anticipated. I didn't need his sympathy, I wanted honesty.

"They were very different people, Mercy. Aadya might have been more powerful, but her jealousy over your mother, Annabel, was extreme."

"Why didn't you tell me?" I asked.

"That your aunt wants you dead? One of your biggest emotional hurdles is family, Mercy. A part of me feared it would make things harder for you—more confusing. I'm sorry I didn't tell you the truth. I'd like to know how you figured it out."

"Besides the red hair and green eyes? Something about one of them felt evil and dark. The other, I can't explain it—I just knew it was my mother. Her calming presence, I suppose. This dream felt stronger than my previous one, actual objects moved after the interference. Is that even possible? The thought is terrifying, Fitz and I. . ."

"Whoa, what do you mean moved afterward?"

"I woke to the sound of giggling down the hall. They were in the activities lounge, drawing and staring up at me. I turned to run out and collided with Sebastian. Then everything disappeared, except a crayon rolling across the floor."

"Sebastian?" His brow wrinkled in thought.

"Yes, Dr. Lee's new patient."

"Ah yes, I remember. I haven't had the chance to introduce myself to him yet. So, the objects they were using remained after they disappeared?"

"Should I be afraid?" I asked.

"Her subconscious powers have strengthened if she's able to be that present." He stroked his eyebrow, then sat up straight. "They're getting bold. The only way to fight this is for you to practice your own subconscious gift, then you might be able to block them. I'll see if Dr. Lee is available today. Don't wear yourself out, you'll need your strength."

I nodded in agreement.

"We're going to do everything we can to protect you."

"I'm tired of people protecting me. I intend to do it myself."

. . .

A FEW HOURS LATER, I waited for Dr. Lee outside his office. Tension rippled on the other side of the door, I could feel it. Someone yanked the door open with force, and Sebastian stepped out, startled to see me standing there.

"Hey, Mercy. I meant to find you earlier to check on you after last night. You seemed pretty shaken up."

"What happened last night?" A deep voice rumbled behind me.

I turned to find Drake standing behind me, staring intensely at Sebastian. Sebastian's eyes shifted toward me as if he didn't want to announce my personal business. The silence made things worse. It made us look guilty of something completely innocent.

"Mercy?" Drake questioned again.

"It was nothing. I had a nightmare, and I ran into Sebastian in the hall. I went back to bed and slept well afterward."

"Glad to hear it," Sebastian said with a knowing smile. "Talk to you guys later."

After excusing himself, Drake turned to look me in the eyes, his hands on each side of my face, affectionately. "Sometimes I wish you were a better liar, so you didn't embarrass yourself. You want to tell me the truth?"

I grinned. "Later, I promise."

"How about tonight?"

"Tonight?"

"I have plans for you. Be ready by six." His lips quickly met mine before leaving me with Dr. Lee.

. . .

THREE HOURS. I spent three hours diving into my subconscious, learning to block, focus, and amplify. The pain in my head throbbed brutally, and my eyes swelled from pressure. I felt as though I had a hangover. Dr. Lee decided it might be best to bring in a sensory interferer to help with the pain during training. My gift wasn't numbing like it did last time and I couldn't focus. Dr. Lee stuck his head outside the door and yelled, "Ah, Sebastian, come here for a minute."

"What now?" he asked, full of attitude.

"I thought you could help a patient of mine. Her training has caused some discomfort. Do you think you could take time out of your busy schedule to assist a fellow Regalian? Since you seem to excel at sensory—really, one of the best I've seen." Dr. Lee cocked his head to the side and glared.

Sebastian's jaw clenched but looked over at me with kindness and sympathy. "Of course. Anything for Mercy."

"It's not a problem. Drake is in his room, and he'd prefer to do it anyway," I explained.

He smiled. "No need, I'm standing right here. It won't take but a minute. Close your eyes, okay?"

I did what he instructed and felt his hand rest on the back of my neck and the other on my forehead. Nothing happened.

"I'm proud that you've learned to block so well, but I need you to let your guard down, or I can't help you," he explained.

I tried to relax, but couldn't let go of the defensive hold I'd clung to.

"Think of something that relaxes you, go to your happy place and breathe for me. That's it, good girl," he whispered. "Almost done."

The pain dissipated, and my eyes no longer felt as though they'd pop out of my head. "Thank you, I really appreciate it."

Sebastian stood with his arms crossed in front of me. "Anytime. Out of curiosity, what made you relax so quickly?"

I cut my eyes toward Dr. Lee, then back at Sebastian. "It's um, well it's personal."

"Drake," he guessed. He stared at me with a half-grin. "I get it, you know. I felt like that about someone before."

"What happened?"

"Long story." Sebastian's eyes darkened. "I gotta get to the tennis court. Kellan is waiting for a butt-kicking." He stopped at the door frame and grinned over his shoulder. Then he left without another word.

Dr. Lee watched us from the window with a thoughtful expression. "Head back to your room and get some rest, Mercy."

. . .

I TOOK a long nap and woke eager to spend the evening with Drake. Since we had given in to our connection, my body craved him—needed him near. I showered, and for the first time in a while, took extra care shaving my legs and applying makeup. I wanted to feel beautiful for whatever he had planned. My wardrobe consisted mostly of jeans and cotton shirts, nothing fancy or pretty. So I called in backup, and Neela sorted me out. She loaned me a red ruffled top with black jeans and heels. I fell in love with the outfit and told her she'd been promoted to my personal stylist.

"Seriously, Mercy. We have to update your closet. It looks

as though a twenty-year-old guy lives here," she grumbled while sorting through my clothes.

"Thanks, Neela."

"I'm just saying." She shook her head, a mortified expression on her pretty face.

A few minutes before six, a note slid under my door, instructing me to walk to the rooftop. A smile broke across my face, and I left the room, eager to see what Drake had planned. As I opened the door, Ren and Sebastian stopped in their tracks at the sight of me.

"Wow. You look hot, Mercy," Ren called out. His gaze took me in from head to toe, and Sebastian slapped him on the back of the head.

"Thanks, Ren. See you guys later."

I took the stairs to the roof, and as I opened the door, the sight took my breath away. He'd strung lights on all four corners of the roof, and soft music played from his cell on a table in the center. A white tablecloth, candles, flowers . . . it was all there. I couldn't move. I've never considered myself a romantic before, but tears welled up in my eyes when I saw the effort he put into planning this. He strolled toward me as if I was a wild animal he'd frighten.

"You like it?" he asked.

"This is unbelievable. How did you manage it?"

"I had some help. I wanted to actually take you out, but it's too dangerous right now."

I smiled, still shocked at the effort. "This is perfect."

"Would you like to dance?" He held out his hand for mine.

"I'm in shock, and I'm not sure if I can move."

He bent over, placing his shoulder against my stomach and stood, carrying me.

"Drake! Put me down! I can walk! I can walk, please!" I screamed. "I'm too heavy, please put me down!"

"You are perfect in every way."

He stopped at the table and slid me down the front of his body, grinning that adorable half-smile I loved so much. We danced, just the two of us, and the sound of traffic in the distance was the only thing that kept me grounded. I quickly realized that I'd never felt happier than I did at that moment with him.

We ate take-out from an Italian restaurant next door, and he'd ordered a special dessert from Arin's Bake Shop, giving full credit to Ren for the idea. We stood beside the brick wall, looking over into the crowded city. I felt his emotions swirl, and I don't think he even realized how intense they were that night. Happiness, contentment, adoration, and fear. Terrified that something would tear us apart.

I whirled to face him, wrapping my arms around his neck. "I'm scared, too, you know."

His eyes narrowed on my face, knowing I'd read his feelings.

I continued. "I don't want anything to happen to us. I've never been this happy before."

He cracked a smile, then his mouth crashed down on mine, my back pressed against the rough brick wall. One hand protectively cupped my head, the other ran down over my hip and up my shirt, resting on the bare skin of my lower back. I didn't want him to stop, I wanted him all over me.

His mouth ran down my neck, and I pushed my body into him, needing the contact. His hands clung to me, touching and pulling me against him. I gripped his shirt in my fist, desiring everything I could get from him. When the connection became too intense, too close to crossing the line, Drake pulled back and took a deep breath, "I was wrong. My strongest gift is resisting you because that took everything I had."

"We don't have to stop, we could stay up here away from everyone, just the two of us."

"It wouldn't take much for them to find us with you moaning."

I narrowed my eyes. "Moaning?"

"You make little moaning noises when you're happy. Eating dessert, reading, when I kiss you . . ."

His eyes darkened, and I leaned into him, pushing those boundaries.

"Mercy, I'm barely hanging on here, and I need you to help me. This is not an eighteen-year-old guy bringing a hot girl to the roof to make out, and I refuse to treat you that way. I'm going to take my time with you because that's what you deserve. We have our entire future to be together, and more than anything, I want you to feel cherished for the first time in your life."

"Just being with you makes me feel that way."

"Glad to hear it, but I want to make sure it stays that way." He kissed me once more, then rubbed my bottom lip with his thumb. "You look beautiful tonight. I hope you've had a good time."

I froze at the change in the air. My gaze searched the rooftop, but we were alone.

"What's wrong?" he asked.

"Something feels off—suspicious." I tilted my head to the side and expanded my senses. "It's like, I feel something dark, almost like evil intent."

We both turned and looked out around the building, searching for any sign of trouble.

"I don't see anything. Do you still sense it?" Drake asked.

"No, it's gone. Weird, right?"

"Hopefully, it's nothing. We've had a lot to deal with lately. Let's talk about your mood earlier today. Tell me about the nightmare that wasn't a nightmare."

"Long story short?" I asked.

He nodded for me to continue.

"Aadya paid me a visit while I slept last night in the form of two young red-haired girls. One sweet and innocent and the other evil, who happened to be coloring a picture of me dead."

Drake's jaw clenched, and I could have sworn the brown of his eyes turned red. "Wait—two little girls? Why is that?"

"Apparently, Aadya and my mother are twin sisters. "

He leaned back, meeting my eyes. "Please tell me this is some kind of sick joke."

"No, it's not. Dr. Lee is trying to teach me to keep a subconscious guard so she can't enter my thoughts. It is exhausting, I thought I might pass out from a headache earlier."

"Why didn't you come to find me? I could have helped."

"Well, Sebastian walked by his office at the right time, so Dr. Lee asked him to step in."

His eyes narrowed on my face.

"It really wasn't a big deal, Drake."

"No? I've seen the way he looks at you. There's a fascination there I don't like. Plus, I want to be there for you. You want Cassie putting her hands on me?"

I dipped my head and swallowed hard, the thought crawling under my skin and lighting a fire.

"That's what I thought," he mumbled.

I put my hands up, defensively. "I'm sorry. I didn't think of it that way. I did offer to find you, but Dr. Lee insisted on Sebastian helping."

"So you're saying I need to blame him, that you're a helpless bystander?"

"Exactly." I smiled innocently and batted my eyes.

"Don't give me that look, Mercy." He leaned into me once more, kissing the tip of my nose. "You are a lot to handle."

"You have no idea."

"*How* ow do you know he's the one?"

I glanced over the top of my book while Neela waited patiently for my response. She chewed her pitiful fingernails as if the conversation was too much for her nerves.

"What's going on in that head of yours, Neela?" I closed the book, accepting the fact that between my lack of sleep and Neela's love life, I wouldn't accomplish anything.

"Nothing. It's nothing." She opened her book, pretending to push the matter to the side, then closed it again, looking up at me.

I waited.

"Well, I guess I want to know what you're feeling, you know? I remember the obvious connection the first time you met, and I want to know how you knew, despite your Allegato mark."

"Okay, well, I'm honestly not sure he is my forever," I said.

Her mouth fell open like I'd admitted murder.

"Don't get me wrong, I want to spend the rest of my life with him, but he hasn't been forthcoming about his mark, and I think it's for a reason. We obviously have someone out there we're meant to be with, but our connection is too strong, and we're tired of fighting it."

"What will you do when they show up?" Her eyes were sad, as if she knew this would be a problem one day.

"Drake says he'll fight for me, but I know that if he meets the one, I can't force him to stay. I guess I'll battle that heartache when the time comes."

Her eyes turned sad. "Just know how brave I think you are, fighting for something you want even when everything around you screams it probably won't end well."

"I'll take my temporary happiness while it's here, Neela. I may never find it again."

She nodded at my reasoning, and a single tear escaped down her cheek. "Did you know my father and mother weren't matches? They both have psychokinetic interference, and he wears an eye while she's marked with water lines. They both wanted children and were never able to find their mate. So they left Seregalo, determined to leave it all behind. I think the concern will always be there, you know? If a mate shows up, will they be able to stay or will the connection be too strong. It's always hovering over them, even now. Do you think the Allegato can be wrong?"

"I wish I knew, Neela. I'd like to think so. I want to know that the person I share my life with is my choice."

"I got curious when I heard Sebastian had sensory power, with my mark being an eye, but there's nothing, not even a small connection. He looks at me like a young, immature kid sometimes. Now, I definitely have a strong connection with Kellan. I think it's more lust than anything. Did you know he asked me out?"

"No, I didn't. You gonna go?" I asked.

"I don't know. I'm so scared of messing up someone's life. When my family comes back, I want to leave guilt-free, nothing holding me to Fremont. Long term, that's the best thing, even if that man is fine." Her attempt at joking was futile and did little to ease my sympathy for her. I knew she missed her family.

"Tell me about them." I hoped talking about them would bring her comfort.

"My family?" The thought brought a smile to her pretty face. "I have two older, rambunctious brothers, Caleb and Colton, who treat me like a princess. It's hard to believe they'll turn twenty-one and twenty-five this year. Colton is the older, more mature sibling. If trouble is brewing, Caleb has something to do with it," she chuckled. "I wonder about them, you know. Have they fallen in love? Are they even alive? The thought of losing my family . . . it's unbearable."

"Don't think like that, Neela. When did you see them last?"

"Five years ago, when my parents dropped me off with Fitz. They wouldn't tell me what happened, but they insisted I stay with him until they come back." Her head lowered, trying to hide the loss of five years, as though all of this was perfectly normal.

Something tormented me. Five years. Drake's family died five years ago. I tried to push the thought aside, hoping it was a coincidence, but something inside said otherwise.

"My brother's were so protective, especially at school. I can't imagine what you went through without anyone to have your back," she said, softly.

I sat up straight. "School? You had issues, too?"

She nodded. "Dad said they knew we were different—special. He said the weak become jealous and defensive around the strong. I miss him so much." She took a deep breath.

"Have you asked Fitz for updates?" I asked.

"I did the first couple of years, but then I tired of the

disappointment, so I quit asking." She closed her book with a hard bang.

I glanced up to the fakest smile I'd ever seen. She leaned toward me and whispered, "Let's sneak into the kitchen for ice cream." Neela needed a distraction. Her emotions were all over the place.

I smiled. "Sounds perfect."

"Are you talking about me again?" Drake leaned down and kissed my cheek."

"I'm sneaking into the kitchen for ice cream with Neela."

"I'm better than ice cream, you know. If you'd like to stay behind with me."

"Are you covered in whipped cream and cherries? Because if you aren't, this conversation is over."

"I can be," he whispered.

I shook my head and walked out of the activities lounge—as Drake chuckled behind me.

. . .

THAT AFTERNOON DRAKE and I ran for almost two hours, then sat on the rooftop staring out over the busy city. The orange glow of sunset dimmed as it hid behind the skyscrapers in front of us.

Our situation was so different compared to most couples our age. In another world, we'd be dating, making dinner reservations, and showing up at parties. In a different time, he'd meet my parents, promising to have me home by midnight and my father would threaten him if he didn't.

We'd make out in his car, skipping school, and heading off to college to start our future together. But that wasn't our world, and we were both realizing the misfortune of it. We craved normalcy.

Needing a shower before dinner, I ran inside to clean up. I tossed on jeans and a black tank top, pulling my hair in a messy bun. I noticed Nora had already left, so I must have been running behind. Ren stood there waiting as I opened the door.

"Hey, what's going on?" I asked.

He bowed. "I'm here to escort you to dinner."

"Escort me? When did Fremont become so formal?"

He didn't respond, but stared with the warm gaze I'd become accustomed to as he held out his arm. I played along, but rolled my eyes along the way.

I leaned in toward him. "What is this about?"

As we turned the corner into the dining hall, the lights flipped on, and everyone screamed, "Surprise! Happy Birthday!"

My eighteenth birthday. I couldn't believe I'd forgotten my birthday. Drake came toward me, grabbing the sides of my face and kissing me enthusiastically. I heard someone clear their throat, and I was almost certain it came from Sebastian.

"Happy birthday," he whispered, then kissed me again.

I stared at all the faces around the room. "I can't believe you did this."

He shrugged. "We all did."

My gaze traveled to the table behind him, covered with a variety of snack foods, and I instantly started salivating at the sight of the pink cake topped with strawberries.

"What is that?" I shouted louder than necessary.

"Isn't it beautiful?" Neela asked. "Sebastian picked it out."

"Is that strawberry?" I asked.

Sebastian chuckled, "Yes. Strawberry cream cheese."

"Did you know it is my all-time favorite? I've only had it

at someone else's party as a child, well, because I've never actually had a cake, but I loved it!"

Sebastian's hand swung out, halting the conversation, "Wait a minute, you've never had a birthday cake?"

"No, I haven't. This is amazing! Thank you all so much!"

I couldn't say for sure, but the undercurrent of anger rolling through the room felt as though it came from Sebastian. I knew the guy was temperamental, I saw it when he first arrived. But sometimes he seemed over the top.

We devoured the cake, all except Cassie, who said she still couldn't eat, and Cyrus, who was allergic to strawberries. Kellan and I chatted about the latest tennis rankings when a sizable pink gift bag dropped in front of my face. Neela stood over me with a smirk.

I stared at the gift bag in shock. "What is this?"

She shimmied from side to side and grinned. "Happy Birthday, Mercy."

Again, my eyes darted from the bag to her face. "Why do I feel so nervous?"

She chewed on her lip without answering.

I dug into the bag, eager to find out what put that mischievous look on her face. "You didn't!" I exclaimed.

Neela clapped. "I did. It's only a starter wardrobe, but you have at least three outfits."

I jumped from my chair, crashing into her with excitement. New clothes were rare for me, and I couldn't wait to try them on."Thank you so much!"

Grateful seemed like such a petty word for what I felt. Nora gave me a journal, something to vent my emotions, and Ren brought a box of blueberry scones from Arin's.

"Here's another." Drake handed me a small box wrapped in teal paper.

I ripped open the packaging with enthusiasm. A small gold chain lay inside, attached to an oval plate with a beautiful cursive M engraved on the front. Drake flipped it over to reveal an intricate design of an eye.

He leaned forward and whispered, "One way or another, you'll have my mark."

I took the necklace out of the box and held it at my neck while he clasped the back. I didn't know what to say, and I almost feared I'd cry if I spoke. He kissed me on the side of the head and moved out of the way for Fitz.

Fitz spoke quietly. "Mercy, this is something your parents wanted you to have."

"My parents?" I asked.

He handed me a small white box, and my hands shook from nervous energy. I opened it to find a delicate gold band. The antique design held a combination of small round diamonds and an oval emerald in the center. It was gorgeous.

"My birthstone," I mumbled to myself.

"Hers too," Fitz whispered, referring to my mother. "When she was pregnant, the swelling forced her to remove it. Your father would wear it on a chain to keep it safe. Now, it's yours."

I looked up at him with wide eyes. "How did you get this?"

Fitz tilted his head and grinned. "That's a story for another day."

I nodded, full of emotion, then reached down to pull the heirloom from the box. It slid over my finger with ease—perfect fit. Heat engulfed my hand, and I almost removed it when it became uncomfortable. It subsided, and I could have sworn the brilliance increased as it settled into place on my finger—as if the ring accepted me. Words stuck in my throat as Sebastian left the dining hall, leaving a wake of sadness, pride, and fear around us. Nora followed him.

Fitz's expression was full of emotion, "Keep it safe, Mercy. Take it off for no one."

. . .

I TURNED the ring around my finger, the small strip of moon-light shining through my window glinting off the stones. I couldn't sleep. Unanswered questions burned through my mind, and three words, in particular, ate at me. Five years ago. What happened five years ago to alter the lives of two friends I love dearly? There's only one person who might have the answer, and I knew even if asked, he might not be honest with me. Fitz.

Raising up on my elbows, I listened for Nora's even breathing, wanting to make sure she slept soundly. I slipped on my clothes and left the room as quietly as possible. Thankfully, the dark halls of Fremont were empty. No matter the time, there was usually someone up.

Fitz's office was at the end of the hall on the right—never locked. Shouldn't there be files or something private to guard? Then again, he probably saved everything on a digital file somewhere. I slowly turned the doorknob and pushed on the heavy wooden door. The blinds were open, moonlight shining throughout the office. The light wasn't great, but I feared the lamp would bring too much attention to the room.

I started toward his desk, the top middle drawer locked. I felt underneath for a key or release like they did in the movies, but came up empty. Psychology books, notebooks, and office supplies filled the side drawers of the desk. Could Fitz really be this boring? I went through everything in the cabinets, shelves, and books. I told myself this was a waste of time, so I turned to head back to my room. That's when I saw it.

A small black trunk, maybe two feet long, sat on the bottom shelf. Hidden in plain sight between two sections of encyclopedias. I pulled the trunk free and turned on the desk lamp to rummage through Fitz's belongings.

Papers and pictures toppled out when I lifted the lid. I found college degrees, old mail, and a few photos of him and Dr. Lee when they first opened Fremont. They both looked younger, less stressed. I couldn't imagine what they'd been through over the years to protect their students, especially Fitz.

When I finally decided to give up, a picture of two boys, maybe eighteen or nineteen, fell out of an envelope. A house stood behind them, made from smooth stone with a wooden arched doorway. Willow trees on both sides were blowing with the breeze, and the sky was bluer than I had ever seen it. Something inside me whispered, "Seregalo." Fitz had to be the guy on the left with curly dark hair and eyes that turned down when he smiled, but the one on the right . . . he looked like . . . it wasn't possible. Had I lost my mind?

I flipped the picture over, and the words written on the back would forever change my life.

Brian M. Fitzpatrick and Noah Sebastian Monroe.

I flipped the image back over and looked at the face I'd seen for weeks, Sebastian's face. My father's face. How could this be? My palm flew over my mouth to mute the sob, climbing up my throat.

"Now you know." Fitz leaned against the doorway with his arms crossed in front of his chest.

"How could you not tell me?" I whispered.

"I'm ashamed to say I just recently found out. I honestly thought he'd died, Mercy. I knew Dr. Lee had a new patient, but I was so involved in your training and protection, I let him handle all of our new residents. I searched him out after speaking to you about your nightmare. I couldn't believe it.

My mind is still blown, but my heart is full. We stayed up all night, reminiscing and talking about you."

Fitz squatted down in front of me. "He had to stay hidden, Mercy, and it takes his entire sensory gift to project his younger self. He was heading toward lunacy when Dr. Lee brought him in—found him in an alley out in the open, mumbling about an attack. Using his gift constantly for the last five years had taken a toll on him. All he's ever wanted was to protect his family, you must know that."

I struggled to swallow as bile burned my throat. "And Dr. Lee? Does he know?"

"He does. Dr. Lee knew he was hiding something, and figured it out rather quickly. It's imperative we keep your father's identity hidden. Aadya doesn't need to know he's alive."

"What happened, Fitz? Five years ago, something went down to alter my friend's lives, and I know you know. I'm sick of the secrets and the lies. If I'm such a major part in all of this, then I deserve the truth. My friends deserve to know what happened to their loved ones. Just be honest with me. Did it have something to do with my parents?"

"Yes," Fitz sighed. "I swear, Mercy, I'm getting these details along with you. If I had known any of this, I would've come for you much sooner, I promise. I would never have left you with that horrible woman. Your father wouldn't have either if he had known what it was like."

I nodded that I believed him, because I genuinely did.

"When you came of age, another ripple of power ran through Seregalo. A reminder of sorts that you were still here, alive and well. The evening of your thirteenth birthday, a wave of magic ran through the city, then the news broke the story about an explosion at a local school gym. Aadya sent every Custos available to New York to sniff you out. Your father, along with the Morenos and Parkers, held them off to protect you. They believed in your future, and I know they would do it all over again."

"They . . . all died? Protecting me?"

"The Morenos died, yes. The Parkers helped your father diminish the threat, then they went into hiding with their two oldest sons, waiting for the time Aadya would attack again. We all know it's coming, Mercy."

"The ring, did my father give it to you?" I asked.

"Yes."

I lowered my head, crying for my family and Drakes. What would Drake think when he found out I was responsible for their death? Would he still want to be with me? I shook my head back and forth, telling myself that this couldn't be real. Thinking back, all Sebastian had done since he arrived was take care of me. I needed to see him. I needed to meet my father.

"Where is he, Fitz?"

Fitz stared down at his watch and sighed. "Lee put him on the security rotations. He'll either be on the roof or in the courtyard right now."

I took a deep breath, then walked out of his office without another word.

❖

13

I didn't have to search for my father. I felt him. His warmth. His fierce determination to protect me. An awareness of the truth sharpened my intuition where he was concerned. I walked out the backdoor of Fremont—a crisp cold wind grazing across my skin as I stepped onto the courtyard.

Just like Dr. Lee instructed, I blocked. This time, I didn't focus on shielding myself from a subconscious power, I blocked a sensory interferer—my father. The moment my eyes found him, the breath left my lungs. He stood with his back toward me in the center of the yard, looking up at the stars. My shield blocked the image of his younger self he'd fought so hard to conjure.

The moonlight lit up his salt and pepper hair. His left shoulder that sat just a smidge higher than the right—similar to mine. The way he focused on the sky, as if he begged for answers he didn't have. How many times had I done the same?

The crunch of grass under my shoes rang out through the

quiet of the night, and I knew he was aware of my presence. His emotions were all over the place—joy, fear, gratefulness.

"You've been practicing. I haven't had any real competition from a shield in quite some time."

His deep voice soothed my soul. I couldn't speak for fear of crying.

He still hadn't turned around to face me. "I wanted to tell you, but I didn't know how. I'm not sure I've always made the smartest decisions where you're concerned, but everything I've done—everything—is because I love you and want to protect you."

Warm tears left paths down my cheeks at his words. It was the first time someone had told me they loved me. I'd always wondered what it would feel like.

My father turned and met my gaze. Tears filled his eyes, but he didn't move. The heart-shaped face, eyes, dimples . . . We looked so much alike.

"My mother—is she alive?" I asked, softly.

His eyes darkened and his chin trembled at my question. He shook his head. "I'm sorry," he whispered.

My shoulders slumped in defeat. I pursed my lips and wrapped my hand around my neck as if I could relieve the tightness in my throat. I knew it wasn't likely she had survived, but I'd hoped.

"The night of my thirteenth birthday—I felt an emptiness. A loss of someone important. I remember it so clearly." My eyes filled with tears.

The stress of using his gift was obvious in the dark circles under his eyes. "Yes," he whispered. "I should have been there." His guilt was evident in the shakiness of his voice.

My father's presence pulled a vulnerability from me. One I fought everyday to hide from my friends. "I'm glad you're here."

"Mercy . . ." He stepped forward and wrapped his arms around me.

I buried my face in his chest and a comfort I'd never experienced consumed me. I breathed him in, as if relishing every detail of our private moment. I'd never felt smaller.

He kissed the top of my head, then whispered, "You're insecurity, your self-doubt—it all stems from your lack of connection to your power growing up. You're stronger than you know. I'm going to help you. Alright?"

"Is Aadya coming for me? Is that why you're at Fremont?" I had so many questions—I blurted them out as they came to me. "Will you leave again?"

"Honestly, Mercy, I don't know what she will do. I do know that you need to be prepared for anything. Now that you've demonstrated multiple gifts, she will attack eventually. If she finds out I'm here, she will show herself sooner rather than later."

"I don't know how to be this person," I cried. "This powerful individual that's supposed to lead our people." I hiccuped as the sobs kept coming. "What am I supposed to challenge her to? Kinetic-tennis?"

I glanced up as my father fought a smile. "Come sit down."

We walked to the side of the courtyard where a small concrete bench sat between two shrubs, shielding us from the garden entrance. We both sat silently, staring up at the beautiful night sky. Not a cloud in sight.

"The day you were born—when we realized the extent of your power—Annabel fell apart. The thought of you being anywhere near her sister terrified her. But I told her, if nature trusts Mercy for this destiny, then we will too. The struggle was keeping you alive until you were old enough to take over."

Then, I asked the question I wasn't sure if I wanted him to

answer. "How long have you been in New York?" My gaze focused on the crisp blades of grass between my feet.

He cleared his throat. "I never left."

Confusion and frustration overwhelmed me. I stood and paced the courtyard, my fist balling up at my side. "You just left me alone? All this time? You left me with her?" The night sky dimmed as clouds stole the pristine starlight. I breathed through my anger, trying to see it from his point of view. I couldn't. I didn't understand.

"No. I never left you, I promise." He stood, placing his hands on my shoulders as he turned me to face him. He bent slightly, just enough to look into my eyes. "Going in and out of school, watching you work with children in the evenings, following you home to make sure you were safe. I was there. I never left."

I blinked as tears blurred my vision. His hazel eyes softened and his thumb swiped across my cheek. "I'm so scared," I admitted. "Please don't leave me."

"I'm here, Mercy."

. . .

LEAVING him in the courtyard was the hardest thing I'd ever done. As if he would disappear or maybe I would wake, realizing it was all a dream. A wonderful, beautiful dream. We sat together under the stars for hours, discussing everything and nothing. Sometimes we grew silent, just grateful to be sitting with each other.

Adrenaline flowed through my veins. I wanted to scream and shout at the top of my lungs. I couldn't. Fitz told me my father's position was delicate. If Aadya got wind of his whereabouts, it would have put everyone in danger.

I walked up and down the hallway, unable to force myself to bed. I couldn't relax and there was only one who could calm my mind and heart.

My knuckles lightly tapped the wooden door. I was grateful he didn't have a roommate. I heard shuffling on the other side of the door before it opened. Drake stood, his hair sticking up in all directions, wearing nothing but shorts.

Good Lord.

He struggled to focus. "Mercy? What's wrong?"

His deep voice clouded all rational thought as I absorbed the sight in front of me.

"Mercy?"

"I, um, I'm having trouble sleeping," I mumbled.

His eyes softened and he opened the door wider as he stepped to the side. He closed the door behind me then took my hand, leading me toward his bed. The twin bed appeared much smaller in his room, with his large frame stretched out from top to bottom. I crawled underneath the covers and laid my head against his hard chest, absorbing his warmth—his strength.

"Do you want to talk about it?" he asked.

"Now that I'm laying beside you, I seem to forget what brought me here to begin with," I mumbled.

A deep chuckle resonated through Drake's chest.

I closed my eyes, as peace flooded my mind. Snuggling deeper into his side, I grazed my fingers across his hips.

Drake pulled my hand toward his face and his lips skimmed my knuckles. "Let's not push my control."

I grinned as my eyelids became heavy. "Control is over-rated," I whispered.

"Says the girl with no control."

. . .

For the first time in my life, I felt on top of the world. Being able to have breakfast with my father, practice my elemental gift, and experience a parental bond I never knew existed—it was more than I had ever imagined.

I felt Drake's eyes on us, watching and wondering about the unusual friendship that had blossomed. But he also showed trust and understanding–he knew I needed the support of my friends at that confusing time in my life.

A couple of days after my father's reveal, he asked me to dress inconspicuously for a quick outing. I was too excited to ask questions, so I braided my hair in the back and put on Drake's Yankees cap. After lacing up my boots, the awareness of being watched pulled my attention toward the open door.

Drake leaned against the frame, his eyes dark and his mouth tight. "Are you sure you can trust this guy?"

I grinned, "I'm positive. You know I wouldn't go otherwise."

He nodded, then stepped inside the room. "Make it quick, or else I'll go crazy." He wrapped his arm around my waist and jerked me to his chest. His lips softly brushed across mine, teasing me.

As my teeth grazed his bottom lip, a deep growl vibrated throughout his chest and the kiss deepened. After what felt like several minutes, someone, sounding quite irritated, cleared their throat in the hall. I'd forgotten the door was open.

I pulled away and looked up into the wide eyes of Sebastian. "So–we need to go. You know, if you're finished."

Fitz walked up and slapped Sebastian on the back. "Want me to come?"

Sebastian didn't take his eyes off Drake. "This is something I'd like to do alone, if you don't mind."

Fitz nodded and smiled. "Of course. See you this afternoon."

Drake's eyes narrowed. "Take care of her."

"Always."

. . .

ALTHOUGH WARMER THAN USUAL, the morning air revived my energy. I thrived on being outdoors and the added security at Fremont had kept me limited to the courtyard.

My father stayed close to my side, keeping an eye out for threats. Although watchful, there was peace and contentment in his eyes that wasn't there when he arrived. As if our connection had filled a void inside us both.

He stopped at a nearby food cart, ordering coffee—then whisked around the corner to an older lady selling bouquets of flowers. My brows raised out of confusion, but he only smiled and asked the woman for pink and green peonies.

We walked for what felt like a mile, before turning down a quiet street in a residential neighborhood. It was actually very close to our old apartment. After a few more blocks, our destination came into view and I froze.

My eyes widened and I shook my head, as if my mind struggled to accept the reason for our trip that morning. My father looked back and his eyes softened. "Come, Mercy." He stretched his hand out for mine.

My shaky hand in his, we walked through the black iron gate of the cemetery. Tall headstones were scattered underneath an expanse of hovering trees, shading the green lots before me. The smell of freshly cut grass combined with the decay of flowers overwhelmed my senses. Everything felt amplified as my emotions welled to the surface.

Toward the back right-hand corner of the graveyard, an oval headstone sat under a sliver of sunlight breaking through the trees. Simple and elegant. My father didn't speak —he kneeled, placing the bouquet of peonies in front of the stone. I watched as he closed his eyes, then I sensed the longing in his heart as he took a minute to remember the love of his life—his everything.

"Mercy?"

I eased toward my father, somewhat hesitantly. Something about seeing the engraving made it too real—which seemed ridiculous considering I already knew she was gone. But when my eyes traveled over *'Annabel Claire Monroe- Beloved wife and mother'*— I felt her loss all over again.

"She would have adored your spunk. Annabel was quiet and sweet-natured, not as out-going. I think it was hard for her growing up beside Aadya, who demanded everyone's attention."

I clenched my teeth. "What makes a person so demented, that you can only be happy if others are suffering?"

"Honestly, I've never known her to be any other way. Annabel spent most of her life trying to understand her. She never gave up hope that she would change."

"Aadya's visited me in my sleep. Did you know that? Having someone else in my head—it feels dark and intrusive."

He nodded. "Because it is. Subconscious interference empowers a Regalian more than any other gift. Manipulation of the mind is not to be taken lightly, Mercy. I've never met a Regalian with the power that hasn't abused it."

I swallowed, nervous about manifesting the gift myself.

"I know what you're thinking," he whispered. "You can choose to be different. You can be an example to others."

"I refuse to violate someone's mind that way." I shook my head, angry. "It isn't right."

He grinned at my words. "I want you to take in this moment, Mercy. How you see the world, the passion you have for others. Always keep this level of love and respect in your heart. That is what makes a leader. Not the level of power you were born with."

I studied the headstone, vowing to never forget those words. "I'm glad you're here."

He took a sip of coffee and smiled. "Me too."

. . .

MY FATHER, still under the disguise of his younger self, sat across from me in the library—the table in front of us piled high with books he wanted me to study. 'Regalian history', 'Uncovering the Origin of Elemental Interference', 'The Role of a Custos'. The past couple of weeks had been grueling—he pushed me more and more each day.

He pointed out pictures in the open book in front of me. "Here, in Ireland, is the entrance to Seregalo. There are rumors of other hidden lands, but if they are out there— we've never found proof."

"Other than Seregalo? That's interesting. Do you think they hold the same power we do?"

"If they exist, and that's a big if, I would think so. Although there are tall tales of Regalians with gifts such as healing, invisibility, or shape-shifting."

My eyes widened in surprise. "How have I never ran across these books before?" I asked, shaking my head.

"You won't find these in your everyday library, Mercy.

This is the only set I know outside of Seregalo. Practicing everyday will build your power, but knowledge is the root of control."

I slammed the book closed in front of me and my father sighed. "I want to hear about my family. Tell me about Mother," I insisted.

He grinned. "Your mother was just as bright and beautiful as you—and just as stubborn." His eyes lit up. "I miss her so much."

I propped my chin on my clasped hands in front of me. "How did you meet?"

"In Seregalo. Fitz told me he had met someone and he seemed more preoccupied with her, rather than causing mischief with me. I wanted to meet this girl. What could be so special about her?" He chuckled and shook his head. "As soon as we laid eyes on each other, we knew."

"And Fitz?"

My father's face fell. "Brokenhearted. He didn't admit it, but I could tell. There wasn't anything I could do, Mercy. We were a perfect match."

"So you just knew? Without seeing each other's marks?"

"We did. There's an electric pull that isn't quite normal, but not unnatural either. My power intensified around her."

I glanced down at the table, feigning interest in the texts. "I heard some never find their match."

"True. They still find happiness though. You can't grieve for a connection you've never experienced." He cleared his throat. "Is there something you want to talk about?"

"I'm just trying to understand. I thought Dra—nevermind." I shook my head, feeling awkward. "It's nothing."

He grinned. "Some things can't be found in a book, Mercy. Listen to your heart."

I sighed. "So you're telling me I won't find Mr. Darcy in these texts?"

He grinned, shaking his head. "You are so much like Annabel. That sounds like something she would have said."

"My mother had good taste."

Dad closed the book in front of him and sighed. "She married me, didn't she?"

I threw my head back and laughed at his witty response.

The humor in his eyes turned to worry as he sat up straight. "Mercy, there are things we need to talk about. I didn't want to overwhelm you, but you have the right to know."

The abrupt change in his demeanor worried me. "You're scaring me."

He slid his chair closer and lowered his voice. "I don't mean to. You've had a lot to process and this isn't something that is easy to talk about. But you need to know. It's imperative you understand the true meaning behind your mother's ring and also . . . you have a right to know about Marl—"

"I've been looking for you," a deep voice rumbled.

My father's voice halted as he sat up straight.

I looked over my shoulder to see Drake leaning against the doorframe. "What are you doing over there?" I asked.

"Keeping an eye on Sebastian," Drake mumbled, smiling. "Would you like to see a movie tonight?"

"I've never been to a theatre. Can we do that?" I sat up straight, grinning.

"I'm not sure it's safe enough for that, especially after our trouble at the ballgame. We can watch one in the activities lounge though."

I deflated.

"I promise as soon as I'm allowed, I'll take you. You have my word," he promised.

My father spoke up. "I remember my first movie. Nothing like the excitement of a new flick and the smell of buttery popcorn in the air."

"Flick?" Drake asked.

"Yeah, you know. A movie," Sebastian explained.

"What was it? What was your first movie?" I asked.

"Back to the Future. I was so excited. My father and I snuck out of the house the weekend it released." He grinned at the memory.

"Back to the Future?" Drake asked. "Didn't that come out like over thirty years ago? Before we were born?"

Sebastian pursed his lips. "Well, guys. I have a meeting with Fitz. Talk soon." He abruptly stood, making his way toward the door.

"Wait—I thought we needed to talk." My brow raised at his quick exit.

He looked at Drake, then back at me. His eyes softened and love filled the air around me. "Find me later. I'll give you guys some time." He winked before leaving me alone with Drake.

"That guy is strange," Drake said. "He appears to be smitten with you." He raised one brow and smirked.

I smiled. "You would know all about that."

He smirked. "You've been in here all morning. Don't you want a break?"

"No, I really want to get through these passages. Wanna keep me company? I can read to you in my sultry voice."

He kissed my cheek and smiled. "Never thought I'd look forward to Regalian history."

✦

14

"*Y*ou do realize you have to eat and sleep, right?"

I looked up from the grueling passage on Elder history to find Fitz at the doorway of the library. "Just think how well I'll sleep after reading this horribly boring chapter my father insisted upon."

"Noah loved Seregalo history. I despised it—cheated off his paper in class." He chuckled. "Don't tell him I said that."

My brows raised in shock. "Your secret is . . ."

Fitz held up one hand, halting me. "Did you hear that?" His eyes scanned every corner of the room—every window.

I didn't hear anything, but I felt it. Malevolence hovered around the Fremont building, ill intent hanging in the air like a morning fog. It reminded me of the eeriness I felt on the roof with Drake. All at once, alarms sounded from every corner of the building—the security system.

"Stay here, Mercy. Don't come out of this room," Fitz ordered.

Fitz closed the library door, telling me to lock it behind him. We'd gone over what I needed to do if there was ever a security breach—hide and shield my subconscious. Alarms echoed throughout the building, leaving me in a pent-up state of fear and desperation.Tucking myself under Fitz's desk in the corner, I found a comfortable spot to concentrate and created a bubble around my mind.

A few times, my shield would waver as my thoughts drifted to the others. Where were they? Were they okay? The alarms were silenced and the building was too quiet. Too— vacant. A shadow passed over the window, causing me to jump. I slowed my breathing and waited. Fitz would be back soon, right? Fremont had several rooms, so I knew it would take a while to secure the building.

What is that noise?

Clomp. Clomp. Clomp.

Something that sounded like boots drew near. My breaths became quick and shallow, and my hands clenched in fists. The squeak of the doorknob made the hair on the back of my neck stand up. Fitz knew it was locked, he wouldn't be trying to open it. I reached out to see if I could sense anything, and I felt them . . . the remorse for what they were about to do, but satisfaction in doing it. There's only one person I knew that could feel so twisted—Asher Moreno.

If Drake got a hold of him, he'd wish he was dead. I stayed frozen and shielded my mind as much as possible. The sinister soul outside the door drifted further away, and in its place, a timid and sweet presence stood. Nora. I'd know her anywhere.

I tip-toed to the door and whispered softly, "Nora? Is that you?"

"Mercy! Thank goodness. Please let me in."

I cracked the door open, and Nora looked up at me with swollen eyes—she'd been crying. She hurried into the room and I locked the door behind her.

"You weren't there. I woke, and you weren't there. I didn't

know what to do, so I hid in my closet until I sensed you," she explained.

"I'm so sorry, Nora. I was studying when Fitz went to investigate a noise."

Nora wrinkled her nose. "Studying what?"

"Long story. I'm not sure what to do now." My emotions were all over the place, as lightning struck in the distance, creating an electric path across the sky.

"See if there's something in Fitz's desk. If nothing else, an envelope opener or pocket knife. We can't go out there empty-handed," I told her.

"Go out there? Are you insane? No, we should wait here. He'll be back soon, Mercy."

"I refuse to abandon everyone, Nora. Aadya's guards are here for me. Me. I have to fight back, but I won't ask you to go with me. Stay here and lock the door."

Her shoulders relaxed, and she released a heavy sigh. "I'll go with you."

I gripped her hand. "You don't have to, you know that, right?"

Her face softened, trying to comfort me. She didn't have to speak, I knew she'd never let me go out there alone.

I pulled at the top drawer of his desk. As stressed as Fitz had been about security, he'd surely keep something. "Locked. I bet he has the key."

"Key? Mercy, what do you need a key for? You're psychokinetic." Nora smirked as if it should have been obvious.

I'll admit, that was embarrassing. I sat in front of his desk on my knees and willed the lock to release. Nothing happened.

"Don't think about unlocking it. Picture the lock in your mind and force it through the motions."

I thought about the inside of the release and moved it

around as if I had inserted a key. It wobbled, but never fully turned. I continued to focus and finally, the drawer popped free.

I dug around the papers in the drawer, and located a small handgun in the back.

Thank you, Fitz, I thought.

I checked to see if Fitz had loaded it, then motioned for Nora to follow. Her petite frame shook from unease, but she loved me enough to go with me.

A loud crack of thunder echoed over the building as we opened the door. The hall was pitch black, and the creak of the old wooden floor the only thing we could hear. Where had Drake and the others gone? Where was my dad? We eased down the hall and crept up the flight of stairs. Nora reached out to stop me in my tracks.

"I feel someone, up ahead." I reached forward, straining my senses, and wishing my emotional gift was as sensitive as Nora's. I caught the slightest presence of fear up ahead, possibly in the lounge.

The black of the room kept us from being able to see more than a few feet ahead. I could have tried using my sensory gift to increase my night vision, but the fear of needing my power for something else weighed on me. Tiptoeing forward, I held the gun at the ready. A sniffling drew us over by the bookcase where a figure huddled under a blank in the corner.

Nora pulled the blanket off an inconsolable Cassie. Mascara ran down her face, and she shook all over. "What the hell is going on?" she said through tears.

We both knew we couldn't tell her the truth. Even though Regalian, she wouldn't be able to handle it.

"Someone broke in, Cassie. We need to get out of the building, alright?" I told her.

"Are you crazy? I'm not moving!"

My eyes widened. "Shh! Be quiet before you get us killed."

Her face went pale at my words.

I shook my head, annoyed. "If you want to stay here, fine, but don't come out until we come back for you."

"Where are you going?" she asked.

"To look for the others," I told her.

"Well, I'm not staying by myself." She ungracefully staggered to her feet. "Plus, at least you have a gun."

We crept back into the hall, making our way to the stairwell. We were about twenty feet away when Fitz stepped in our path with his hand up, silently telling us not to move. He listened, as if sensing someone close. The relief of having him with us released a tightness in my chest I didn't realize existed.

His eyes were hazy from the extreme focus it took to sense everything around him. His expression turned to confusion, as if he didn't understand an emotion he had picked up on. All at once, a baseball bat swung out, smashing Fitz in the side of the head, his body falling limp on the floor.

"No!" I shouted.

I raised my head and looked eye to eye with the most sinister and devious person I'd ever met. Bile crept up my throat at the thought of confiding in him. We trusted Dr. Lee with our lives. An evil smile spread across his face as he threw the bat to the floor.

"Hello, Mercy. I've been looking for you."

"You . . . you said you would protect us. You were his friend," I cried.

"Friend?" He threw his head back and laughed. "I've put up with his ramblings and nonsense for years! Do you have any idea how many times I've wanted to kill him? Do you?" His shouts echoed down the hall.

"You're working for Aadya?" I asked.

"We're working together. We are in love, Mercy."

"In love? It's funny you think either of you are capable of love. You honestly don't know what will happen to you when she's finished using you, do you?" I shouted.

Dr. Lee's fists clenched and unclenched as I spoke. He knew I was right. His nostrils flared, and the veins in his neck developed a cord-like appearance.

"I've known it was you all along. I told her so, but she wanted to wait to see if Noah showed himself," he spat. "And of course, he did. Now you can die together."

A loud cackle erupted from his throat before he threw his hand out toward my head. His power collided with my shield, and he pushed harder to search for a crack in my armor. I'd barely put forth any effort to thwart his advances. He thought he'd taught me enough so he didn't blow his cover, but that was all I needed to perfect the wall I'd built. I had worked on this with Drake for hours, and I was ready for him.

Desperation fueled his source, and frustration controlled him as the defeat in his expression transformed into a treacherous sneer I couldn't interpret.

His voice became angry. "She knows you'll come for her —for Marley. Will you let her die too? How many, Mercy? How many people have to perish for you? Is that what you want? Could that be what fuels the source of the great future queen? To live off the suffering of innocent lives around you?"

"No!" I shouted.

"Isn't that what you're doing right now? Guarding yourself while the magic rebounds into poor, pathetic Cassie. Such a horrible trait, to care so little for those weaker than you."

My head jerked to the left, and Cassie wobbled back and forth. She slowly turned to look at me, blood dripping from her nose and ears. Her eyes were bloodshot and swollen.

She'd taken everything that he intended for me—he made sure of it. A small pale hand reached out for me as she fell forward.

I caught her with my free arm to break her fall and eased her to the ground, keeping the gun pointed at him with the other. The light in her blue eyes faded as she cried out for me to help her, and I watched as she took one final gasp, squeezing my arm, then releasing it.

No matter what she'd done, she didn't deserve this. Anger flowed through me for what he'd done. I made eye contact with Dr. Lee, and he smiled as he cocked his head to the side. My father's words about abusing subconscious interference echoed in my head.

A horrible high-pitched yell came from my right as Nora threw her palms over her ears.

"Sweet, angelic Nora. Poor thing. Too pretty for her own good, you know. Couldn't even get the older men to leave you alone, could you sweetheart?" He chuckled.

The combination of Nora's screams and Dr. Lee's laughter swirled inside my already overwhelmed mind. I wouldn't let him do this to anyone else—one innocent life was bad enough. The gun shook in my hand as I stumbled to my feet. His laughter escalated as I pointed it in his direction.

Another yell from Nora—that's all it took. I pulled the trigger.

Click.

His laughter died as he stared at me, amazed I'd tried to fire at him. He didn't think I'd do it. The gun didn't fire and being inexperienced, I didn't know why. His cackling continued, louder than before, mocking me.

I felt the energy around me stir as my fear and anger collided. My chest heaved, struggling to take a breath as the air electrified. My kinetic power exploded into the gun, and pushed the bullet out with force. No one in the room realized what had happened until his shirt stained red, and he collapsed to his knees in shock. I stood over him with the gun, shaking and panting.

I couldn't hear anything around me, no voices, footsteps —nothing. My pulse pounded in my ears, drowning out the gasps from Dr. Lee. He reached out for me, then fell face down on the floor. I didn't snap out of my daze until familiar hands pulled the gun from my grip. Drake checked the chamber to verify there were bullets and turned the safety off. He tucked it in the back of his pants and forced my eyes up to his.

"Mercy, stay with me. We gotta get everyone out of here, and I need you to focus. Do you understand what I'm saying?"

I nodded, unable to speak.

"Get to the roof. A chopper is on the way." Drake helped Nora to her feet, sparing a quick, sad glance toward Cassie. He looked over at me with sympathetic eyes. "This was all him. Not you, Mercy." He pulled us toward the stairwell. "I have to search this floor, then I'll meet you up there."

"Fitz! We need to check on him!" Nora panicked.

"Ren's got him, Nora. Don't worry, he's alive," Drake answered, before turning back toward the hallway.

I took the stairs, one shaky step at a time, with Nora gripping my hand. We pushed through the door at the top of the stairs, and froze. Stella, Cyrus, and Kellan all stood in the corner huddled together. Neela stood in the middle of the roof, rain pouring down her face. A Custos guard stood behind her with a knife at her throat. I scanned the length of the roof—at least fifty Custos were waiting, and Asher Moreno stood in the center with a cocky smile.

Asher yelled over the pounding of rain on the roof. "If any of you try anything, we will kill her. You wanna take that chance?"

The charge of magic dissipated as the fear of harming one of our own took root.

Asher's gaze swept the roof. "Now then. Where's that brother of mine? Anybody?"

Silence.

"Nobody? Alright, then. Maybe a death or two will bring him forward." Asher nodded toward the guard and Neela gasped as the blade pressed against her skin. She clenched her jaw, as if fighting the need to release her power.

"Right here." Drake pulled a gun free and aimed it toward his brother.

Asher grinned. "Drop the gun, Drake. You know I'll kill her and sleep well afterward."

Drake took a deep breath, then slowly dropped it on the ground. "That's fine, Asher. I think we all know I don't really need it," he responded.

Asher tilted his chin up defiantly, and the surrounding Custos shuffled nervously. "You're on the wrong side, brother. There are things you don't know."

Drake laughed. "Oh, really. You have all the answers, I presume?"

"I know what happened to our parents," Asher admitted.

Sweat ran down the back of my neck, and my heart felt as though it would beat out of my chest. I wasn't ready for Drake to know the truth, not from Asher. Drake stood silently, but continued watching him.

"Why don't you ask your girlfriend who she's gotten killed? She has to have the record, right? Her Mom. Our parents. Who else?" Asher continued to speak, taunting him with a twisted variation of the truth.

"That the side you wanna be on? The one that got mom and dad killed? It's not too late, Drake. You can do what's right."

Drake's eyes met mine, and I knew his feelings for me were unyielding. No matter the circumstance.

"It's true. I'm so sorry," I whispered as tears ran down my face.

Drake's focus turned full force on his brother, and I knew there was enough emotion in his power to kill them all. The moment Asher came to the same conclusion, he nodded toward the guard. Mine and Neelas's power collided, halting the blade at her neck as Drake took the feeling from the guard's limbs. The blade fell to the ground along with the Custos, and Neela bolted across the roof toward me.

Completely focused on Neela, we never saw the gun until it was fired. When Asher's bullet left the chamber, I knew with all of my heart I was too late to stop it. Drake collapsed to his knees, as blood soaked through his shirt. I knelt beside him, crying—holding pressure on his chest as his black shirt morphed into a white one, and the black of his hair transformed into the salt and pepper I'd grown to love. I shook my head in disbelief. My father had conjured the appearance of Drake.

The intensity inside of me at that moment was triple what I'd felt on the subway. Love, heartache, and fear entwined for a vicious explosion of power. A massive bolt of lightning struck overhead as my back arched painfully, and my head shot up. I couldn't hear anything around me. Neela's mouth opened as if she yelled my name, but there was no sound.

Drake and Ren burst through the door, right as Stella dove on top of the other students, protecting them. An eruption of energy rippled across the rooftop, knocking every Custos, including Asher, off the ninety-foot building and onto the street. The sickening sound of bodies hitting concrete echoed around the block.

I fell to my knees, sobbing. My father focused on me, as if absorbing everything in the last few minutes of his life.

"No. No, please!" I placed my hands on his chest, putting pressure on the wound. Drake knelt beside him and pushed my hands away, taking over. He, Ren and Neela pulled from their gifts, attempting to control the bleeding. It was no use. He had lost too much blood.

"Elise! Where is she? She has to help him!" I cried out.

"She stayed with Fitz." Ren bolted toward the stairwell to find her.

I brought my palm into the air, twisting my wrist like I'd seen Elise do. Nothing happened. The silence of my gift told me what I already knew—I wasn't in touch with the interference of time. I screamed out in frustration and cursed my lack of control.

"Mercy—" Drake's voice was barely a whisper as he continued holding pressure on his chest. "He doesn't have long."

I glanced up and Drake nodded toward my father, silently telling me to take advantage of the time I had left.

My father's eyes were focused on my face. There was no fear—no panic. "I'm so proud of you," he gasped.

"I'm so sorry," I cried. "I'm so—so sorry. I'm not strong enough."

"You are so much stronger than you know. I love you, Mercy. So much." He lifted his hand, and I held it against the side of my face. He took several deep breaths. "Never give up —that's what she wants."

"Don't leave me, Dad. Please! You promised!" I screamed over the loud crack of thunder.

He breathed in slow and deep, as if relishing the last few seconds we had together. "You know, strawberry cake was Annabel's favorite too." He closed his eyes as his palm fell from my face.

All at once, a feeling of despair and loss traveled through my body, just as it did on my thirteenth birthday. As if a piece of me died along with him.

I sat there for several minutes—uncertainty and confusion hovering in the air from my closest friends. No one knew what to do for me at that moment.

"All this time? All this time your father was at Fremont?" Drake stared down at my father in shock. I wiped the tears rolling down my face. It was futile—more followed. I climbed into his lap, not knowing what else to do.

A gentle hand rested on my shoulder as Fitz stumbled to my side. Bruises shadowed his face and dried blood matted his hair. He looked as if he could pass out at any moment.

Elise kneeled on his other side, tearful. "I'm so sorry, Mercy. I'm sorry I wasn't here."

"You can try now, right? It might work, Elise. You have to try." I begged.

"Mercy, we can't bring people back from the dead. He's gone," she whispered sadly. "Noah was a good man. I can't imagine how hard this is for you, but you've got to leave, Sweetheart. I promise I'll take care of his body, and I'll do it respectfully, but I've got to get everyone out of here before more Custos show up."

"One more minute," Fitz mumbled.

Elise shook her head. "You look as though you might collapse, Fitz."

"He was my best friend, Elise. Mercy's father. Give us a minute," Fitz snapped. His face softened as he took in my father's lifeless body before him. "Rest well, my friend."

I leaned forward, kissed my father's brow, then whispered, "Thank you for loving me."

I looked up as the rain slowed, almost hovering in mid-air. Sirens wailed in the distance, no doubt on their way to the disruption at Fremont. A helicopter landed on the rooftop, and Stella gave the group their orders. Elise, Cyrus, Kellan and the others would go with her on the next chopper, and we would take the first. I gave Elise a small nod to let her know I trusted her with my dad. As the helicopter landed, Drake picked me up and carried me over to board.

"Wait."

"Mercy, we need to leave now," Drake insisted.

"My dad's picture and quilt. It's all I have."

He knew by the look on my face there would be no compromise.

"I'll be back." He took off running toward the entrance while the others jumped aboard, and Ren helped Fitz into the front. Drake returned at lightning speed with the items and promised that Elise would send the rest. The aircraft shook slightly as it hovered above Fremont, and I noticed Drake staring down at the dark pavement, no doubt mourning the loss of his brother. His brother I had killed.

I squeezed his hand, not knowing how to comfort him. "I'm sorry about Asher."

"No way around it. He wasn't the same person he once was, Mercy."

"He was still your brother."

"Yeah, he was."

We weren't in the air long before I felt the helicopter descend. Surrounded by tall buildings and busy streets, it was apparent we were still in the city. We landed on the roof of an old brick apartment and soon learned it belonged to Fitz.

"It's a Brooklyn loft I keep for emergencies. I've only ever told a handful of people about it. Elise is taking the other group to an apartment in Jersey for protection. We will report it as gang violence so they don't suspect anything," he explained.

After walking down two flights of stairs from the roof,

Fitz unlocked a heavy metal door to a large open living area. Exposed air ducts, brick walls, and black iron fixtures reminded me of Fremont. You could tell it stayed empty the majority of the time, with only the bare essentials scattered throughout the room. Fitz looked worn and struggled to focus. Ren and Drake were on each side, balancing him as he stumbled into the room. Fitz directed them to his bedroom, and they assisted him in laying down to rest.

I stood in the middle of the room, the night crashing down around me. I slowly turned, taking in the surrounding space, but my mind was back on the roof at Fremont. How many? How many people had to give their life for Aadya's thirst for power? The room shook, paintings fell from the wall, and cabinet doors swung open. All I could hear was the inhale and exhale of my breath as destruction continued around me.

A cold hand rested on my cheek, and the room settled. Nora's blue eyes stared up at me sympathetically as she invoked calm into my madness. Tears filled my eyes.

"I killed them, Nora. It's my fault they're dead. Cassie, Dr. Lee, my father, Asher. All those Custos have families somewhere. I took their lives."

"No, Mercy. She took their lives," Nora told me.

Another set of arms came around and picked me up from behind. "Come on. Let's get you in bed before we have another earthquake. Ren? Can you show the girls where to sleep? Mercy can stay with me."

Sadness filled Ren's eyes. "Sure thing."

Drake pulled the blood stained shirt over my head and replaced it with one of Fitz's he found in a drawer. I laid on the bed—unmoving—watching the fan above me as it blew a light breeze over my skin. Drake pulled my shoes from my feet, one at a time, and tucked the blankets around me.

"I lost my father tonight." I thought if I said it out loud, it might help me process what happened. It didn't.

Drake exhaled and kneeled down to kiss my forehead. "I don't know how to help you."

I continued to stare at the ceiling fan, the way the blades angled to direct the air toward me. The perfect speed to cool the small room. It's purpose fulfilled. Unlike myself. "Crazy, isn't it? The amount of power our small group has, and we still can't save someone's life."

Drake climbed into bed, holding me against his chest, and sighed. "Get some rest, Mercy."

. . .

I HEARD IT AGAIN. Giggling woke me in the middle of the night, taunting me with the knowledge she'd somehow gotten into my head again. I was too exhausted to shield, and she had gotten through. I swung my tired and heavy legs off the side of the bed, and my feet hit the cold wooden floor. I knew it could've been a trap, but I had to know. I wanted to know everything I could about her.

Light shone underneath the door, and the laughter of a child echoed from outside my room. I crept out of the bedroom, quietly. Drake needed his sleep as badly as the rest of us. The loft was silent—everyone sound asleep. The only thing separating the living area from the kitchen was a granite-topped bar. The giggling continued, and I turned to search out the little girls I knew would be there.

This was different. The egotistical redheaded child from my previous nightmare sat cross-legged in the middle of the cold tiled floor. Her head tilted down, and her eyes focused up at my face, waiting for me. Kitchen knives were splayed along the floor like puzzle pieces, with the largest blade clenched inside her palm.

Beside her sat a little girl with long brown hair and hazel eyes. Her mouth opened as if screaming, but without sound. Blood ran down from a gash in her neck, and cuts criss-crossed her hands as if she'd fought the knife. I looked back at the little red-haired demon, grinning.

"Aren't you going to come for Marley? Don't you care about anyone else?" She whispered in a sickeningly sweet voice. Her eyes traveled down to my hand, the one that wore my mother's ring. The grin vanished, and she screamed, "That belongs to me!"

I stumbled backward and ran into Fitz, almost knocking him to the floor.

Bruises shadowed the left side of his temple and he squinted as if in pain. "Mercy, what's going on?"

I looked down at the blood covering my palms.

"What happened?" He asked.

I held my shaking hands in front of me, then glanced down at the kitchen floor smeared with blood. Fitz pulled me toward the sink and turned on the faucet to look for wounds.

"Fitz, I'm fine."

He scrubbed the blood away and continued to search frantically.

"Fitz, look at me."

He paused and raised his eyes to mine.

"I'm okay."

His relief was audible throughout the kitchen. "Then whose blood is this?"

I stared down at my hands, then back at him. "I don't know."

"**I** have to go," I told them.

The distress was so thick in the room, I thought I might choke. Everyone sat throughout the living room, listening to the latest vision I'd had. Everyone, except Drake, who stood staring out the window with his hands behind his head. Disapproval clear in his rigid posture and refusal to acknowledge the conversation.

Aadya wanted something from me, and she wouldn't stop until she got it. I didn't tell them I'd heard the name Marley twice in the past two days—once from Dr. Lee and now from the vision. I knew what they would say—it was a trick, not to fall into her trap. Also, something about the name felt personal and I wasn't ready to share the information until I knew more.

"She's going to kill you." Ren said from across the room. "This is what she wants."

"Aadya will try to kill me no matter where I am. This is about cutting the casualties, Ren. Plus, I can't keep running."

"You know none of us will let you go alone, Mercy," Nora said.

"I'm sorry," Fitz said. "I'll never make it through Stonedell until I heal from the concussion. Only a mentally and physically strong individual can pass those trials. Aadya doesn't make it easy for people, other than Custos."

"I'd never ask you to go in your condition, Fitz. Just prepare us. Tell us everything we need to know. I don't feel like time is on our side."

"I'll do the best I can, Mercy." Fitz answered. "You need to know that getting there isn't for the faint of heart." He shook his head, disapprovingly. "I'm not sure your father would agree to this . . ."

"He isn't here," I whispered. "Plus, I don't feel like there's another option."

Drake stomped off to the bedroom and slammed the door without a word.

"He's scared of losing you," Fitz said, sadly. "We all are."

I sighed, then stood to follow Drake. I knew he worried, and I'd feel the same way about him. But this was something I had to do, and I needed Drake to support me.

I expected him to be lying across the bed, angry, with his arms above his head like usual, but the bed was bare. The rush of running water came from the bathroom, and I knocked gently but never received an answer. I cracked the bathroom door, and my heart slammed against my chest.

Drake stood in the glass shower with his hands against the tile, head lowered. The muscles in his back were flexed from tension, and water trickled down the ridges in his arms. I could barely make out the Allegato mark on his shoulder, but it didn't make sense. It looked jumbled, almost as if it wasn't complete. I didn't really care. I knew who he belonged with.

Handsome didn't seem like the right word. Drake was a work of art—but that alone didn't keep me standing there, interrupting his solitude. It was the magnitude of how much this man worried about me. It took my breath away, and the fact that his feelings for me could get him killed weighed heavily on my heart. Why would I put him in that situation? I didn't want Drake or anyone else risking their life for me.

The groan of the faucet being turned pulled me from my daze, as Drake stood facing me. I couldn't speak, all I could do was stare at him—admire him. He opened the glass door and reached for his towel, completely uninhibited, watching me. He wrapped the towel around his waist and walked toward me, causing my lower belly to clench and my palms to sweat. Stepping forward, he pinned me between his body and the wall.

Placing his hands on the wall beside my head, he caged me in. He leaned forward and grazed his nose against my jawline, breathing deeply. All at once, he kissed me with passion and anger fueling his every move. My hands roamed over every inch of his back while he pushed himself against me. His hand cupped my face, and he separated his mouth from mine, nipping at my bottom lip.

"One day, when I'm not so stressed about your survival, I'm going to have you, Mercy. You will be mine." Then he abandoned me, walking back toward the bedroom.

My head fell back against the wall, slightly flustered. "I know what would help my stress," I whispered, inappropriately.

"I'm guessing you've learned how to take care of that by now," he responded from the other room.

. . .

"Ren secured you a passage to Ireland with his father's shipping company. I think it's your best shot, considering you will have him to protect you if needed. They will try anything to keep you from leaving New York. Aadya has spent years trying to find you—she doesn't want to lose you again. Custos are camped around the city, watching for you, and we have to be careful. I think you need to split up to make it across town."

"What if they follow us after we board?" I asked.

"When you board the ship, the Custos will be powerless. There's nothing they can do. Mr. Williams is a powerful elemental interferer—there isn't anything Aadya can do with water that he can't counteract, if you have issues at sea."

"Fitz, I don't understand. Isn't there an easier way to get to Seregalo?" I asked. It sounded extreme. "Can't we take the chopper?"

"Do you really want to be in the air for a long period of time if she can control the wind? This is your safest route, Mercy. Ren's father can protect you far better than I can. Plus, arriving in Ireland on a ship is less noticeable than a chopper." Fitz frowned. "There is no easy way to do this while they are searching for you."

Self-doubt crept in, but I pushed it to the side. "And when we get to Ireland?"

"Understand that not just anyone can walk into a magical underground world. Security, including spells, are in place to keep that from happening. I know a family that can help you, but you must be resourceful to find them."

"Resourceful, how?"

"Ask around town, quietly, of course. It has been years since I left, and I have no idea where they live now. Pubs and local stores are a good start. Ask for Quinn McDonnell."

"So let me get this straight, we're getting on a cargo ship owned by Ren's dad? Then it's gonna take us a week to get to

Dublin, but we have nowhere to go once we arrive or have no idea where these lost friends of yours reside?"

"That's right." He nodded as if proud I remembered everything.

"I'm completely confused why you were so worried, Drake," I offered, with more sass than I should have.

"Your idea, Babe. Let the man know if you have a better one," Drake said.

Heat flooded my face at his words. The room grew quiet, and when a calm smothered the flames in my chest, I knew Nora had intervened.

"Thank you, Nora."

She tilted her head in my direction.

"Gee, thanks, Nora. No love for me?" Drake asked.

"Have you seen her when she gets upset? I think she's a priority," she whispered.

I jerked my head in her direction. "Hello? I'm right here."

"Look, Mercy. My dad takes this trip every few weeks, and he's leaving tomorrow. This could be our only chance, not to mention we'd have him with us."

Ren was right. We probably wouldn't get another opportunity like this.

"You're right. I'm in if you guys are. I would never ask any of you to put yourselves in danger, though. I want to make that clear. If anyone wants to stay behind, then I wouldn't blame you."

The stomp of boots pulled my attention to the right, where Drake walked off toward our bedroom . . . again.

"We need him with us, Mercy. I'm not sure we'd make it without him," Neela said.

My heart hurt for him. "I know."

I followed him to the bedroom, hoping to ease his mind. The tension had been unbearable throughout the day, but I wasn't sure what to say. He took what little clothes Elise had sent over and stuffed them in his bag.

"What are you doing?" I asked.

"Packing," he mumbled. "I think it might be best if I slept somewhere else. The loft over the living room is empty."

"Are you abandoning me?"

"Nope. I'll apparently follow you to our death because I'll be with you tomorrow, even though we all know your powers aren't ready. What the hell? Nobody else seems to care."

"Aren't ready? Did you forget what happened on the roof?" I yelled.

Drake looked up, angry. "By accident! You don't have a clue how to conjure that kind of power on demand yet, Mercy. I wouldn't be so worried if you had control, but you don't and you know it. You've had three months of training, and you're ready to put everyone at risk. And here I am, following you into the pit of the unknown, knowing you're keeping something from me."

My mouth fell open. "Keeping something from you? What are you talking about?"

Drake charged across the room and tilted my chin up to look into his eyes. "Tell me you aren't lying to me. That the feeling you've been dishonest is ridiculous. If you tell me that, then I'll stay."

I opened my mouth to deny it. To tell him I'd never lie to him, but he was right. The color in his eyes faded at my silence—the word Marley sitting on the tip of my tongue—that I was responsible for his parent's deaths. I felt like a coward.

He turned and walked out.

. . .

"ONE MORE TIME, guys. Let's make sure everyone understands," Ren instructed.

It was five o'clock in the morning, and Ren's father had sent a driver to pick up our bags. They would store them on the ship, so we weren't traveling across town with visible luggage. We needed to blend in as much as possible.

"We'll split up and meet at the Seaport District on Fulton. Mercy's taking the subway with me, Drake and Neela are on the bus, and Nora's taking a taxi—which will drop her off right at the door of the port. Everyone in agreement?" Ren asked.

We all nodded, but nerves kept us from answering. Nora was the youngest in our group, just sixteen years old, so we planned the safest route for her. Even though everyone else was only a few years older, we felt that our powers were more defensive.

"Elise and I will fly overhead in the helicopter. We'll keep an eye out on the port. I purchased everyone a cell phone, and the numbers are programmed for you. If I see anything, I'll send a warning," Fitz explained.

"Fitz, we're ready," Elise announced.

Fitz looked around at each face as if memorizing every detail. "I believe in you, all of you. I hope you know that," he said.

Nora went first, a taxi waiting at the door. After a few minutes, Drake looked back at me before walking out the door with Neela. What if I never saw him again?

Fitz leaned forward and kissed my forehead. "Everything inside of me says I'm stupid for letting you go. What would your father think?"

"He would tell you that you couldn't stop me."

Fitz cracked a grin. "That sounds just like him. When this

is said and done, we'll have a proper memorial for Noah, alright?"

"Thank you, Fitz—for everything."

"Time to go," Ren called out from the door.

We took the stairs, neither of us speaking. Ren and I were dressed in dark colors to blend in with the other New Yorkers, but I wore a hood over my head so I'd be less noticeable. Fitz said they'd be on the lookout for my long dark hair, so we did our best to hide it.

As we exited the building, the helicopter's engine roared to life, hovering over the rooftop. They circled, looking for any sign of trouble, and when Ren and I made it to the subway terminal, they took off downtown to watch for Nora's arrival. Fitz had planned this exceptionally. My phone beeped, alerting me of a group message, Drake sent the all-clear for him and Neela. They were on the bus. I hadn't received anything from Nora yet.

Ren and I stood to the side, waiting for the train to arrive. My lungs felt tight, as if they fought to expand, and sweat coated my palms.

"Mercy, are you okay?"

I nodded. "I'm fine."

He scoffed. "You don't look fine."

"Such a charmer, Ren."

He smiled at my remark. "Try to relax. You look like you're up to something, and someone might notice."

I took a couple of deep breaths and willed myself to relax. I leaned into him and put my arm through his, looking like the happy couple.

"Drake's gonna kick my ass."

"He had the choice to go with me, he chose the bus."

"Are you guys alright? The tension's been thick."

"I don't know, Ren. He doesn't agree with this excursion. I need him to support me."

"I guess it's hard to support you when he knows you're keeping something from him."

My head whipped around at him in surprise, and he grinned.

The train arrived, and he jumped on without another word. We found a seat in the far corner and tucked ourselves in tight, out of view.

We rode for a few minutes before I made the decision to address his comment. "I'm not purposely trying to lie to him, or any of you. There are things I'd rather not talk about yet, that's all. Sometimes, I need to process it before I hash it out with you guys, you know?"

"Have you told him that?" he questioned.

"The things I need to say, well it needs to be the right time. I'll talk to him, I promise."

We sat for several more minutes, as the train stopped to pick up early morning passengers. The closer we got to the financial district, the busier it became. The hair stood up on my arms after the last stop, and two men in black stepped aboard the rail. "Ren, I think two Custos are here."

Ren turned his back on the crowd to hide me in the corner. The men were slowly making their way toward us, looking over each face in the crowd suspiciously.

"They're coming, Ren," I whispered.

Ren clenched his jaw, going over our options. He made eye contact with me and said, "I'm sorry, Mercy. Please forgive me."

My eyes narrowed. "What are . . .?"

All at once, Ren grabbed the back of my head and slammed his mouth over mine, kissing me. My body froze, and my first instinct was to hit him, but I quickly realized his plan. If they saw us making out in the corner, they wouldn't suspect us. I closed my eyes and wrapped my arms around his neck. I did the only thing I could think of—I pictured Drake. The kiss intensified, and more of Ren's body pressed into mine as his palm came up to cup my face. We stayed locked for several minutes, and when we finally broke away from each other, I took a peek over his shoulder. They had moved on to another car.

"I think it worked," I whispered.

Silence.

"Ren?"

"Yeah, good. That's good." He turned around—his body rigid—and took a deep breath. "Let's keep that between us, alright?"

"Of course. Quick thinking on your part—that was genius," I offered.

Still no response.

My heart ached for him. Even though I'd pictured Drake, I knew that Ren kissed me, seeing no one else.

"This is our stop." Ren stood, and I followed him to the sliding doors, waiting for them to open.

"Ren, I'm sorry. . ."

"Mercy, I'm fine, really," he said.

Again, I put my arm through his, walking toward the Seaport. The bus pulled away when Drake and Neela turned on the sidewalk, keeping an eye out for a threat. Drake's gaze instantly found me, and I saw them shift, taking in my arm wrapped around Ren. He turned away from us, and they walked off to their designated spot.

"He may not talk to me after this, Mercy."

I stopped in my tracks, unable to move forward.

Ren looked apologetic. "Hey, it was just a joke. I didn't mean to stress you out."

I lifted my finger and pressed it against his lips, listening. "Do you hear that?" I asked.

We closed our eyes and reached out as far as we could.

Our phones dinged, and we looked down to a message from Fitz.

"RUN!"

We took off, but not fast enough. I glanced over my shoulder at what appeared to be a massive tornado, ripping through the concrete and buildings toward us.

Rain poured down as people everywhere screamed and cried, grabbing their children and running, while the funnel of wind swept up an older man pushing a hot dog cart. I vaguely heard my name shouted, but I wasn't sure by who. Ren and I were both gifted with elemental, so if we could get control of it we could stop the devastation.

We came to that conclusion at the same time and stopped in our tracks. Turning toward the funnel spinning our direction, we reached out, forcing a calm over the angry storm. The rain turned into large hail, beating down around us. It was too much—too powerful. Ren reached for my hand the minute the tornado hit us, pulling us upward in a spin of confusion.

I couldn't hear anything except what sounded like a freight train in my ears. Anger resonated from the wind, and I knew this was the result of Aadya's attempt to keep us contained in the city. Ren's grip on my hand grew tighter, determined to hold on. The storm made its way toward the Seaport, and if she succeeded, she'd ruin our chance of escaping the city.

"We have to fight harder!" I screamed.

Ren controlled the spin that had overtaken us, and we were now upright in the eye. We stayed connected and placed our palms out to slow the wind. My heart cried out as adults and children were still being swept into the vortex, crying with fear. Blood covered faces screamed as I tried to concentrate on what we had to do. The only way I could focus was to close my eyes and not absorb the wreckage.

Our powers fused together, and my hand warmed around my mother's ring. The emerald gleamed brightly as the whirl slowed substantially. At once, Ren and I stood in the middle of the street, surrounded by the city's destruction. Calls for help sounded under the rubble, and sirens wailed in the distance. I fell to my knees at the catastrophe around me.

"Are you hurt?" Ren asked from beside me.

I couldn't speak—my heart hurt more than anything.

"Mercy, look at me. Your head is bleeding."

I reached up to the top of my forehead, where warm sticky blood coated my fingers. I looked down at my hand, and it rippled, the blood disappearing and reappearing in a flashing scene before me.

"Is that Fitz?" Ren asked.

The chopper had landed on the tall building beside us. Fitz, Elise, and four others I didn't know were standing on the rooftop looking out over the city. Elise and the other strangers all had their palms out, turning, erasing the damage before our eyes. Even with all five of them, the struggle was apparent—but they were doing it. Structures slowly pieced back together, and individuals returned to where they were before the destruction hit. Food carts reappeared onto the street, and glass meticulously put itself back together. I breathed deeply, and relief overpowered everything else at that moment.

Drake and Neela ran over to where we sat and helped us to our feet. His hands searched my body for injuries, "You're good?" He cupped my face, forcing my eyes to his. "Are you hurt?"

"I'm okay."

Drake pulled me to his chest and kissed the top of my head.

"That has to be the craziest thing I've ever seen," Neela said. "And I've seen a lot."

My phone rang out as I pulled it from my front pocket.

"Fitz? That was insane!"

Fitz's voice was stern, "Board the ship right now—all of you. If you don't leave now, I'll never be able to get you out of the city." He ended the call.

"Wait, where's Nora? We can't leave without her." I looked around, frantically.

"Maybe she's already on board. She should have arrived before us," Neela reminded me.

We quickly made our way to the entrance of the pier where two men in black and gray leaned against the gate, grinning. Fitz was right, they had been waiting for us.

"Now, that's what I call entertainment," the first one called out. "Impressive, you guys have skills."

"I don't have the patience for this today," Drake mumbled.

A snarl crossed the Custos' face, then he cut his eyes to us mischievously.

"You know, I scoured the subway for hours, all morning, searching for you, Mercy. I couldn't figure out how I'd missed you." He grinned.

My stomach dropped, and my mouth tightened.

"Then, I remembered you guys. Tucked in that little corner, making out. Arms wrapped around each other. Lips and tongues locked. I'm getting hot just thinking about it."

Fear kept me from looking toward Drake, but I could feel his emotions—the rage and jealousy transformed into pain. The two men fell on their backs, slamming their heads against the boardwalk. Drake leaned over them, narrowing his eyes.

"It's amazing how easy it is to take the feeling from your legs. Do you think you could swim that way? Let's find out." He kicked both men into the water as if he'd kicked a rock. As he turned back toward us, his eyes were once again tinted red. "Let's go."

Ren looked over at me, concerned.

"We'll explain it to him. He'll understand, Ren."

"I hope you're right. I can't swim without my legs, Mercy."

Ren's father, Mr. Williams, met us on the pier. "Did everyone make it?"

"This is it, and Nora should have arrived earlier."

He shook his head. "You guys are the first. I started getting worried."

"Wait, Nora never arrived?" I pulled my phone out, texting Fitz. The phone pinged quickly, stating that they had lost her taxi during the storm. No, no, no. We can't lose Nora. Where could she be? My phone rang as if Fitz knew my mindset.

I answered, "You lost her? I'm not leaving her behind!"

"You don't have a choice. If you don't get out of the city, you may not get another chance," he explained.

Neela put her arm around my shoulders, urging me forward as the phone disconnected.

I shook my head. "No! You can't expect me to leave her behind. I won't."

Neela whispered, tearfully, "She would want you to go while you still can."

"We need to get out of New York." Mr. Williams pushed me forward, forcing me to board the massive cargo ship, where large cranes hung over our heads and shipping crates piled high on top of each other.

Several men were on the top deck, securing the shipments and preparing for our trip. The inside of the freighter was simple and clean. Two rooms were side by side with bunk beds and a small square window looking out toward the water.

Mine, Nora's, and Neela's bags were in one room, Drake's and Ren's in another. I couldn't help but feel sorry for Ren—sharing with Drake wouldn't be easy.

"You guys get settled and I'll send for you when it's time for dinner. It's nothing fancy, but it's food." Mr. Williams clapped his son on the back and gave us privacy.

We went our separate ways without a word and I crashed down face first on the bed, groaning. I turned my head to the side, absorbing the sight of Nora's suitcase. My heart ached and I wanted nothing more than to go find her.

"We'll find her, Mercy. There are tons of reasons she didn't make it to the port—especially in this city."

I didn't respond.

"You wanna talk about it?" Neela asked.

"No."

"Well, tough. You kissed Ren? You better explain yourself." Neela was angry for Drake.

I rolled over, staring at the ceiling, annoyed.

"I hate how everyone assumes we did something wrong. You don't even assume we might have had a reason? Because Nora would have. She, at least, has faith in me."

Neela's face fell. "I'm sorry, you're right. I worry about Drake right now. Something isn't right with him."

"A couple of Custos were on our train, and we were trying to blend in, hoping they'd overlook us. Ren grabbed me and started kissing me. And it worked, but. . ."

"But what?" she asked.

I exhaled, annoyed. "I know that it meant something to Ren, and I'm not sure how to address that."

"What about you? How did you feel when he kissed you?"

"It shocked me at first. When I realized his plan, I pictured Drake. That was the only way I could get into it." I wrinkled my nose at how horrible it sounded.

"Drake is your man, girl. That's how it's supposed to be, and Ren knew that before he kissed you. The only person you need to worry about right now is Drake. He's your priority, not Ren."

"You're right. I'll talk to him."

We unpacked, and I decided to take a shower before dinner. A shared bathroom was across the hall and surprisingly empty. Everything I needed had been stocked, and I stood under the hot water much longer than I intended. My body, a constant state of pent up stress and fear, relaxed under the hot spray. When I turned the faucet off, I stood in the shower, my safe space, not wanting to return to reality.

I wrapped a towel around my torso and tucked it in tightly. Upon opening the door, I came face to face with Drake, apparently having the same idea. He took in my current state, wet and wearing his necklace, and his eyes heated. I didn't know what to say. He tried to step around me, but I reached out and put my hand across his waist to stop him. He paused but didn't turn to look at me.

I hated the tension between us. "I want to explain what happened."

The muscle in his jaw clenched tight. "You don't have to—Ren already did."

"You're still angry with me."

"I'm struggling with the image of another man's tongue down your throat. Give me a few minutes to get that out of my head, okay?"

I leaned toward him, pressing my body against his chest as I whispered in his ear, "You need to know that I couldn't kiss him. When I figured out what he'd planned, the only way for me to go through with it was to picture you. You're the only one I want."

He took a deep breath and leaned toward me, losing the battle within. Needing the contact as much as I did, his feet shuffled forward. My back hit the door frame as the towel slid slightly lower. I fisted his shirt, pulling him closer.

"Would you like some company in the shower?" I asked. Standing on my toes, I kissed underneath his chin as he closed his eyes. His hand snaked around my waist and his head lowered, looking me in the eyes. As soon as my lips grazed his, a voice interrupted us.

"Hey guys, is the bathroom empty?" Ren called out.

I jerked my towel up higher, covering as much as I could.

Drake leaned back, growling deep in his throat. "I'm grabbing a shower, then it will be."

Ren came closer, and his eyes widened at the sight of me in a towel. Drake seethed, staring a hole through Ren. This didn't help anything.

"Mr. Williams sent me down to see if you had everything you needed," an unfamiliar voice called out.

I turned to see a beanpole of a man, maybe early twenties, with wavy blonde hair and a genuine smile. He stopped in his tracks when he saw me standing there half-naked.

"Wowza. One of the crew members told me about you. He wasn't lying." His gaze took me in from head to toe.

I crossed my arms in front of my chest, standing awkwardly between the three men. I eased behind Drake, attempting to shield myself. "I, um. I think I'm going to put on some clothes." I spun toward my cabin.

"I think that's smart," Drake muttered.

The poor guy swallowed and excused himself. "Just let us know if you need anything. I'm David." He bashfully waved once more, but as soon as he saw the look on Drake's face, he tucked his tail and ran.

. . .

I THOUGHT my day couldn't get any worse. It wasn't possible, right? Wrong. I'd messaged Fitz twenty times for updates on

Nora. Still nothing. Mr. Williams sent his assistant down to escort us to dinner, which happened to be Alexa, the blonde Swedish assistant with legs up to her neck.

I walked behind her, my face scrunched up as if I'd eaten something sour. She had an obsession with Drake's arms and liked to graze them while talking. I'd considered breaking her hand—her slim, smooth hand with the perfect fingernails. . .

"After dinner, I must take you on a private tour," she told him. "Show you all of my favorite, more hidden spots on the ship." She winked toward Drake.

The loudest crack of thunder I'd ever heard struck over the freighter, and all heads spun toward me. Drake looked pleased with himself.

"You know, Alexa, that sounds nice," Drake answered.

I hope Alexa can swim.

"Oh, I didn't realize it was going to rain. Maybe it will be a quick shower," she said.

"I doubt it," I mumbled.

"Well, you guys have a seat here, and someone will bring your food. I hope you don't mind eating with the crew. I'll see all of you soon." She smirked at Drake as she walked away and. I had a fleeting vision of throwing her overboard.

We sat down together, Neela and I on one side, the guys on the other. Four men brought dishes and cups toward our table, showering Neela and me with affection. David went to extreme lengths to straighten my fork beside my plate and place my napkin in my lap. I was a little afraid to move. Drake and Ren glared. I wondered if he planned to feed me as well.

"Is this the one you met . . . you know, in the hall?" One guy asked.

I turned toward Neela with wide eyes and she bit the side of her lip, fighting a smile.

"Yes, this is her. Isn't she fantastic?" David beamed.

Drake twirled his knife around his fingers, watching.

"Guys, sit down and leave my guests alone," Mr. Williams called out. "Sorry, ladies, they don't get a lot of interaction with women. All except Alexa, and they don't seem to care for her."

Well, I liked them already.

The crew finished bringing out plates of pasta, and everyone ate in silence. My attention bounced like the fake boobs on Alexa's chest, all over the place. Thoughts of Nora, Fitz, my relationship with Drake, and the mystery of Marley haunted my quiet dinner. The weather worsened, and the ship rocked from side to side.

"Mercy, if this is you, please get a grip. I'm getting sea sick." Neela's face paled.

My eyes drifted over to Drake, and his wall quickly covered his concern.

"I'm finished. I'm going to take a walk." I threw my napkin on the table and stood.

They didn't argue, just silently watched as I walked the wrong direction—into the kitchen—then turned to exit the correct door.

I made my way to the deck as the rain poured steadily. My fists held tight to the railing as the ship rode the giant waves of the ocean. My body felt like a tea kettle, ready to blow from the pressure. I took a large breath, filling my lungs with salty air. As I exhaled, tears came with it. I bent, resting my forehead on the railing as I let the emotions take control.

The problem lied in the fact I still couldn't control it. Drake was right. The more I let loose, the worse the water became. Large swells of blue and white smashed into the boat as rain swept sideways against my face. The side of the freighter tilted up, forcing me to grip the railing with both hands—then crashed down after the wave rolled by, similar to my emotions.

A sense of peace had built inside my chest, and the thought occurred to me, maybe this release would calm the storm inside my heart—until the sight ahead took my breath away. A rogue wave, rolling fiercely toward the ship, threatened to overturn the vessel, putting everyone onboard at risk.

The turmoil that churned within my heart and mind continued to put people's lives in jeopardy. I reached out with my mind, using elemental interference to battle the devastation my own feelings had caused. The wave slowed, but continued toward the ship. I took a deep breath and placed my palms out in front of me, begging psychokinesis to combine with the magic of elemental interference.

The wave stalled a couple of feet in front of me, and at least thirty feet over the ship. Moonlight shone through parts of the water, with shadows of sea life swimming leisurely. It was as if time had slowed for everything around me. I lowered my hands gracefully, and the wave followed suit. The size of the swell rocked the cargo from side to side and nearly knocked me from my feet.

"Very good, Mercy." Mr. Williams stood behind me, bracing himself between two shipments.

When the vessel settled, he stepped toward me, leaning on the rail in front of me. Water drenched every part of my body, and I shivered in the night air. "Don't worry, if you hadn't figured it out, I would've helped. Fitz talked to me about your predicament. Hell of a life you've had, but you're doing it. You're learning to control a multitude of gifts in a short amount of time. That's impressive."

"Why can't I do it anytime? People have died in front of me, and I can't seem to pull from my source to help them."

"That, my dear, is a question only you can answer. Something is holding you back, whether it's fear, confusion, lack of self-confidence, I'm not sure." He placed his hand on my shoulder sympathetically. "Plus, sometimes things can't be altered. People die everyday, Mercy. Nature is stronger than we'll ever be."

"I don't want anymore suffering, Mr. Williams. I want to help."

He smiled. "Your parents were good people, and you are too. You'll figure it out, but you need to take some time for yourself, instead of trying to fix things for everyone else."

Mr. Williams walked back toward the door. Basically, I stood in my own way. I cared too much about those around me and didn't pay attention to what my heart and mind needed. So, what? Should I shut myself off from everyone around me for a few days? Focus on my strengths and control? Something told me that was exactly what I needed. No distractions.

"Mr. Williams?" I called out.

"Yes?" He asked as he opened the metal entrance.

"I think I need a private room. Away from everyone this week."

He nodded. "I'll take care of it." He smiled and left me with my thoughts.

I stayed out less than an hour, meditating in the salty night air. I knew I needed to rest, so I made my way downstairs to grab my bag. Surely he'd arranged for a private room by then. I walked around the corner and stopped, stepping back behind the wall.

"Where are you going with Mercy's bag?" Drake asked.

"Mr. Williams asked me to fetch her things. She moved to a different floor," David announced.

"Where exactly would that be?" Drake sounded pissed.

"I'm not at liberty to say," David responded in a shaky voice.

Drake's voice deepened. "I'm not going to ask again."

"Drake, this must be for a reason, it's not the guy's fault," Neela interjected.

Doors slammed, and the hall went silent. I crept around the corner and came face to face with Neela.

Her brows raised. "You suck at hiding. What's going on?"

I sighed, "I'm struggling with control."

Neela scoffed. "This is nothing new."

"Exactly. I need to make some changes and try to concentrate. I think a few days alone might help."

Neela nodded and gave me a half-smile. "Whatever you need, but just so you know, Drake isn't going to handle this well."

"Maybe it will be good for him too."

❖

*I*t had been five days since I'd seen Drake, Ren, or Neela. Ren's dad told me to call him Marcus, and I learned all about his wife, Anzu. He moved me into the spare bedroom in the master suite since he never used it. Attached to the suite was a weight room that overlooked the sea, an excellent way to expel energy build-up from exercising my gift. He created a plan consisting of meditation, exercise, and eating—along with practicing control. All day long, I repeated the schedule. I ended up in the gym twice a day, and he had me running on the top deck during the evening when the others were at dinner.

I'd never felt stronger, mentally, or physically. His staff prepared high protein food for me daily, and Marcus even taught me basic hand to hand combat. I couldn't imagine how I'd feel after a month with him. The progress that week had been startling. I'd lost down to less than fifteen percent in body fat and had increased muscle definition in my arms and legs. Energy buzzed through me, always at the ready.

More than that, I had control and balance. Marcus's tactics were brutal, but effective. He'd use his elemental gift to attack at any given moment, forcing me to pull from my source on demand. I learned to use one gift while backing another off. The clarity and conciseness in my gifts made so much more sense. It wasn't that I couldn't use two at the same time—it was about learning to balance them. Give and take for the better of those around me.

Drake. My heart ached to see him—to touch him. He had no idea how much I needed his presence around me. When he looked at me for the first time in five days, I wanted him to see the transformation. Not only on the outside, but the inside as well.

Fitz messaged me with updates every day, but there was still no sight of Nora. He didn't have to tell me what I already knew—he was losing hope. I refused to give up on her.

I pulled my favorite sleeveless romper from the bag and applied more makeup than usual. I knew we'd be traveling, so I fixed my hair in a bun on top of my head and wore the necklace he gave me.

"Mercy?" Marcus knocked twice before easing the door open. "I have something for you."

"Please, come in."

"Listen, I hope this doesn't upset you, but I confided in Anzu about your issues." His eyes held an apology I didn't feel like he owed.

"I'd never expect you to keep anything from your wife, Marcus. That wouldn't be fair. Especially since you've spent so much time with me."

"Well, Anzu isn't gifted, but she's very intuitive. Her culture believes the signs from above are here to guide us. She had a dream about you last night, Mercy. She didn't go into great detail, but fire surrounded you. Not to harm you, but to protect you. She goes on these trips with me now and again, and she always keeps a few belongings on the ship. She asked me to find these earrings and give them to you before you left. They're firestones."

The square diamonds radiated a reddish-orange hue that changed with the light—they were exquisite. "Marcus, I can't accept these. It's too much."

"That's a mighty big insult to refuse a gift like this, Mercy." He gave me a partial grin, and he knew he had me.

I smiled and put the earrings on. They were perfect.

"Beautiful, just gorgeous. I'll let her know you loved them."

"I'm not sure how to repay you for everything. You and Fitz have supported me and taught me more the last few months than anyone has my entire life. I know my father would be grateful I had both of you."

"Proud of that." He nodded and hugged me. "Let's get you off this old cargo ship, what do ya say?"

The bright sunlight hit my eyes, and it took a few minutes to adjust. My friends waited by the exit, looking out over the city of Dublin. I couldn't believe we were in Ireland.

"Damn girl, no one told me we had a personal trainer on this freighter. Who worked you over?" Neela called out.

Drake's head spun my direction, and the desire in his eyes glided over my skin from head to toe. I knew exactly how he felt.

Ren ran over, picked me up, and swung me around. He stepped back, looking me over. "My dad did a number on you, didn't he? I should have warned you." He chuckled, "It's good to see your face."

"It's good to see you too." I smiled at the faces I'd missed so much over the past week. The family I wanted to protect. The reasons I isolated myself to begin with.

Ren grabbed my bag and left to stand with Neela. Drake hesitantly walked over with his hands in his pockets.

I smiled. "Hey."

"How are you?" he asked.

"Better than I've been in a while."

"You seem different—happy." His eyes cut to the ground. "I've missed you."

I stepped forward, wrapping my arms around his waist. My body melted into his. Drake held me tight against him and kissed the top of my head.

Taking a deep breath, I forced myself to pull away. I looked over the city, and excitement buzzed through me. "You ready for this?"

He nodded and motioned for me to go ahead of him.

Marcus had told us to start at some local pubs. The legal drinking age was eighteen, so that wouldn't be a problem. Before we left, he whispered in my ear, "Stick to your routine, Mercy. You'll need the structure."

Dublin was lively. People and cars in every direction as we walked along the cobblestone path. Gorgeous green mountains created a picturesque backdrop behind busy streets and establishments. We tried a few local shops, but untrustworthy eyes stared us down, not wanting to converse with foreigners. We had to find the right place.

A small establishment sat in the corner of a busy street, adorned with dark wood accents and a green sign that read Connolly's Pub.

"Is this next?" Drake asked.

I shrugged. "I guess so. It's as good as any."

The dark wood continued on the inside with a wall of whiskey behind a long wooden bar. A handful of tables were scattered around the pub haphazardly, and the lunch crowd consisted of several older men yelling at each other between drinks.

"Mate! I'll bate the bag outta ye!" A drunk, older man stumbled to his feet defensively.

"Flynn, you'll get Brennan all hepped up, and he'll lose his head!"

"Saunter off, Connolly."

The bartender rolled his eyes and continued wiping down the counter.

I reached down, grabbing Neela's hand. "Maybe this isn't the best place. I'm not even sure what they're saying."

"Take the weight off yer legs, knackers. Pull a chair."

"I think he's talking to us," Ren mumbled.

"Nah, not knackers—blow-ins," the man they called Flynn, shouted.

We didn't move, just stood, staring at the chaos. Suddenly, Drake stepped toward the bar and sat down. I swear, nothing phased that man. We followed him over, and I sat between him and Ren, while Neela sat on the other side of Drake.

"It be a naggin or a shoulder?" the bartender asked.

I looked from side to side, confused.

"Pint of gat," Drake answered. I looked up at him, and he winked.

"Same for me," Ren said.

I remembered what Marcus told me about alcohol. My power was too strong to risk impairment. "Can I get some water, please?"

The bartender dropped the glass he held, shattering it on the floor. A hush ran through the pub as everyone turned their head in our direction. His mouth opened in shock, dismay evident in his eyes. "Water?"

"Yes, please." I smiled kindly.

"That one has the bright eyes on her, she does," Flynn called out.

Connolly leaned across the bar as if we were sharing secrets. "Fall pregnant, did ye? That's a fret."

Drake's head turned in my direction, amused interrogation in his eyes.

"Don't tell my secrets, Connolly," I whispered. If I didn't make friends, I'd get nowhere.

"Don't you worry yer pretty lil' head lass'. Which bloke done the deed?"

"Not me!" Ren shouted, louder than necessary.

I looked over at him, surprised by his outburst.

"I mean, not that there's anything wrong with Mercy. I'd totally do the deed, but she's not with me. . ."

The look on Drake's face shut him up rather quickly.

"Ah, so yer likin the big lad, here. Congrats, mate."

Drake sat silently, and I grabbed the top of his thigh, causing him to flinch.

"Thank you. I'm so . . . so lucky." He turned his bottle up, ignoring my glare.

"Flynn! Brennan! Sling yer hook before I sort you out!" Connolly screamed at the old men, a poor attempt at defusing the argument.

My grip on Drake's leg tightened and he placed his hand on top of mine—his thumb rubbing back and forth over my skin. My body soaked in the contact, the warmth and power radiating from him, and the need was overwhelming. My source was in overdrive after having no contact with him the week before. I excused myself and hurried toward the ladies room.

My back hit the bathroom door—eyes closed. I tried to meditate like Marcus had taught me. After a few minutes, breathing became more manageable, and I settled. That was until I opened the bathroom door and saw Drake leaning against the wall with his arms crossed in front of him. He watched me, silently, as if deciding what to say.

"Being this close to you is calming, yet overwhelming." I admitted. "It's hard to describe."

He ran his hand through his hair and sighed. His eyes

looked weary. I could tell he hadn't been sleeping well. "I can give you space," he offered.

I shrugged. "I don't know if I want you to." I smiled and his eyes softened.

He pushed off from the wall and placed his hand on my lower back, leading me toward the bar.

Ren had struck up a conversation with a local about the McDonnell family. "We're looking for someone named Quinn McDonnell. Do you know him?"

"Don't ask Flynn, he's had a drink in him!" another man shouted.

"Brennan, yer face that sour ye could make yer own yoghurt!" Flynn shouted.

"McDonnell, ye say?" Connolly asked. "I know Quinn. Fine lad. Moved his family out to Astriawell some years back."

"Do you know how we could reach him?" Ren asked.

"Feck, I can drive ye!" Flynn offered.

"There we go, now." Connolly rolled his eyes.

Flynn stood, defensive. "Careful, Connolly, I'm all hepped up!"

"Yeah, yeah." The bartender rolled his eyes and continued wiping down the counter.

"If you have a car, I can drive," Drake said. "I just need to know the way. I can pay for your time."

Flynn rubbed his chin as if he considered the bargain, but we all knew he'd say yes. He'd already offered.

"Ye got a deal!"

. . .

"WHAT IS THAT?" I asked.

"Ye needed a car." Flynn said, louder than necessary.

"Does it run?" Neela questioned.

Flynn's eyes widened. "Wind yer neck in, lass."

Neela looked over at me with wide eyes, "What did he just say to me?"

I shrugged my shoulders, baffled. "What kind of car is this?"

"She's a '59 Austin A35. A beaut!"

The compact car had two doors, and it could've possibly been black at one time, but now the metal showed through. The leather seats had splits in some places—the carpet worn to the frame.

"So, how far is Astriawell?" I asked.

"Couple hours, now," Flynn replied.

We piled into the Austin as Drake and Flynn sat up front. I shoved in between Ren and Neela in the narrow back seat.

"Mercy, your butt cheek is on my leg," Ren chuckled, but then locked eyes with Drake in the mirror. "Sorry, man."

Flynn gave Drake simple directions, then passed out for most of the drive. The countryside was beautiful—lush green fields, hundreds of sheep, and mountains that went on for miles. I couldn't imagine living there.

Flynn woke after a bit, then told Drake to pull to the side of the road so he could ask a farmer where Quinn lived. We were close. We drove for about ten more miles and came upon a charming stone cottage, surrounded by a wooden fence and farmland.

"There ye are, now." Flynn got out of the car, pulled our bags out, and tossed them on the ground.

We followed as Drake handed over several bills. Flynn got in the car and drove away without another word. We stood, in the middle of nowhere, watching the drunk Irishman drive away.

"What just happened?" Neela asked.

We busted out laughing at the absurdity, recalling our first day in Dublin with tears rolling down our cheeks. Neela held her stomach, and Ren attempted to speak like the men at the pub, yelling offensively at Neela. When the delirium died down, Drake softly knocked on the old wooden door. We could barely hear the folk music in the background. Drake knocked louder.

The old hinges creaked as the door swung in. The woman that answered the door had her caramel blonde hair piled high on top of her head, and a colorful head wrap tied around the back. Big blue eyes landed on each person, taking in the scene, as a whiff of marijuana flowed out from behind her. She was high. She pushed back the small tendril of hair that had escaped her wrap—her wrists inked in tattoos, and colorful bracelets dangling from her arm. She was spectacular.

"Can I help you?" Her accent surprised me. She didn't sound Irish.

"Hi, we're looking for Quinn McDonnell."

"Who's asking? He belt at the pub again?" She asked, already getting angry at Quinn.

"No! Well, I guess not. I don't know what that means," I said.

"I'm Hilary McDonnell, Quinn's wife, but you can call me Hillie."

"It's nice to meet you. I'm Mercy Monroe. Brian Fitzpatrick sent me."

"What did you say?" Her eyes widened and she stepped back in shock.

"Um, well, I'm Mercy Monroe. . ."

"Mercy! Heavens, Child! I can't believe you're alive! Let me look at you."

She spun me around slowly, but she probably thought it was fast. The effects of the pot still lingered.

She threw her hands dramatically over her heart. "You look like your dad."

"Wait, how do you know who I am?"

"Our mothers were first cousins. We're family, Mercy."

. . .

HILLIE GRACIOUSLY INVITED US IN, and we sat around the living area while she 'wet the tea,' whatever that meant. I couldn't believe I'd met my cousin in Ireland.

"Am I the only one getting high?" Neela asked.

"Nope." Ren snickered.

Hillie walked back into the room, the smile on her face unnaturally wide, and handed everyone a cup of hot tea. "Drink up, drink up. This is my special recipe." She waited patiently for all of us to take a sip. "I use honeysuckle and orange blossoms."

"It's lovely, Hillie. Thank you so much," I said.

She beamed at the compliment. She told us all about her paintings on the walls, and the farm she and Quinn ran. She met him when she was my age, and married soon after.

"When you know, you know," she said.

I felt the intensity of Drake's eyes on my face but I didn't look up. I couldn't. He deserved the truth from me before we could move forward.

Ever the gracious host, Hillie offered us a tray of sandwiches while telling us all about the history of Astriawell. She radiated a light to those nearby, a brightness we desperately needed.

"You must be wrecked. Quinn won't be back until late, so let me show you to the loft. It isn't much, but it'll do. We'll talk more tomorrow when Quinn returns and you've had a rest."

Hillie led us upstairs to a large open loft. Wooden floors against stone walls, the loft couldn't have been larger than a college dorm. Simple and bare, two twin beds and a bunk bed sat side by side with a lantern in the window.

"The toilet is at the bottom of the stairs. I know it isn't much . . ."

"It's perfect. I can't thank you enough."

"We're family, crazy girl. That's what we do." She hugged me once more, then turned to leave.

We all took a bed—Neela on the top bunk and me on the bottom—the springs squeaking loudly in unison. I covered my mouth to keep from laughing, while Neela cackled above me.

I knew I wouldn't be able to sleep. My thoughts turned chaotically, refusing to let me rest. I grabbed a set of clothes out of my bag and snuck toward the stairs.

"Where are you going?" Neela asked.

I looked over my shoulder. "Running."

"By yourself?" Her brows pulled together in concern.

"I'll be fine, Neela."

I pulled on my tank and shorts in the restroom, then stepped into the crisp night air. Light jogging turned into a full-on sprint. Miles and miles, the pent-up stress released into the cool breeze like fallen leaves. The relief was immediate. After running down the road and back, I walked the property until my heart returned to a normal pace.

A barn in the back housed several horses and a chicken coup where a ladder led to a loft full of hay and painting supplies. Hillie was sure to get high and paint up there—probably naked. I fought against that image as I sat up in the loft, thinking of the days ahead. The barn door slamming startled me, and I looked over the edge to see Drake climbing the ladder.

"What are you doing here?" I asked.

"You didn't think I'd let you take off running in another country by yourself, did you?"

"Well, I'm finished so you can go back to bed. Get some sleep."

He shook his head. "I haven't slept soundly in two weeks, Mercy."

I knew he wasn't lying. I saw the truth in the dark circles around his eyes.

"Are you ready to talk about it?" he asked.

"About what?" Even though I had decided to come clean, the immature part of me insisted on playing dumb.

"What you're keeping from me."

I sighed. Drake had been through so much in his life. I wanted to be the one who brought happiness—not pain. The truth about his parents wouldn't be easy. On top of that, all this way for a person I'd never met? That seemed a little crazy, and I hated that I couldn't explain it. But if I ever wanted to mend things, I knew I'd have to be honest with him.

"Promise me you won't think I'm naïve or ridiculous," I said, softly.

"Is that what's keeping you from being honest? You should know me better than that."

He was right. I did know him better than that.

"The night of the attack at Fremont, Dr. Lee said something to me about knowing I'd come for Marley. The last vision I had, the child mentioned Marley again, right before she claimed ownership to my mother's ring."

"You want to know who Marley is," he guessed. "You want to find her."

I bit the inside of my cheek. "I do."

He shook his head. "Why didn't you tell me this?"

"I didn't want you to worry about me falling into Aadya's trap. I need to find Marley, but I don't know why." I swallowed. "I know you would have tried to talk me out of it."

"Maybe. It wouldn't have stopped me from coming with you though." He tilted his head, thoughtfully. "Is that all?" he asked.

"There's something else."

Drake waited, patiently.

I closed my eyes and blurted out the truth. "The night your parents died—they were protecting me from Aadya." My voice cracked. "It's my fault, Drake."

He took a step back and shook his head, confused. "What? How do you know this?"

My voice was barely a whisper. "Fitz told me. I'm so sorry. I wasn't sure how to tell you."

He stared at the hay under his feet, but his eyes were vacant, as if transported to another time and place.

I tried again. "Please—say something."

"You, um. You caught me off guard, Mercy. That's not what I expected." He slid down to the floor, sitting with his elbows propped on his knees. "I've thought of that night so many times. Wanting to understand what could have been so important for them to risk their lives. Leave their sons behind to fend for themselves."

"Please don't hate me," I whispered.

Drake's expression softened. "I could never hate you. At least I know they died fighting a worthy cause. A cause I'd lay down my own life for." Drake looked up at me. "I just need some time to process, you know?"

"I understand."

"This trip could've gone differently for us if you had been

honest, Mercy. I'd follow you into fire, nothing you can say will change that."

"I'm sorry, Drake."

"I'm glad you told me." He stood and dusted the hay from his jeans.

"Where are you going?"

"To bed. Let's see if I can sleep now that my imagination isn't running wild from your dark secrets."

"I'll be there soon," I told him.

"Goodnight."

. . .

FLAMES LICKED at my skin without burning. Once again, fire danced around me, protecting me from the beasts. I could hear screaming in the distance—my name yelled from what sounded like Nora. I had to reach her. We needed to save her. The echo of laughter rang out around us and crawled under my skin. The pain, suffering, and heartache were enough to last me a lifetime. I screamed, my back arched and my head back, expelling every bit of power I had inside.

Sitting straight up, I barely missed the bunk above me as I gasped for air. Drake, seated on the end of his bed, watched with his forehead creased and mouth set in a grim line. He stood and handed me a glass as he pulled his shirt over his head. I drank the water, calming the remnants of the vivid dream. My shirt stuck to my back, wet from sweat. He bent, lifting it over my head, and slid his Yankees shirt on me.

"Better?" he asked.

"Getting there. Thank you."

He turned, heading back to bed.

"Drake?"

He paused.

"Please stay with me. I relax when you're with me."

He looked down at the small bunk, skeptically.

"Please," I begged.

His face softened, and he climbed in bed beside me, wrapping his arms around me from behind. The stress dissipated, and a peace settled over me.

"That's much better, thank you."

"You're welcome. I love it when you beg."

I fell asleep, smiling.

I could hear whispering the next morning, but I wasn't awake enough to care. Warmth surrounded me, and I'd finally slept peacefully. I drifted in and out until the sound of music crept up the stairs to our loft. My eyes opened, and memories from last night hit me. The nightmare. Drake.

Drake laid flat on his back, and I had stretched out on top of him. His hand drifted underneath my shirt and held tight against my lower back. The warmth of his chest filled the empty void that appeared since he last held me. I missed him. He stirred beneath me, and his other hand reached for the back of my head, entwining his fingers into my hair.

I felt it when he woke. He froze as he realized where he was. His body stiffened, then relaxed as he slowly slid his hands away from me, leaving me cold. I sat up and stretched, barely missing the top bunk. I smiled shyly at him, still wearing his shirt.

"Thank you for last night. I haven't slept that well in a while," I admitted.

His gaze took me in, the morning light shining through the window. "I didn't mind. I can't remember the last time I slept that good." The dark circles under his eyes had vanished, and the heaviness gone.

"You guys coming down for lunch?" Neela called from downstairs.

I looked at Drake, shocked. "Lunch? How long did we sleep?"

"I don't know, but I have a feeling we needed it."

Drake left so I could change in private. I wasn't sure if last night meant anything, but I'd hoped we had made progress. I wanted him to trust me. As I started to join them downstairs, Neela and Ren huddled at the bottom of the steps, unaware their voices carried up the stairs.

"It sure looked like they were back together. Do you think he told her?" Neela asked.

Ren sounded pissed. "It isn't right if he didn't. You know how much she disliked Alexa."

"I'm staying out of it. Those two are complicated enough." Neela's voice trailed off as they snuck back into the kitchen, leaving me devastated and angry.

So much for honesty. Alexa? I kept to myself for five days and he couldn't wait for me? He couldn't give me the time I needed to collect myself before moving on? The last thing I wanted was a tornado to hit the McDonnell's home. I needed to get out of there and clear my head—quickly.

I changed back into running clothes, my face flushed and heart-pounding. I didn't need distractions like this. I couldn't afford to lose control. Running down the steps, I pulled the front door open, only to run into Drake with a wildflower in his hand.

"For you." He held the daisy, waiting for me to accept.

I took the flower, but couldn't look him in the eyes. Alexa? Seriously? I tried to keep walking, but he grabbed me by the arm, forcing me to face him.

"What's wrong?" he asked.

Using my sensory gift, I lit my arm up like a hot iron, burning anyone who dared touch it. He jerked his hand back and stared at me with hurt and confusion. He didn't know I could do that. I said a silent thank you for Marcus' training.

I turned and ran as if I could leave my problems on that stoop. I sprinted down the country road, needing the wind in my face and the crunch of gravel under my shoes. What exactly happened with Alexa? It had been obvious what she intended, but I would've never imagined Drake going there. I thought back to the day when I walked in on him in the shower—when he refused me. The crippling betrayal flooded my mind. I needed to stop and breathe. I needed clarity.

A lush field surrounded an ancient-looking tree that shaded the center of a meadow. The trunk appeared massive, around six feet in diameter, and I chose that spot to spend some much needed alone time.

The beauty of Ireland called out to me—this place in particular. I closed my eyes and the atmosphere soothed the anguish that Neela and Ren's words had caused.

I loved Drake with everything inside me. There wasn't any part of me that doubted it. Maybe he was tired of waiting for me to get my crap together. Perhaps he felt lonely and took an opportunity. The thought hovered in the back of my mind that she looked an awful lot like Cassie.

I needed Nora. She always knew what to say, and she'd been on my mind morning and night. Fitz still hadn't found her, and I couldn't imagine a world without Nora.

"Feel like company?"

I opened my eyes to Hillie—smiling—but less stoned that day.

Her carefree personality was contagious. "Sure. This place is amazing, Hillie."

"Yes, it is. Helps you clear your head. Am I right?"

"Clarity comes to those who seek it, isn't that what they say?" I grinned.

"Don't listen to that crap, cousin. Clarity comes to those who discuss it. That's the only way to get past something. I heard Neela and Ren talking when I was in the jacks this morning."

"The jacks?" I tilted my head, confused.

"The toilet," she clarified.

Ah, yes. The jacks.

"I have to tell you that Drake was pretty upset after you left. I told him to stay, and I'd go after you."

"Thanks for that. I just needed some space."

"What's the deal?" she asked.

"My attraction to him is so intense—I'm terrified of getting hurt. We want to be together but the hurdles that lurk down the road are a constant shadow on our relationship."

Hillie propped her head in her hand, intrigued by our issues. "Hurdles? What do you mean?"

"Allegato marks. I carry the mark of Rage Fire. Drake is sensory."

"Mercy, that doesn't mean it isn't Drake. Fire is a scarce sign in Seregalo. He could have another gift that hasn't presented itself. What's his mark?"

"I'm not sure—when I've seen it, it almost looks unfinished—chaotic."

She raised her brows. "Sort of like your powers?"

My head popped up, and I stared at her like she was the most brilliant person I'd ever met. "Do you really think so? What I overheard this morning . . . I'm not so sure."

"There's always more to a story, Mercy. You should've learned that by now. If you and Drake run into a problem, you confront it. Never run from it."

She was right. Drake deserved the opportunity to defend himself, and I needed to fight for our future. I shouldn't have jumped to conclusions, but every time I pictured him with that long-legged bombshell, I couldn't help but fume. And maybe sulk a little.

She stood, dusting the grass from her dress. "Let's get back to the house. You've been out here all day, and it's almost mealtime."

"All day?" I questioned.

"That's right, so get your fanny moving. You're going to love skinny-dipping in the creek at sunset. That's something else entirely." Hillie wagged her brows.

I ignored that last tidbit of Hillie and Quinn's life. It wasn't something I wanted to witness. It did amaze me how time could get away when I shut the rest of the world out.

"Plus, Quinn arrived back home and is eager to meet you."

❖

*N*ext to the creek, a bonfire blazed, and our group circled the flames, chatting over bowls of what looked to be stew. Hillie pulled me over beside her, knowing I needed the comfort of her kind and understanding presence. Her intuition always amazed me.

"Mercy, this is Quinn." Hillie giggled.

Holy smokes. Quinn had to be at least seven-feet tall. He had dark hair, with a rough-looking beard. The man was twice my size, and tattoos covered both arms. I looked over at Hillie with wide eyes and an opened mouth.

"I know, right?" she mouthed.

Drake cleared his throat, watching our exchange. Hillie stared at Quinn like she was seeing him for the first time.

"What brings you to Astriawell, cousin?" His deep voice startled me.

I cleared my throat before I spoke. "We need help if we're going to find Seregalo."

He didn't react at all. "And why do you think I'll help you?"

"Brian Fitzpatrick sent us."

Quinn leaned back with his hand on his chin, contemplating my answer. "Is that so? Well, it must be important if Fitz sent you. How is he these days?"

"Recovering from a concussion, given to him by his partner, Gavin Lee. It has been a rough week," I explained.

Quinn sat forward, angry at the revelation. The man was intimidating. "Where's Lee now?" he grumbled.

"Mercy shot him," Drake answered.

He nodded, pleased. "Why would you want to go to Seregalo? It isn't what it used to be."

Quinn and Hillie's eyes became heavy as they focused on the ground at the mention of the hidden land.

I closed my eyes, and prayed for strength. I wanted to be honest with them. With everyone. "I want to change that."

Quinn burst out laughing, the sound echoing along the creek. "How are you planning on doing that, little one? Please, do tell."

"So far, I've manifested four of the six gifts. There's a strong probability that I could be the next leader of Seregalo."

It was the first time I'd said it out loud. Pride ridden smiles graced my friend's faces at the acceptance of my future. Quinn sat back, drink tilted up to his lips. He watched me, taking his time to respond.

"So, it's true then," he mumbled.

Drake's rough voice surprised me. "It's true."

"Four, huh? I thought you were supposed to have all six—that's the rumor." Quinn turned his head to the side studying me.

"If I have the gift of time, I haven't figured it out yet. It doesn't matter if I'm subconsciously powerful. I refuse to ever use it."

Quinn raised his brows. "Have you learned to shield your mind?"

"I have, but I refuse to violate another's subconscious."

Quinn smiled. "Smart girl." Quinn stared around our small group, sizing us up. "It's not for the faint of heart—the journey."

I chuckled. "I'd be disappointed if it was easy."

"Alright, future leader of the Regalians. I'll take you to the entrance at Stonedell. The rest is up to you. We leave in two days."

"Wait, why two days?" Ren asked.

"The entrance only opens during a new moon, when the sun aligns with the moon. So, we leave in two days."

We sat by the fire for hours. Hillie told us stories about her and Quinn and how they fell in love with Astriawell. Their connection, so apparent in every move they made, caused me to long for Drake. First, I needed to look at him without picturing Alexa. Lightning flashed in the distance, and I knew I needed to excuse myself before I caused a natural disaster. One thing Marcus told me repeatedly, "When you feel yourself spiraling, know when to walk away."

I stretched, then pushed up from the ground. "I'm going to bed. Goodnight, everyone."

"Goodnight, Mercy. Sleep well." Hillie called out.

I walked back toward the house as the rain slowly sprinkled to the ground, strengthening with every negative thought. Everyone took off for shelter, and I snuck to the side of the stone cottage, creeping toward the barn entrance. The loft quickly became a quiet space for me, a place of comfort. Wet clothes plastered to my skin by the time I climbed the old wooden ladder, but I didn't care. I sat alone in the hay, watching the storm roll in.

Thunder provoked snorts and grunts from the horses, as the chickens prepared to roost. Rain clattered on the roof, and I closed my eyes, letting the sound drown out everything around me. I reminded myself to let go and breathe—quit thinking—stop hurting. The storm dwindled.

"You know, I went to great lengths to pick that flower for you." Drake's voice carried through the night air.

Words failed me and I could tell by the tone of his voice that my silence annoyed him.

"Why won't you talk to me? I thought we made progress with each other last night."

"I thought we did too," I muttered.

"So, what's changed?"

I stood to face him. "Alexa," I admitted.

His eyes widened, and his visible swallow told me my words hit home. As if waiting for the chance, thunder rolled overhead and rain pelted the ground.

He blinked. "What about her?"

"What happened, Drake?"

"Nothing happened, Mercy. I swear."

"I was honest with you last night, Drake. This is your chance to come clean. I overheard a conversation between Neela and Ren on the steps discussing whether you'd been honest with me about Alexa. How do you think it made me feel?"

"Probably very similar to when I heard about you kissing Ren."

Ouch.

"Did you sleep with her?" I asked.

Drake's eyes flamed at my words, and he took a menacing step toward me. "What did you say?" he asked.

I couldn't keep my chin from quivering. "She looks an awful lot like Cassie."

"So, now I've slept with Cassie too? Is this who you think I am?" he shouted over the unrelenting storm.

"I don't know who you are!"

Another step forward, Drake grabbed me by the back of

my neck and covered my mouth with his. I pushed against his chest, but my heart refused to fight him. My fists clenched his wet shirt, and I pulled him as close as possible. His hands were everywhere—wanting every inch of me. We were starved for the connection.

My legs buckled and Drake came down on top of me. He stayed up on one elbow attempting to keep his weight off my chest, but I needed to feel him. His size made me feel small and protected. One of my legs wrapped around him as I pushed up against him. Drake moaned and I could feel the muscles in his back tighten.

Our kiss slowed, but the pull between us only strengthened. His hand cupped the side of my face as he pulled back. "You know who I am, please don't say that. You know me better than anyone."

His lips grazed mine once more.

"I love you, Mercy. I've always loved you, and there will never be anyone else for me. Do you understand that? If you don't feel the same, now is the time to tell me."

Tears rolled down my cheeks as his thumb wiped them from my face.

"I love you, too." I admitted.

He kissed me again, soft and leisurely.

"No more running. For either of us, right?"

I nodded. "Right."

We sat in the loft together, his arms around me as we watched the abrupt storm transform into a soft rain. We were quiet for several minutes when he finally spoke.

"Alexa followed me into my room after I'd taken a shower. By the time I realized she was there, Ren came through the door to find her there, with me half naked. It didn't look good, especially since you and I were on the outs. He stomped off mad, and I never explained when I should have. I kicked her out, and I never touched her. I swear."

"I believe you."

"I have to say, jealousy is hot on you. Let me know if you want me to rile you up again sometime. We can make it happen."

I shoved him. "I think I'm good."

"Just offering." He grinned and kissed the top of my head.

I sighed. "Why is everything so complicated? Life, relationships, family, friends."

"Talk to me, Mercy."

"All I've ever wanted was to have a loving family. Right after meeting my dad, he dies in my arms. One of my best friends is missing. Even though you and I love each other, something unknown lies between us. Will our mates show up down the road? Could we really be fated?"

Drake's eyes met mine. "Wait, what do you mean could we be fated? Our marks don't match."

"Hillie thinks there's a chance my mark could still be yours," I told him.

"How's that possible?" Drake's eyes brightened.

"Apparently a fire sign is a secondary, rare gift, that's all I know. She thinks it could be undiscovered, and the reason your mark looks unfinished is that my powers are still evolving."

"Is there any way to know?" he asked.

"I wish I knew. Hopefully, time will tell. I think she doesn't want us to give up."

"I'm never giving up, Babe. I promise." Drake pulled me against his chest.

A little while later, we crept back into the house, soaking wet. It was late, and Neela and Ren were already asleep. Stripping off wet clothes, I stood in front of him in my bra and panties. I pulled his shirt from my bed, and he watched as I pulled it over my head. His eyes darkened at the sight of me wearing it.

Piled up on his small bed in shorts, Drake smiled at me from across the room. I couldn't resist climbing in beside him. He wrapped his arms around me, one hand resting on my hip. I closed my eyes, letting sleep take me as a contented sigh escaped from his lips.

. . .

THE NEXT DAY, Quinn took Drake and Ren with him to mend a gate in the fields. Hillie worked with me for hours on subconscious interference, which apparently had been a family trait. She and Quinn met when they were both escaping Seregalo, and the connection was instant. The beluas, boar-like magical beasts that were created to protect the land, attacked them by Aadya's command, and Quinn saved her life. Which explained why she kept a smitten look in her eyes—he was her hero.

She taught me about my heritage, the gifts my grandparents held, and where everyone lived now. Most of my family had passed, especially the ones who disagreed with Aadya's ruling. She couldn't tell me much about my father's family, but I enjoyed hearing what she knew. Hillie was thankful for Quinn but craved the intimacy of close family, especially the last few years. I knew exactly how she felt.

"Why did my parents leave Seregalo? Or why couldn't they have lived in Astriawell? There must be more to this story, Hillie. They didn't know I had multiple gifts until after I was born, right?"

"That's right." Hillie looked uncomfortable. "You know Aadya's your aunt, right?"

I nodded. "Yes."

"Aadya and Annabel were both in love with the same man, Mercy."

I jerked back, shocked. "My father? Aadya loved my father?"

"Fiercely. She swore he was her mate. Your father feared for Annabel's safety, so he snuck her out of Seregalo and ran. I was a child, but I remember Annabel telling us before she left that if their baby turned out to be a girl, she'd name her Mercy. Fitzpatrick, for a boy. They wanted their happily ever after, Mercy. Same as you and Drake."

Aadya took everything from my parents over jealousy. Her quest for power left a wake of destruction and death, leaving her alone and unloved. To wreak havoc among so many lives, all in the name of power, is something I couldn't fathom.

. . .

THE REST of the day flew by with discussions of beluas, Custos, hidden spells, and the people we should search out if we found ourselves in need of help. The domicile of Seregalo, where Aadya lived, and the Elder's village were locations she wanted me to memorize. The Seregalo River ran behind the domicile and the mountainside was a reasonable escape if we needed to be out of sight. Hillie and Quinn prepared us the best they could, but the creases in their forehead and down-turned mouths gave away their unease. Quinn explained that we'd leave after lunch the next day, putting us in Stonedell at nightfall, in time for the new moon.

After dinner, Hillie announced she'd made special

brownies for everyone, and I knew exactly what that meant. I found Drake sitting in the kitchen area, talking to Quinn.

"Drake, can I borrow you for a moment?"

"You can borrow me for as long as you like." He grinned as he stood from his chair.

Neela and Ren, unaware of Hillie's recipe, dug into the tray of dessert.

"Oooh, somebody's having fun tonight!" Hillie giggled.

We walked out the back door as the music turned on and the brownies came out.

"Perfect timing," Drake mumbled.

I'd built a small fire by the creek and spread out a thick quilt on the ground.

"What's this?" he asked.

"Well, I hoped you'd help me with my sensory gift," I admitted.

Drake laughed. "And here I thought you were being romantic."

"Do you not know me at all?" I asked, shocked.

Drake smiled and sat beside the fire. "Whatever the intentions, it's nice to have some time with you."

I smiled at his honesty.

"What do you want to work on?" he asked.

"Marcus taught me to use feeling as a defense approach, so I feel like I'm strong in that area."

"I agree, the third-degree burn on my hand would attest to that."

"Sorry about that," I said.

He raised his brows and fought a smile.

"Do you remember when you evoked a beach scene in my mind? How did you do that?" I asked.

"The key is that you have to visualize it for the other person to see it. I can't make you see something, without seeing it also. Does that make sense? I can take your sight away completely, but if I want you to see the inside of that barn, I must go there myself."

"Can I block you from altering my senses? Similar to the subconscious block? I blocked my father's shield at Fremont the night we met. I'd love to learn it defensively if possible."

"I'm not sure, but we can try."

Drake and I practiced for hours, evoking and blocking. He proved to be a distraction, sending images of himself in the shower, working out, or anything that involved him half naked.

I sighed, but couldn't hide my amusement. "Would you stop?"

"What?" How did he manage to look so innocent?

"You know." I wave my hand in front of him. "I can't think when you're . . . you're . . ."

He raised his brows. "Shirtless? Sweaty? What? Please, tell me."

I closed my eyes and pictured myself in a red bikini on the beach, glistening sweat dripping down my chest from the scorching sun. I moaned from the warmth.

"Can you focus enough to block that image?" I asked.

"Point taken."

The productive night had been good for both of us, and we discovered more control in our gift than we'd ever had before. Time had not been on my side as far as preparing for Aadya, and I wanted to soak up as much knowledge as possible before we arrived in Seregalo.

"It's getting late," Drake said.

The night air grew chilly, and the fire died out. I focused on the flames, igniting them strongly enough to burn for hours. He looked up at me and smiled, my intentions clear. Leaning back on the quilt, he opened his arms in invitation for me to lie down.

"Remember I'm here to protect you. I need you to work with me, not against me, Mercy."

"What are you talking about?"

"I don't know what we'll come across, but you'll have three other gifted individuals with you that have studied this their entire life. Don't forget we're here to help."

His words comforted me. Sometimes it was easy to forget that I wasn't alone.

"I won't," I promised.

We grew quiet and I attempted to focus on his emotions —anxiety and agitation—an undercurrent of fear in what tomorrow would bring. Something else radiated from Drake, a possessive and territorial energy.

"What are you thinking about?" I asked.

He propped up on his elbow, looking down at me.

"Tomorrow, we'll arrive in Seregalo. Over two-thirds of Regalians still live there, Mercy. There's a good chance you could meet your intended mate. I want you to know that I don't care what the Allegato marks say. You've always been mine. Mine to love. Mine to protect. I guess I need to know, well, if that isn't my mark on your back, will it change anything for you?" he asked.

I wanted to be honest with him, because I promised I would. Digging deep, I ran through every scenario in my head. Could anyone ever take me away from Drake? Would it change anything?

"Nothing." My fingers gripped the back of his neck.

"Me, either."

He grabbed the side of my face and kissed me roughly. He didn't care what the mark said. He knew as I did—we belonged together. Lips made their way to my neck as he came down on top of me, the thick blanket protecting us from the ground. My hands clawed up his back, and he groaned deep in his throat as he let go of his control. He kissed me as if he feared he never would again. The flame inside my chest raged from need—my power craved him.

Drake tossed our clothes haphazardly along the bank, and pulled the extra blanket from the side to cover me.

We kissed and touched for the longest, relishing the moment we'd both wanted for so long. When the intensity became too powerful, he pulled back to study my face.

"Mercy, if you aren't sure about this, we can stop now."

The thought of him pulling away caused physical pain. I couldn't imagine wanting anyone as much as I wanted him right then.

"Do you have any idea how much I've wanted this? This connection with you? Whether it's now or next year, it's always going to be you, Drake."

"I love you, Mercy."

"I love you, too."

. . .

I PULLED THE BLANKET HIGHER, shielding my eyes from the bright rays of the sun. It could never compare to the warmth in my chest—a comfort that could only come from being held by the one you love. We needed to leave after lunch, and there were things we had to do. Letting go of our private moment was difficult. Something had changed inside me. The unstable center that needed structure, meditation, and exercise calmed. Soft lips kissed up my back, forcing a grin to break through the haze of sleep.

"You look peaceful. Relaxed," Drake observed.

"I'm happy."

"You can say it. It's me, right?" He winked, teasing me.

I now understood the smitten look on Hillie's face.

"Last night was perfect. On the creek bank in Ireland, beside a fire . . . I'll never forget it."

Drake swept the loose hair from my cheek. "One day, we'll defile every creek bank I can find. I promise."

I rolled on my back, smirking. "That is the most romantic thing you've ever said to me."

"It's a gift." Drake came down on top of me and I wrapped my legs around him, rubbing against him as his lips left a hot path down my neck. "I don't want to hurt you," he whispered around my mouth.

"You could never hurt me. Please Drake . . ."

He gripped my hip, then slid his hand down my thigh, lifting it over his back. "I can't wait to hear those words for the rest of my life."

. . .

WE STAYED TANGLED a little longer until we finally dressed, drowning in the disappointment of losing our moment.

I had just finished folding the quilt as Neela and Ren walked out to meet us.

"If I had known you guys were camping, I'd have come out here. Quinn and Hillie kept us up all night. I could hear everything," Ren complained, shaking his head.

"I don't even remember crashing last night. Those brownies put me in a food coma," Neela replied.

Drake smirked but didn't respond.

"You guys almost ready?" I asked.

"I guess. It makes me sad to leave, though," Neela said.

"Me too," I said while staring out at the property. "We'll

change and meet you guys back at the house."

Drake and I climbed up to the tiny loft and looked around at what we called home for the past few days. So much had changed for us there, and we'd both carry a piece of Astriawell with us forever. Strong arms came around me, and Drake's chin rested on my shoulder.

"What are you thinking about?" he asked.

"Fireside by the creek," I admitted.

I felt Drake smile against my cheek before he kissed me.

"I'm afraid to leave. Worried things will change when we do. Can't we stay here and have our happily ever after?" I turned to face him and wrapped my arms around his neck.

"And give up your fate?" he asked. His hands skimmed up the back of my shirt, lightly rubbing my skin.

I shook my head and grinned. "You're my fate."

"What about the Regalians?" Drake's lips created a path down my neck, and his hands pressed my body against his.

I closed my eyes. "I know, you're right, but I would love to have a few more days with you."

"Me too, babe." He kissed me again before he turned to change clothes. I watched as he removed his shirt, and his Allegato mark gleamed in the sunlight.

"What do you think it means? Your mark?" I asked.

"I don't know. I have a feeling we'll find out soon enough."

. . .

"WAIT A MINUTE. I'm confused. Can you repeat that?" Neela asked with attitude.

"Horses. We'll ride horses to Stonedell." Quinn looked at

her as if she'd lost her mind.

"I've never even been on a horse, mountain man. And it's an all-day ride, correct?"

"That's right." Quinn nodded.

"Somebody call Flynn. I'll ride in that death trap!" Neela shouted.

"Neela, calm down. It can't be hard." Even though I tried to talk her down, I wasn't at peace about the situation.

These horses were enormous, like Quinn-size huge. He sat upon a massive black stallion in front of us while Hillie stared at him like she could eat him up. He had two other horses with him. Drake grabbed the reins of the extremely agitated brown one and jumped right into the saddle. Show off. He took the horse around the property and rode it back toward me.

"Did you have to pick the horse that has an attitude?" I asked.

"I apparently like challenges." He cocked his head to the side, giving me a meaningful look as one of my eyebrows rose at his remark. He slid back in the saddle and held his hand out in invitation. Once my foot was in the stirrup, Drake picked me up and set me in front of him. My back pressed up against his chest, and he rumbled appreciatively in my ear.

"You've got to be joking!" Ren and Neela were on a horse, galloping awkwardly around the meadow. My eyes watered from the all-consuming laughter from the crowd, which only fueled her anger. Hillie covered her ears, shocked at the negativity and filth pouring out of Neela. The girl was not happy.

"Don't forget me, Mercy." Hillie looked at me with wide, bright eyes, and I realized that she was stoned again.

"We'd never forget you. We'll be back soon, I promise."

She blew a kiss as we left. We followed Quinn, with Ren

and Neela running circles around the meadow behind us.

. . .

THE MONOTONOUS CLOMPING of horse hooves and the heat radiating from Drake relaxed me into a lull. I leaned my head back and closed my eyes. We'd been riding for hours. At one point, Neela had fallen asleep over Ren's back, a small amount of drool escaping from her lip. It was sexy.

Drake stayed aware of everything around us, and I could feel the energy buzzing from his body. He kissed my forehead as I found a comfortable position by his neck and drifted off to sleep. At first, the rest was peaceful, but it soon changed to a disturbing reflection of myself.

The image that forced its way into my mind didn't feel like interference. It felt like a vision. A man's hand, with an intricate and delicate D tattooed on his wrist, reached out, waiting for me to accept him. I placed one hand in his palm and stepped forward in front of a large crowd. My eyes cut to the left, where Drake watched, angry and helpless. An evil giggle erupted behind me as a knife appeared, slitting Drake's throat. The blood-thirsty crowd cheered at the sacrifice. The man leaned forward and whispered in my ear, "Now, nothing will stand between us."

I bolted upright, startling the horse and causing him to rear back on two legs. He kicked against the panic radiating from me and knocked us onto the ground. The horse galloped away from the threat, and Quinn ran after him. Drake and I lay flat on our backs, gasping from the adrenaline.

"What happened?" Ren and Neela trotted over, taking in

the scene before them.

"Mercy decided it was time for a break," Drake replied calmly. He sat up, giving himself a chance to recover, then looked over at me. "Are you hurt?"

"Just my pride," I admitted. I threw my arm over my eyes.

"What was that about?" he asked.

"Can we talk about it later?" I whispered.

He didn't answer but stood and reached for my hand, a reminder of the man's invitation in my vision. I stood on my own, ignoring his offer, and he narrowed his eyes, unhappy with my response. Guilt over something I hadn't even done caused tension throughout my body, and it didn't matter how much I hid from everyone else, I couldn't fool him. He stepped in front of me and wrapped his arms around me tightly.

"You were asleep. I'm not sure what happened, but it wasn't real. I need you to center yourself and come back to me. Alright?"

I nodded.

Quinn returned with our horse and checked to see if we were okay. When we convinced him we were fine, we started back on our path to Stonedell. I didn't fall asleep again. I made sure of it. An eeriness enveloped me as we approached Stonedell. The fog of magic thickened as we got closer, and my powers strengthened as if they sensed we were close to home.

In the distance, a rock structure appeared through the trees, covered in vines and moss. It was difficult to tell how tall it was, considering how much lush, green foliage had attached itself to the exterior. Massive trees surrounded the area, and if there was an entrance, I didn't see it. The visible stones had a shiny film looking texture as if a bubble protected the rock.

"Welcome to Stonedell," Quinn announced.

"Where's the entrance?" Ren asked.

"You won't find a front door if that's what you're looking for," Quinn answered. "Not just anyone can find their way into Stonedell."

"So, now what?" I asked.

He waved his hand toward the shimmering stone. "Give it a reason."

"Give who—what? I've been in a constant state of confusion since I stepped off that blasted cargo ship," Neela complained.

"Stonedell. It needs a reason to invite you in. The magic must consider you worthy. If it senses aggression or evil intent, you can't enter. Aadya forced the elders to place a spell on the entrance to protect herself."

"Damn. That's a waste of a trip," Ren responded.

"Well, obviously, lad, you don't go up there thinking about how you're gonna murder their queen. There must be good intention in your heart for passage to be granted." Quinn rolled his eyes.

"Ok, ok. I got this. How does it work?" Ren asked.

"Walk up to the stone and lay your palm against it. Stonedell will assess your intentions."

Ren swaggered to the stone wall with his game face in place. He cleared his throat and straightened his spine as he lifted his hand to the wall. At first, nothing happened. He waited for several seconds until finally glaring over his shoulder toward Quinn. "This damn thing is brok . . ." Ren flew back against the tree with so much force, I thought he'd broken his back.

We lifted him to his feet as he shook his head, stunned and slightly pissed off. He stomped over to the wall again, determined to gain entry. Angrily throwing his palm forward, the stone wasted no time in tossing him back on his rear.

"Are you tryin' to get yourself killed, lad? Why are you here? Let the wall see your purpose, if there is any." Quinn shook his head, exasperated, and turned away from Ren.

Again, Ren stood in front of the wall, contemplating his plan of action.

"Search your heart, mate. Gotta be some love in there somewhere," Quinn yelled.

Ren's eyes found mine. Breathing heavily, he focused on me. He placed his hand upon the stone, and the rock shimmered as if it had gone invisible. Ren stepped forward, his body crossing the barrier to the enchanted land.

Drake's mouth tightened as he balled his fists. "If we survive, he and I will have a lot to talk about."

"Lets focus on the surviving part," I mumbled.

Neela stepped up next, as calm as I'd ever seen her. This woman didn't have a drop of ill intent in her body—she had nothing to worry about. Her palm calmly raised toward the stone, and it immediately shimmered, letting her through.

I glanced up at Quinn. "If I don't see you again, thank you

for everything. We wouldn't have made it this far without you and Hillie."

Quinn smiled, "Anytime, ruler of Regalians. You change things, we may move back."

I grinned. "You better."

"Don't forget, Mercy. This place will turn you inside out before it's done with you. It only allows the strongest to pass, and it's different for everyone. Use your power in every decision you make."

I turned toward Drake, my heart full of emotion. "See you on the other side."

He grinned, but it didn't reach his eyes.

The wall was much more intimidating when you stood right in front of it. The power it held intimidated me, and my palm shook as I raised it forward. I had to bury my hatred for the aunt that destroyed my family—hide the hostility I felt every time someone mentioned the word Seregalo. Concealing my hatred was my only option.

I thought of my parents and the land where they first met, and being there with Drake warmed my heart as happiness drowned out everything else in my mind. A power I wasn't expecting reached out, tickling my palm and calling for me. I stepped toward it, hypnotized, and found myself in an empty stone room, the lack of windows shrouding it in darkness. A thin layer of dust covered the stone flooring—not a footprint in sight. Large rectangle stones created a fortress type atmosphere, and although I couldn't see outside, I felt as though we were in a tall tower—isolated from anyone that could hear my call for help. My stomach dropped at the thought.

"Ren? Neela?" I called out, but only the echo of my voice responded. I waited a few minutes for Drake, but quickly realized that Stonedell had separated us. Fear crawled up the back of my spine and tried to belittle my power, telling me

I'd never make it alone. Whether or not this was part of the spell, I had to forge on, ignoring anything that could hinder me from succeeding.

I could barely make out a small entrance, maybe two feet across, on the other side of the room. The air pulled at my magic, inviting me toward the tunnel. The black hole of death was about as inviting as Central Park at midnight. Cold stones emitted a chill throughout the tunnel, and a constant drip of water kept a steady rhythm in my ears.

As if carried by a breeze, a whisper traveled past me, "You shouldn't be here."

It disappeared as fast as it arrived. I closed my eyes and breathed, reaching out for any sign of another presence up ahead. It was vacant.

My fingertips grazed the stone wall, feeling for a shift in the rock—or anything to guide me. Claustrophobia kicked in as the walls tightened, and hot breath blew across the back of my neck. My upper arms pressed against the cold rock, and I had to turn sideways to fit through the tunnel when a pain-ridden scream reverberated throughout the corridor. Neela.

Panic overwhelmed me and I closed my eyes at the memory of Quinn's comforting voice. "Use your gift, Mercy."

I pleaded for my emotional interference gift to calm me. My mind needed to maintain clarity. Concentrating on night vision, I expanded my senses until a hint of light shone from the tunnel behind me. That wasn't possible. I had come from that direction.

I inched my way back, the walls tightening around me, and after what felt like an hour, I found myself surrounded by a circle of tall, narrow mirrors bordered in thick gold frames. The glass ceiling displayed the new moon above, taunting me with the trials of Stonedell. Every reflection in each mirror conjured a unique image of myself at different times in my life.

The first reflection, on my knees, crying over my dying father. My eyes swollen and wet—my posture defeated. Next, my expression slack and my eyes lifeless, pointing a gun toward my head. The weapon shook, but my face showed nothing: no nervousness, no fear, and no doubt. I looked dead inside. So many times through childhood, I imagined this very image and the painful reminder brought forth buried memories. It seemed like a lifetime ago.

The images continued on and on. Kissing Drake on the roof, holding a dying Cassie, hugging Nora, screaming on the subway—then—a small child sat on the ground all alone. Her long dark hair matted, and her clothes worn and dirty. A trio of girls stood behind her, laughing and pointing at the sad, deprived soul.

I repeatedly watched this image, sympathizing with the girl and not knowing how to process it. I didn't even remember this time in my childhood. I'd put it out of my mind—learning to do that early on saved my sanity.

The last image held the most important piece of myself, and the gratefulness I felt at witnessing the moment overpowered the sadness brought on by the mirrored room.

My parents cried over a dark-haired baby, naked on my mother's bare chest. Sweat rolled down her face from labor as my father leaned forward, kissing the top of my head with tears in his eyes. They stared at the child in wonder as a ripple of current ran through the room.

The smiles turned to shock as they realized what that meant for me, and my mother shook her head fiercely, mouthing the words, "No. No, please." She wrapped her arms tight around the small newborn—then her eyes widened in surprise at something happening in the room.

Shouts of pain from my mother replaced the calm. Then, rejoicing over a second, beautiful, red-haired newborn laid beside the first. Twins. A whisper ran through the tower, "Marley."

I took a step back, away from the confusing vision. How could this be possible? Someone would have told me, wouldn't they? Memories surfaced of my father trying to tell me something important in the library that day. My knees hit the hard floor, and my body shook. A sister. I had a sister. Did she know I existed?

My heart squeezed painfully at the thought of missing out on a sisterly bond. One that would have made my life a little less lonely. Dr. Lee said Aadya knew I would come for her. Was she using my twin as bait?

As soon as I made the decision to save her, small cracks in the glass appeared, then shattered around me in slow motion, flying throughout the room. I turned, my gaze taking in the small slivers sitting frozen in the air. Then, the bottom of the floor fell out from under me.

Bright white light replaced the darkness, blinding me as I fell through the air. After several seconds, my face slammed against hard ground as pain and warmth shot through my bottom lip. Blood dripped down the front of my shirt as I pushed up from the ground and fought to see in the blackness surrounding me. It was nightfall. Gigantic trees hovered over me, roots as wide as my waist. The trunks were large enough to drive a small car through, and it reminded me of pictures I'd seen of the redwoods in California.

The glint from the stars appeared abnormally bright, and the moon looked close enough to touch. From the clean, crisp air to the green grass, everything was too perfect. At first, the thought crossed my mind that I'd arrived in Seregalo, but I soon realized that Stonedell was just getting started.

The quiet forest observed my every move, waiting and watching. Bright yellow eyes perched on the limbs of trees—

my only companions—and I talked to the creatures as if they understood.

"Alright, guys, Help me. Can you point me to the way out?"

A slow blink was my only response.

"Bored with me already? I'm offended."

Surveying my location, there wasn't an obstacle in sight. No tunnels, no mirrors, just the pitch black sky hovering over me like a shroud. I walked for what felt like several miles, searching for a way out. A stream appeared in front of me as it ran over smooth round rocks and disappeared back into the trees. I bent on one knee, cupping my hands to drink from the stream and regroup.

Rustling in the distance gave me pause—the pounding of my heart echoing in my ears. I reached out, the source of the noise directly in front of me. I expanded my hearing range and detected someone running toward me. The shuffling of feet indicated more than one set, so I kept low to the ground and crept back into the camouflage of the trees.

Hiding behind the trunk, I pressed my body as flat as I could against the bark. A petite figure in a gray hooded shawl ran out into the clearing and skipped across the stream, cradling something to their chest. Fear and desperation rippled through the air around them as they bolted toward the other side of my tree, concealed by the wide width of the trunk. I peeked toward the hooded figure as they pulled the blanket tight around the bundle. A hint of red hair peeked out from the women's cloak as her green eyes searched for an unknown threat.

My mother, but who did she cradle? More footsteps followed, and she closed her eyes as a shimmer surrounded her, shielding herself with her gift. Four men—Custos— rushed through the trees with rage-filled expressions. Angry shouts echoed through the night air as they ran past us, searching for the mother and baby on the run. My mother released the shield she'd put in place and leaned against the tree, sliding down to the ground, sweaty and exhausted. She pulled the blanket back and rubbed the thin red hair of the infant.

"Please, God. Please protect Noah and Mercy, as you have Marley and I. Please protect my family."

Tears rolled down my cheek as the vision dissipated in the night air. Seeing first hand, the desperation and despair she went through as she fought against Aadya, brought a sense of sadness, but also pride I couldn't describe. I stood for several minutes, digesting what I'd witnessed. The crackling of firewood and smell of smoke pulled me in the direction I came from. A soft humming drifted in the breeze, seeping into my soul and calming my nerves.

I tiptoed toward a campfire, constructed in front of a giant tree trunk used as shelter. My mother sat beside it, drinking from a hot mug and cooking over an open fire. A thin twig snapped underneath my shoe and her head popped up.

"Who's there?" She called out.

Something told me I'd never get the opportunity to speak with her again, and I should relish it. I wanted it—the chance to meet the woman who sacrificed her life for her daughters.

I stepped out of the shadows and her shoulders relaxed. "Who are you?" she asked.

"My name is . . . Nora. Nora James."

A hint of a smile broke across her face at the sight of me, as if we shared the secret of my true identity. She didn't call me out, but love and adoration filled her eyes.

"Are you alone, Nora?"

"Yes. I smelled the smoke and hoped someone would offer food and shelter," I lied.

"I'm Annabel. The fish is almost ready. You're welcome to eat with me. Please, come and sit."

I sat across from her, and I couldn't help but stare. Older than the previous vision, but still beautiful.

"How old are you, Nora?"

"Eighteen."

"So young to be out here alone. The forest can be a dangerous place at night. Where are you headed?" she asked.

"I, um . . . I got lost. I thought it would be a nice evening for a walk, but I guess I went too far."

My mother scraped the fish from the pan and slid it on a tin plate. "It isn't much, but it's better than nothing. Eat up." She smiled.

"Did you catch this yourself?" I asked.

"I did. Fishing used to be mine and my husband's favorite pastime. We'd spend hours on the bank, catching and releasing —just being together." Her head dropped thoughtfully and sadness filled her eyes. "Do you have a boyfriend?" she asked.

"I do." The realization that I could talk to my mom about my boyfriend stirred emotions deep inside. I paused for fear of crying. "His name is Drake."

"What a unique name. Some friends of ours have a son named Drake. He's only fourteen or fifteen, but there's something special about him. I can feel it. Someone will be lucky to have him one day."

I swallowed the lump in my throat, "My Drake is pretty special, too."

"He's good to you? Takes care of you?" she asked.

"He does. He'd lay down his life for me."

Mom grinned at my response and nodded, as if she were pleased. She studied my features, entranced by my eyes, then quickly turned her attention to the flames. "You remind me of someone, Nora. Someone I love very much."

"Do you and your husband have children?" I asked.

Her gaze never left the fire. "Twin daughters actually, thirteen years old today. We have to watch them from afar, though. We would give up our lives to protect them."

Tears streamed down my face at her words, "So, you're able to see them?"

"I watch over Marley here in California and Noah is in New York. He stays with the oldest, Mercy. She's a unique girl, and it's important she's protected."

"They are very lucky to have someone that cares so much," I cried.

"Oh, dear. I'm so sorry. I didn't mean to upset you. Sometimes my mouth runs away from me."

"I know a little about that," I chuckled.

We ate our dinner together in silence and my heart swelled at the precious gift. What had I done to deserve this? A question nagged at me, and I knew if I didn't ask, I'd regret it for the rest of my life.

"Tell me, Annabel. If you could tell your daughters one thing, what would you want them to know?" My voice faltered on the last word, but I recovered.

She smiled in my direction, and for a few seconds, I felt as though she looked straight into my soul. Not at Nora, but at Mercy.

"I would tell them we were always with them. We never abandoned them. I would tell Mercy that one day, she will have to make a very important decision about who she is and what impression she wants to leave on the world. Seregalo needs her."

"That is beau . . ."

"And I'd tell her to stay strong. There isn't anything wrong with breaking down from the stress that awaits, but afterward she must rise up and take what is hers." A tear glistened as it rolled down her cheek. "Rise within the Rage Fire child, it will protect you."

Her form shimmered as a single tear rolled down her beautiful face. Everything around me shattered into tiny sharp fragments and evaporated into thin air. I sat in front of the tree, cold and alone as I broke down. Sobs escaped my throat as I leaned forward, gripping the green grass in my fists.

An ear-splitting scream reverberated throughout the trees and I jumped to my feet. I ran toward the noise, unconcerned about the danger that awaited. In the distance, two Custos guards held my mother against a tree as she fought their grip. Her body sagged, tired and weak, as Aadya stood before her with her palm on my mother's head. Mom screamed against Aadya's intrusion.

"You might as well tell me where she is, Annabel. Don't you want the torture to end?"

My mother stayed silent, never breaking eye contact with Aadya. Her misery continued as Aadya dug deeper for information until mom's eyes met mine, almost apologetically, before she fell lifeless in their arms. An evil smile broke across Aadya's face.

"Get Marley, it's time to go home." Aadya ordered.

They turned, leaving her body unmoving on the ground. I rushed toward her, but within a few feet of picking up her limp frame, the scenery vanished.

New York. I'd know this city from anywhere. Car horns blared on the crowded streets and the smell of food trucks hovered in the air. I sat in a small alley, huddled against a brick building. Across from me, a homeless man with a scruffy beard stared out onto the streets, stretching his neck and keeping a watchful eye. Something about the man looked familiar, and I realized who sat under the torn clothes and filth—my father. I followed his line of sight, and we were sitting across the street from my school.

"Stonedell can be brutal. Am I right?" he asked, continuing to watch the doors of the high school.

My head spun in his direction, surprised he'd addressed me so openly.

"It can be. It can also offer gifts such as this," I whispered, tearful.

"I sit out here every day, waiting for you to leave school. Sometimes you've been crying. Your eyes will be swollen and red. I've watched you run from the building, laughter echoing from the halls behind you. It was all I could do to stay seated by this old building. Watching the torment on your face nearly tore me apart, and if I had known what you went through at home—I would have swept you away in a heartbeat. I hope you know that."

I blinked, attempting to clear my vision. "I do."

"On the rare occasion, I've gotten to see a smile as you walk by. What a gift that is." He smiled at the memory.

"I wish I'd known you were here. If nothing other than a wink now and then, well, it might have changed things for me." I admitted.

"I'm so sorry, baby girl. You and I have lost so much. Family, friends, love . . ."

"She'll pay, Dad. I need you to know that she'll pay for what she's done."

"I believe you, Mercy."

We sat between the filthy brick buildings, relishing the time we'd never get again. My life was so different from what I thought. Leaving school, hopeless and alone, to arrive at a home I didn't belong—but all of those years, love surrounded me. Love watched over me and protected me. I just didn't know it.

The buildings moved inward, threatening to crush us. I

placed my feet against the brick wall in front of me and pushed as hard as possible. My father never budged as the walls enclosed. I reached forward, gripping his hand, not wanting to let him go.

When I knew my time had run out, I whispered, "I love you." Then, I fell through the dirty concrete and hit hard dirt.

As I struggled to stand, the hair on my arms stood up. I listened carefully, attempting to detect which direction the threat would come from, but they were all around me.

Massive black beasts, with coarse hair and long teeth, growled fiercely from all sides. Beluas. Hillie warned me about them—the same creatures that graced my nightmares. In my dreams, the fire protected me. I fought fiercely for my elemental source but conjured nothing. There was something magical about the place, and my power didn't exist there. That's when I knew it had to be another test.

Low to the ground, they inched toward me. Growling and slobbering uncontrollably, they craved and hungered for blood. Two on my left were on edge to the point of attacking each other, blood lust taking over all reason. As one sneaked up close, almost catching my leg with its sharp fang, another belua tore its neck out with strong jaws, territorial and starving. I saw a small opening to the right, between two trees, and I did the only thing I could think of. I ran.

My legs pushed harder than ever through the thick forest. I could hear the clomp of hooves, and somehow I knew they enjoyed the chase—the thrill. Jumping wide roots and dodging low-hanging vines, I made my way toward . . . where? I had to think of a plan but couldn't get my bearings while running. Snarling and nipping drowned out everything else as I approached the edge of a rocky cliff. If my only two options were jumping or being dinner for beluas, I'd jump in a heartbeat. Rushing water slammed against rocks and pulled my attention to the edge of the cliff where a waterfall poured into the river.

That was my only chance. I forced my legs to run faster, needing the speed to make the jump. If I didn't get distance, I'd end up too shallow and break my neck. Just as my feet left the ground, a sharp bite of pain swiped my leg as a belua gave one last-ditch effort before falling down the cliff after me. Jumping toward the water, I heard the hard crunch of bone as the beast tumbled against the rocks below.

Cold water swallowed my weak body and pulled me downstream. It felt as though the current had a hold of my feet, pulling me further into the water's dark depths. A tingle of magic burned in my chest, and I pulled from my source, begging it to awaken. All at once, I broke through the surface, gasping for air. Controlling the current, I pleaded with the water to direct me, and before I knew it, I landed on the side of the bank, alive.

Coughing up water, I collapsed on my back to catch my breath. The blue of the sky was vibrant, as if hand-painted, and a memory pulled at my mind. Then, I recalled the picture I'd found of Fitz and my father—the sky was the same shade of blue. *Seregalo.*

Clear, crisp water ran over smooth stones, and the fluffiest white clouds I'd ever seen were painted against a turquoise blue sky. Not a dead tree or wilted flower in sight. Perfection.

I had no way of knowing how long I'd been in Stonedell, or if the others made it through. Waiting for them seemed pointless—so I walked. Worn paths throughout the trees made it easy to maneuver. Keeping my senses sharp, I sat every hour to meditate and center myself to my surroundings. Birds sang, frogs croaked, and squirrels jumped from tree to tree. I couldn't pick up on anything else in the area.

Another mile or two, the trees opened up to a clearing

with stone cottages in the distance, exactly like the ones from Fitz's picture. It amazed me how Seregalo looked like Ireland, with a filter. The countryside was similar but flawless and vibrant. I took one step outside the tree line, and a knife appeared in front of my throat, freezing me in my tracks. So much for staying focused.

"I'd advise you not to move," a deep voice rumbled.

"And I'd advise you to take the blade from my neck," I replied.

He chuckled lightly, amused by my boldness. The knife pressed into my skin in warning, and I decided I'd had enough. A girl could only take so much in one day. Using the energy around me, I forced him on his back and took the feeling from his limbs. As if that isn't embarrassing enough, he yelled for help.

"Seriously, Caleb. You scream like a girl. Shut your face before someone hears you," another masculine voice called out.

"I can't see, you ass goblin. Don't let her kill me. This would be a humiliating way to die," Caleb cried.

"I'd let her do anything she wanted to me."

"Are you two finished?" I asked.

"You must be Mercy. I'm sorry about my brother. He bet my dad he could take you. I'm Colton."

My breath left my body, and tears filled my eyes. "You're Caleb and Colton."

"Um, yeah. We just told you that." Caleb rolled his eyes as if I were slow.

"You're Neela's brothers," I exclaimed. "Where is she?"

Colton shook his head. "We don't know."

. . .

CALEB AND COLTON led me back to their cottage, and Ren waited at the door.

He bolted forward, wrapping me in his arms. "What happened to you? I've made myself sick worrying the past few days."

"Days? It's been days?"

"Yes. I almost left thinking you guys never made it. The Parker's convinced me to give you more time," Ren explained.

"I'm guessing you haven't heard from Drake, either?" I asked.

"Nothing," he said. "What happened?"

"I honestly don't know. I went through several trials, but it only felt like hours." My time with my parents was private. I wasn't ready to share that.

"Interesting. I wondered how detailed Stonedell would be with someone as powerful as you." A deep voice sounded. A tall, intimidating man stepped forward, studying me. "I'm Joseph Parker, Neela's father."

Mr. Parker, a large, wide-shouldered man, with dark eyes that could see straight into your soul stood in front of me. I took a step back at his intensity.

A high-pitched voice, laced with authority rang out. "For heaven's sake, get out of the doorway. The poor girl looks as though she's been through hell."

We all moved into the cottage, and a petite woman with smooth dark skin, who reminded me of Neela, led me to a dining table. "Sit, sit. I'll get you something to eat. I'm Naomi."

"Thank you. It's nice to meet you." Everyone sat down staring at me, the silence awkward and tense.

"When's the last time you saw everyone else, Mercy?" Mr. Parker asked.

"The entrance at Stonedell. After Ren made it through, Neela entered, and I followed her. Do you have any idea where they could be?"

Mr. Parker sighed. "There are a few drop spots after people enter Seregalo, depending on the trials they went through. It's not something you can predict. Some are in the trials longer than others."

Mrs. Parker sat a plate on the table with fruit, bread, and cheese. "Eat, Mercy. You need your strength."

I stared at the food, but I couldn't force myself to pick it up. "I need to find Drake and Neela. We've already lost Nora —I won't lose them too." I met Mr. Parker's eyes.

"They're smart, Mercy. I wouldn't worry too much. They could be headed toward the domicile to find you."

"What's the best way to get there?"

"You're sure you want to do this?" Mr. Parker asked.

I nodded. "I'm sure."

"It won't be easy. Custos guard the Seregalo domicile, and Aadya has forced the Elders from their homes to live under her ruling. She likes to keep an eye on them."

Of course she does, I thought. "I never expected it to be easy, but there has to be a way." Mr. Parker contemplated my answer. I could almost see his wheels turning as he considered all of my options.

"How long can you swim underwater?" he asked.

"However long it takes." I answered.

"The main channel that washed you up runs behind the domicile. To get past security successfully, you'd have to swim at least a quarter of a mile."

"Done." I forced myself to pick up an apple slice and take a bite.

His eyes widened in surprise at my boldness. "Done?"

"Yes. It's not a problem," I said.

"Alright. We'll get you to the river—as close as possible. The rest is up to you."

"Do you think I should give Drake and Neela a chance to find us?" I asked.

"No, we've been searching since Ren arrived. Not a sign of them anywhere," said Mr. Parker. "I'm afraid we can't wait. Aadya could pick up on your presence at any time. If you're hell bent on walking into the fire—then it has to be now."

"We're coming." Caleb and Colton spoke up from across the table. "Our sister is out there. You can't expect us to sit around and do nothing."

Naomi's eyes filled with tears. "I can't lose another child, Colton. My heart can't take it."

"You haven't lost any of us, Mom. Neela is still out there, I know it," Caleb told her.

"I'm not sure I can disguise all of us. I've never attempted to use my sensory on more than one person," I admitted.

"I can disguise them as Custos easily," Mr. Parker spoke up.

Naomi looked over at her husband with disbelief in her troubled eyes.

"We can't bubble wrap them forever, dear. Our youngest is out there right now, working toward a better tomorrow," Mr. Parker said. "It's going to take all of us."

"We'll need to get Mercy as close as possible. The only way to do that is through the market, to the river bank behind the Elder's abandoned homes," Colton said.

"I agree. They won't question a couple of Custos walking through, but they'll interrogate a strange woman." Mr. Parker continued, "Unfortunately, that's the Seregalo that Aadya has created."

I remembered Drake's sensory instruction—I had to visualize what I wanted them to see. "I don't think I could keep a disguise up for long. If someone stops me, I might be able to change their view, if it's only for a few minutes."

"I say we dress her as a Custos along with Colton. If someone stops her, she can use it if she has to. Caleb, you follow, but not too close. Over two will look suspicious."

I would have never been able to do this without them. "Thank you, Mr. and Mrs. Parker, for everything."

"For heaven's sake, call us Joseph and Naomi." Joseph smiled.

19

I sat in front of a mirror, my mind a million miles away while Naomi braided my hair. Drake and Neela's absence weighed heavily on my heart. I fought against the need to find them, knowing Mr. Parker was right. It was now or never.

She raised the hood of the black cloak over my head. If I had to use my gift, I'd only have to alter my face. Colton stood well over six feet tall, and I hoped the size difference wouldn't be too noticeable walking through town.

Joseph worked on our disguises, but insisted I rest. Color returned to my cheeks after eating. I had to admit—he was right. I already felt way better than I did on arrival.

"Evening will be best. Several shops are closing up for the day. That will be the safest time for you to travel, then you can swim at night," Naomi explained.

Caleb and Colton walked into the room, dressed in the same cloak, only gray.

"Out of curiosity, why do some wear gray and some wear black?"

"Rank. Gray is for the more experienced or powerful

guards."

My eyebrow raised at his remark and I looked down at the black cloak around my shoulders. Colton grinned.

"Is there anything I need to know about being a Custos? How they act or what they're allowed to do?" I asked.

"Not really. They throw around more power than they have, but the safest bet is for you to keep your head down. They'll assume you're new in the position," Colton answered.

"Alright, let's do this." Adrenaline flowed through me as my magic hummed in the air around us. Reaching out to sense my surroundings while shielding my own mind would be the only way to get inside. I had to stay focused.

"Colton and Caleb will see you to the river safely, then it's up to you. The river behind the domicile is spelled. If you come up for air, it'll trigger security. You've got to swim past the domicile to at least the dock. That's where the spell ends." Joseph explained.

"How do you know the spell hasn't changed?" I asked.

"Because the Elder that put the spell in place is a close acquaintance, but his assistance only goes so far, due to his allegiance. He isn't too happy about being forced from his home."

Naomi spoke up, "Plus, changing a spell is difficult. To place one, an Elder representing each gift comes together with a common goal for the good of Seregalo. Otherwise, it won't work. From my understanding, there isn't much to agree on these days inside those walls."

Ren sat across the room, his brow furrowed, and his knee bouncing.

"Can you guys give us a minute?" I asked.

The Parkers filed out the door to give us privacy.

"What's up?" I asked.

"What?" he asked. "I mean, I don't understand why you'd think something's up. Besides the fact we're in freaking Seregalo, disguised so we don't get killed and you're planning on walking into the lion's den. Sounds perfectly safe." Rage had built up until he exploded. "Apparently, I'm the sane one!" He screamed.

"Ren, please calm down. I know this is a lot to take in, but I'm nervous too."

"Are you? Because you don't look nervous at all. You look thrilled—excited, even. Does the anticipation of death do something for you, Mercy?"

"How dare you? I never said you had to come! You knew I came here to confront Aadya, so don't blame me if you're a coward! Do you think I should continue letting her wreck the lives of people I care about? So she can continue to rule?"

"Why not? We can escape, far away from here. Let her believe you're dead! She wouldn't be killing people if you weren't alive, Mercy. Maybe you're making it worse!"

Ren's words sliced through my heart like a knife. I knew my existence had been the catalyst for all the destruction. Does that mean I should let her get away with it? My family escaped Seregalo before I was born, and that alone told me what kind of leader Aadya had been to the Regalians. No. I had to take a stand.

"I can see it in your eyes," Ren said. "The need to prove yourself, the fear of failure."

My expression never wavered. "Then you don't know what you're talking about."

"Really?" Ren shook his head, annoyed.

I stepped forward. "Yes. Maybe if you were in my shoes, you'd see it differently."

"You mean, maybe if I had multiple gifts? Is that what you're referring to? I'm sorry I'm not all-powerful, and I only hold one gift. I guess some of us are just mediocre, right? Maybe if I were more like Drake, things would be different."

I threw my hands up, exasperated. "Is that what this is

about? Drake?"

"I saw both of you—did you know that?" he asked. "Down by the creek, him stripping you bare. It should have been me. You were matched to me, not him."

"You watched us?" I asked, appalled. "What I did with Drake is none of your business, and I'm sure he'll feel the same way!"

"Don't threaten me with your boyfriend," he growled. "You know what? I'm done. I can't believe I followed you into this disaster like some lovesick puppy. Good luck surviving, Mercy." Ren stomped out of the room, and the slamming of the cottage door echoed throughout the house.

He left me. I couldn't believe he actually left me.

The bedroom door opened halfway, and Naomi leaned against the doorframe with sympathetic eyes. "Better he leaves now, instead of abandoning you down the road. You need to know who you can count on."

I sat in the chair Ren had occupied minutes before. "You're right, but the truth doesn't make it any easier on my heart."

"Do you want to talk about it?" she asked.

"No, I want to put it out of my mind and focus. Thank you for offering."

Caleb yelled from the kitchen, "Do you want to talk about the creek? Because I'm here for you."

After everything that happened, a small smile broke through my despair. I shook my head at Naomi. "How do you do it every day?"

"I meditate a lot," she replied.

. . .

COLTON and I walked toward the market, him oozing confidence and attitude, me with my head down, refusing to make eye contact. Hopefully, they'd never look past him when they saw the sneer he sported.

"We're going to have to make a few stops to blend in," he told me. I had to admit, I was curious. What type of shops did they have in a world created for gifted individuals?

Cobblestone streets lay out before me, and the buildings were a combination of stone, brick, and stucco. Everything was pristine, not a piece of trash in sight. Brooms swept the sidewalks by themselves, and one man stood in the street, his graceful hands orchestrating them. The turquoise sky took on an orange hue from the sunset, and a light breeze blew down the streets.

Colton turned to the shop on our left. "If you want to fit in, better hit the Boozer."

"Boozer?"

"Yep, Custos love to drink."

Get plastered, then meet your aunt. It was like a holiday to-do list.

I pictured more of a pub scene, but this was nothing like the taverns I'd been in. Everything from the floors to the countertops was pristine copper. Standing room only, there was no space for tables. The room had a long bar on each of the four walls, and the bartenders stood behind the counters, watching the drinks pour themselves. I imagined most bars to be similar in noise and laughter, but the magic inside Boozer created a hypnotizing atmosphere.

Colton ordered a couple of shots, and we stayed a few minutes after—long enough to make an appearance and not bring unwanted attention our way. We made our way out into the fresh air, and Caleb stood across the street, chatting up a cute girl. He straightened when we caught his eye and he continued following behind us at a safe distance.

Pink and yellow flowers bloomed along the sidewalk while residents smiled and waved at passing neighbors. Children laughed, chasing each other down the street. They appeared to be content. I doubted the case I'd made to Ren about creating a better Seregalo, until I walked past an older woman with a muffin cart. Her frail, wrinkled hand reached out and clung to my arm through the cloak, nails pressing into my arm. I paused without turning in her direction. My heart pounded against my chest as an instinct to fight took over.

"I knew you'd come one day. I prayed I'd be alive to meet you," she whispered.

I took a deep breath and turned to face her, revealing my true identity. I can't say why I trusted her, but I did.

Her face softened—tears filled her eyes. "You look just like your father, did you know that?"

I grinned. "I've heard that a time or two."

"My goodness at the power coursing through you, Child. My prayers are with you." She gently patted the side of my face.

"Thank you," I whispered.

"When all is said and done, you know where to find me." The woman turned back to her cart as if we'd never spoken.

Colton and I continued down the sidewalk, the kind lady's words replaying in my head, giving me the courage to do what I needed.

"Do you know her?" I asked.

"Yes."

"Well? Who is she?"

Colton sighed, "Mrs. Monroe."

"Wait. You mean she's. . ."

"Noah's mother. Your grandmother."

I swallowed the large lump in my throat and kept moving. I couldn't show emotion—not then. A warmth ran through me at the thought of still having family. I had a grandmother.

Colton led me into another store, the window filled with crystals and jewelry. The lights were low, and as soon as I entered, a peacefulness washed over me. I looked around at the rock-lined walls and ceiling, and it hit me. We were in a cave. Carved rock shelving graced the stone walls where large crystals emitted power and energy throughout the air. You could walk through and feel the power in your chest. Almost a recharge, which could've possibly been his intention.

"Can I be of service?" A tall, thin woman peered over her glasses as she stood at the counter.

"We're cooling off, if that's okay," Colton answered.

She smiled, but it didn't feel authentic. "Take your time."

Colton leaned in carefully, "The cave is always cool, so Custos stop by to take a break from the heat. If you're gifted, you can feel the charge in the air. I hoped it would help."

We walked around for a few minutes, but the owner never took her eyes from me—watching my every move. Colton led me to the door, and another Custos waited on the sidewalk. Colton never faltered as he kept walking, ignoring the threat that loomed.

"Hey! Do I know you?" I knew that voice. It couldn't be. . . Could it?

"No, Man. We just joined. I'm Colton."

"Good to meet you, Colton. I'm Asher. And you are?"

I froze. I concentrated on my gift, conjuring the first image that came to mind, "Cyrus. I'm Cyrus." The image of the skinny, allergy-ridden kid at Fremont was the first person to pop in my head.

"Well, Cyrus, if you wanna make it around here, you might wanna beef up. You're frail, my friend," said Asher.

"Will do. Thanks." I fought to alter what Asher heard so

he didn't recognize my voice.

"See you around," Asher called out.

Walking toward the end of the cobblestone street, I whispered toward Colton, "I thought he was dead."

He scoffed. "Looks alive and well to me."

Dusk settled over the town, but not dark enough to hide us. Voices pulled our attention back from where we came. Caleb stood outside of the store listening to the owner while Asher's eyes watched over the city. She appeared to be describing someone, and my stomach dropped. The moment Asher realized what had happened, I felt it in the air. Anger over my deception, embarrassment that I'd fooled him. His head whipped in my direction and he made eye contact with me.

Colton shoved me forward. "Run, Mercy."

We turned right, out of the line of sight, and dashed down the street into what looked like an abandoned cottage. Glass covered the floor from shattered windows, and the door hung loosely on one hinge. Broken and splintered furniture littered the floor. Pictures had fallen from the walls and a few clothing items were strewn around the destruction.

"Where are we?" I asked.

"An Elder's home. Take off your cloak. The river runs directly behind us. You're gonna have to swim a little earlier than expected."

I shed the cloak and boots Naomi gave me, leaving me in a tank top and leggings. Colton escorted me to the back door, and as my hand wrapped around the broken handle, the front door crashed in. Asher, along with Caleb and another, had caught up to us. Caleb looked as though he could puke and didn't know what to do.

Asher smiled, looking me over. "Been thinking about you, sweetness."

"It's a shame. I thought you died," I replied.

"I did, too. Fortunately, you tossed me in the back of a dump truck instead of the road. I'm guessing it was on purpose. Can't deny our love?"

My fists tightened in anger. "You killed my father."

He held his hands up, smiling innocently. "Well, technically, I was trying to kill Drake."

A voice told me to back away while I could. Asher would pay, but that wasn't the time. "It was nice seeing you, Asher, but I have somewhere to be."

"How's my brother, Mercy? I don't see him here, so that means he is dead or in the area. Did you kill him too?" he asked.

Although I refused to show it, his words crushed my spirit. I didn't know where Drake was or if he had survived Stonedell.

"Have you ever wondered what if?" I asked.

"What?" His face scrunched up as if I spoke German.

"What if? Sometimes I think, what if I'd never been born a Regalian? What would my life be like? Do you ever ask yourself what if? What if you hadn't turned your back on Drake? What if there was someone out there that could have helped you control your gift? Would you still be with your brother? Would you be on the other side of this war?"

Asher's chest expanded from breathing heavily, and his jaw clenched with irritation because he knew I was right. He'd asked himself 'what if' many times, but he was too proud to admit it.

My voice turned sad. "You're nothing to Aadya, Custos are expendable to her, but you were someone to Drake."

Asher never responded, but the combination of anger and pain in the air was all-consuming. I could feel the turmoil. He hated who he had become—despised how far he had fallen.

"Goodbye, Asher."

He stepped forward just as I took their eyesight. They reached out, trying to get their bearings as I opened the back door to escape. I looked over toward Colton and Caleb, "Run. When I leave, they'll get their sight back."

"Mercy. . ." Colton started.

"Thanks for everything." I needed them to hurry—I wanted them safe.

He nodded and pushed his brother out of the cottage.

"You know I'll find you. When I do, I'll tear you from limb to limb, like I promised on the subway," Asher threatened.

"Keep trying, Asher. It keeps things interesting."

I turned to sprint for the river. By the time they could see, I had dove into the water. It was almost too easy.

I had devised a plan for swimming underwater, which wouldn't have been possible without my energy and elemental gifts combined. Using the surrounding air, I created a pocket of oxygen so I could breathe. It would hopefully last the full distance, so I wouldn't need to come up to the surface. I also focused on increasing the current, so I could swim faster. I'd never tried it before, but I wasn't about to tell Joseph and Naomi. I wanted them to feel confident in my plan.

The swim went smoothly, the current of the river pulling me downstream. Watching the fish and turtles swim by my personal energy bubble was like gazing into an aquarium, and I could only imagine what this would be like in the ocean. Halfway through the swim, the images in front of me transformed. The fish and reptiles surrounding me rippled— morphing into visions of horror.

My father, bleeding out in my arms because I was too weak to stop it. My mother, alone and desperate, crying in fear over the family she would never see again. Breathing became difficult as the bubble wavered under my hold. The images evaporated and Drake's sexy smirk replaced the violence—until a trickle of blood dripped from his nose—then the corner of his mouth. Then his eyes. Blood eventually covered his entire face and he screamed in agony as fire scorched his skin. The bubble I created heated around me, and I fought to take a breath.

Then, something dark around me whispered, *Rage Fire*.

I gasped as the bubble cracked, threatening to expose me to Aadya and her guards. Flames engulfed my body, swirling fiercely around me in the river. I closed my eyes against the vision, and pushed forward. My head throbbed from the pressure of the magic and the muscles in my legs cramped. My skin felt blistered from the heat, but I knew it wasn't. It was part of the spell.

I knew I'd made it to the domicile because the tightness in my chest began to retreat and a familiar sensation pricked the back of my neck. The flame inside me ignited at the presence of Drake nearby. I could feel him.

The pressure completely faded as I passed the domicile, and the wooden posts of the dock came into view. I had to make it to the other side, and I'd be in the clear. My lungs strained for the last bit of oxygen, but I swam past the posts for ten to twelve feet to make sure I'd gone far enough. Then, the cool breeze hit my face as I inhaled fresh air. I eased over to the bank, slowly raising my head from the water.

The grass beside the bank was tall and green, creating a whimsical landscape, but the domicile was darker than I anticipated. The black stone looked almost evil. Not dark gray, black. Each stone looked to be about three-foot square, and the building was at least fifty feet high. Massive single-paned windows surrounded the top of the building, and guards stood watch along the back entrance.

I didn't feel as drained as I expected after the swim. I tried to think of a distraction to get rid of the guards, but their focus was unyielding. I couldn't use the typical sensory impairment, as soon as I entered the building, they'd get their sight back and call security. I had to be more creative.

Come on, Mercy, they're men. You know how to distract them, I thought. I closed my eyes and conjured up three beautiful women, half-naked, about 40 feet down the river bank. I kept the vision vibrant and real in my mind so they would see it just as clear. The women waved seductively, teasing them.

It took all of ten-seconds for the Custos to take the bait. As they drifted toward the women, I snuck across the lawn to the door. Easing the heavy door open, I slid through the crack, unseen. My blood boiled at the presence of Drake. Knowing he survived comforted me, but I didn't want anyone I loved close to that evil spawn.

The same black stone on the outside composed the interior of the building. Large squares of what looked like black granite covered the floor and walls, sleek and extravagant. A glass ceiling allowed for natural light, and the white light of the moon shimmered overhead, beaming off massive glass chandeliers. There wasn't a piece of furniture in sight. No tables, lamps, or pictures on the wall. The building spoke for itself. There also wasn't a soul nearby. Where were they?

I quietly stepped down the hall, my wet footprints capturing my attention. The last thing I needed to do was leave breadcrumbs. Concentrating on the elements, I pulled the river water from my clothes and watched as the droplets gathered together, then collected the remaining water on the floor. Now, what did I do with it? I looked around the corner into a parlor and tossed the water in a vase by the window. Pictures on the table caught my eye, and before I knew it, I had walked across the room.

Framed images of Aadya were everywhere. The day she took over Seregalo, a celebration in her honor, and even one of my father. Not a single picture of my mother on display.

Bitterness devoured any sympathy I could ever have for her. My parents would be alive if it weren't for her. I turned away from the history I cared nothing about, unable to look at any more reminders of what she had done.

I left the parlor and crept down the long, dark hallway. Movement ahead forced me into an alcove, and I reached out to listen.

"Can you please take this to Marley's room?"

Marley. My sister was there.

"I took breakfast to that brat this morning, and she threw the tray at my head. It's someone else's turn," an angry voice spat.

A smile broke out across my face. She really was my twin.

"Just sit the tray outside the door and knock. That's what they did last night."

"I better get hazard pay. I'm not joking."

I followed the footsteps toward the opposite direction, keeping a safe distance. Dark, narrow steps spiraled above us, and we climbed at least three floors before he cut to the left. I stayed hidden around the corner until I saw him place the tray on the floor.

A decorative brass number seven adorned the large wooden door. Seven. Ironically, my room number at Fremont. He hesitated, knocked once, and took off the way he'd come. I plastered myself against the wall, unseen. As soon as the hall was clear, I tip-toed across the floor to room number seven.

I picked up the tray and attempted to turn the door handle. Unlocked. The wooden door creaked as I slowly stepped inside, closing it quietly behind me. My gaze traveled around the room, as the tray fell from my hands. I couldn't believe my eyes. A red-haired girl staring out the window turned in shock. Her eyes were wide with . . . not fear, but disbelief. Awkwardness hung in the air as she blinked several times and took a step back. Number seven—the room looked exactly like mine at Fremont.

Two twin beds, separated by a small table. Plain white walls, and even a replica of my black and white quilt laid across the bed. Our father's picture sat on the bedside table. How could this be possible?

She stepped forward. "Mercy, is that you?"

I reminded myself to breathe. "Marley?"

She smiled and exhaled loudly. I imagined she feared I wouldn't know her. I stared, unsure what to do. I recognized her. After all, she was my twin. My other half. But there was no instant connection like I'd anticipated. No fireworks. Just years of confusion and loss between us.

"I'm so happy you're here. We have to get out of here. I can't stay here any longer with this horrible woman. Please help me!" Marley's eyes were wide with anxiety, desperate to get away.

My heart ached for her. "Calm down, alright? I'm going to get you out of here. How long have you been here?"

"Five years."

Aadya succeeded that day in the woods—the day she killed our mother. The day she took Marley and so many people died protecting me. Guilt overwhelmed my heart at what Marley had been through because of me. She lost just as much as I had.

I shook my head. "I'm so sorry. If I had known the truth, I would have been here sooner."

"How did you find me?" she asked.

"We have so much to talk about, Marley, but it's going to have to wait, okay?"

"Yes, we have much to discuss," a familiar voice came from the door. "I suggest you cooperate if you want to see your friends alive."

Thu Dang. The day kept getting better and better.

20

*M*y body instantly went on defense.

"Now, Mercy. We won't have any issues, right? Your loved ones are few. You wouldn't want to lose anyone else."

As much as I despised this man, he was right. I relaxed my shoulders and took a deep breath. I could take him—my power was eager to lash out. But I also wanted to hear what he had to say.

"Good girl," he whispered.

I narrowed my eyes, remembering the suffering he induced in the alley. "What do you want from me?"

"We want to chat. Aadya is very excited about meeting her other niece."

I laughed. "I bet she is."

Thu Dang's evil grin widened. He came toward us, and I stepped in front of my sister protectively.

"You'd put your life on the line for someone you don't even know?" he asked.

"She's my sister, that's all I need to know."

Thu Dang kept his gaze focused on me. "Marley, stay here. Aadya wants to see Mercy."

"I'm staying with her," Marley demanded.

"No, you're not. If Mercy wants to see her precious Drake again, she'll come alone."

There it was, the only thing that could ever make me abandon Marley in this horrid chamber they had created. I looked over at her, full of regret. "Marley?"

Her head was down, eyes focused on the floor. She knew what I was going to say.

"Marley, I promise I'll be back. I need you to stay and wait for me. I can't . . . I can't let anyone else die. I hope you understand that."

Marley raised her head, standing up straight with resolve in her eyes, "I'll wait. Please, Mercy. Please come back."

"You have my word." I wouldn't fail her.

I followed Thu Dang out of Marley's room and into the hall. He turned toward the opposite direction I came and took me around the corner to a set of stairs. The black granite stairs soon turned into wide blocks of gray concrete —rough and cold. We walked down five stories before stepping into a dark, chilly dungeon.

Rows of cells were lined down the dark enclosed space, secured with massive locks that shimmered in the shadows.

"No one's ever escaped." I glanced toward Thu Dang as he continued, "I'm sure you're wondering."

I wouldn't admit it. I could feel my source as it struggled to stay lit. Something about the dungeon dampened my strength, and if I didn't stay focused—I wouldn't be able to use my gift at all. The first couple of cells housed strangers, dirty men who looked as though they hadn't eaten in days.

They threw themselves against the bars, begging me for help. Thu Dang's eyes lowered to the first man, and the prisoner screamed uncontrollably. He begged him to stop, crying out until blood dripped from his eyes, and his body fell limp.

"He's been getting on my nerves lately." He walked away from the unmoving body without another thought.

That prisoner was a Regalian. A blood-born native of Seregalo, and Thu Dang threw him away like a piece of garbage. He could have had family—people who depended on him. Now, he'd rot in a dungeon at the bottom of the domicile. What kind of future would these people continue to have under Aadya?

Screams echoed throughout the darkness, and my stomach dropped at the sight of the beaten and abused Regalians, clawing their way toward me. Walking forward, a small hand reached out and grabbed my ankle. I looked down into the most beautiful blue eyes I'd ever seen. The little boy huddled close to the cell door, begging me for help.

I leaned over and gently took his hand. "Hi, I'm Mercy."

"Do you have food?" he asked, desperately.

"What's your name?" I asked.

Confusion crossed his face. "I don't think I have one."

"Where are your parents?"

Again, he shook his head as if the question was absurd. "I don't have any."

I couldn't imagine how long he'd been there not to remember having parents.

Thu Dang stepped forward to chastise him, and I intervened. "Leave him," I demanded.

Thu Dang's head turned to the side, like a puppy, not understanding the command.

My stare never faltered, and he eventually turned, continuing down the aisle. My chest tightened, and I knew we were getting close to Drake. Thu Dang stopped in front of an empty cell, gesturing with his hand for me to step forward. I gripped the cold, metal bars, looking for any sign of movement. Then, two red eyes appeared in the far corner.

"Your boyfriend has quite a temper. Ripped the arm off my best guard, and I haven't forgiven him for it."

"Drake? Is that you?" I called out into the darkness.

Red eyes moved toward me, and I found myself nervous, removing my hands from the bars and stepping back. He never spoke, but when he became visible, my source fought against the spell to ignite. I reached through the bars and palmed his warm face. He closed his eyes and breathed. When he looked back at me, the red tint in his gaze had faded.

"Are you alright?" he asked.

"I'm okay." I breathed a sigh of relief that he wasn't hurt.

I turned toward Thu Dang, angry. I couldn't focus in the dungeon, and the confusion kept me from defending myself as two guards grabbed each arm and threw me into the open cell beside Drake, locking the door. The bolt shimmered brightly, then settled into place.

"Now, that's better. Make yourself at home, Mercy. We'll be with you shortly." Thu Dang and his guards walked toward the steps without another word.

"When we get out of here, I'm going to break his neck." Drake's words were lethal. He turned toward me with bright eyes, a hint of red returning. "You have no idea how worried I've been, Mercy."

"How long have you been here? What happened, Drake?"

"Honestly, I have no idea. Time is not the same after you walk through that portal at Stonedell. I swear I was there for weeks trying to get back to you. I found my way out of caves, fought fires, and suffered through the mirrored room a dozen times before I realized I had to alter my reaction to the images. I've never been through anything like it."

"Mazes and fires? I experienced the mirrored room, but I

didn't have the others. And I went through that only once. I had other trials though."

"Once? Are you joking? That was miserable, Mercy."

"Memories were all it showed, some more painful than others, but nothing I couldn't push through. They showed me the identity of Marley." I admitted.

"Well? Who is it?"

"My twin sister. I met her upstairs before Thu Dang interrupted and brought me here. I have to get her out of here, Drake. I have to help her."

"We will, I promise." He took a deep breath and massaged his forehead with his fingers.

"What are you thinking?"

"Just stressed. I can barely keep up with one of you, the thought of having two . . ." One of his eyebrows raised in my direction, and I couldn't help but smirk.

"Jackass. What did the mirrors show you?" I asked.

Drake's eyes squinted as if the reminder caused him pain. "I had visions. Horrible visions of the future. Fire consumed you. It surrounded you. Flames licked at your skin, and I couldn't reach you. As if they protected you from me and everyone else, the fire owned you."

"How did you get past the trial?" I asked.

"It took a while. My fists were bloody from bashing the glass, but I had to repeat it over and over. I knew the only thing I could do was accept fate. When that happened, the fire became part of me, and Stonedell moved to the next trial. Embracing that future was the hardest thing I've ever done."

"It means nothing, Drake. The purpose of those trials is to take you on a head trip."

"It does, Mercy. There's something very significant about that vision, but I'm not sure what."

I reached toward his face and he gripped my hand, kissing my fingers.

He sighed "It felt as though I fought for weeks. Stonedell tossed me in an empty cave on the mountainside. Ancient by the looks of it. Bones piled in the corners and a foreign language had been carved into the walls. The only word that I could make out was Moreno. I felt like they were trying to tell me something, you know?"

"Tell you what? Something about your family?" I asked.

"Maybe."

"How did you get here?" I asked.

"I snuck down the mountainside and dove into the river. They had to have someone monitoring the water, as quick as the guards were on me. They were there before I broke the surface."

"Spelled. The Parkers warned me in advance," I explained.

"Neela's family? You found them?"

"Well, technically, they found me in the forest. Ren was already at their cottage, waiting for word from us, but we haven't seen Neela."

"What happened to Ren? Is he here?"

The thought crossed my mind to share as little as possible. But this was Drake, and he would know if I lied.

"Ren left." I lowered my eyes to the floor, knowing he wouldn't take it well.

"Left, where? Is he alright? Mercy, look at me."

I peered up at his tense expression. "He stormed out before I came to the domicile, quite upset I might add." My anger toward Ren was one thing, but it didn't compare to the hurt.

"He left you unprotected?" He asked.

"I had Caleb and Colton, but yes, he left. He asked me to run away with him and leave everything behind. When I refused, he walked out."

Drake paced the cell, fuming.

"And . . ." I added.

"What?" He snapped.

"He watched us . . . down by the creek. The bitterness and resentment he carries, Drake, is much worse than I imagined."

Drake didn't speak, but his hands tightened into fists.

"Don't worry about Ren. I'll deal with him." His words sliced through the air.

"Drake. . ."

Heavy boots clomped into the dungeon, several pairs by the sound of the shuffle. My stomach turned at the thought of them coming for him. I stood, my body already on defense. The fully cloaked Custos walked by my cell without a glance. The guard in front stood shorter than the others but directed them to the cell down the aisle.

The creak of metal rang through the air as the door hinges whined. The guards shuffled into the dark space, dragging out a small, huddled form. I watched in horror as they carried the body, led by the short, demanding leader. As they passed my cell, a blonde head fell back out of the blankets. Nora.

"Nora! Nora, look at me!" I screamed until my lungs burned.

Dark circles lined her eyes, and bruises ran across her cheek. What had they done to her? My power remained on the sidelines, eager to play at any moment, but the dungeon's spell kept me from using it.

"Where are you taking her?" My outbursts went unanswered.

"Mercy, calm down." Drake called out.

"Drake, where are they going with her?"

"Listen to me, that was for your benefit. All of it. If they wanted her dead, she would be. Do you understand?" Drake asked. "Calm down."

I knew it made sense, but I couldn't get over her lovely

face, battered and weak. Nora had become family, and I refused to lose her too.

My hands gripped the bars in frustration. I had to get out of there. I wasn't any good to anyone in the dungeon.

"Mercy. Babe, look at me." Drake's soft voice broke through my panic and my eyes drifted to the cell beside me.

"I'm not giving up. Alright?" he told me.

I nodded. "Okay."

I slid to the floor exhausted and covered my face with my hands. *Think, Mercy . . .* Why hadn't she killed me? What good am I to her? If I worried about someone taking over my position, the obvious thing would be to get rid of them, but she hadn't. A part of me knew the answer. This was part of her sick, twisted game—a cat playing with her catch.

Drake and I sat for several hours, going over possible scenarios that ended with our survival. What power we could generate dissipated in a matter of minutes. The occasional cackle of a captured Regalian rang out across the damp, cold basement, reminding me of the lives at stake.

High heels slapped against the stone, and I ungracefully hurried to my feet. Sensing my frustration and anger, my power fought against the dampening spell—eager to escape. Finally, the woman I'd come here to see showed herself. Aadya slowly stepped up to face me. Her eyes swept me from head to toe, lips smirking at my current predicament.

She had beautiful, long red hair and bright green eyes identical to my mother, but a devious and evil spirit lurked behind the physical features. I observed the wrinkles around her eyes and down-turned mouth, a sign of her stress and age. It had to have been difficult on the soul, taking the lives of so many. Her long, red dress dragged the floor, embellished with black crystals around the neckline. She looked seductive without effort.

"Are you certain this is her? She doesn't look like much." Aadya sneered at my appearance.

"Oh, that's her, alright. I've been up close and personal several times, Madam. Though, not as close as I'd like." Asher stepped out from behind her, looking me over.

Drake slammed his hands against the bars, shaking his cell. Aadya's eyes widened and she stepped back surprised. "Are the spells still intact?"

Asher nodded. "Yes Ma'am. Thu Dang tested them before bringing her down." Asher turned toward Drake. "Hello, brother. I tried to tell you—this girl's gonna get you killed." Asher laughed.

"She doesn't look like us," Aadya observed.

"That's her. Jumped into the river to escape." Asher mumbled.

Aadya's eyes widened. "Did she now? Tell me, how did you manage the spell?" Aadya clasped her hands together. "Was it everything I wanted? I always imagined underwater visions of horror to be thrilling." She grinned.

My eyes widened. "Oh, yes. You should try it sometime."

"Snarky like her mother," she spat. "But she looks like Noah. Yes, I see it now." For a split second, her eyes turned kind, remembering my father's face, but after seeing her kill my mother in cold blood, I had no sympathy for her. I never would.

"Tell me, Mercy, where is Noah? We must contact him and let him know you're safe."

I glanced over at Asher, my eyes narrowing in question, "You didn't tell her?"

Asher's back straightened as he stood silent and nervous.

"Tell me what?" she snapped.

"My father is dead."

Aadya's palm braced her belly as she took a step back in

shock. Her pale face shook, refusing to accept it. "What? No. No, he can't be dead."

I wouldn't have believed it if I hadn't seen it for myself, but the woman truly loved him. At least, she believed she did.

"He is. Didn't Asher tell you? He shot him," I admitted.

Aadya stared at me for several seconds, her chest rising and falling with the deep breaths it took to control her rage. A single tear escaped and traveled down her cheek, but she never moved.

Her hand slowly lifted toward Asher's head, and then her power seized his body. I could feel the energy, a dark vibration reaching forward, eager to take anything she would allow. Aadya's magic was just as evil as her heart. Asher, shaking and helpless, looked over toward Drake with sorrowful eyes as he landed on his knees before toppling to the ground.

She used subconscious interference to kill Drake's brother in front of him.

It only took seconds until Asher's body was limp and unmoving. Drake looked away, gripping the bars in front of him as another guard dragged Asher across the hard stone. The spell might have kept me from sensing Drake's pain, but I knew it was there nonetheless.

She clapped her hands together. "Now, back to business."

This woman had no soul.

"I'd like to introduce you to someone extraordinary, Mercy."

She stepped aside, and a tall, blonde-headed man stepped forward. His wavy hair curled around his ears, and blue eyes shone through the darkness. Strong and muscular, he stood at least a foot over Aadya.

"This is a very close friend of mine, Felix."

Felix reached through the bars to shake my hand, and my

eyes zeroed in on the tattoo on his right wrist. My belly clenched at the memory of my vision.

"Now, don't be rude. Shake the man's hand," Aadya insisted.

I reached forward, and he gripped my hand softly. "It's very nice to meet you." He turned back toward Aadya, "Does she have to be in here with the criminals? I want her in my room, right now."

Drake stepped forward at his words.

Aadya patted Felix's face and smiled, "My friend Felix dreamt of you, Mercy. You are to be his." She clapped her hands in front of her, a proud aunt doting over her niece.

"You're insane. I don't even know him," I blurted out.

"Are you saying you don't hold an elemental mark on your shoulder?" she asked. Venom laced her words, the insinuation clear. She knew exactly what marked me. I didn't even realize I'd been holding my breath until my lungs burned for release.

"That means nothing," I whispered.

"Doesn't it? Felix has elemental interference, so I think it's perfectly clear. You've never dreamed of him?" Her hostile eyes bored into mine, stripping away any deception.

"I . . . I may have had one," I admitted. My eyes cut toward Drake.

He took a step back, surprised.

"Ah! There you have it, then. I'll plan the mating ceremony at once. And don't fret, my dear. I'll be there in place of your sweet mother and father. I'm your family now." She grinned sadistically as they turned to leave. "We'll take you to Felix's room in a bit." The echo of their departing footsteps amplified the discomfort between our cells.

"A vision? Is that what threw me on my ass on the way to Stonedell?" Drake asked.

I bit my lip, looking away from Drake.

"Mercy . . ."

"I saw a ceremony with him," I painfully admitted. "It didn't end well."

He nodded at me, understanding my lack of details.

"She's a powerful subconscious interferer, Drake. There is no doubt she orchestrated the vision."

He exhaled. "So, what's your plan?"

"I wish I had one. Getting out of this dungeon is a good start."

"Are you saying I need to calmly stand by while they escort you to his room? Not quite my nature."

"I don't know what else to do, Drake. I can't use my power if I'm stuck here."

Custos marched around the corner, charging toward my cell. My eyes cut toward Drake, and he exhaled.

"Trust me," I pleaded. "Please."

Slowly stepping back, he sat in the far corner. The effort it took in restraining his fury was impressive—his eyes the only sign of his wavering control.

There were ten Custos lined up outside the door as they waited for me to step forward.

I met Drake's eyes one last time before following them out of the dungeon.

❖

The silent walk upstairs took forever—or maybe the knowledge that we were going to Felix's quarters made it feel that way. Five floors from the dungeon and I could still feel Drake seething. He carried enough aggression to tear the domicile apart. If they weren't careful, he would.

A colossal set of gold-trimmed double doors on the left side of the hall came into view. The frame shimmered against the light, evidence of the spell protecting it.

"Ah, is this the chamber of the mighty queen? The spawn of Satan. Wearer of slutty clothes and thick concealer. Anyone?" I glanced around at the Custos escorting me.

Silence followed my attempt at humor until a soft snicker erupted through the crowd of guards. I couldn't be sure, but it almost sounded like it came from the front. Someone had a sense of humor.

We stopped at the next door on the left. Although less regal, it still portrayed a sense of entitlement with gold embellishments along the frame. Did Aadya keep Felix this close to her? And why? A shiver ran up my spine at the thought of her mating me to someone she's already had her way with.

"Wait inside," a guard announced.

I opened the door to a large bright bedroom—the floor and walls composed of sleek white stone. My stomach turned at the sight of the massive bed with thick black posts in the center of the room. Black curtains framed tall floor to ceiling windows overlooking the Seregalo River.

A large tiled bathroom, complete with soaking tub and walk-in closet, took up an entire side of the room. There wasn't a towel or washcloth out of place. Sorry, Felix. We'd never work out, I thought. A click echoed throughout the large room as the door opened, and I spun to see Felix smiling boyishly.

He stepped forward. "Finally, I thought they'd never get you out of that horrid cell. My apologies, my love."

Oh, dear.

I clasped my hands together and spoke as if he were a toddler. "Felix, while I appreciate your kindness, you don't even know me."

"I know everything I need to, Mercy. I've seen a vision of our future, and it's everything I've ever wanted in a mate."

I knew Aadya had orchestrated our union, but Felix believed in us with all of his heart.

"You don't think there's the tiniest little chance that Aadya had something to do with our vision?" I placed my index finger and thumb in front of his face, measuring out the possibility of that scenario.

Ignorance shined from his eyes like a lighthouse. "Oh, she did," he insisted.

My eyes widened, surprised at his admission. "I think so, too."

"She sat down with me and interpreted the meaning of it

all. If it weren't for her, I might have never known it was you, Angel-cakes."

I puked a little in my mouth.

"Plus, my Allegato mark is the combination of the moon and water. Do you have any idea how many people I've met with more than one gift?"

"Um, five?" I guessed.

"Two. My Aadya and my mate." He grinned.

His Aadya? What the hell?

"We have a surprise for you." His excitement caused my stomach to clench and my heart to race.

"A surprise? Awe, Felix, you shouldn't have." I rolled my eyes.

"Aadya has arranged for us to have a mating ceremony along with a wedding since you're used to formal customs. She planned it all for tomorrow. I thought it was very considerate—the thought of you missing out on anything had my knickers twisted, if you know what I mean." He winked.

"What, um, knickers . . . wedding?" Just stop talking.

"A Regalian mating ceremony is very private, between the man and woman in their bedroom, exchanging vows before they consummate. We're going to incorporate a wedding ceremony for you. Aadya has it all planned out, Mercy. She's going to give you away, and Marley will stand by your side."

I watched his face, lit with enthusiasm over my perfect day. "Wow, Felix. That all sounds like a dream. I'm curious, then what?"

"What do you mean?" His brows pulled together in confusion.

"After tomorrow, will we live together at the domicile?"

"Oh, heavens no, Cupcake. Our mansion is far greater in Dolderia. You'll love it, I promise."

"In Dolderia?" I asked. "Where is that, Felix?"

"Well, under the Swiss Alps, of course."

"What?" I sat down on the side of the bed, stunned. Then quickly stood when I realized what had probably happened on that mattress.

He stepped forward and wrapped his arms around me. "Dolderia is our hidden underground land in Switzerland. I will be the next ruler, and you will be by my side."

My father had told me there were rumors of other hidden lands, but he said there was no proof. "I had no idea Dolderia existed," I admitted.

He leaned forward as if sharing a secret. "No one does. Our world has been kept secret for over a hundred years. You can only enter at the permission of our king—my father. Unlike Seregalo, nature will not dictate who rules our country," he spat.

That's when it clicked. Every attempt Aadya made at getting rid of me had failed. So she planned to mate me to another, far away, to eliminate the threat—and she wanted it done quickly. She knew if Felix took me to Dolderia, he'd never let me leave.

"I'll teach you everything you need to know, I promise." He leaned in further, studying my mouth. Right before he kissed me, my hand pushed against his chest, halting him.

"What's wrong, angel?"

"I, um, well," I stuttered.

Felix's face fell. "You don't have to say it. I already know about Drake."

"You do?" My eyes widened.

"He won't be a problem any longer. Nothing will keep us from being together. I promise you."

. . .

I STOOD at the window all night—thinking, planning and worrying. No matter the situation, I'd always been able to come up with something on the fly. Every scenario I conjured placed someone I loved in danger. If I made a wrong move at all, they'd kill Drake or Nora. I still had no idea where Neela was—what if they had taken her too? I had to be smart.

I couldn't lose them. I wouldn't allow them to die by the hands of my malicious aunt. I didn't know what to do, so I prayed for guidance. I prayed for grace and protection over my loved ones. I prayed for the people of Seregalo and all the innocent lives that Aadya had tortured. I knew I didn't have long before she would summon me to the ceremony, so I stole a few quiet moments to think about everyone in my life that had molded me into the Regalian I was in that moment.

I could feel my source, awakening as the effects of the dungeon dissipated. A storm raged within and I had to wait —choose the perfect time to unleash the fire within.

As the sun rose over the mountain, the bedroom door opened without so much as a knock. Aadya rushed in, over-joyed, with a group of women trailing behind her. Marley stood in the back—her eyes full of sorrow.

Aadya announced, louder than necessary. "It's your big day! I have a lovely surprise. Marley, come here."

Marley hesitantly shuffled forward and handed me a garment bag.

"What's this?" I asked.

"Open it," Aadya demanded.

I unzipped the garment bag and pulled out a long ivory silk dress. My gaze took in the thin fabric. I blinked hard, controlling the tears that fought to escape.

"It was Annabel's favorite." Her voice took on a sickeningly sweet tone that made me want to stab her in the eye.

I glanced up at my sister. A combination of sadness and anger surrounded her.

"Can I go back to my room now?" she asked.

She didn't want to be a part of this any more than I did. Marley didn't wait on a response, she turned and left the room.

"You won't be going to the party if you keep acting like that, Little Miss!" Aadya screamed—then quickly turned toward me with a toothy grin. "Can you excuse us, ladies?" The women filed out of the room.

I zipped the dress into the bag as rage built within me. How far would she go?

"Why are you doing this?" I whispered.

"Don't be selfish, Mercy. Think of the good you'll do. Ruling your own country instead of stealing mine . . . and you get to live. Win-win." She giggled as she threw her hands in the air.

"And Marley?" I asked.

"I haven't decided." Aadya's long red fingernail tapped her chin, thoughtfully.

My eyes narrowed. "You can't force people to stay with you. I assumed when my father left, you would have figured that out."

Contempt filled her eyes as her mouth drew up in an evil sneer. "You don't understand what you're talking about, you little brat. You think you know what it takes to rule a hidden land like Seregalo? You don't know the first thing."

I tilted my head to the side and whispered, "I think you feel threatened that I'd make a better leader than you."

Her back straightened as she jutted her chin forward. "We'll see about that." She stomped off toward the door. "Get dressed. Do something with yourself—it's your wedding, for heaven's sake." Before slamming the door, she looked back and sneered, "Don't worry, I'll keep Drake company in the meantime."

. . .

MY FEAR for Drake and Nora persuaded me to take a shower and look presentable. Aadya had left a bag of hair and makeup supplies along with the dress, so I styled my hair in waves down my back and attempted to hide the exhaustion on my face. The dark smokey makeup that outlined my eyes reflected the grim and depressed soul within. I chose the brightest red lipstick I could find and stepped into the silky gown. Perfect fit. I still wore the firestone earrings, my mother's ring, and my necklace from Drake. She couldn't take those away from me.

I'd always dreamed of slipping into something like this one day, but it felt wrong. There were no friends styling my hair and gushing over the way I looked. I didn't await my father to kiss me on the cheek or walk me down the aisle, and the man of my dreams wouldn't be waiting for me downstairs. This was just another nightmare.

"Hello? Ms. Monroe?" I turned at the unfamiliar, deep voice at the door.

"Yes?"

"I wanted to introduce myself. I'm Josiah Foster, an Elder in Seregalo. I, well, Noah was like a brother to me. We grew up together, and I just heard of his passing. A good man, your father."

A middle-aged man, average height, with sandy blonde hair stood calm and confident in the doorway. His dark suit and white dress shirt fit as though it had been custom tailored.

"Aren't you a little young to be an Elder, Mr. Foster? I imagined them to be the oldest in the city."

"Aren't you a little young to lead the elders?" He smiled.

"Point made." I grinned. "Forgive me, but why are you here?"

He stepped forward and lowered his voice. "Because I believe in you. I have faith in our way of life and her time has run out, Mercy. She's failed us."

"What do you suggest?" I asked.

"I don't know what the answer is. We're tired, Mercy. Exhausted. If we don't do something, there won't be any Regalians left. Just know some of us are prepared to fight with you if it comes to it. That's, well, that's all I wanted to say." A kind, half-grin spread across his face as he walked out the door. "And, Mercy? Noah would be proud of you. I know he would." He turned toward the door.

I took a deep breath. "Mr. Foster?"

He glanced over his shoulder toward me.

"I have no intention of going to Dolderia. I can promise you that."

He exhaled, relieved. "Good to know." Then the door closed with a final click.

The noise outside beckoned me to the window, and I glanced out onto the lawn of the domicile. Such a strange, beautiful sight laid out in the enchanted land. They constructed an extravagant white platform, centered in front of the building, and rows of chairs perfectly lined around the stage. Wine and champagne circulated among the dreary crowd, hoping to revive their spirits about marrying off their next chosen leader. Or did they even know?

"Get a move on—your mate is getting restless," a snappy voice called out.

Aadya, dressed in a tight, black dress with a slit up one leg, looked as though she already wanted to strangle me. She'd piled her hair loose on top of her head, and a large emerald necklace nestled low in her cleavage.

"Where's Marley?" I asked.

She feigned interest in her perfect nails. "She decided to stay in her room."

"She decided?" I asked.

"I don't have all day, Mercy. Let's go."

"Have you told her?" I asked.

Her eyes narrowed. "Told her what? We don't have time for this."

"How you killed our mother in the woods that day and left her body on the ground. Does she know? Have you explained how you ordered two guards to hold an unarmed, weak woman, while you played with her mind until her body crumbled? Does she know our parents hid, watching over us our entire life so you wouldn't kill us? How you tore our family apart because you were jealous? No? I guess it hasn't come up."

Her eyes widened in shock, but she quickly recovered. "Time to go," she sneered.

Aadya led me outside, the sunlight glinting off the emerald around her neck. An icy hand grabbed at my palm, forcing me to portray unity that didn't exist. Lifting the skirt of my dress with one hand, I stepped onto the stage, and cheers rang out among the crowd. Aadya waved, smiling brightly at the applause. A sharp pain ran through my hand as she twisted it, hinting for me to portray the joy of a happy bride. I couldn't even force it.

My sensory gift reacted, burning her hand as her grip tightened. She hissed, then jerked away, her eyes filled with anger.

My gaze caught sight of Drake at the left side of the stage, identical to my dream. Shimmering shackles gripped his biceps, and the muscles in his chest tightened from his heavy breaths. We made eye contact for all of three-seconds before she pushed me forward. There, in the front row, Nora sat hunched and weak, a Custos on each side. A threat, in case I didn't cooperate. Nora's weak gaze lifted toward mine and nodded once.

"Let's be smart, Mercy. For once in your life, do what's right for everyone else," Aadya whispered. "After today, we'll never have to see each other again."

Felix's hand swept out in front of me, the intricate D visible on his wrist. The tattoo I assumed symbolized his country. He waited for me to accept him as sweat broke out across my neck and chest. My eyes cut toward the domicile where Marley watched from her window.

Her pale, sad expression was visible from the lawn, as her palm pressed against the glass. I wish I'd known what went through her head at that moment—it might have saved me heartache down the road.

Mr. Foster sat with unwavering eye contact from the Elder's private section. At least a dozen men and women sat within the roped off area—posture straight and heads held high. An air of importance surrounded them as the people of Seregalo nodded their greeting in the Elder's direction —respectfully.

One to two hundred guests sat before us, excitement humming through the air. She impressed me by throwing everything together so quickly. It looked beautiful, but no amount of beauty could wipe away the despair and darkness in my heart at that moment. Gray clouds blocked the sunlight and the wind whispered gently through the strands of my hair. My gaze roamed to Drake—then Mr. Foster.

I closed my eyes, remembering my vision so clearly. Mr. Foster nodded, knowing exactly what needed to happen. His hand reached forward, and he began turning clockwise, slowly. I felt the vibrations of magic in the air and a spark of energy that carried an undercurrent of determination. He didn't turn it back. He slowed it down.

Every second dragged around me, and I could see the perfect time to make my move. The combination of adrenaline and Drake's need for violence fueled my power like never before. I slowly slipped my hand into Felix's, taking advantage of the shift in time while I could. Could Josiah stall the moment long enough for me to do what I needed?

I glimpsed at Nora as the short, fearless Custos beside her lifted the hood of their cloak. Neela. My heart cried out in relief. Neela had survived and waited for the right time to expose herself. Caleb and Colton stood in the back, waiting for my move.

As soon as Felix gripped my hand, my mother's ring illuminated under the glint of the sun. My palm warmed, and I couldn't breathe from the energy pulsing through me. A satisfied cackle erupted behind me, and a blade emerged at Drake's neck. It was the only chance I'd get.

I let the power flow through me—from my chest outward. I gave it everything I had. What started as a mild burn, turned into raging flames as heat ran down my arms angrily. An explosion of magic released in that moment, knocking down anyone within a fifty-foot radius, including myself. I barely remembered the surge as I raised up from the hard ground, shaking off the dizziness and double vision. My hearing faded in and out like a radio station with a poor signal—as if a bomb had struck the domicile. Neela had dove on top of Nora protectively, and the spell holding Drake's shackles dissipated as panic broke out across the lawn.

That moment would change everything for us, for all of the Regalians, if we could stay focused and rally against Aadya. The explosion confused the people of Seregalo, and they were unable to tell the difference between a leader and a villain. Some ran and others stayed behind to take a stand against the unknown force.

The sky blackened as a storm swirled overhead. The wind picked up, whipping chairs and flowers from side to side. The power of the Regalians blew along with the breeze, wrapping around me and fueling my flame. Energy from all sides collided mid-air as rain poured down onto the city. Fighting broke out, magical and physical, as I fought my way to Aadya.

Anger, fear, and confusion made a catastrophic mix in the magical world. Large-scale tornadoes devastated the domicile, trees lifted by their roots, and people stumbled across unmoving bodies throughout the lawn. Emotional interferers evoked fear into the citizens nearby and some absorbed panic from those surrounding them.

An intense push from the subconscious interferers caused pressure to build inside my head, forcing me to shield my mind. Unable to handle the energy assault, the weaker Custos sat brain dead from the power colliding around them as blood dripped from their ears and nose. Drake fought his way toward us, fighting multiple Custos at any given time.

Lightning struck overhead, splitting a massive tree over the Elders. With one palm shielding a small child from debris, I forced my other one toward the council, lifting the fallen trunk away from their heads. Raising it high into the air, I twisted my wrist and hoisted the tree into the approaching tornado, then coerced the wind funnel across the Seregalo River.

"Look around you! Nothing but fear and death as always, Mercy," Aadya screamed from the stage. Her hair fell loose around her face, and a large rip ran across the front of her dress. "This, ladies and gentlemen, is your fearless and gracious leader," she screamed over the wind and rain.

"No," Mr. Foster shouted. "You're the root of this. We've had enough, Aadya!"

Aadya cocked her head to the side and leaned in aggressively. "We? I only see you, Josiah. You shall die for treason."

Several Elders walked over to stand with Josiah. Aadya's face fell, but her chin remained high. "Fine, you'll all die."

The devious smirk remained as her nostrils flared, and veins distended in her neck. A rumbling, of sorts, captured my attention from the outlying meadows. A dark cloud of dust rolled fiercely toward us, threatening to smother us all. I reached for elemental interference until I realized it wasn't dust. They were beasts. Hundreds of beluas charging wildly —responding to their master's call.

Snarling ripped through the wind as dirt kicked up behind them. Aadya had risked everyone's life to keep her throne, even if it meant there was no one left in Seregalo. Our gifts collided to stop the massacre as the beluas attacked. I launched one beast into a tree, breaking its neck, and then created a water spout to trap several others. I spun to toss another one off a child, and that's when I saw it. Two beluas jumped for Neela simultaneously, and she'd only been able to hold off one.

It latched itself around her throat, fangs sliding all the way through. Her knees hit the hard ground, and her dark brown eyes searched for comfort in mine. She knew it was the end. As the beast released her, I caught Neela in my arms, begging her not to leave me. The color in her beautiful face faded as her chest heaved.

Blood rushed through my ears, and my jaw clamped down painfully. I wouldn't lose her. I couldn't. I'd never been trained, but I'd witnessed it several times. I placed my palm in front of her, and focused on the moment right before she was attacked. I strained and pushed at my source, then time began to turn back slowly. Heat crackled in the air, and the blood running down her neck and chest blurred. My hand shook from the effort to hold it. If I could turn back time far enough . . .

Sweat poured from my face as the wounds sealed themselves in her neck and Neela gradually rose to her feet, the beast hovering back into the air above her. That was as far as it would go—I didn't have the strength to take it further.

The horror at not finding an alternative path for Neela's fate led me to my next move. I was out of options and my power had weakened. I refused to let anyone else die. Holding on as long as I could, I knew I couldn't turn back time any further. As I released the hold, I jumped in front of Neela protectively against the charging belua.

Another body struck mine, slamming me forward to the ground. Scrambling upright, I took in the Regalian on the ground behind me, covered in blood.

Ren.

He pushed me out of the way. The belua pulled free from Ren's chest, but immediately lit up in flames—squealing from the agony of the fire. Felix stepped up beside me with his palm out until all that remained of the beast were ashes. I scooped Ren's head into my lap, while Neela sobbed beside him.

"No. Please, Ren. Please don't leave me."

I tried to turn it back, as I did for Neela, but the air only fizzled.

"Mercy . . ." His chin quivered as he cried, but whether it was fear or pain, I didn't know.

"I believe—I believe in you," he whispered while his eyes fought to stay open.

"Ren? Ren, please open your eyes," I cried.

Reaching out, I turned my palm again. Over and over—I put everything I had into saving him. My source fought for strength—for energy.

"I'm sorry, Mercy. Time interference drains you faster than anything. It's not possible to do it again so soon, not yet," Josiah said.

I did the only thing I could. Using what power I had left, I pulled from sensory interference to take the feeling away, to relieve him of his pain as his body fell limp. Ren's love for me killed him, and I could do nothing to stop it. The image of him taking his last breath, so I could live, would haunt me for the rest of my life. Felix kneeled beside us, his eyes full of pain as he took in the massacre around him. Had he finally witnessed the evil that existed inside of Aadya? I hoped so.

Whispers traveled throughout the crowd, "Did you see that?"

"Mercy saved that girl," a woman called out, pointing toward Neela. "She sacrificed herself."

Regalians stood in awe of a leader putting themselves in danger over another, something they weren't used to witnessing. Yes, I'd saved Neela, and put another dear friend in danger doing so. Defeat washed over me as another life drifted away in my arms.

Sharp pain pulled at my scalp as Aadya yanked me to a standing position by my hair. With a knife at my throat, everyone froze around me. Drake seethed—fury vibrating through the air, as the magic of Regalians crackled around us. They were ready to fight.

Aadya leaned in close. "See what these people are, Mercy? They're distractions. That's what happens when you care too much." She whispered in my ear, "You didn't even see me coming."

The beluas stood at attention, waiting for her command.

"Seregalo is mine!" she screamed. Deranged laughter echoed around the land.

Heat surrounded me like a furnace, and I struggled to breathe. Consumed by my source, the flame raged inside my heart. Drake stood across from me, eyes red and chest heaving. Something had changed within him. An internal war brewed and clawed, begging for release. He fought against it, losing the battle within.

As Aadya swept the blade toward my throat, Drake fell to his knees with a roar. His face contorted in pain as his body arched away from the ground. My legs threatened to collapse at the sound of skin ripping down his back, and his spine shattering. Confusion paralyzed me, and I hadn't seen genuine fear in Aadya's eyes until that moment.

"What is happening to him?" I screamed.

Josiah whispered in disbelief, "Rage Fire."

My throat tightened at his words.

Fire overpowered his body, his skin burning dark red. Flames engulfed him. The Drake I knew no longer recognizable. The screaming and clawing ceased as I feared the worst. As the blaze simmered, the silence was eerie around us.

Smoke and ash dissipated, and where Drake fell to the ground moments before now stood a fierce dragon that stood at least twenty feet tall. His scales were deep scarlet and red tinted the black of his eyes. He took intimidating steps toward us as his head swept from side to side, studying the crowd defensively.

"A dragon," Aadya stated, amazed. "I never believed the tales."

Drake came closer as we took a step back. I had no way of knowing if he still existed inside the beast, but I wanted to believe he did. A gruesome snarl revealed massive teeth as he came eye to eye with me. His head swung to Aadya and lowered, showing respect to the leader of Seregalo.

Her hand drifted up, caressing the dragon's scales as he leaned into her.

"This is what I've needed by my side. You. You will take my power to a new level. I will be unstoppable. I will be. . ."

Drake swung his head back into the air and descended with his mouth open, teeth bared. Aadya's words were cut off as the dragon bit into her neck, ripping her head from her shoulders. He tossed it onto the stage, followed by a blaze of blue and red flames, leaving it in ashes. Her headless form fell to the ground, as silence fell over the crowd. My gaze ran over the emerald necklace at my feet, glowing as if it called to me. As I reached to pick it up, a powerful pull between the necklace and my ring took my breath away. There was a definite connection—I just didn't know how significant.

All at once, Aadya's beluas attacked, avenging their master. The dragon turned, growling, and breathed a circle of fire around Neela, Nora and myself, protecting us.

Gusts of wind blew against my face as heavy wings beat against the air. The ground shook as he leaped into the sky and soared overhead. The dark shadow swarmed above us, breathing fire upon all the remaining beluas.

I looked around at the once lush green lawn, now ravaged from our battle. Regalians were dead, lying haphazardly across the ground. Blood covered the torn and twisted tent, and ashes were scattered across the stage. It was over. Aadya was dead.

Drake circled the sky and landed on the ground in front of me with a loud boom. He looked me in the eye and slowly knelt before me, and the crowd followed suit, showing respect to the new leader of Seregalo.

❖

J collapsed to the ground. I never wanted this. The deaths. The innocent lives crying out for compassion. I wanted to wrap everyone in my arms, evoking peace about their future in Seregalo. Things would be different after the devastation. I would make sure of it. Neela wrapped her arms around me, unable to speak. Weak and vulnerable, Nora could barely hold her head up, but conjured as much comfort into our hearts as her little body could withstand.

The Elders escorted Nora, Neela, and myself inside while the remaining guards assisted the survivors. I looked back one last time at the friend who gave his life for our cause. He believed in me. I never loved Ren the same way he loved me, but I cared for him more than he knew. He would be honored in Seregalo for his bravery—his loyalty.

Before walking inside, I looked back at Drake as he flew overhead into the woods.

"He'll be back, Mercy. He's got quite a bit to process," Josiah told me.

I knew he was right, but Drake's emotions were a blur of confusion and fear—I wasn't sure how much time I could give him when I knew he needed me. Josiah led each of us to a room similar to Felix's to get cleaned up, and Marley offered to bring clean clothes. My mother's ripped dress fell from one shoulder, and blood smeared across the side of my face.

I stood under the hot spray of the shower, still in shock at what I'd witnessed. My boyfriend literally bit Aadya's head off.

I fell to my knees, head bowed, and cried. The heat of the running water rinsed the dirt and tears from my eyes as blood circled the drain, along with the last remaining doubt of what I needed to do.

Fall apart now, Mercy. Then, it's time to rise up.

My mother's words echoed throughout my head.

The tears dried as I forced myself to stand up straight. I could do this. I jumped from the shower to dry off, and as I turned from the bathroom, an unfamiliar mark caught my eye in the mirror. My Allegato mark had transformed. Was that even possible? The flame now blazed behind a dragon, fierce and strong, surrounded by all six gifts. The dragon I understood, but the gifts?

The only thing I knew is that we were destined to lead together. A smile broke through my distress, as the truth finally emerged. A truth we knew all along.

Clean clothes were on the bed, thanks to my sister. I slipped on the jeans and sleeveless top, pulling my hair up wet. I had things to take care of, matters that couldn't wait.

Josiah exited Nora's room as I walked into the hall. "How is she?" I asked.

He frowned. "Better, but she needs rest. Aadya wasn't kind, Mercy. I'm not sure what she's been through, but I hope she'll eventually talk to you about it."

I hoped she would. Nora deserved a happy and secure life, and I would do whatever I needed to make that happen.

"I'll let her rest, then be back to check on her," I said as I walked toward the stairs.

"Where are you going?" he asked.

"The dungeon," I answered.

Josiah sighed, but quickly followed behind me.

A sinister sensation enveloped me as my bare feet hit the cold stone. A faint drip of water echoed throughout the space as I made my way through the dungeon toward the small boy. Josiah handed me the keys as I opened the cell and found the child curled into a ball.

He'd weakened since I saw him last, and my heart broke for the life he must have lived. "Get this child food and water, Josiah. His time here is over."

"Of course. We'll get him in a room at once."

"Free the others, as well," I demanded.

"All of them?" he asked.

"Every single Regalian will have a chance to start a new life. I'll make sure of it."

Josiah shook his head. "There might be some push back on this, some of these men are criminals."

"Aadya had her own definition of criminal. They will start new with me."

Josiah nodded in agreement. "The Elders are gathered in the dining hall. They'd like to meet with you as soon as possible, Mercy." Josiah said quietly.

"Guess I should've seen that coming. I'm going to check on Nora, then I'll find you."

. . .

NEELA'S FAMILY HAD ARRIVED, greeting me with hugs as I entered Nora's room. The relief in her parents' eyes was evident, but distress and anxiety was palpable from the bedside.

"How is she?" I asked.

"Weak, but resting comfortably. I think she'll recover fine," Mr. Parker said.

Confusion crossed my face at the sense of agony in the room. I stepped toward Nora and stopped dead in my tracks. The pink in her cheeks had returned, the dark circles diminishing around her pretty eyes. Caleb sat beside her, holding her hand and watching her sleep. He agonized over every whimper, every deep breath.

Neela stepped up beside me, "It was instant, Mercy. As soon as he walked into the room, the connection was obvious. And . . . their Allegato marks match."

"I didn't realize Nora was even marked. She never mentioned it," I whispered.

"No, she didn't," she smiled.

I hugged Neela and turned toward the door. "I have a meeting, but I'll be back to check on her later, alright?"

"Sure, but I think she's in good hands," Neela responded.

I smiled at the sight of Nora having someone for the first time in her life—someone who'd put her before anyone else. I left the room, promising to return soon.

It took me an hour to find the dining hall, and it felt as though I was late to class, walking in as everyone stared. A dozen or so men and two women sat around the long wooden table, impatiently. I wasn't going to apologize and hide my face. The Elders needed to respect me.

"I'm Mercy. I'm grateful for the opportunity to meet with you and answer any questions you may have. I'm sure this is very confusing after working with Aadya for so long."

"We never worked with Aadya. We worked for her." An

older man at the end of the table spoke up. "Are we supposed to believe it will be any different with you?"

"No, you're not. And I would never expect you to take my word on that. I'll have to earn your respect as you will have to earn mine." I glanced over toward Thu Dang, his eyes glaring in my direction. "Tell me now if you have a problem with that so we can settle it."

After several long seconds, he submitted, eyes focusing on the table.

"I'm eighteen years old and learning every day. I'll need guidance and patience from each of you, but I was born with these gifts for a reason, and I want the opportunity to prove myself. I have a couple of requests, or I refuse to be a part of this council."

"Here we go," someone mumbled from the crowd.

I ignored the comment. "No one will die at the hands of this council."

A few men shifted uncomfortably in their seats and swallowed visibly.

"If you have a problem with that, I'll introduce you to Drake." I narrowed my eyes.

"So, when things don't go your way, will you always threaten us with your boyfriend?" Thu Dang asked.

"Only the murdering of innocent people. It's non-negotiable," I told him.

Several members nodded their heads in agreement.

"Second, the domicile will pay for the repairs of the Elder's homes so you can move back immediately."

"You're not making us stay here? What if you demand a spell? What will you do?" A well-kept woman with gray hair quietly asked. One brow raised, skeptical of my requests.

"I'll never demand anything except the promise for the Elders to protect, not harm. If a spell is required, we'll meet and discuss it, making that decision together. I'm part of this council. I refuse to be a ruler."

"We're supposed to trust that the dragon won't burn us to the ground the first time we disagree with you? I'm not that naive." Thu Dang laughed.

Josiah stood, and a hush fell over the crowd. "Mercy was chosen for a reason, and we'll respect that. As far as Drake goes, he's a Moreno. One of the most respected and upheld families since the creation of Seregalo." He cleared his throat. "I believe we can all agree that Asher was an exception."

Chuckles followed his comment.

"We've all heard his ancestors' stories, and I believe our land is blessed to have him. There is no greater protection for our land than Rage Fire."

Several heads nodded at Josiah's words and silence remained for several uncomfortable minutes.

"Alright, Mercy Monroe." A feeble old woman stood on shaky legs. "You have my support."

. . .

I HAD NEVER FELT MORE overwhelmed. For the most part, the Elders seemed relieved, but I knew it would take time for them to trust me.

Josiah asked to speak with me after the council dispersed. As we entered the parlor, a kind-looking couple sat, their excitement buzzing through the air.

"Mercy, I'd like you to meet the Hughes Family. They are the first people I thought of when you released the boy."

I searched their eyes for intent, only finding a deep-seated need for a son. Josiah was right, he would be safe with them.

"Can you call him?" I asked.

"Sure," he smiled.

"Mr. and Mrs. Hughes. . ."

"Please, Ma'am. Call us Gary and Alysia."

"Of course. I want to thank you for opening your home to him. I'm sorry to say I don't know anything about his family or heritage. If it's not too much trouble, I'd love to hear from you now and again, for updates."

"We'd be happy to," Alysia said. "Our daughters are thrilled to have a younger brother. Maybe you could visit him."

I smiled at the thought. "That sounds wonderful."

Josiah brought the boy into the room, fed and dressed in clean clothes. You could already see the color returning to his beautiful face, evidence of how much better he felt. Gary kneeled down and asked, "What's your name, Son?"

The tiny face peered up at me, nervous and embarrassed at not having one.

"His name is Ren," I said. "Ren Hughes."

Alysia smiled with tears in her eyes as she wrapped her arms around him. "Welcome to our family, Ren."

. . .

THERE WAS SO MUCH I needed to do, so many people I wanted to speak with. Riots broke out in the city at the knowledge of Aadya's death, especially when they heard the rumor of the terrifying Dragon that killed her. I sent the remaining guards to establish control in the city and reassure the Regalians.

They needed to know they were protected. My mind was consumed with finding Drake, taking care of my friends, and sitting down with my sister.

I'd already told Marley I'd have lunch with her the next day, so we could get to know each other. Having a sister was the greatest gift I'd ever been given and I couldn't wait to bond with her. The Parkers kept an eye on Nora, and I knew I had nothing to worry about with Caleb around. But I needed Drake, and the thought of him being alone in Seregalo somewhere made my chest hurt. I recalled our conversation about Stonedell—*the mountainside.*

Drake said Stonedell dropped him in a cave on the cliffside and a small voice told me I'd find him there. I borrowed Marley's shoes and walked out behind the domicile, looking across the river toward the rocky cliffs. I didn't even think about it. I jumped into the river, only focused on getting to Drake.

I wasn't sure what direction to go, but I followed my intuition across the river and toward the cliff ahead. The trek up the rocky mountain wasn't horrible until I reached the top half. Stepping on the flattest rocks I could find, I slowly climbed, reaching out for Drake's presence. Something familiar pricked the back of my neck, and a touch of fear lingered. What would I find? Would the same Drake exist? I used my power to search him out, for any sign of the direction I needed to go.

He didn't hide his thoughts. They were like a beacon calling out to me. Confusion and pain overwhelmed his emotions as I made my way up to the opening of the cave. I glanced in, almost afraid of what I'd find, but there he was—sitting in front of a fire—unaware of my presence.

The inside of the cave wasn't stone as I had predicted. Blackness shone around the walls and ceiling, as if lava had created his dark hole for him to wallow in. The carvings along the cave wall stretched from one side to the other, just like he had described in the dungeon.

The transformation ruined his clothes, but he didn't seem to care. Glaring into the fire before him, he battled the rage within—a gift he never wanted and didn't know how to control. His eyes, now outlined by the glowing red ring, made his features even more striking. A war raged within Drake, but I couldn't help him with this one. There were so many questions with no one to guide him. Then, I felt what he needed most—me.

I stepped into the archway. "You know, you're way hotter now. No pun intended."

He didn't move, but his face relaxed at my joke. "What are you doing here?"

I shrugged. "Looking for you."

"Where's your mate?" he asked.

I grinned. "Sulking in a cave, somewhere."

"You know who I'm talking about," he mumbled.

"Felix? Ruler of Dolderia? Future Mr. Mercy?" I joked.

"That would be the one."

"Probably on his way back to Dolderia by now."

He glanced up at me, his eyes dark and heavy. "Why are you here, Mercy?"

He stood, angry for what he'd become, and walked over to the cave wall where a steady stream of water flowed from the side of the rocks. He placed his hands on the stone, bracing himself, as he lowered his head under the cool water. Steam rose as it ran over his hot skin. I followed, and he flinched at the feel of my fingers running across the long, white scars on his back from his transformation.

My eyes traveled up to his shoulder, the Allegato mark complete. The tattoo portrayed a dragon centered over a flame identical to mine, intricately surrounded by all six gifts. Had anyone's marks ever matched as ours did? What did it mean?

"You know, the first time Nora saw my Allegato mark, she called it Rage Fire. When your body went up in flames today, the Elders told me you had the gift of Rage Fire."

He looked over his shoulder with hopeful eyes. "After what I've become, do you even think that's possible?"

"Now that you've shown your true self and my powers have evolved, your mark is complete. Do you really think that's a coincidence? We are a perfect match, like we've always known. I accept you for who you are, Drake. You're not getting rid of me because you can breathe fire."

Drake didn't take time to think about my words. There was no hesitation or moment of self-discovery. He turned, pulling me against him. His mouth devoured mine, hungry for anything I would give. His hands roamed, needing to feel my skin against his. He craved this connection, and the longer his mouth was on me, the more at ease he became. I stepped away from his hold. His eyes blazed as his chest heaved for air. He reached to pull me back when I halted him with my hand.

I pulled the shirt over my head and threw it to the side. I turned, showing the evidence of our match. His lips grazed across my mark as a territorial contentment radiated throughout the cave.

"You're really mine," he whispered as if needing to say it aloud.

"Unless you know any other dragons I should be searching for."

That was as far as I'd gotten before he couldn't restrain himself any longer. He spun me around and lifted me into his arms. I wrapped my legs around his waist as he carried me to the fire and gently laid me on the ground. Drake knew how I felt about him, but he also needed to hear it. I never wanted him to doubt it.

"I love you for who you are. All of you. It's in your blood. It's your legacy."

Drake's eyes glowed in the firelight.

"I love you, Mercy. No matter what happens, I'll always protect you," he promised.

"Always."

Marley

❧

I reached out subconsciously—needing to find her. A part of me demanded to know where she went. I could feel the coolness of the cave walls and the warmth of the blazing fire. Drake. She'd found him.

"I'm sorry, I tried. She has, unfortunately, won over the other Elders. I won't stop. You have my word on that. She'll pay for what she has done," Thu Dang said.

"Thank you. It may take time, but we'll figure something out," I said thoughtfully.

"Do you need anything else from me tonight?" he asked.

"No, that is all."

The bedroom door shut, and my frustration built to violent levels. I looked around bedroom number seven, the twin beds and the replica of the family quilt. The quilt that I should have had. She had everything—like always. The powers, the boyfriend, my father. She even had my mother's ring.

I'd heard stories about the ring, the power it held. They never intended on giving it to me. Aadya promised me the necklace one day and now Mercy had that also. I was the unworthy, weak sister, and Aadya understood how I felt. My mother, Annabel, always outshined her. She stole the love of her life and moved away from Seregalo. Aadya's family abandoned her—I knew what that was like. Tucked away in California, they hid me from everyone. Aadya told me my lack of power embarrassed them, but she could help me. She would make me strong.

I'd lived with my cousin in San Francisco growing up, oblivious to this life until Aadya found me and explained what happened. She wanted me to be as close to Mercy as possible, developing a genuine understanding of her life. She recreated her bedroom and taught me about subconscious interference, and visiting Mercy as she slept. How to invoke visions and nightmares . . . She said I'd be more powerful—more loved than Mercy ever was.

I reached forward into her subconscious once again, sensing what she felt as her guard lowered. She was distracted—not shielding herself like normal. A warm, strong hand slid up her thigh as wet lips traveled down her neck. Her stomach clenched as her nails dug into his back. Safe, loved and adored—that's how Drake made her feel. I deserved that.

She better enjoy it. Soon, it will be me ruling Seregalo during the day and lying under Drake at night. I will be the biggest interference Mercy has ever dealt with. She just doesn't know it yet.

TO BE CONTINUED.

FROM THE AUTHOR

Writing isn't always easy. Sometimes, I can type for hours—thrilled at the stories that seem to roll effortlessly from my fingertips. Other days, I sit frustrated and question my abilities as an author. One day I realized, we all do that to ourselves, everyday. Whether I'm exhausted from a long day at the hospital, or overthinking my decisions as a wife and mother, I will always doubt myself.

That's why my village is so important.

Brian, Roman and Isaac—I love you more than you know.

My family for their love and support.

The greatest friends, coworkers, and ARC readers anyone could ever ask for—thank you for encouraging me to write the novel I would want to read.

Thank you all for going on this journey with me.

ALSO BY A.F PRESSON

BLIND TRUST: Book One of the Trust Series
(Available on Amazon)

BROKEN TRUST: Book Two of the Trust Series
(Coming soon!)

INTERFERENCE: Book One of the Interference Trilogy
(Available on Barnes & Noble, Amazon, Apple & Kobo)

Printed in Great Britain
by Amazon